I0768804

LIONE

FALLING CITY BOOK 1

LIONE

D. LAMBERT

4 Horsemen
Publications, Inc.

Lione
Copyright © 2025 D. Lambert. All rights reserved.

Published By: 4 Horsemen Publications, Inc.

4 Horsemen Publications, Inc.
PO Box 417
Sylva, NC 28779
4horsemenpublications.com
info@4horsemenpublications.com

Cover & Illustration by CD Corrigan
Typesetting by Autumn Skye
Edited by Kris Cotter

All rights to the work within are reserved to the author and publisher. No part of this publication may be reproduced, stored in a retrieval system, or transmitted in any form or by any means, electronic, mechanical, photocopying, recording, scanning, or otherwise, except as permitted under Section 107 or 108 of the 1976 International Copyright Act, without prior written permission except in brief quotations embodied in critical articles and reviews. Please contact either the Publisher or Author to gain permission.

All characters, organizations, and events portrayed in this novel are either products of the author's imagination or are used fictitiously. No generative artificial intelligence was used in the creation of this book or its cover.

All brands, quotes, and cited work respectfully belongs to the original rights holders and bear no affiliation to the authors or publisher.

Library of Congress Control Number: 2024952328

Paperback ISBN-13: 979-8-8232-0816-1
Hardcover ISBN-13: 979-8-8232-0817-8
Audiobook ISBN-13: 979-8-8232-0819-2
Ebook ISBN-13: 979-8-8232-0818-5

DEDICATION

This book couldn't have survived to publication if it wasn't for many people! Thank you, Curran for giving me a safe place to explore fantasy stories, Josh for listening to the rambling, Rachel for questioning me when I needed to slow down and be realistic, and many others! Thank you for waiting.

CONTENTS

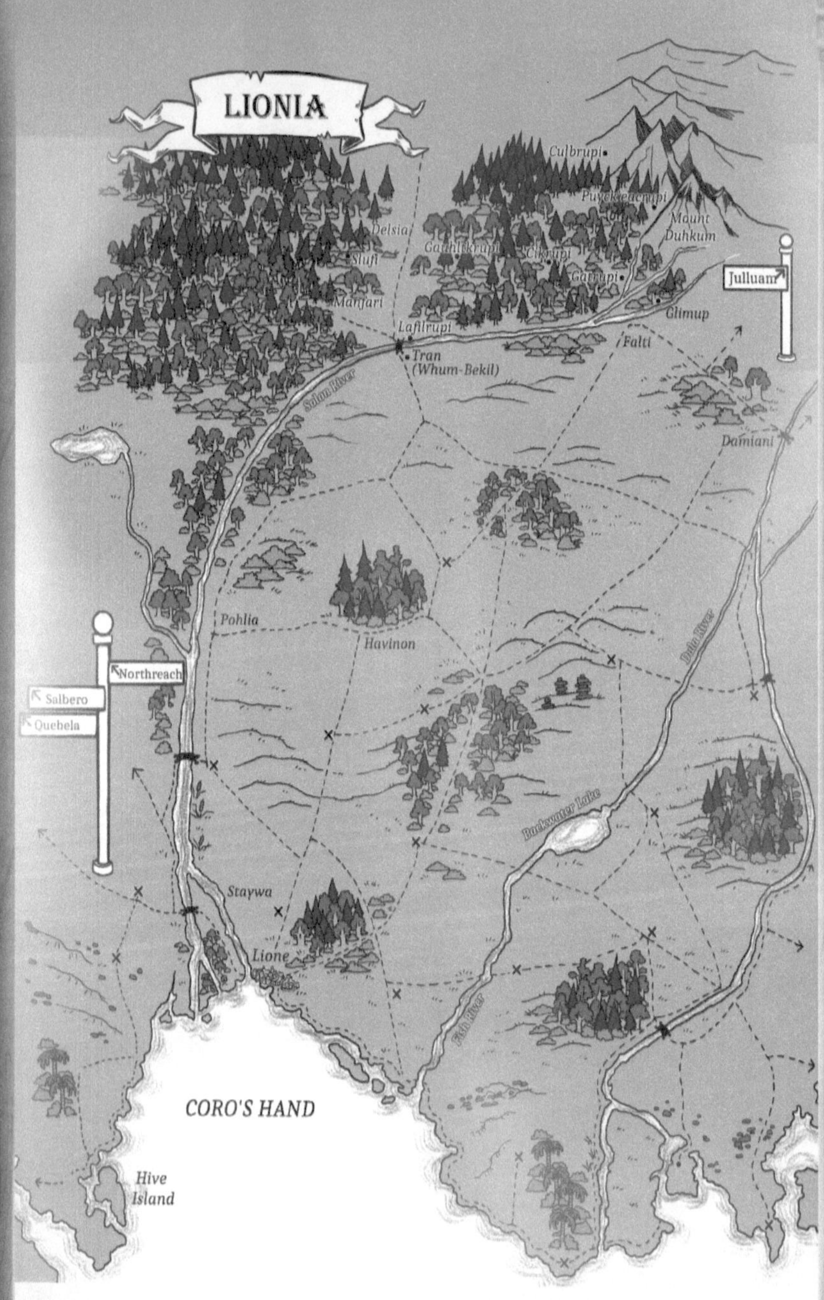

LIONIA
Culbrupi
Puyckreucrupi
Mount
Duhkum
Delsia
Gaichliskrupi
Cikrupi
Slufi
Garrupi
Julluam
Manfari
Lafilrupi
Glimup
Tran
(Whum-Bekil)
Falti
Salan River
Damiani
Pohlia
Havinon
Dula River
Northreach
Salbero
Quebela
Backwater Lake
Staywa
Lione
Feln River
CORO'S HAND
Hive
Island

PROLOGUE

There was no panic.

At the heart of the grove, Tril found Vela sitting serenely in her habitual cross-legged position. The gentle tides of her breathing were unhurried in the cold air despite the screams in the distance. They would worsen soon. Neither prophet needed visions to know as much.

He knew she felt his presence on the edge of trees, but, in her resignation, she did not open her folded eyes. It was not until he moved—when it became apparent that he was both alone and not a soldier—that she peeked out from her meditation.

"Tril!"

For as long as he had known her, Vela had never failed to greet him with a smile. But this evening, with enemies moving in under the fall's thinning canopy, her expression fell to see him.

"You should not be here!" She pushed herself up, her long robe falling around her. "Beloved, please! You must…"

Her lip trembled in anticipation of tears, but he defused both her misery and her fear with a toothy, playful grin.

"The greatest prophetess the Nurmi has ever known, and you did not foresee my return?" Tril teased.

Vela weakly smiled in return, still mindful of the plans it seemed he was abandoning. "The box?"

"Hidden, of course," he replied, taking her outstretched arms in his own. His hands were weathered, and the hairs on his arms were as white as his arctic wolf pelt, but his strength had been something more than natural for years, and his grip was still firm. Tril squeezed her arms in excitement. "It is hidden in a place I know they will find. I even know who will find it!"

He felt the tension fade from her arms once he assured her the box they had so laboriously fashioned was safe. She did not seem to hear his other claims. Instead, Vela ran a delicate finger over his cheek and let her smile drop, her eyes wistful. It felt as though the sun had passed behind the hills.

"Beloved," he said, shaking her slightly, "I know. I have seen it."

"Greatest prophet the Esparans ever had," Vela mumbled. "You should go, Tril. Soon they will be here." She lovingly ruffled his gray-blond hair, the features that would betray him as not Nurmi. "If the enemy finds you, they will go north in search of your people. Who then will open the box? If the dragons..."

At long last, she met his ice-pale stare, and her words fell off. He needed no reminder.

"I came back to tell you, Beloved. I will go, I swear, but first..."

In the corner of his mind, carefully controlled by decades of guidance, Tril saw his *visaln*, the visions, answering his thoughts. A little woman, her hands tattooed with holy symbols of the One God, pulled his precious puzzle box from the roots where he had buried it. He had left no clues for her; she needed none. Like him, the girl would be a prophet.

The sight of the woman, dressed in the un-dyed wool robe of a Nurmi priestess like that of his lover, made Tril's face brighten.

"The Twins, Beloved. The Priestess will find the box. I have seen it."

Through the apathy she was using to shield her breaking heart, Vela eagerly looked up. "But that legend predates the Demon Wars! We thought they were to chase back the demons, but the war ended, and they had not come."

Unable to bear holding her at arm's length any longer, Tril pulled his priestess against him. Her head found a place on his chest obligingly.

"The Twins were to save the Nurmi from their darkest days. They will free your people, Beloved. They will return your people to their homes." It was a daunting prospect, and Tril knew the task would only grow more difficult as time went on. Already, every Nurmi in the Corelands had been taken captive by the black-haired invaders. One grove remained, but even that would be lost by the end of the day and, with it, the last free Nurmi.

A shout went up in the distance, one of battle and rage. The grove's priests were making their final stand.

Tril felt tears against his chest.

"We know nothing about them," Vela whispered. "We do not know when they will come or their names…"

"They will be daughters of Maltor, the first freed slave of the age. You named him. The drop that makes a ripple. The ripple…"

"The ripple that begins a flood," she finished. She sat in the grove here to fulfill that prophecy.

"They are the flood."

Her head snuggled into his chest. Powers she had trained him in warmed the air between them, pushing aside the chill of the coming winter. For a few moments, they forgot about the enemy.

Tril could see her visions in his mind, and he briefly worried she would stumble into the parts of the future he had deliberately withheld from her. But time was short, and she only focused on the part she had to play. She sought a way to make the likely future more certain.

"I will tell them," she decided, looking up at him from within the fold of his arms. "I will tell them of Maltor, and his name will give him courage. I will tell them the Twins are coming, and the promise will strengthen their faith. When the prophecies are fulfilled, the people will be ready."

A new voice, this time closer, reached them, but neither prophet understood the coarse language. When there was no sign of opposition to the orders of the invaders, Vela pulled away.

"Tril..."

His arms cold, he let them fall.

"I will go. I just..."

Knowing the longer they delayed, the harder his promise became to keep, Vela sat on the forest floor once more. Around them, the voices had softened. They did not need to shout orders. Even the drums had faded.

A man stepped into the grove behind Vela, armored and broad. He wore a plumed helm and carried a long spear, too long for hunting beasts. His head turned to the priestess seated in the holy grove.

It was over.

In a thought, Tril disconnected himself from the golden light of the Dreamworld, where he knew his lover would soon be walking in death, and opened himself to the spiral of magic in the darkness. Wrapping the magic around him, he erased his presence from the mind of the intruder and hid.

The first invader was followed by a dozen more, all standing ready for more desperate priests to fling themselves onto their spears in defense of the grove. But only Vela remained. She did not flinch as they surrounded her.

There were too many possibilities for Tril to be satisfied with just walking away. Drawing in magic for a second time, he formed a thought and sought the man with the gray plume on his helm.

Take her captive. Let her be paraded before her defeated people, mocked and ridiculed. Take her to Lione.

Thoughts needed no language. The man snapped orders to his soldiers, and they picked up Vela despite her passivity.

He let the thought magic drop. *Let her tell her story,* he thought to himself. *Let her spread the word.*

He dared not follow as they left the grove, fearing he would break to see her captive. He was the last of the Northlander Circle of the Eidenlandsa, and he wielded the arts of both Dreamers and Wizards. He could have destroyed their invasion. He could have freed her. He could have stopped everything.

But the lines of possible futures that flooded his senses every day showed the world he would be creating if he let his heart's pain decide his course. They had set things in motion. His duty to Vela and to the world was finished with inaction.

As the sun sank behind the trees in earnest, the invaders marched away. Their celebrations rang through the forest. The old Northlander lowered himself to sit under a red-leafed maple tree. By morning there would be frost. He had endured worse, certainly, but tonight was different.

He had no need to see the morning.

There would be freedom, as he had promised her, but it would be in a time when his legend had been forgotten. His meddling, he thought with a smile, would be forgiven by ignorance in the eight hundred years it would take to free the Nurmi.

One last time, he looked into the future the Dreamworld powers revealed.

The Twins would be born, two halves of the same soul, and they would fight for the freedom of all people. His homeland, the Esparan kingdom hidden by walls of mountains, would be conquered by then. The heart would lead the way, as it always did among the Nurmi people, but the heart Tril saw beating in the chest of the Warrior of the Twins was not the pure one Vela expected. The Warrior, when she came, would be hardened by her hatred and driven by more than one call for vengeance.

And the Twins were just human. There would be mistakes and many of them. If things went wrong...

Thought I did not know?

Hearing Vela's voice, Tril sat up. While her body went with the soldiers, her soul reached through the golden light of the Dreamworld and settled with him. In his fatigue, he had not noticed her arrival.

Dejectedly, he admitted, "They are not your heroes of old. They might fail. The Warrior—"

She follows her heart.

"She follows her fierce heart to multiple tragedies. Her choices are heavy. Love is a dangerous thing, especially for one such as her."

But love...

Tril felt Vela's caress through the Dreamworld and leaned back against the tree trunk under the pressure.

There is only love. When the blackened shaft flies, when the Twins stand side by side, when the Corelands are filled by friendly strangers, when the box is opened and the dragons clear a path, there will be peace.

On the edge of consciousness, Tril answered, "But without a villain, who needs a hero?"

There was no answer for a long moment. The wind of the woods wrapped itself around the auburn leaves and dropped them around him.

Do you ever regret coming with me? Vela asked. *You can return home now.*

He heard her smile like a tease. Tril reached back through the golden Dreamworld to answer. *I have outlived all I knew, even those who were so much younger than me. Now I am just a tired old man.*

My tired old man, she corrected.

Very glad to be your tired old man.

The golden light reached out once more, engulfing him in a warm embrace. Alone, Tril slumped against the tree, the loose red leaves falling around him.

The cold set in. The day was done.

PART 1

MY ENEMY

CHAPTER 1

In the dense forests by the Solon River, Lania lay atop a warm boulder, reveling in the sun on her exposed skin. She thought herself like the firedrake sprawled across another boulder on the far side of the pond, basking in the light as the season changed, trying to leave behind all other responsibilities for a time. They might both be wild, she mused, but only the firedrake was free.

Across from her, the stubborn maple tree's leaves were a red so dark, the canopy looked black in the fading winter. The scent of the evergreens mingled with the cold water that swirled in the nearby pool before, like a child called to chores, reluctantly wandering back to the main river.

On occasion, Lania tricked herself into dipping a foot into the cold pool while the firedrake watched on with an expression of sarcastic disproval, yet it did not fly off, as if amused by the antics of the strange human. Now stretched out on the boulder with both hands tucked under her chin, Lania contemplated using one of her remaining arrows to spear a fish, but her hunts had been successful, and she had no need for the meat. Seemingly knowing they had nothing to fear, the silver fish flitted about in the clear water directly below her. The firedrake likewise looked on, seeming curious but not interested in hunting.

There were so few of the blessed creatures on the Lionian-controlled side of the river, Lania would not dare harm the firedrake either. These little dragons, the size of a large dog, were the biggest of the dragonkin in the Corelands now. Their larger cousins, true dragons, had been chased away or hunted by the black-haired Lionian conquerors long before Lania's birth. Seeing the brightly colored dragon lounging comfortably in her presence was a blessing from the One God, she was certain. Although what that blessing might lead to, she did not know.

Her eyes drifted up to the old maple tree as one of the leaves released, and she followed its lazy fall to the surface of the water. Seeing the ripples, she experimentally squeezed a few drops of water from her hair, let them trickle into the pool, and compared.

The firedrake sat up and stretched its wings, contemplating her and the ripples she made in the pool.

Lania met the yellow gaze of the reptile, and she thought she saw it smile. It was not the first time she had seen the beasts, but it would be a long time before the next; war was in the wind, and the dragonkin would flee the region, likely to migrate south. This last glimpse, however, inspired her, and she nodded to the animal in thanks. It gave a shriek, stretched its wings one last time, and took off through the canopy as a pink and green streak lost in the sunset.

In the wake of the flying reptile, a wind blew over the water, and the maple shook. For a second time, leaves fell like drops of blood to spread their ripples over the roughened surface of the pond. Bleeding, legends said, to die and then be reborn, the maple shed the blood of the forest. This one had clung through winter in this tiny sanctuary. Lania passed a prayer to the tree in thanks for its selfless act. Perhaps if it bled, she would not have to.

The warmth of the sun vanished, and a brisk winter wind blew over the thinning branches of the maple. She could not stay. She had not so much as a cloak to keep back the night's freeze. There would be frost by morning, but that same frost would melt as soon as the One God's right eye again rose over the eastern horizon. Before long, the cold would persist, and should she stay, Lania would freeze. But for now, she could return in the morning, which set a relaxed smile on her face. The fighting was still a long way off. Even if the Black Arrow decided to march the army in the morning, she could sneak back down to the river before they left.

She stretched idly on the rocks to absorb the last of the warmth from the stone before standing. Despite having spent the day with her bow, she did not feel sore. Strained muscles were too relaxed after the time swimming to complain.

It was time to go back. The Nurmi scouts should be returning, and she dearly wanted to hear their reports. How long would the Lionians pursue her father's forces? They had to make it to the far side of the Solon River, where the mountains of the Corelands could swallow them up, but Lionians marched swiftly. They were already too close, although the Black Arrow himself insisted there was still time.

She had to believe in him. Her father had been fighting Lionians for decades now. He knew how the enemy thought. *Conquerors, all of them,* she thought. *As if they think at all.* The monsters of the south fought. That was all the men of Lione were capable of.

As Lania reached for her hide trousers, a chill ran up her spine like the creep of a spider. Her stomach crunched into a stone, and panic flooded over her. She stepped back and shook her head, spraying cold water. Before she could center herself entirely, she was overwhelmed by a sense of undeniable anxiety.

The feeling was not hers; it belonged to her twin sister.

Fearing Akara had come under attack, Lania dropped her clothing. Pausing only long enough to snatch her bow and quiver off a nearby tree branch, she bolted from the pond.

She was not shy about wearing no clothing, not even boots to cover her cold feet, but she immediately missed her hunting knife. The bow would have to do, as she dared not delay.

Without slowing her pace, she swung the quiver into place on her shoulder and snatched an arrow. She burst from the woods like a stone from a sling and rushed across a field. At the base of the hill where the Nurmi forces had set camp, the meadow was wide and empty. Despite the fear shared from Akara, no enemies filled the view. Lania slowed, confused. She saw no threat to the Priestess. Warriors milled behind barricades at the crest of the hill, but they watched with lowered weapons.

Although Lania could not see her, she knew Akara was among the onlookers; she felt the urgent emotion lessen when her sister saw her. At the same time, the reason for the feelings became obvious.

A single Nurmi scout broke from the cover of the forest line on the far side facing the camp. Glancing often over his shoulder, he fled into the grass like a hare chased by a wildcat. Before the Nurmi man could duck into cover, the pursuing Lionian rider broke from the shadows of the trees.

Angling toward the east with speed blessed by the spirit of the firedrake she had left behind, Lania broke into a sprint, aiming to set herself between the fleeing scout and the Conqueror hunting him.

The Lionian conqueror rode with his long spear lowered to his horse's knees. His thick leather armor was broken by flashes of starlight in the sunset; metal bands were woven between the leather to cover the chest and abdomen. Done in black, the eight-pointed sun symbol of Lione took up most of his chest, stark against the blue of the metal-leather composite armor. His gray-plumed helm glittered, identifying him as a yoraci, the lowest rank of officers for Lione.

He must have been wealthy; the horse was huge, dappled brown, and partially covered by dark red leather. The monstrous beast reminded Lania of legends of demon-horses bred beyond the Gate and brought to the world to serve the Conquerors. But those were creatures of myth. Years of experience allowed her to recognize the sizeable south-bred warhorse for what it was.

The mounted Conqueror paused at the edge of the forest, in no hurry to catch the doomed scout. For a moment, he seemed to admire the situation.

An instant later, Lania accepted her error. He was not admiring. He was waiting for his yorac, his group of underlings.

One by one, five more Conquerors joined the first. Each rode a horse, simple ponies or long-legged racers, not at all like the warhorse. Their armors were identical, although those of the diasists were ill-fitted and new, awaiting when the recruits would broaden their shoulders and fill them out.

Monsters, each of them, although they looked like men under their armor. They were slave-masters, murderers, destroyers of the One God's world, and heartless beasts. They were Lionians, the Conquerors.

Lania drove her feet faster, feeling like an owl swooping toward an unwary mouse. The Nurmi scout would never get within range of the camp in time. Only Lania was close enough to save him.

At a gesture from the yoraci with the gray plume, a diasist with his white plume kicked his horse into a run and brought up the heavy spear.

Lania threw herself to her knees, skidding through the cutting blades of dry grass, and brought up her bow. Just as the Conqueror reached the upward climb of the hill, he flew off his horse and thudded into the field. She did not doubt her arrow had cut into his throat, piercing under the chinstrap of the helm.

The world paused for a unified gasp. The five other riders, having trotted in formation behind the charging Lionian, came to an abrupt halt.

Some logic, the last of its kind to filter into her mind, told Lania to hold off the attackers until others from the camp could join her. The world narrowed into the five men in the field below.

As the five other Conquerors circled to adjust their formation, Lania began a slow march down the hill. The first of her arrows bounced harmlessly off one silver helmet, but the sound of it seemed to shake the Nurmi scout to his senses; he took off up the hill with a yelp of delight and a skip of joy. A second arrow slid narrowly into the eyehole of the helm and killed another attacker.

They finished formation, their shields now raised. Lania paused, seeking an opening; she was low on arrows.

"It's just one Nurmi! And she's naked!" one diasist shouted.

"You take her out then!" the other answered. "Did you see that shot?"

"Fine!" the third called. "I'll do it!"

Her target chosen, she put her last iron-tipped shaft into the shoulder of the brave diasist who moved to advance. The Conqueror let out a shout and let fall his spear, although he retained his seat.

"With me!" the yoraci called to the diasists, finally getting his wits about him. Unified, they brought their horses to a slow canter, keeping in a line. The diasist she had wounded reached for the sword on his saddle, his double-edged dius, and followed his companions forward.

Lania had made her way down the hill and to the first Conqueror she had slain. Not bothering to mutter a prayer to counter the pollution of the Conqueror, she pulled the dead diasist's dagger from his belt. She felt the chill of the metal creep up her arm and let it feed her smile. Distantly, she felt the Priestess whisper a prayer for her. Polluted or not, she again had a weapon.

Poised, she waited for their foolishness. Even the yoraci did not scare her; she'd kill his ilk before. She knew where to put her blades.

As the first horse raged past, Lania sidestepped, switched the blade to her left hand and aimed it low, letting the horse's speed drag the knife across the animal's side. Enraged, the horse threw its rider, then bolted, the girth cut and the saddle falling to the side. Riding horses made for poor warhorses.

Before Lania could deal with the downed man, the second Conqueror was bearing down on her. She lifted the dagger in a feint. Anticipating her stepping aside once more, the inexperienced Lionian pulled wide to his right, driving him into Lania when she came up on the other side. She brought the blade down into the rider's hip and sent him to join his companions in the dirt. He quickly bled out into the grasses.

When she landed, she had traded the dagger, carried away in the blood and bone of the second rider, for a sword. The easy positioning of the dius had been intended to allow the rider to switch between weapons during battle rapidly. It had placed the blade's grip in easy reach of the Warrior's right hand as her left dug home the borrowed dagger.

In his haste, the gray-plumed yoraci overshot his target when she leaped aside. Neither Lania nor the yoraci were able to turn fast enough to press the attack.

The first downed diasist rose, brandishing his dagger. He waved the blade in the air like a priest casting a spell, as if entertaining a child, but battle fury burned in her blood and drove her to action. When he brought his dagger down to block her dius, the diasist grunted in surprise to find Lania's sword in his gut.

His step back had not been enough. One lunge had easily slipped the blade under the layers of metal armor, cutting just over the pelvic bone and deep into the abdominal cavity.

As soon as she pulled the dius free, the monster collapsed.

As the yoraci turned his horse, the final diasist—with an arrow sticking out of his right shoulder—reached her. He slashed down as she rose from her latest kill, and Lania threw herself into a roll. Coming up as the newest rider wheeled his horse, she tried again to dodge aside, but, as she turned, she found the horse and rider once more too close for a swing of the sword. Keeping the horse in a tight circle, the Conqueror pinned her.

Like a cornered animal, she lashed out.

Lania's first strike landed on the protective coverings of the rider's leg, but on the second, inspired, she struck the foot, cutting to the bone and distracting the diasist. Given its head, the horse shied away from the spinning blade, carrying the diasist away from Lania.

Infuriated, Lania threw her dius into the back of the wounded diasist. It hit point first and cut between the strips of metal woven into the blue and black armor. The fifth Conqueror fell from his horse.

The world cleared in an instant. Lania met the eyes of the final Conqueror, still mounted and unwounded, as he positioned to charge her unopposed.

The bottom of her stomach dropped out as she realized that her hands, for the first time since she had bolted from the tranquility of her pond, were empty. She stood alone, unarmed, and naked before an armored yoraci, the most experienced of the soldiers here. She was too far from the fallen Conquerors to steal another blade, and he would overtake her before she reached the safety of the forest. There was nothing to stop him.

Lania suddenly knew what the target felt like when the archer aimed his shot.

The yoraci was in no hurry; she saw him scan the area, giving Lania a moment to release her breath. A spark of hope flashed as the Lionian glanced up the hill. Her father would have sent fighters down the hill and, by now, they should be well within dangerous proximity for the Conqueror. If the Lionian was threatened, he would have to flee.

Her hope was crushed when she looked up the empty hill. The only thing between her and the sharpened logs of the camp defenses was grass. The camp, and every one of its members, remained safely behind the barricades. Her father had held the warriors back.

She was alone. She had been abandoned. Nothing stood between her and the Conqueror.

She should not have been alone! How could the Black Arrow ignore her? He must have known she could do little more than hold them. He could not have expected her to slay all six! She was the Warrior, but that was a lot, even for her.

The feeling of sickness vanished as her rage surfaced. A growl escaped as she bared her teeth. She snarled a curse up the hill, knowing he would never hear it. He'd put her on display, showing her off, using her to build up the morale of the fleeing army encamped above. She was their Warrior, as foretold by the One God. She could not fall here!

Her attention snapped back to the Conqueror when the horse stamped its foot impatiently. Lania's rage was transferred from the man watching from the top of the hill to the black-haired invader fool enough to stand in her path.

"Come on!" Lania shouted in her best Lionian. To her astonishment, there was no tremble in her voice. Her fear buried by rage, she threw her arms wide in invitation. "What are you afraid of, beast? Come at me, you coward! Come on!"

The Conqueror flinched, his head turning to search the field.

Lania's Lionian words became interspersed with Nurmi. "Attack me, you coward!" she screamed, taking several steps forward. "Have you no soul?" she accused, using the Nurmi word for "soul" as she did not know the Lionian one. "Have you no courage? Where is your glory now? What is it you fear from a lone woman? Come on!" As she shouted, she ran forward. Although the sane part of her mind was appalled that she would be so reckless, it was silenced by her fury.

With her next step, the yoraci started as if suddenly noticing his downed companions and the madwoman in front of him. With a quick jerk of the reins, he directed his horse down the hill and disappeared through the trees in full flight. Lania, still screaming insults at the departing Conqueror, was truly alone.

She did not stop. After kicking one of the corpses, she snatched up a long spear and snapped it across her knee before throwing the pieces toward the camp where the crowd, the predicted crowd, was watching. *A show.* She was naught but a show.

"Demons take you!" she shouted before breaking into a run and running blindly across the field, back into the sanctuary of the forest. She did not stop until she found her way to the pond where her afternoon had been interrupted.

She dove in and let the cold water slap her with reality.

Lunch could be outside now that the winter rains had ceased. While fellow councilmen took their meals in sequestered corners of the Councilhall, Aurion Arrius Illica Polfius left the smooth white building and sat on a bench under the swaying poplars. To get to the top of the mound over the half-buried hall, he had to use the upper public doors, not the hidden lower doors reserved for the councilmen. That suited him.

The people attending the Councilhall varied. On justice days, the unscrupulous made their required appearances to be judged. On holy days, the priests flooded the space with festivities, trying to attract new faithful with promises of blessings. On council days, the wealthy arrived in carriages pulled by purebreds, seeking to buy influence with thinly concealed bribes.

Following these were the spectators. The public was admitted through the upper doors to fill the benches and judge the actions of their governors. They were a mixed group, from vagrants looking for a warm place to rest to the haughtiest of the upper class. Only slaves were forbidden within the wizard-stone walls of the Councilhall.

The flux meant anyone could be on the mound above the Councilhall at any time. A person could get lost in the crowds. Many tried to do so.

In his white and black robes, the chain of his district hanging from his neck, Aurion was far from inconspicuous. House guards, familiar faces he fully trusted, flanked him. Sitting to the side in the cool spring air, he hoped to avoid notice while he memorized all he saw.

The largest group was the slaves. Awaiting the return of their masters, they staged wrestling matches in a nearby yard. The competitors had stripped, Aurion presumed to protect their uniforms from tears or mud, leaving their sun-burned backs open. Their tones ranged from the pale freckled skin of an Esparan's to the Santanese's coal-black color, all made bare by their games. To his surprise, they were taking bets, but, lacking coin, they shouted out deals of knickknacks from thread dolls to carved buttons to each other in Lionian. He wondered what value the items had between the races of slaves. Would a Windraso's button be worth a Santanese's beadwork? It was fascinating to see them treating such frivolous things as valuable.

An older man passed between the guards and sat beside Aurion. With fingers stained black from ink, he took an olive off Aurion's lunch platter.

"You didn't eat before coming?" Aurion said, suppressing a smile.

"You eat better than I do," Grizzle replied, his voice a characteristic grouse. He popped the olive into his mouth.

"And whose fault is that?"

The old spymaster pursed his lips under his salt-and-pepper beard, then spat the pit from the olive. He reached for another, his eyes squinted near-closed due to the sunset. His eyebrows united over his brow. "I'd hate to burden your coffers by stuffing myself on mango and quail lunches."

Aurion snorted. "I'm sure the budget can afford getting you your own olives." He pulled the platter away from Grizzle. "Council's rejoining in ten minutes. I'll need my strength. Volustio's speaking next."

Grizzle grunted. "You'll need your patience, you mean."

"That too." Aurion wrapped a flat bread around a chunk of cheese. "I assume you have a reason to interrupt my reconnaissance?" He chewed the wrap hastily, having been distracted by the happenings atop the mound. The cheese was as salty as the olives. Thankfully, the Councilhall provided wine. He would need it.

"Is that what you call this?" Grizzle cast his gaze around skeptically.

Aurion nodded his head to the side. "Master Gitarius has been arguing with his wife for an hour. He's run out of money for flattering councilmen and now his daughter needs a new dress for courting." Grizzle did not turn his head to look at the blustering man in his signature two-colored garb of red and black by the stables.

"She needs more than a dress. He spent most of her dowry too," Grizzle replied.

Course Grizzle knows, Aurion mused.

"He doesn't need much for that," Aurion pointed out. "Councilman Dracus has a nephew whose prospects are increasingly limited as the slave trade in Santan dries up. Dracus and Gitarius were talking earlier; probably why Gitarius' wife hasn't stormed off yet. If that falls through, they'll have to reconsider Tanfius Galfium and I know Bellavina would hate to have her daughter marry into that family. Speaking of which…" Aurion tilted his head in the other direction. "Councilman Galfium is behind the pinnacle there. Met one of his slaves. I suspect he'll be out in a minute. He doesn't have a lot of stamina." One of the councilman's slaves, a large, hollow-eyed Santanese with a shaved head, stood by as a lookout, but his uniform gave him away as one of Galfium's slaves.

"One of his slaves, or someone else's?" Grizzle asked.

Sensing the question was a trick, Aurion reviewed what he'd seen. The young man had been a small Nurmi slave, but the uniform had been large on her. Although that commonly happened when someone purchased a Nurmi without thinking about sizing uniforms correctly for the child-sized people, Galfium owned many Nurmi. He would not have had issues outfitting a new slave in his tri-colored white, black, and green. Her brand…

"No brand," Aurion realized aloud. "Demons, I just about missed that. She's a prostitute then?"

Grizzle gave an exaggerated shrug, frowning dramatically. "Might be owned by one of Cansi's priests. Might be I followed her here."

"I knew there was a reason I keep you around," Aurion admitted, chewing quickly on the flatbread.

A shout of victory rose over the din of the wrestling circle where a large Windraso was declared the winner. Considering the man's size, it was no surprise he had tossed the smaller curly-haired Yeahsin out of bounds within seconds. Around them, new bets were made, and a woman stepped up as a challenger. A Windraso as well, her long red braids were tied behind her head. Although she was slightly shorter than the victor, her fists were as big as his. When they clashed, it was like the crashing of ships.

"What's got your attention with the slaves?" Grizzle asked. He was following Aurion's stare, somehow another olive in hand again.

Aurion swapped the platter to his other side, pulling his eyes from the slaves.

"High Councilman Meltatio's slave is consistently placing bets with Maurio's," he said. "Every few matches, they meet by the gate."

Grizzle nodded. "Since I'm here, I'll find out what they've been discussing."

Brushing his hands off, Aurion stood. "I'd appreciate that. That's what your budget is for, after all."

A servant threaded between the guards to retrieve the dinner platter from where Aurion left it on the bench. Grizzle leaned down the bench and snatched another olive before the servant could whisk the plate away. The servant glanced over his shoulder as he left, eyeing the strange man in black and the placid councilman. The guards were tolerated because each had been vetted by Grizzle himself before being accepted into the household, but Aurion and Grizzle waited until the servant was out of earshot before speaking again.

"You'd better speak your business, Grizz. I need to get back in there."

"Always about business, eh? Well, the East Army reported the Black Arrow was south of the Solon River as of five days ago."

Aurion raised an eyebrow at the spymaster. "The rebel does that a few times a year. Why does it matter now?"

Grizzle cracked a wide smile, teeth bared like a bear as he contemplated his stolen olive. "He's got his daughters with him."

Despite himself, Aurion snapped to attention. "The Twins?"

The spymaster grinned. "Both."

"Is my horse ready?"

Grizzle tsked at him, his broad mouth turning into a long frown that stretched his beard to his sternum. "The sovereign won't want his councilman gallivanting into a war zone."

"He can yell at me when I get back. Grizz, if we take either the Black Arrow or the Twins, this threat is over. If we got all *three*..."

"Not that much of a threat. They're a rabble."

"For now. They get organized, and we'll lose holdings in Namera."

"Doesn't mean you have to go in person."

"But it means I want to."

Aurion met the spymaster's dark eyes. He had not given Grizzle a formal order since the man joined the House of Illica three years prior. As Master of the Household and a ranking councilman, Aurion could insist on obedience, but he wondered how that would affect their relationship. Grizzle had chosen to work for Aurion and proven himself efficient, even ruthless, when necessary. To survive in the Council, Aurion didn't just need a spymaster; he needed one as good as Grizzle.

But Grizzle cracked a crooked grin and said, "I've got Balvor putting on his loraxi tabs and assembling his men. Horses await you at the house. Ride hard if you want to catch them."

Aurion clasped Grizzle's shoulder and squeezed. "You know me too well."

The old spymaster shrugged and spat another olive pit. "That's my job."

Aurion spurred out of Lione within the hour, the council meeting abandoned.

CHAPTER 2

Lania sat motionless on the northwest tower in the light of the sunrise, her legs properly folded beneath her. She had laid her weapons near the ladder, hoping they would not interfere. Her callused hands clenched and unclenched on her lap, conscious of her sword's absence. Comforting her, black paint drew a mask over her eyes and traced a line from her forehead to her chin, connecting her mind to her body.

She tried to work through the breathing exercise to clear her mind, but failed. The part of her that wanted to pick up the sword, the same part that wished the Lionian army would hurry up and attack, was too eager. *Patience*, she told herself. Every moment the Lionian monsters hesitated at the fort Lania defended was time bought for the retreating Nurmi forces.

Breathe in. She focused on the breath and held it. The air smelled of perfumes from the evergreens surrounding the fort, flavored with new-budding flowers. It tasted sweet but chilled from the dew. It barely held her attention for a moment.

There had been commotion in the Lionian camp the night before. After mooncycles of waiting, they'd raised an additional banner, which meant a high-ranking galeni had joined them. Whoever it was, they'd come with two new war machines and a handful of soldiers, which would matter little to the already extensively equipped army surrounding her fort. She had to conclude the new commander brought something else of value. Why send such a senior officer into battle with so little?

She had exhaled without thought and lost the meditation. She could feel her twin scoffing through their linked spirits, but knew Akara understood. Even when Akara had been trained as the Warrior and Lania as the Priestess, Akara had proven adept with prayers and meditation while Lania had been more interested in fighting.

Breathe in, Lania tried again.

The defenses were ready, as they had been every day since the Nurmi army had snuck away from the fort, named *Glimup,* or "Freedom" in Nurmi, three nights earlier. Regardless, Lania would do her rounds. The enemy's sentries would have changed with the dawn. Did she have time to sneak out before they sent their scout? She would like to get a second look at those machines.

She snapped her thoughts back to meditation, scolding herself. *Breathe in.*

If the new arrival was what the army had been waiting for, she would see action soon. The Nurmi army should be near the base of Mount Duhmkun by now. The Lionians may yet catch them if they figured out where they had crossed the river. Lionians knew how to march swiftly, even over land. The Nurmi needed the safety of the Corelands forest to evade them. They were close, but...

The breathing technique was not working; she had lost concentration again. Her mind remained tangled with the tactics to keep the enemy at bay when they finally figured out the men and women propped up along the wall would never fire a shot or lift a sword. Perhaps they would smell the rot if the wind shifted.

In the end, the Lionians would come, and Lania would have to flee or fall. That was her fate, and she had accepted it. The part of her that itched for the feel of a weapon in her hand knew it would take control then. When hesitation meant death, the meditative mind would disappear entirely. Balance was not possible. She was the Warrior.

Lania opened her eyes. Although clouds waited on every horizon, she sat under clear skies more reminiscent of a summer day. But spring arrived with trepidation in the far north. The melting snows lingered in the shadows of the conifers.

She rose slowly, and her right hand touched the silver torque on her arm reflectively. The simple band was a barbarian's unattractive ornament to any not of the One God's children. Although it had lost its smoothness to nicks, bends, and stains from battle, the symbol engraved on the widened end of the armband remained perfect; a circle with four lines extending from it. As long as she wore the One God's eye, she was blessed.

From the tower, the Warrior looked down into the valley below the fort. The day began for the army encamped there. As she watched, a lone rider headed up the hill.

No time, she decided. The scout was early.

After collecting and then sheathing her sword, Lania retrieved her bow and smiled as she notched an arrow. *What an entertaining dance*. He knew the range of her bow and slowed, wary, once he reached it. Lania fired her first shot high, following quickly with a second, low arrow. Both arrows struck near the scout, one after the other, as if shot from two different bows. Although accuracy was impossible at the range, the arrows made him jump. As tempting as it was to let him close enough for her arrows to find the gaps in his armor, he might spot or smell the dead men on the wall and recognize her ploy. She could not allow that.

He studied the fort's walls from a distance, looked to the forests nearby for the signs of a Nurmi raiding party or ambush and, finding nothing, rode back to camp.

Another day. They had stopped sending parties through the forest to spy on her, accepting that a soldier in the woods was an easy target for a Nurmi hunter like her. Would they notice that the warriors along the walls were the same ones that had been there for the last three days? She had changed their helmets again overnight, trying to make it look like the watch had changed, but she knew the trick was hardly more than a wish. She was alone. They would figure it out once the clouds of flies became obvious. Then, they would come.

She headed back along the wall, barely remembering to grab the remaining food by the ladder, but her sister had warned her not to let her health suffer while she guarded the fort single-handedly. She shoved the bread into her mouth and chewed self-consciously.

She was feeling out of shape. Three days without fighting made the Warrior feel stiff and weak.

Patience, she reminded herself.

She could sneak out to take another look at the Conqueror's demon-cursed machines. There was one fire-launcher—she had learned to recognize those from the battles fought at her father's side—and one she assumed was a ram for breaking down doors. If nothing else, she knew the launcher took time to set up. She would have plenty of warning should they decide to use it.

As she stood watching from her lookout, riders left the camp for a second time. The new banner flew above the group. There were only nine of these Conquerors—a yorac—but one of them must have been a leader of some kind to have a banner. The new officer?

Lania notched another arrow. She would show him why no one had dared venture too close to *Glimup* Fort. But the party stopped beside the arrows that had scared off the scout and did not approach for her to take better aim. Were they as impatient as she was? So many days without any activity could be destructive to an anxious army. Would they come?

The party turned back to camp without ever stepping within her range. She replaced her arrow with a disappointed sigh.

But upon their return, the Lionians pulled the machines forward. Her heart leaped. *At last!*

Lania rushed around the fort, checking everything was ready, but nothing had changed. Desperate for something useful to do as she waited for them to climb the hill, Lania put down the bow and drew the familiar weight of her sword into her hand.

Training took over, and her anxiousness faded. Moving unconsciously, she fought the shadows near her, lunging, blocking, and stabbing at nothing until her muscles warmed and her mind cleared. When at last she stopped, she was ready.

Battle was her meditation, and far more effective than any of the teaching from Akara's grove.

Lania took a place on the wall between the corpses, her bow at her side and a pile of Lionian spears at her feet. Horns and drums reached her ears, and the perfect lines of armored invaders began the march up toward the ready Warrior. Farther back, the launcher threw a container of flaming oil.

The first shot crashed into the woods behind the fort. The second blasted into the central tower behind Lania and rained fire into the courtyard. Bow in hand and arrow notched, the Warrior did not flinch, except to smile briefly.

She had no intention of going down into the courtyard, but the Lionians would have to pass through the mess of debris and fires. The fort had been doomed since the Black Arrow and the Priestess had led the people out. Fire would cleanse it nicely.

Erasing her smile, Lania waited, as unblinking and steady as the bodies around her. By the time the Lionian monsters were close enough to see the blank faces of the dead Nurmi on the ramparts, the Lionians' perfect formation was relaxing. They could tell the bodies were just that; dead propped up to give the semblance of defenses. Some of them got sloppy, opening a hole in their shield wall.

This time, Lania kept the smile from creeping onto her face. In one action, she lifted her bow, aimed, and loosed. Her arrow struck a white-plumed diasist, the lowest rank sent to test the advance. Before his neighbors could bring the shields back into the solid wall, her second arrow passed between them, killing the Conqueror behind.

The wall of shields closed once more; the threat was now apparent.

She lowered her bow to take up her spears.

The first three spears bounced off the shields, but the fourth one embedded into a soldier's foot, who fell. As with all those who had fallen before him, he was quickly replaced. There were plenty of diasists to fill in the gap.

Lania saved the remaining spears and instead headed for the main doors. Once the Lionians had brought up their next machine, pounding the ram into the blocked entrance, Lania dumped a pile of rocks over the edge of the walls. Those who had neglected their defenses were knocked unconscious even through their silver-colored helmets by the heavy stones. The second pile of rocks followed quickly, but it had less effect as the enemy brought up their shields.

The ram slammed solidly into the doors.

Lania had no plans to ever use the main gates again and had blocked it with everything possible. The walls would have been easier to crack than the solid oak doors reinforced by piles of stones, bodies, and wagons.

Once they had replaced their dazed companions, Lania dropped her next defense.

The black, sticky liquid was no longer hot, but it poured down on the enemy, coating everything with darkness. With a quiet thanks to the One God for her access to fire, Lania tossed a burning scrap of wood over the edge in the wake of the tar. Although cool, the black liquid burned well. Flames spread quickly among those who had been coated.

But for each fallen Lionian, another stepped up. Their numbers seemed never-ending.

They renewed their attack on the door. Below her, the pile of debris blocking the doors shifted under the force of the demon-damned machine.

Lania's spears found every opening they gave her. By the time the Lionians had pushed the doors out of their frame, a dozen more Conquerors lay dead or wounded, and Lania was gone.

She ran for the far wall and retrieved her bow. The first man through the door was dead before he set his foot down. With the debris to clamber over, the shields wavered, exposing holes she filled with arrows or spears. Unable to reach her, the Lionians hacked their way into the heart of the flaming fort.

Once in a cleared space, the Lionians wheeled into a turtle formation, defended on all sides as a unit. Shuffling as one, they advanced, extinguishing the smoldering fires nearest them with stomps and shouting commands from behind their wall of shields.

The fire slowly moved toward the invaders, and Lania waited.

With no response from within, the formation paused. A horn sounded from behind.

The earlier group of riders entered the fort, their strange banner flying high. Proud and pompous, the broad Lionian sat tall on his warhorse and shouted: "We know you are here! Surrender now, or your life will be forfeit!"

Lania smiled from inside the tower where she had taken refuge. *Surrender? Laughable.* No Nurmi surrendered. She would die first.

From the covered window of the tower, she aimed her arrow at the man with the black plume adorning his helm. She had not killed a braxi before. He would be replaced from the carefully controlled ranks, but she could still be proud of the death of a black-plumed Lionian.

He turned his horse to pace across the courtyard. "There is no escape from here! You cannot hide from fire!"

She ignored him, lost in contemplation. The gaps in his leather and metal composite armor were few and tricky. His movement made a heart shot unreliable; there was a plate over the sternum in their armor directly behind the black sun on the chest that her iron-tipped arrows would struggle to pierce at this distance. She needed flesh. The legs were plated in parts, but that would not kill. Their healers were too good. The base of the neck gaped when he turned: that would work.

As she considered her options, a new Conqueror arrived under a plain eight-pointed sun banner that made her pause. The sun marking meant Lione. What did it mean when it was used as a banner?

The new arrival was older than any Lionian she had ever seen. The typical black hair of the Lionian was pure white with age and stuck out from a non-standard half-helm that left his face open. His expression, wrinkled with age, was grim and knowledgeable as he rode briskly, dressed in bright, polished armor. The four Conquerors around him in formation, wearing a scorpion-within-the-sun marking on their chests, bore the brunt of many battles on their dented and blackened armor. Each was dressed in the typical black and blue of the Lionian army, but had a red plume atop their helmets. She knew the ranks of Lione, but did not know what a red plume meant.

Between the older monster and his escort of red-plumed Conquerors rode a woman.

Unlike the Nurmi, Lionian women did not fight. But this woman was dressed in partial armor, her black hair pulled back from her face. Although her armor was blue and black, she wore no sun on her chest and carried no weapons.

Lania consciously shrugged to herself. Lionian women kept slaves. Lionian women killed slaves. They were as guilty as their men. Still, it was better to kill the officer if she could.

It was only then that Lania noticed the color of the old Lionian's plume: blue.

A *galeni*, she recognized. The old Lionian was the commander of at least half of the East Army.

Lania adjusted her aim. The death of a galeni trumped a braxi by far.

She fired the arrow through the crack in the shutter but missed the small gap in the galeni's neck plate. Her position revealed, Lania did not have time to acknowledge her frustration. The Black Arrow himself had taught her the bow. It was generally known she had the same sharp eyes as her father. She never missed! She cursed the Lionian's luck.

The guards with their red plumes blocked any further attempt against their leader, although she shot many more Conquerors before they located her trap door and brought a ladder.

The diasist who opened the door fell on his comrades below with blood spilling from his split neck. The next three fared no better. Down in the yard, new orders came from the galeni, and the Lionians brought burning planks to the base of her tower. As the fire began to rise, she pulled a cloth from her belt to cover her face, but it helped little to filter out the smoke.

The door below was surely being watched. There was only one other way to go.

Lania kicked open the shutters, slid out the window, and pulled herself onto the roof of the tower with her bow in hand. Hidden by the smoke, her arrows rained upon them. They returned fire into the smoke with their crossbows, but the fire meant to trap her now defended her perch.

Pain lanced through her leg, and she collapsed onto the roof. Battle rage still in her blood, she pulled a strip of cloth from her belt, yanked the bolt from her leg, and tied the fabric around her wound. By the time she stood again, bow in hand, the excitement had erased the pain from her mind.

The flames drew near, forcing her to jump from the tower like a dancer at the evening fire. Balancing first on her good leg before standing firm, she landed on the outer log wall of the fort. Now clear of the smoke, the spears and bolts chased her along the wall to a second tower. Shouts continued below, and she vaguely heard something about taking her alive, but she paid it no mind. When she reached again for an arrow, she found only one in her quiver. Without hesitation, she fired it off.

She now had a choice. Before her, a horde of black-haired monsters sought to take her down. At her back, the forest beckoned her. She could jump to the trees, away from the fire, swords, and spears. She had lived her life in the woods; they would not catch her once she was under its protection, even if their forces were milling among the trees beyond.

But she had to delay the Lionians and buy time for her father's forces to escape.

She drew her sword. The defenses were done. She had no more tricks. There was nothing to stop the Lionians now except her and her sword.

It was time to dance.

Leaping from the wall, Lania landed on her good leg and threw herself against a Lionian shield, knocking the monster down. Without a pause, she leaned back and slashed at the arm reaching for her, cutting it open and forcing the enemy back. She jumped the prone man and shouldered a Conqueror aside to let her sword strike the neck of another. It was not a lethal blow, but it caused him to stagger away. She ducked next, and her feet turned with the accuracy and grace of a performer on Spirit Eve. A quick sidestep put her out of the way of the responding down-thrust.

They were everywhere.

Recognizing that they were trying to disable rather than kill her, Lania began to laugh. Their formations were designed to surround her, but she danced out of their reach. With a thrust that set a man on his rump, she jumped free of their circle, ready for another.

She landed on the wrong leg. Interrupting her strike to the enemy's neck, Lania's leg gave out under her.

From the ground where the wounded leg had sent her, Lania could not escape the hands reaching for her. She swung blindly, not caring who she hit or how hard. A weight knocked her to the ground. Gloved hands stole her sword. She expected a beating to follow, or perhaps death, but the voice of the old galeni cut through before the soldiers landed more than a few kicks.

"Alive, you oafs. Bind her!"

Ropes followed.

After three years of catering to the crowds and rules of Lione as a councilman, Aurion found it refreshing to ride through the countryside. It would have been better alone, but a councilman was never alone.

"That's us past the border," Balvor shouted over the clatter of hooves. "Falti's up next." The red-plumed helm muffled his voice, but his southern accent stood out among the bodyguards.

"Hardly a border," Aurion shouted back.

The loraxi commander of his personal guard laughed loud enough for his subordinates to hear and join in. The full loraxan, over thirty soldiers, had been assigned to getting Aurion into the north and back alive, making the road crowded and noisy with armor and weapons.

The "border" was a point where the Nurmi presence began but was not marked by towers or defenses. The odds of running into a band of the savages were still low; it was unlikely any Nurmi had snuck past the city of Falti, but the diasists with him kept their hand crossbows readied as they rode. It would not do for a Councilman of Lione to fall prey to a Nurmi hunting party. It would get worse the farther north they rode, but Aurion was unwilling to allow the threat of enemies to block him from reaching the East Army, which was engaged with the Nurmi forces.

As they crested a rise, Falti appeared ahead of them, and Aurion pulled his horse to a walk to better examine the surroundings. The small town had grown from its origins as a rudimentary fort. Trapped in the dense forest, they relied heavily on the road for food supplies, and the depth of the ruts for the wagon wheels showed it. At a distance, the dents and scorch marks on the gate of Falti were still visible. According to the original report, this was where the Black Arrow and his savages had started their attack. The East Army had driven them off, then harried them north, making their retreat into a race for the mountains.

He needed to update his information, and those closest to the events were the best source. Aurion approached the gate of Falti instead of riding past. The soldiers matched Aurion, their protective formation uninterrupted. Balvor had trained his soldiers well.

"Face it," Balvor said as he brought his horse next to Aurion's, "you'd be disappointed if you didn't get to see a savage."

Aurion chuckled. "I've seen plenty of Nurmi, but I'll be disappointed if I don't see the Black Arrow or one of his daughters. They say he's been cornered."

Balvor snorted. His expression was hidden within the closed helm, but Aurion heard the mocking smile in the voice. "Oh yes, cornered in the fort, the impossible fort that didn't exist until the Nurmi hid in it! The magical fort! The invisible fort, or so Braxi Hanseri would have you believe. He couldn't have missed it, after all."

The men around them did not join in the humor, their heads turning to watch the roadside woods.

"Who goes there?" a sentry on the wall shouted down.

"Use your demon-cursed eyes!" Balvor yelled back before Aurion could reply. "White and black robe! Open the damned gate for the councilman."

A hundred apologies followed as the guards on the gate struggled to crank the rusted entrance wide. In the many years since Falti's construction, it seemed no one had tended its gate mechanism; it creaked loud enough to be heard in distant Lione.

"Diasist Narum, could you freshen that mechanism up, please," Aurion said as he passed into the city. "No one wants the gate to be slow when it matters."

The diasist on Aurion's left bowed his head and peeled off from the group, sliding tools out of his saddlebags as he dismounted. Narum had been an engineer in the South Army before Aurion had brought him to Lione. He was one of the best Aurion knew.

His guards at his back, Aurion brought his horse to a halt once he was through the gatehouse. Falti's guards had assembled, with the commander of the city, a worn paki, striding purposely across the central yard to greet Aurion.

While they waited, Balvor added, "But I guess if the Nurmi weren't a threat, they wouldn't have sent Galeni Lonthius up. They don't send the highest-ranked galeni to take command of the army directly for fun. You hoping to see him too?"

Aurion never missed an opportunity to meet with his old mentor, although it had been at least a year since he had seen Galeni Tactus Lonthius. He did not know if Lonthius would have time for a social call. He'd noticed on the report that Galeni Lonthius' daughter Olena was still with her father, a fact Aurion needed to verify. Despite being of a highly marriageable age, Olena had been a fixture in her father's company. Aurion had a suspicion he knew why, but those were questions for Lonthius himself.

"Councilman, we are honored to—"

The greeting was as far as Aurion let the paki get. "Relax, Paki Carothan," he soothed. "I'm not here for official inspections. The gods know I never do those bloody things."

The paki's stance eased.

"I am Councilman Aurion Arrius Illica Polfius, Councilman of the Freeman District and Master of the Household of Illica," Aurion fully introduced himself. He had already shown he knew the paki's name, but giving his full name and position was a compliment. Further, it allowed them to recognize him, and Aurion saw the soldiers immediately release their collectively held breath. Other councilmen enjoyed making those beneath them squirm; Aurion worked to maintain a reputation for the opposite. "I'm passing through on my way to join the East Army. I thought you might have some recent reports."

Paki Carothan's voice was cheerful. "We just had the messenger through. The East Army broke into the Nurmi fort this morning, thanks to Galeni Lonthius and his soldiers. The Warrior has been captured after holding the fort for at least three days alone. The rest of the Nurmi forces are unaccounted for." There was no shame in the man's voice; he trusted delivering the information was valuable despite the unfortunate outcome.

"Unaccounted for?" Balvor barked.

"Probably heading to the mountains. I must be off quickly if I am to catch them up," Aurion interrupted. "Thank you very much for your help, Paki Carothan. I'll stop in on my way back."

Turning his horse, Aurion headed back out the gate, collecting Diasist Narum as he left. The gate slid shut without a creak behind them.

As soon as they were again on the road, Aurion kicked his horse into a trot. The packed earth under the hooves had been patched in the bow wave of the army, giving them a smooth run between the wagon ruts.

"You in a hurry, Aurion?" Balvor called, matching the change in pace.

"I've been stuck in Lione for years, Balvor! I've missed out on everything. The Warrior's been captured!"

"And the rest of the army is 'unaccounted for.' You figure that you can find them if you get there fast enough?"

"Gods no," Aurion replied, goading his horse to a canter to spite the loraxi. "But if I hurry, I might catch sight of the Warrior. I wouldn't mind that! Come on, boys! Keep up!"

The better part of an hour passed, the group alternating periods of trotting with long lopes when the terrain allowed. The trees flew by, unimportant, except when roots reached the edge of the road and made the horses skip. At last, a train of people and wagons, as well as a slow jail cart, trundled into view, heading toward them. The bodyguards created their circle of defense around Aurion, requiring no instructions from Balvor.

"You seem keen to look at this Warrior," Balvor commented, moving in protectively. He had his dius, a short double-edged sword, in hand now. "Is he that special?"

"She," Aurion corrected. "The Nurmi believe that the Warrior and the Priestess will destroy the Lionian Sovereignty, a prophecy dating back eight hundred years. She's described as a predator of supreme strength and cunning, often compared to the mountain cat of the north."

Hearing Balvor snicker, Aurion shrugged. "An exaggeration, I'm sure, but she is particularly proficient at killing Lionians, at least a hundred of us, single-handedly. Plus," he added, eyeing the pyre smoke on the horizon, "however many she killed today."

Once they reached the column, Aurion and his escort pulled to the side. It took some goading from Aurion's bodyguards to keep the soldiers marching, the train's initial response being to clear the road for the White and Black. But once they moved on, the pace picked up.

"Putting on a good show," Aurion dryly commented. He'd been on the other side of the exchange before. The presence of a superior pushed fear into each step. They didn't know his face and couldn't see his chain and seal well enough to recognize him. He could be the Councilman of the East Army, their ultimate superior short of the sovereign himself. He resisted the urge to smile at them, knowing it would increase their apprehension.

"We rush and rush and rush, just so you can wait," Balvor grumbled.

"*Watch*," Aurion corrected. "So I can watch."

They let the column pass until the jail cart came into view, then fell into the ranks behind it. The defending soldiers were forced to spread back, leaving Balvor and Aurion closest to the cart.

A paki with a green plume walked alongside the jail cart. As they reached hearing distance, the man shouted at the prisoner, demanding the location of the disappeared Nurmi forces.

Aurion checked the banners and cross-referenced them to the lists he had memorized. The paki would be Paki Dulci, a hot-tempered mid-class soldier Aurion had dealt with in his early career. But while Aurion had moved up the echelons, Dulci's temperament kept him in the paki rank.

"Speak Lionian, damn it!" Dulci snapped.

From within the cart, which was too small for her to stand or lie down in, a woman replied in Nurmi. Aurion assumed she was swearing floridly at Dulci.

When Aurion was much younger, his father had taken him to a circus show in Lione. Visiting the great, distant, and mysterious White City had been an incredible thrill. He remembered being disappointed by the mountain cats; so sick and weak, they had hidden at the back of their cages. He had expected the same from the caged cat before him now, but was pleasantly surprised.

She was, however, not exactly as the legends described her. Nurmi were small in general, and she was no exception, being well below the height of a Lionian. Her matted brown hair contained a handful of braids held by bright threads. These braids danced as she tossed her head in a way that reminded him of a rebellious green horse. The only piece of jewelry was a silver armband on her upper left arm that clearly no one had managed to take from her. Her armor was boiled leather with strips suspended from her belt. It had been badly damaged and repeatedly repaired, but some of the damage was recent.

No one had removed her armor, but her sword was gone from her belt loop. A blood-stained cloth wrapped around her right calf suggested she had roughly treated a wound during the conflict. The fabric was not of Lionian origin.

Answering Dulci's call, a slave came forward, a Nurmi boy who had to jog to keep up with the moving cart. He was probably six or seven, his brown hair cut to forbid him the traditional long hair of his culture. His blue and black shirt and the sun-shaped brand on his right arm identified him as an army slave, but the X brand above it, coupled with the thin scars across his young face, made it clear he had been bred in the southern mines. He averted his pale eyes, accepting his orders without looking up at Dulci. But that changed when the boy glanced at the cart. Instantly, the slave made a sign with his hand in front of his scarred face and said something in Nurmi.

"Bold," Balvor grumbled.

"Impressive," Aurion countered. "He instantly knows her! And now he's broken the Language Law right in front of a paki. That's faith."

"Or stupidity."

Dulci had lost all patience; the paki stepped up and struck the boy across his face, knocking him back several steps. Unfortunately for Paki Dulci, this brought him within arm's reach of the cage.

The Warrior's filthy hand snaked out, caught the paki by the collar, and slammed him against the bars with a resounding "clang." Dulci went down unconscious, his helm rolling off into the grass beside the road.

The senior yoraci immediately called a halt. The entire yorac surrounding the cart drew their diuses and advanced on the cart's occupant. The woman rose into a crouch, eyeing the approaching Lionians with her back to her cage's wooden door and giving them a feral grin.

Aurion kicked his horse forward, and the ranks parted before him instantly.

"Yoraci," Aurion snapped at the man with the gray plume, "call off your men."

The order was passed on as if by reflex. The Warrior laughed from behind the bars, harsh and mocking. A shiver ran down Aurion's spine, and he fought the instinct to back away. Some of the soldiers overtly flinched. "Send a man to get Paki Dulci," Aurion ordered, staying on task, "and keep people at least a stride away from that cart."

"Yes sir, er... Councilman," the yoraci said, having recognized the robes. Once a man was dispatched to see to the fallen paki, Aurion released a reserved smile. Paki Dulci was going to have a terrible headache, both from the blow to the head and from having to explain the event to Galeni Lonthius. It was vital, and Aurion was certain Dulci was aware of it, that the Warrior reach Lione alive.

"I have been out of the service for three years, and yet people still call me 'sir,'" Aurion said to the yoraci as the lower-ranked diasists pulled away from the cart as ordered. "I never get tired of it."

"I served with you in Santan, Councilman Polfius," the yoraci replied. "The army is loyal to their man." The yoraci removed his helm briefly, allowing Aurion to recognize him and his broad smile.

"Of course you did, Yoraci Falcium! I had not forgotten, but even I cannot see through those helms. You have done well for yourself. Last time I saw you, you still had a white plume."

As he replaced the helm to ensure his men saw he was still in charge, the yoraci shrugged. "Lione takes your recommendations seriously, Councilman."

"Demon shit," Aurion answered with a laugh. "The army takes my recommendations seriously. Lione tries to ignore me." He glanced at the cage to see the savage watching him as he finished. "Of course, I spend my days making sure they cannot get away with it."

The pale eyes of the Nurmi had always astounded Aurion. Hers were a particularly brilliant azure that rivaled the most vivid stained glass he had ever seen. Although someone had wiped much of it away, the remaining black paint on her face gave a solid contrast to the brightness of the eyes. He saw daggers in that potent stare, promising him death at the first opportunity.

"Amazing. Is she truly the Warrior?" he asked.

Her silent stare was the only response.

"She does not speak Lionian, Councilman, but the boy here can translate for us," Yoraci Falcium offered.

Aurion deliberately turned to face Falcium, although he watched the Warrior out of the corner of his eye. "Is it true she held the fort alone for three days?"

The yoraci found something interesting at his feet to look at. "Yes, Councilman," he admitted in an uncommonly low voice.

"Commendable," Aurion added, glancing back at the savage to register her reaction. "Not many could fool the Lionian army for that long."

Her lips peeled back in a predatory grin. It spoke volumes that the woman could smile under these circumstances. More importantly, it meant she had understood him.

"Is she the Warrior then?" the yoraci asked.

"Good question," Aurion said. "She speaks Lionian, Yoraci Falcium, but chooses not to answer. Let us try something different." He met her stare once more. "If you do not answer, I will assume you are not the Warrior, and your name is not Lania."

Her eyes narrowed as though peering through his armor. "I am," she said.

Aurion knew the Nurmi traditions: her name had been bestowed by a priest reading augury stones on the eve of her birth. The name was sacred to her and her people. She could not deny her name.

"Good," he answered. "You see, Yoraci, she can be reasoned with." The yoraci leaped at the opportunity and demanded to know where her escaped army had gone, just as Dulci had.

She paused as if considering how to phrase her response in the foreign language but then blankly looked at the yoraci and answered frigidly in Nurmi.

The Nurmi boy failed to stifle his giggle at what was said. Unfortunately for the boy, the sound attracted Falcium's attention. Yoraci Falcium scooped the slave under one arm and placed his camping knife to his throat.

"Tell us," he commanded.

Aurion had the urge to shrug. He doubted they would get any result this way, but he was sufficiently attracted to the mystery of the Warrior to await the response. If nothing else, he would learn more about this so-called legend.

She answered in Nurmi at first, the words a rapid string of nonsense. In the next breath, the Warrior brought her glare onto Yoraci Falcium.

"I will tell you what I told him," she said in halting Lionian. "I will not sacrifice the lives of many for the life of one, be it another's or my own. I will not tell you what you want to know. If the boy dies, the Priestess will ensure his place beyond the Gate. If he dies, he dies to protect his people."

Her Lionian was imperfect and offensive, but she spoke with such confidence Aurion felt obliged to believe everything she said.

The translator stopped squirming, although he was silently crying. For the Warrior he had only ever heard stories about, the Nurmi slave was being brave. It amazed Aurion that their faith could have such a strong effect.

"Leave the boy," Aurion interrupted. "It is not worth the bloodshed. Paki Dulci would be disappointed if he lost a slave needlessly. Your efforts are noted, Yoraci, but there are other ways of getting what we need."

The yoraci roughly swung the boy down and ordered him to be gone.

When Aurion looked back at the Warrior, it seemed some of the daggers in her eyes had dulled ever so slightly.

"Yoraci Falcium, provide food and water for the prisoner. A dead Nurmi does me little good," Aurion commanded.

"Councilman, captured slaves do not eat, and they spoil the food. Giving her food would waste it. She will be weak when she arrives, but she should survive."

"Most Nurmi would rather die than become a slave, but this one expects to escape. She will eat," Aurion corrected.

He left Balvor and half of his loraxan with the jail cart, taking the other half south ahead of the column. There was much he had to prepare.

CHAPTER 3

When Aurion rode out from Lione, his house loraxi, Antori Yeon Trailuse, escorted him with a dozen defenders. But once they met with Balvor and his team, Aurion nodded dismissal to Antori. The younger loraxi saluted deferentially and backed off to allow Balvor to take over. Aurion had questions for the men he had assigned to ensure Lania made it to Lione; Antori gave him the space to ask them.

"You had fun," Aurion remarked to Balvor. He had intended for the words to come out dry, but he found himself incapable of concealing his delight.

"The demons nearly got us," Balvor answered. He held his helm under his arm and grinned from ear to ear as he rode. The bodyguards fell in around him in a familiar pattern as they rode past the encamped army's pickets. Aurion spotted various cuts, scrapes, and bandages on his bodyguards, although all rode proudly on duty between the campfires and tents. These red-plumed bodyguards were some of the finest warriors Lione had. The force confronting them must have been formidable if they had been tested.

Aurion eyed his loraxi. "How many?" The number of enemies could be easily confused in the fog of battle unless one had the good sense to kill them all. Counting bodies was simple.

"Average count is a party of twenty-three Nurmi." With a low chuckle, Balvor added, "But I'd say probably fifteen. A few people saw a lot more Nurmi than there really were. They were some of the best I've seen. The Black Arrow himself joined in."

Balvor tilted his head to a side and led Aurion to the left, toward the center of the forces. Soldiers were noticing him and his robes; whispers followed him. It meant most got out of the way quickly, which was helpful.

"Four of the would-be rescuers dead, but three times that of our own," Balvor continued. He dropped his voice. "We lost Warain."

"How?"

"They popped out of the hills, leading with arrows. Wouldn't have been so bad if that mountain cat of yours hadn't grabbed some diasists through the bars. By the time they turned back around, they were dead." Balvor's eyes went distant, a thought turning over as his horse picked its way along the cleared track. "Those arrows were strange. Two of Paki Dulci's boys only got grazed, but they dropped dead minutes later, just when the fighting was hottest."

"Poison," Aurion confirmed. He had expected as much. The Black Arrow's arrowheads seemed to lose their potency by the time they reached Lionian hands, so no one knew what the Nurmi leader used to lace his arrows, but everyone knew it was nasty. "Potent poison," he added.

Balvor nodded sadly. "One of those shots took Warain, but the rest of the arrows weren't black. Most didn't get through the armor, anyway. While we chased the Black Arrow, one of his vermin got the cage lock off, but Yoraci Palin's crew got against the door before she got out." With a sidelong glance at his superior, Balvor added, "My commendations to Yoraci Palin."

Aurion nodded in promise to pass the word on. The sovereign was undoubtedly going to ask him his opinion on what happened.

"Your mountain cat's been uneasy ever since. Must have been quite the disappointment," the loraxi finished. "I'm just glad we had a chance for a workout."

"I'm glad you made it on time. They are assembling the parade in the Stadium District already. We must be quick," Aurion answered as the central column of soldiers came into view. Despite the early morning, none were sleepy. When so close to home, little direction was required from Paki Dulci; they had a spring in their steps.

But before they arrived, they had to be presentable. The sovereign wanted the Warrior's reveal to be perfect.

"Couldn't cut it much closer," Balvor agreed. "We had to stop in Havinon for medical help after the attack. Could have been worse. We could have missed your parade."

"This is not my parade," he replied.

"Whatever," came the snide reply as the jail cart came into view.

Aurion approached, and the soldiers around it saluted sharply in recognition of the white and black robe, then parted to give him a clear view of the prisoner. Everything about Lania seemed a little less bright in the morning light. She had added mud to her face paint, although he did not know how. Her braids were now tipped with crimson or black, and her clothes were darker from the mud spattered across them. It must have been deliberate. How had she gotten so much dirt on her?

The Warrior sat at the front of the cart with her back to the door and her legs folded under her. When she glanced his way, it was a slow movement, as if looking at him was not worth her time or effort. Despite the calmness of her posture, her eyes had lost none of their glory.

"So, you are still here despite a valiant attempt," he told her, not expecting a reply.

She snorted at him. "*Ug fehuyl ouy vcub cukracs.*" She faced forward once more, fixing her eyes ahead of her.

A Nurmi reply was as useless as no reply.

"Councilman!" a new voice called.

Aurion faced Paki Dulci with an indifference similar to that which Lania demonstrated. *Fast runners*, he thought. It had taken the paki no time to acknowledge the presence of a councilman. *A good smith too.* The dent in Paki Dulci's helm had been skillfully hammered out.

"Get the men moving, Paki," he ordered. "Lione is ready for you."

"Yes, Councilman!"

"Hardly the work of a councilman to give that message," Balvor muttered as Paki Dulci turned his attention to the horns and drummers following him. The call went up; the troops rushed to assemble.

"I was heading this way to collect all of you. Sovereign Polfius asked me to pass it on."

"I assume he reminded you to be back on time," Balvor said.

Aurion nodded. "I must go straight back once I have all of you."

His eyes went to the penned Nurmi, his curiosity piqued by her feigned disinterest. No doubt, she was listening closely to every word.

"Do you fear what awaits you, Warrior?" he asked.

She did not turn her head but said, "Just because you fear your future, *Ducqyilul*, does not mean I should. You have reason to fear."

He smiled. "You have never seen the White City, have you?"

Her shoulders tensed briefly, like a twitch to disturb a pestering fly. She quickly reestablished her firm, straight-backed posture. *The name?* he wondered.

When she gave him no reply, he shrugged. "I do not think you will like it."

His men gathered around him, all thirty-five. Although he could not see it, he suspected she watched him as he rode away. *Probably wishing me dead.*

He rode back to Lione flanked by Antori and Balvor. Both were veterans who had earned their ranks with sweat and blood and expected the same of any of their subordinates. Boxed between them, Aurion had never felt safer.

As they rode, Balvor gave a complete account of the battle based on what he had seen and what he had been able to get from others afterward. He finished his briefing as they reached the city.

Even on the festival day, the celebrating throngs parted immediately to the White and Black.

They traveled to the Prison District in silence, the city's noise too great for conversation. When he dismissed the soldiers, Antori calmly bowed out. Balvor refused to be released, citing his current duty as head of the bodyguard. Those who could go home now departed. They might catch the parade pass through the Freeman District if they hurried.

It was going to be a long morning.

Aurion was looking toward the back of the parade for the white, black, and gold banners of the sovereign when he heard a woman call his name.

"Loraxi Giesela," Aurion said warmly, his annoyance buried without thought. "You are stunning, as always." Balvor rolled his eyes.

The young woman staring up at him from the ground was far from what Aurion would consider his taste in women. She was short and thin and had pulled her long black hair back, accentuating her sharp cheekbone. She could have been mistaken for an army slave in her blue and black army garb without helm or sword, except she was classically Lionian. Her collar's two silver rank tabs were lost among enough rings, necklaces, and earrings to make a councilman's wife blush. Each, he was well aware, was magical.

Saltha Lanni Giesela was the Beast Commander. Although Aurion did not know which trinket provided the necessary power, he knew Giesela controlled three red dragons. As no one knew how to transfer the power to someone else, she had been given the rank of loraxi and assigned a position in the ranks of the South Army. Galeni Lonthius had mentioned more than once how valuable the woman and her dragons were.

"I am so glad to see you again, Councilman." Giesela blushed and averted her eyes shyly.

"It is my pleasure, Loraxi. Are you joining us today?" Although he asked the question, the answer was evident.

She beamed up at him. "My Reds will fly over the city as you pass through. We came from Guildar at the sovereign's request."

"Should you not be in your place with your pakan?" Although she could command the dragons from anywhere, he was confident she had a place in the parade. He was also anxious to get on with his duties.

"I will join them when necessary," the woman growled in a distinctly unwomanly manner.

"You dislike your companions?"

"Let us simply forget those louts, shall we?" she answered. "It is more civilized company I seek."

He gave her a kind smile, hoping she would not read into it. "Although I am certain they will never express thanks, Loraxi, I assure you the entire Lionian Sovereignty is grateful for your quick thinking after the unfortunate death of your father. Had you not known how to bind the dragons, I fear they would have been lost to us. We appreciate your efficiency under dire circumstances."

"And your gall in doing it," Balvor added from beside Aurion.

Giesela shot Balvor a scathing glare.

Diplomatically, Balvor added, "I heard you have as many balls as any of us. Any other woman would have fled at the sight of a Red that pissed off."

She settled a little at his praise.

"Forgive me for cutting short our visit," Aurion interrupted, "but I know the sovereign wanted to have words with me. Perhaps we can continue the conversation when you next visit Lione, Loraxi. I would be glad to host you in my home." His invitation, while sincere, would come to nothing. He knew she was being shipped back to Guildar first thing in the morning.

"Of course, Councilman. I would be delighted." She bowed stiffly.

With a slight bow of his head, Aurion kicked his horse on, targeting the golden sun standard he'd spotted above the blue and black soldiers.

"Well?" the older man in white and black and gold asked as Aurion stopped his horse at his side. Although the conversation with Giesela had not been forgotten, Aurion quickly pushed it from his mind.

"Well, they still have the Warrior," Aurion confirmed. "They are on their way."

Sovereign Laxus Vannio Polfius nodded as if he had already known this. *He probably did*, Aurion thought. The sovereign's spymaster was good at his job.

"And the attack?" Aurion had to look up to meet the eyes of his sovereign, seated as he was on a large warhorse in gold armor. It was one of the few times this ever happened, as Sovereign Polfius usually reached only Aurion's shoulder.

"Do you want a full account now?"

The sovereign grinned through his gray beard. "Save that for later. But my curiosity is up. Paki Dulci reported a three-sided attack by groups of twenty Nurmi. I am amazed sixty Nurmi could travel so fast. What do you think?"

"Only two fronts were identified to me; the head and the east flank. A few, probably less than six, were at the head, and all they did was spook the leading yorac into calling the alarm. A single diasist was wounded there. According to men at the front, they never saw a savage, just arrows."

Serves Paki Dulci right for embellishing his report. Aurion had no time for face-saving lies in the army. The truth was more important than anyone's ego.

The sovereign nodded, warning Aurion he had heard a similar, if not identical, account from Spymaster Vannio. "But you knew that," Aurion concluded. "Any of my soldiers would be pleased to give you an account of the battle around the cage."

The grunt of the sovereign was neither acknowledgment nor dismissal. Aurion let it pass.

The Prison District gates opened, ushering in Paki Dulci, his men, and the jail cart. They were quickly directed into a position ahead of where Aurion knew his place would be shortly.

Aurion's place should have belonged to a Councilman of the Army, but Councilman Solorin of the East Army was dealing with the fighting along the Solon River, Councilman Garothis of the West Army was nearly seventy-five and incapable of staying on his horse, and Councilman Dracus of the South Army, had been called away to Santan. As a result, Aurion was to take the place of the Councilmen of the Army and lead the palace guard through maneuvers.

He was looking forward to it. He had not been as out of practice as he had expected during the exercises.

"She does make a good addition," Sovereign Polfius commented, drawing Aurion's attention again to the cart.

The Warrior was hunched at the front of the cage, almost, if Aurion was not mistaken, cowering. He was reminded again of the sick mountain cat for a moment, and he felt, unexpectedly, sad.

"Spoils of war," Aurion said.

"You sound so unexcited." The sovereign laughed. "You know you are the star today. Make sure you put on a good show." It sounded like a threat, but Aurion could not take it seriously. Sovereign Polfius was too pleased today to be issuing threats.

"It has been three years. It was you who warned me that crowds are fickle. Why have they not forgotten me?" Aurion asked the question but knew the answer as surely as the sovereign did.

"You brought them the greatest victory many of them have ever known," Sovereign Polfius reminded him. "I still have been unable to spend all the gold you brought back."

"Not for lack of trying," Aurion replied. "There is also the matter of the statue," Aurion added. "Good timing."

Sovereign Polfius smirked, evidently proud of himself. The statue, dedicated to the defeat of Santan and the riches it had brought, had been erected only a quartercycle ago. Aurion could not help but notice how the bronze soldier, depicted with a Santanese head raised on its sword and severed hands at its feet, shared many of Aurion's features. To further the parallels, it was widely known that Aurion had encouraged stealing the heads and hands of the dead Santanese to prevent the enemy from making good their cannibalistic traditions. He had never held a head on a sword point, that was certain, but the crowd did not care. It looked more impressive that way.

The people still called him Trickster. He had earned the name from the Santanese, who had used it as an insult. Aurion did not care. War was about death. The shorter the war, the better.

"Just a delicate reminder," the sovereign admitted, still grinning.

"Why not? You get as much credit as I do."

High Priest Guital arrived at the sovereign's side to silently indicate everything was ready. The priest's robe was golden from top to bottom, the lightning symbol of the God Lioni set in silver over his chest.

Sovereign Polfius gathered the reins of his enormous horse. "Besides, you must have a lot of support to win a high councilman's seat." Aurion started and opened his mouth to answer, but the sovereign cut in with, "To your place!"

Aurion straightened, bowed from atop his horse, and rode to where the blue uniforms of the Lionian army were embossed with silver, not black. The palace guard looked at him expectantly.

An election was not due for three more mooncycles, but he had not anticipated being promoted so soon. High Councilman! He could go no higher without becoming the sovereign himself! In all likelihood, he would be the youngest high councilman in history.

Some part of him groaned. Not again…

He looked at the sharply-dressed soldiers and focused on the task at hand.

"Ready for some fun?"

He got a boisterous cheer.

Lania had heard the stories: Lione was an enormous city. But having never been beyond the northern villages or raiding the Lionian towns, she had never imagined anything remotely close to the monstrosity that was the capital of the Lionian Sovereignty.

As the jail cart passed through the first gate, the white walls appeared around her like a giant's embrace. The impenetrable stone walls extended as far as she could see in both directions. Above these dragon-sized fortifications, buildings stood taller than trees and one, a thin pillar, reached to the sky like a spike to the heart of the clouds.

Lionians were everywhere: on the gate, on the wall, choking the streets, trampling the fields outside, and marching along the paved roads. Everywhere she looked, people shouted, the noise like thunder. Pieces of colored cloth hung from the corners of buildings and from the wrists of the black-haired Conquerors. Everything else was stone, from the houses to the roads under the feet of the horses. Every corner resembled the one before and the one after.

The sheer size of it shook her. She was nothing; she was a pebble in a river being tossed against boulders and crushed by the water. She did not belong here.

She hid at the front of the cage, the one solid wall of her cart that could shelter her as she suffocated in the noise. For the first time since she had offered to defend the fort, uncertainty filled Lania. Even if she could escape the cage, the city itself was a prison. She could spend years wandering the white streets and never find a way out, drowning in the sea of people that pressed ever closer to her cage despite the soldiers trying to keep them back.

She could not defeat this. She could not even hope to try. There were too many.

She glanced up when the cart stopped. Around her, uniformed soldiers filed in. Drums pounded over the din. A blare of horn answered, and she clamped her hands over her ears to block out the racket, wishing she could disappear and never again surface.

Readied, the cart moved into a rank of people and headed out once more. Peeking out briefly, Lania saw a flood of black-haired invaders choking the streets, brandishing branches and waving ribbons. She buried her head in her knees and pulled herself into a smaller ball. For an eternity, she held back tears as the noise assaulted her and the sea of people overwhelmed her vision.

Then, a cry cut through the noise: "*Reah, Belaul!* Welcome to Lione!"

Lania let her hands fall from her ears as the call found an anchor in her heart and spun, tethered. *Reah, Belaul!* the voice had said. "Hail, Warrior!"

The caller hung off a sale stand, leaning far out. Like the rest of the crowd, he smiled and cheered, but unlike the masses, he was not Lionian. Dressed in the brightly colored uniform of a slave, a Nurmi man waved to her. Catching her eye, he ran his finger from his forehead to his chin in salute.

He knew her, his Warrior. But then, why hail her with such glee? Did he want to see her die?

She moved to the edge of the cart, stared out into the crowd again, and forced herself to see beyond the black-haired flood. A smaller number of brown, blond, or red-haired Nurmi were adrift in the sea of people around her. If she strained, she could hear their hails. More than one ran a finger from their forehead to their chin in recognition. Their Lionian masters did not see the forbidden gestures or hear the illegal words in the commotion.

All over the city, the word spread, slave to slave: Hail the Warrior! The Warrior has come to Lione!

Slowly, she realized their joy was not that she was captured—it was that she was among them. They did not care that she was sitting in a jail cart; she would escape. In their eyes, she saw hope. To them, she had come to bring down the Lionian Sovereignty.

And if they could believe it, Lania could too.

The strength of the One God filled her. She faced the crowd and let herself see the black-haired invaders. For the first time, she counted them as they passed. She saw their old and their weak. She saw their broken beggars and sick. They were laughing at her. They were mocking her.

A stone bounced off the bar above her right hand, a physical attack to match the verbal one thrown at her. A second stone followed. Without thought, she caught it as it slipped between the bars.

It was meant as an attack, but it was an opportunity. The One God had delivered her a weapon.

Lania threw the stone, taking one diasist on the side of the head. The "clang" was pleasantly reminiscent of the helm she had slammed into her bars.

The crowd reacted with screams and fury, although the slaves among them struggled to conceal their cheers and grins. Shouting insults first in Nurmi then in Lionian just so they would know what she was saying, Lania dared the next Lionian to try her.

They responded with more stones.

She caught one but took a bruise from a fourth as she put her back to the door. She grabbed three more, then sent them flying back. One took a horse on the rump, and it kicked, knocking two diasists off their feet. She howled with laughter as they staggered to rise, the parade moving on without them.

The stones came in greater number, and the Lionian's cries built. Their stones were aimed to hurt her, but in the chaos, the Nurmi, their faces alight with wonder, tossed underhanded to land the rock within the cage for her to grab. The shouts reached a deafening level, some encouragement and some rage. She fed both with her throws and curses.

After bouncing a stone off a gray-plumed helm and stunning the hapless yoraci, the crowd went suddenly quiet.

The people paused mid-throw, and the sound of dropping stones replaced the angry cries. Three Nurmi slaves, having stepped out from the crowd to make their toss, froze in place with their eyes wide in terror. The futility of escape kept all three in their places with their jaws slack.

A man in a councilman's long white robe with billowing black sleeves rode up.

Lania recognized him; the man who assigned his soldiers to keep her captive in the march south, the one who had confirmed her identity.

Positioned between Lania and the crowd, he towered on horseback over the three Nurmi slaves. The three slaves stared up at him like deer to a mountain cat. When he spoke, it was into utter silence.

"Arrest these three." The soldiers moved forward like a wave to engulf the three and carry them away. They did not struggle. In a daze Lania did not understand, they allowed themselves to be taken away.

The White and Black again spoke, his voice firm. "Any Lionian wishing to denounce their slave for causing a disturbance is welcome to turn them over to their local barracks. Each will be punished severely." Turning now to face her, he added, "Almost as severely as their Warrior is about to be."

At the cold tone, a shiver coursed through Lania. Instinctually defiant, she squared her shoulders. "Come try," she answered.

He turned away, heading back the way he had come, without reply. The moment he did, Lania realized she still had a stone in her hand.

She was surprised when he caught the throw. Meeting her stare confidently, he held the stone where he had stopped it, a hand's breadth from his forehead. Had it hit, she could have killed him.

The silence deepened.

"Come try," she repeated as he let fall the stone and, with not so much as a grunt of dismissal, rode away.

The rest of the journey seemed quiet. The Conquerors continued to shout at her, throwing curses instead of stones, but she could no longer hear them. As if the cart had ceased to exist, she felt adrift and distant. While a spectacle began in the Stadium where the parade ended, the soldiers turned her cart around and trekked back to the Prison District. The streets were almost empty, but she could still hear echoes of the calls that had inspired her. *Reah, Belaul!*

They took her from the cart with three yoracs of eight sol-diers each as escort, and she sensed their unease as a hound smelled fear. *One day*, she promised herself silently, *I will become all the things you fear.* Her chance would come. The One God ensured it would be so.

In a windowless hallway deep in the prison, they swung a door wide and forced her into a tiny room. She stood silently as they chained her wrists, left, and turned the lock. For a moment, silence fell.

A quick glance around the room was all she needed. All four walls were solid, dark stone. Her hands were shackled, first loosely to each other and then to the wall opposite the thick wooden door. Moldy straw and dirt covered the cold stone floor. In one corner, a hole the size of her head led down. She identified its purpose by the sewage stench.

The heavy door, reinforced with metal and locked securely from the outside, was the only exit. A barred window in the door showed her a depressing view of the stones of the hall outside, barely lit by lamps and eerily quiet. Already the stones against her back had chilled her to her core.

She could escape the chains on her hands—she had little fear of that—but the door was a problem. *Have faith*, she told herself quietly. In the distance, she felt her sister Akara smile.

The door did not open. Once a day, meals slid through a trapdoor at the base of the door. The food was poorly cooked and tasted spoiled, but she had eaten worse and knew she needed strength to escape. She watched the hallway, noting the dimming of the lamps and the passage of the patrols. When her muscles grew stiff from sitting, she danced, fighting invisible enemies within the confines of the chains until she made enough noise for the guards to investigate.

Before long, they stopped investigating. Some part of her knew that was to her advantage.

CHAPTER 4

After three days, the arrangements were made, yet Sovereign Polfius insisted on inspecting the Warrior before giving her over for interrogation. Naturally, Aurion went with him, interested to see whether prison had dampened her fiery disposition.

Aurion walked the prison's familiar cell blocks with an escort of imperial guards, his house guards dismissed when the sovereign's life was the priority. The generic cell selected for the Warrior was deep in the prison complex, far from exits or fresh air. When they reached the cell, the prison guard carefully selected two keys to release the locks, then checked that Aurion and the sovereign were ready before opening the hardwood door.

Lania was chained within, but Aurion sent two diasists in to tighten the chains so she could not reach more than a stride in any direction. They stayed within, ready for her, as Polfius stepped up to the doorway and peered within.

She had not changed, her face still marred with black and her attire filthy. Aurion wondered if she knew the meaning of the white and black robes, or of the black sash and golden chains around Polfius' neck. The sovereign was shorter than Aurion and balding. Without the garb of a sovereign, it would be hard to recognize him as the leader of all the known world.

For a long while, no one moved. But the light of the torch caught something within and Aurion realized she still wore her silver armband.

"Her armband carries the mark of a false god," Aurion said softly to the nearest soldiers. "Remove it from the presence of the sovereign."

Both guards within reached for her and, seeming timid, the Warrior backed up. He was surprised; he'd expected defiance. Surrender in any form would be unacceptable to a Nurmi like her. Still, he supposed she couldn't really resist when chained.

He realized his mistake in the next blink. She'd retreated to get the soldiers within her reach.

As the first diasist reached for her arm, she pivoted away and swung the slack chains into his head like a flail, throwing him back. The second guard lunged in and got the chains to the face, which dented his helm and knocked him out entirely. As the first diasist lurched up and drew Lania's attention, Aurion, still a soldier at heart, seized the opportunity to jump on her from behind. She crumpled under his weight and he was able to pin her under him as she squirmed and cursed him. The diasist pulled the armband free.

He eased off her slowly, but she did not fight him now, perhaps seeing the drawn blades of the sovereign's guard who had moved in from the doorway to retrieve their fallen companions. When she snarled at the soldiers, they scrambled away as if she had snorted fire, and Aurion had to smother a laugh.

The diasist handed Aurion the armband, which he pocketed quickly before returning to the sovereign.

Lania stared at them, seething, until the sovereign decided he had enough and motioned for them to close the door.

The prison guard shut and double-locked the Warrior's cell as one diasist was stretchered away to the infirmary.

"What do you think?" Sovereign Polfius asked, as if he was posing a philosophical question.

"About Lania?" Aurion replied as he tugged on each lock himself, to be sure. They did not want their prize to escape.

The shorter man faked a deep frown. "No, about whether I should upholster the High Seat. Of course, about her! I do not take a trip to the Prison District to talk about the weather, my boy."

"Of course, Sovereign," Aurion answered automatically.

The older man laughed as he headed down the corridor. "Sovereign?"

Aurion gritted his teeth but made to follow. It had been years, and the title "father" still did not fit. He served his sovereign without hesitation, and while he dearly loved the man, Sovereign Polfius was not a fatherly figure. The sovereign came to him for advice, not the other way around.

"I think she is quite a trophy, Father," Aurion complacently replied.

The sovereign smiled at the minor victory as they exited the prison. A covered carriage awaited them with a full two loraxans—easily eighty men—as an escort. The sovereign never traveled lightly. "The question now is what to do with her," he said as he passed through black-covered doors and entered the carriage.

"I certainly do not recommend trading with Councilman Atoron Ganon Galfium," Aurion replied as he followed the sovereign in and settled into a seat by the window. He parted the curtains just enough to let him see the streets without endangering his sovereign. The order to march rang out, and the carriage lurched into motion.

Across from him, Sovereign Polfius' eyes widened. "By the gods! How do you know about that?"

Aurion shrugged. "Isn't that why you keep me around?" As Sovereign Polfius rubbed his gray beard and looked him over,

Aurion's attention went to the window again, where he was putting everything to memory as fast as it passed by.

"I keep you around so you can watch other people's business."

"Well," Aurion said, "the offer was Councilman Galfium's business. He is someone I certainly think we should be keeping our eyes on."

The sovereign sighed and picked a plum from the fruit bowl. For a moment, the only noise was the clip-clop of the horses and the muttering of the streets stilled by the passage of the carriage.

Aurion continued to watch the window, waiting for the question he knew was coming.

"So, what do you think of Councilman Galfium's proposed trade?"

Letting fall the curtain, Aurion faced his sovereign squarely. "Too much could go wrong. If you give Lania to Galfium, the best we can hope for is that he kills her, which would save us the cost of an execution. Most slaves he 'plays' with end up rotting in the garbage trenches within days, but he may not be able to..." He paused, searching for the appropriate word. Councilman Galfium's position was unusual, and there seemed to be no proper way to describe the man's desire for Lania. "He may not be able to handle Lania in the same way," Aurion decided. "She may kill him." He chuckled. "I think that would be doing Lione a favor." The sovereign hid a smile behind the large, black plum. "But if she kills him, she might escape, which would be hard to explain. Then there is the chance she may escape and not bother helping us with Galfium at all. I certainly do not want to have to explain *that* to the Council."

Sovereign Polfius nodded slowly, but Aurion did not sense acquiescence in the gesture.

"Ultimately, we need her out of the way," said Polfius. "She practically caused a riot from the jail cart on her way in. The

Nurmi believe in her. We must show them that their prophecy is empty." His lips hardened into a thin line. "The fall of the Sovereignty is not going to happen."

Aurion nodded, despite knowing it was an empty gesture. The sovereign did not need Aurion's agreement. Polfius knew what he was going to do; he was thinking out loud and expecting a suitable echo.

"We can still use this," Aurion said.

"Executing her publicly would create a martyr. I wonder if they would believe it even if they saw it. No, I think the best thing is to destroy her first. We must ruin the myth before killing the woman. Seeing her on her knees before the Sovereign of Lione will end all talk of legends and prophecy and whatnot."

Aurion nodded grimly. "And broken, she'll talk. She knows many useful things, although that's a secondary goal under the circumstances. Her greatest value is as a symbol."

The sovereign lifted a curious eyebrow as the carriage hit a stone and jostled the occupants. Without thought, Aurion caught the bowl of fruit as it overturned.

"I thought Nurmi did not break."

Aurion replaced the bowl and took a grape. "It has been done," he replied. "But even if it fails, the slaves do not need to know that. We need only to imply she broke. Their doubt does the rest. We can claim we have information from her and make an attack on Namera."

The sovereign nodded, a hand on his thick white beard. "Seeing spoils, even if we take them from the reserves, will lend strength to our position. What do they think of traitors?"

"They have no more tolerance of traitors than we do."

Sovereign Polfius moved to the next step without hesitation. "Then we would be free to let her die, perhaps of a sickness. They will believe her god abandoned her. The legend dies with the woman."

Aurion conceded, trying the window again to avoid the sovereign's confident grin. "It would be nice if we *did* get information. But there are few with the skills to break a Nurmi, especially this one."

The sovereign chuckled. "I would wager my palace that you know exactly who to contact."

Aurion nodded. No Priest of Ramath was pleasant, but the one he had in mind was particularly distasteful. Fortunately, the man was already in the city. The Warrior would take priority over whoever he was currently assigned to.

"So it shall be," Sovereign Polfius declared. "See to the torture. I shall arrange an attack that will spoil their illusions about their Warrior."

The carriage came to a stop. Rather than wait for the servant, Aurion let himself out.

"Be careful," the sovereign added as Aurion stepped out of the carriage. "She is useful alive."

Aurion cut off a helpless sigh. "Sovereign, please tell Councilman Galfium 'No.' When it comes to her death, it will be necessary for her to indeed be dead. We cannot take the chance."

As Aurion closed the carriage door, the sovereign's smile convinced him that he had correctly anticipated Polfius' plans.

As the carriage continued to the palace, Aurion turned to his home. The front door opened before he touched it, but he paused to greet the guards. He was forced to abandon the exchange when the gong of the water clock sounded. As he excused himself and stepped into the entrance, he realized he still had the armband in his pocket.

It was well made, surprising for a race that did not use Lionian forges. The surface was scuffed and pitted, but the finish was without tarnish. She must have polished it, although how she could do so when captured or chained, he did not know.

Guilion, his head footman, arrived holding a block of wood and a piece of paper that Aurion scanned quickly.

"Show High Priest Guital to the garden when he arrives. See that the wine is out for him," Aurion told the servant, indicating that he had finished reading with a nod of his head before turning his eyes back to the armband. Guilion bowed and left.

"Do you have a moment?" a voice asked from the library next to the door, and Aurion jumped, flipping the armband out of view.

"Ailsa?" he managed to stutter, forcibly stopping himself when his feet moved toward her. "What are you..." but his words faltered.

She was beautiful. No matter the time of day, Ailsa's natural beauty was highlighted delicately by paints and colors from Santan desert traders. As the sister of a soldier, she could afford little, yet she created an effect more intricate than the richest ladies of Lione. Her dark eyes were lined in a pale blue that matched the shawl she wore over her navy dress. Her high cheekbones made it seem her face was carved marble with ebony for eyes.

Aurion's breath caught, but he forced himself away from admiration and did his best to sound gentle. By her shy glances, she feared he would receive her harshly.

"I have a few minutes, depending on how late the high priest is."

She dropped her gaze to the tiled floor. "My brother asked that I make peace with you," she said in a whisper.

Aurion forced a careless smile onto his face. It was false, but he hoped she would not be able to tell. "We are at war?" Absently, he drew out the armband once more and handed it to the servant who had come to take his shoes. "See that this is disposed of," he told the man, kicking off his shoes while the servant scuttled away.

"You know what I mean," Ailsa replied.

Aurion smiled a little more sincerely. "Yes, I know. Tell your brother he has nothing to fear from me. The family of Trailus has served the family of Illica for too many years for me to let our disagreement disrupt that." He laid a hand on Ailsa's shoulder as he spoke but removed it swiftly. His thoughts had gone to better times, and he quickly pulled away from the memories. "You and Antori will always be welcome in any Illica estate."

"Thank you."

Although she did not move, the comment seemed to end the conversation, and Aurion considered disappearing to the kitchen to get something to eat before the high priest's visit. "I should..." He gestured down the hall.

Ailsa frowned. "Always busy."

He shrugged. "A councilman's life."

Her gaze rose, and he saw the opinionated woman he loved. Unfortunately, this was a topic they disagreed on.

She grabbed his hands in plea. "Give it up, Aurion, please."

He shook his head and let his smile fade. "Ailsa, we have been through this. You are not made for the life of the Council, I know that now, but I am not going to step down. I can accomplish so much from a Council seat."

"You did not want it when it came to you! I have heard the men talk about how you had to be stopped from fleeing to Salbero! And—"

"That was probably my adoption," he corrected gently.

"Grizzle had to talk you into both!"

"Yes, but the public only knows about the adoption." Presentation and public opinion were everything now.

"So why do you now cling to it? Sovereign Polfius had his fun. Go back. Let it go..."

"Ailsa," Aurion tried, keeping his voice level, "there are fourteen hundred men in Lione tonight who have a place to sleep because I set up the shelters. There are sixteen hundred who got to dispute their land grants so they could be closer to family. I've set up street lighting along all the major roads in Lione and have organized the same in the capitals of every province. I've got soldiers in Santan with twice as many paid sick days as they had last year. Now their families don't starve when the rains bring illness. There are over three thousand children now attending schools with a basic, consistent curriculum, a hundred and sixty-eight of which are only there at all because of scholarships I set up. Can you not see it? This is what I can do!"

"But it is dangerous!" she insisted, stepping forward. Memories flared again to feel her pressed against him, and he fought with them, unable to push her away and knowing he should. "Go back to the army! Go back to being a braxi. At least then you know what enemy you fight. Please, Aurion, leave this."

Aurion's heart ached. He almost said he would, if only she would dry her eyes, but he stopped the words before they formed. He could not abandon Lione.

He pulled his hand from her hold and shook his head. "My heart is lighter knowing I have someone who worries for me, Ailsa, but I will not run from this. My place is on the Council. I am sorry."

She did not follow, not even turning to watch him, as he left her in the entrance hall between carven pillars. He was thankful, for it meant he did not have to meet her eyes and see their pain. Had he waited any longer, he would have run to her, trying to comfort her, but the feelings had to be pushed aside. By the time his guilt made itself known again, he was in the kitchen, gratefully distracting himself with fresh flatbread.

Outside a fine house in the Freeman District, a slave collected the bin of garbage and dumped it into the cart destined for the trenches beyond the walls of Lione. The glint of silver caught his eye. In the moment before the next bin was emptied, the slave snatched up a silver armband and tucked it into his shirt.

4TH DAY OF THE 2ND MOONCYCLE, 994

The day after the sovereign's visit, Lania's door again opened to reveal soldiers. With exaggerated caution, they shortened her chains and added additional ones, hobbling her and binding her hands tightly. They kept their spears leveled as she shuffled out of the cell, a full yorac of eight escorting her. She snarled at them and fed on their discomfort when they jumped. Even their leading yoraci, his gray plume looking fresh, was skittish and worked to keep his subordinates between him and Lania.

At length, they arrived in a small windowless room with a large shielded fireplace and a trio of black-clad men.

The yoraci bowed low and advanced as if expecting the central figure to bite him.

"You are Devotee Seth?" he asked from within the silver helm.

The central man nodded tersely.

"Then she's all yours." The yoraci waved to his soldiers, who immediately secured Lania's shackles to a pole crossing the ceiling, leaving her feet barely touching the ground. They left, the sound of their clattering steps quickly distancing themselves. The yoraci himself closed the door behind them, glancing back as he sealed it but saying nothing.

Lania hated Seth immediately.

He had cropped black hair slicked back with grease that somehow spread and made Lania feel oily in his presence. His crooked smile twisted when he stretched it because of two missing front teeth and a strange pattern of scars over his face that crossed into a star pattern. His hands were squat but strong, and his nails were cut to the quick. She did not know the symbols on the red jewelry he wore over the black robes, but they matched those etched on his oversized ruby earring.

As the devotee settled comfortably into a padded and brightly embroidered chair at odds with the dark decor of the furnace room, the acolytes removed Lania's hobbles. They then retreated to flank their master.

"Welcome, Lania," Seth said through his practiced smile. "I am Seth, follower of Ramath and your host for your stay in Lione." His words implied her presence in the cell, hanging from chains, was entirely voluntary. "I am here to dispel the myths of your religion. I am here to show you the way to enlightenment and worship to Lioni, the true god, and our sovereign, his representative."

"To hell with your god," she answered, using the Lionian word for "god" but calmly saying the rest in Nurmi.

"You must speak Lionian." Seth reached behind him, where an assortment of metal tools waited. "Other tongues are false and evil. You do not wish to be evil." His voice was so sweet, it turned her stomach.

She stared at the white star pattern of scars, trying to ignore the smile that seemed to want to comfort but could only chill. Lania distantly noted that he picked a purple glass sphere from among the instruments. "Curse you, monster," she replied, again in Nurmi.

With one hand, Seth waved one of his assistants, who moved up behind her, forward. With the other hand, Seth lifted the purple sphere.

Lania braced herself, ready for any kind of pain or mind magic. Her connection to Akara would defend her.

She heard her voice, her own voice, speak from the strange purple sphere in perfect Lionian.

"Curse you, monster," it said.

Seth's grin cooled as he closed his squat hand over the sphere and lowered it. "You may do so, but you will do so only in Lionian. Such is our law."

Lania stared at the stone, amazed into temporary silence. She did not understand. It had spoken Lionian. How could a sphere speak her words in another language?

He is a warlock, she decided. That did not matter. Sorceries were broken by truth, and the Priestess was truth, itself. Lania, as the Priestess' soul, could not be harmed by magic. The One God protected her indefinitely from such foulness. The legend of the Twins was clear on this point.

"Never," Lania answered flatly. Focused on Seth's sphere, Lania was startled by a blow to her shoulder. The assistant landed a strike against her upper arm, and a cry, more of alarm than pain, escaped her.

Her voice came from the sphere. "Never," it repeated in flawless Lionian. Her cry had no translation.

"Tac will be responsible for your language," Seth informed her, his face alight. His excitement grew upon her cry.

For a moment, Lania considered speaking in Lionian. If Seth enjoyed pain, he would not hesitate to inflict it. Thanks to the purple sphere, they could force her to obey despite her defiance. The language itself was not evil. She and her sister spoke it often in practice. Why should she fight that?

She squared her shoulders. They were Lionian, and she was Nurmi. She was the One God's child, and she was the Warrior. Nurmi did not surrender.

Soon, he would hate her. She would take the grin from his face.

Lania turned to Tac with renewed resolution and gave him a wicked grin. He was older, his face tanned leather and his nose pox-marked. She found his name particularly apt. While in Lionian the word meant nothing, in Nurmi it was very appropriate.

"Tac," she said. "False name, but appropriately given." Without hesitation, the assistant's fingers flicked along her arm, brandishing a slender knife. She flinched but locked her jaw. The cut was thin enough that it did not bleed at first.

She turned back to Seth and heard her voice repeat the insult, translating the name as well.

"Sin," it said. "False name, but appropriately given."

The smile Seth wore thinned. Before Seth could give further commands, Lania finished her thought, enunciating every word in careful Nurmi.

"Beyond the Gate with you all."

Her calm remained even when she felt a new cut burn and draw enough blood to run down her arm.

Seth waited for the translation from the sphere before he spoke, but the smile was becoming forced. "Rest assured," he told her, "he will stop only when you perform as expected."

She stared at the monster but, in consideration of her arm, did not speak. Her language was a thorn to be twisted into the torturer's side. She savored it.

"Good," Seth said after a moment, seeming to take her silence for the obedience he imagined instead of the defiance it was. "Soon, you will see that our way is the only way."

She barred her teeth like fangs and saw his smile wane again. With her snarl, he recognized the falseness of the previous victory.

"Demons, the Gate awaits you."

Tac's knife cut her shoulder, tiny but deep.

She held her tongue for the better part of the day, her rebellion resurfacing when it could most deflate him. Sometimes, she answered his lies with other lies, sometimes she cursed him, but there was always the resulting cut burning her skin for the crime. After long enough, Seth declared he was bored and left her with two assistants.

She was not told the second man's name, so she dubbed him *Nasib*, the Nurmi word for the dirt in pig pens. He was shorter than Tac and covered in mud like a monster living in the swamp, venturing out to steal bad children from their beds.

Nasib was responsible for her sleep. With him around, she never got any.

She lost track of time. Seth came and went while Tac cut her for each word of Nurmi, and Nasib's impossibly cold hands startled her awake if she drifted, whether from boredom or actual fatigue. Her determination grew desperate as time wore on.

After Seth had taken two breaks and given her none, they came to cut her hair, one little braid at a time. The loss of the braids hurt her more than the little knife in Tac's hand, but she hid her pain, fearing that her suffering would bring her captors joy. Instead, she bit the hand that carried the scissors. To her surprise, her attack took a large piece of the assistant's finger.

They struck her, although if it was one blow or a dozen, she could not remember. The assistant left, and Seth saw the salted leather thong dragged across her back. She bit her tongue to keep from screaming as tears blurred her vision. With the taste of blood in her mouth, her fortitude held. It was a bitter victory.

They fed her once, after her stomach had started to complain, but the scraps did little to help. Sometime later, they generally splashed water in her direction, leaving her parched by the time they released her arms from the bar. The furnace in the room did not help, although her sweat washed the tiny cuts' blood. It stung, but the Warrior knew it would heal them, and she accepted her pain. By the time they lifted her from the bar, the sick smile on Seth's face had faded away.

She hardly registered the walk back to her cell, where she was left with a promise of their return. The food she had eaten sat uneasily in her stomach, and she crawled to the pit to throw it up. Lying sprawled on flea-infested straw with her head beside the reeking pit where her food had tumbled, she finally closed her eyes.

Lost in a dark world of stone and black-haired monsters, with the sound of running water in her ears, the Warrior drifted into sleep.

She dreamed of standing in the golden mist of the Dreamworld and seeing the Priestess.

"I am here," Akara said with a laugh, her long undyed wool robe sparkling in the golden light from between worlds. "I walked to you."

"A great accomplishment," Lania praised her little sister, "but then you were always better at meditations than me. They bore me still."

"And armor is unyielding and uncomfortable to me, dear sister. That is why we are as we are."

"As we chose to make ourselves," Lania corrected.

"Any creature of the One God is capable of ruling its future, or have you forgotten the teachings, big sister?" Akara's voice was childishly sweet.

"If you can tell me Calor's twelve greatest victories, I will answer that," Lania replied, returning the tease. "But did you come all this way through dreams to merely boast, little sister? Do not misunderstand—I am pleased to see you—but I feel something else is on your mind. You are eager, or perhaps nervous. Have you a question?"

Emotions between them were faint when distance separated them, but without the pain of the torture to distract her, Lania recognized Akara's apprehension. It was not bad, merely strange.

Akara's expression became regretful. "I am listening. I can hear our people through their dreams. Will you go to those who call you, Warrior?"

"The Priestess will listen, and the Warrior will answer," Lania answered immediately, aware of no other possible reply. "Yes, I will go to those who call for our help. Guide me, sister."

Although the Priestess wore a thin smile, Lania sensed threatening tears. "When you have found a way out of the shackles?" she asked.

Lania was grateful for the distance between them; Akara would feel little of Lania's pain. Still, she saw her sister touching her wrists where shackles had rubbed them raw. They were bound. When one hurt, both hurt.

"I will find a way," Lania replied with confidence that surprised her. For a moment, it was not a prayer, but a simple fact. "I will do what I have been brought here to do."

The Priestess' smile changed back to the childish grin of a younger sister pleased to be teasing. "Then hurry up. Father says the men much prefer following you. He says it is because you are a strong leader, but I suspect they have fallen in love with you!"

Lania was chuckling when she woke, sore and dirty, in her tiny cell.

Her muscles ached from fingertips to toes, each cut along her arms an individual line of tingling pain. Her stomach still felt like it wanted to climb out of her throat, and her tongue felt a size too big, but she forced herself to swallow and stand up. She had to be strong.

She was the Warrior of the Nurmi people. She would not fail the One God.

With her chains as her weapon, she danced in the tiny room, killing the shadows and wishing they were her torturers. Her mind pushed aside the pain until only her beating heart and steady breathing remained. She reached out to her sister, feeling the calm of the Priestess like a dear friend's embrace, and she found peace as her sister settled into evening prayers.

She was ready for them when they again opened her door, although she had to shield her eyes from the light of the torches.

"Good morning," Seth greeted her. The guards collected her chains and pulled her into the corridor. "Come now, we have a long day ahead of us."

Seth opened his hand from over the purple sphere to hear her reply in Lionian.

"It is evening."

Tac moved at once to her side and reopened one of the many cuts, his bear-like hands clumsy with the thin blade and making a curved line. Lania felt nothing of the sting she knew should have followed.

She enjoyed the twitch that dissolved Seth's smile as the stone echoed the words in Lionian. He replaced the false smirk quickly, but already she could tell he was strained, and she wondered if the reprieve had been for her sake or his. The thought was comforting.

The Warrior had come to Lione, and she was already stabbing her dagger into the depth of the White City's chest.

"Come!" he said, beckoning them into the corridor as he stormed away.

"One day," Lania promised, "I will land the blow that will end your life, Seth." One quick exhale dismissed the pain of the scratch she took for her Nurmi words. "One day," she told Tac, "you will have just enough time to regret your actions here." Predictably, he struck the same place and opened the tiny cut wide enough to bleed down her arm.

It still felt like victory.

CHAPTER 5

Almost a quartercycle after their initial visit, Aurion was surprised to find himself leading the sovereign's second trip into the depths of the prison halls. They had mistimed the visit: as they arrived at the inquisition room, the Warrior was in her cell. Only the acolytes and Devotee Seth himself were present.

The smell of burned flesh lingered like fog in the little room with the furnace. Someone had tried to clean the blood from under the pole in the ceiling, but the dried stains ran to the drain. It had clearly not been empty for long.

Although not his first choice, Aurion accepted torture as an effective means to gain information and influence over a prisoner. His experience with it had forced him to acknowledge Devotee Seth as the finest in the trade. He left cleaning and sharpening to his acolytes, and sat like a ruler in his plush throne overseeing the loathsome work.

Sovereign Polfius did not appear to share Aurion's pragmatic approach and had, by his uneasiness, thus far avoided the art form. His face pale, the sovereign held his ground by sheer determination as the Priest of Ramath sprang from his seat and hurried over. Had the mood been less dark, Aurion would have found it comical. Only a god could frighten a priest as fanatical as Seth, but that was what stood before him now. The sovereign was considered a descendant of the Lord of the Sky, Lioni. Seth, like many, believed he was in the presence of a man and a god in one. It had him flinching like a dog expecting a blow.

"It has been over a quartercycle," Sovereign Polfius declared in a voice dripping with authority meant to disguise his unease. "We have no information. Are you making any progress?"

Seth whined and shied away. Aurion caught his glance and interpreted it as a plea for help.

"Devotee Seth," Aurion intervened, "has been assigned a formidable task. Only a handful of Nurmi have ever bent under torture, and only one with a silver armband. More than half were by his skill, including the one with the silver armband most recently. Breaking one as spirited as the Warrior will not happen quickly." Seth nodded so vigorously, Aurion feared the man would injure himself. To the devotee, that would not have been a bad thing. As any Priest of Ramath, Seth was both sadistic and masochistic.

Aurion gently prompted the torturer, "What progress have you made?"

Seth pushed through his panic and stuttered out, "We first worked with disorientation." His voice gained confidence as he trod into familiar territory. "We used many different rooms and paths, ensuring she could no longer establish anywhere as her own. We also worked at temporal disorientation by preventing sleep and varying food and water cycles."

Sovereign Polfius' expression twisted between confusion, amazement, and disgust.

Aurion intervened again. "The idea is to make her as insecure as possible."

Sovereign Polfius nodded once, confirming that he understood but did not take his eyes off Seth.

"Success?" Aurion prompted the devotee.

So long as Seth focused on Aurion, his words came easily.

"She is a curious one. We have shaken her, of that I am certain. Often, she will touch her upper arm here." He gestured to the place the silver armband had once sat on her arm. "I do not believe she realizes she is doing it. She hardly speaks and will not speak Lionian, although there is no doubt she understands it. We are discouraging her through pain, but her determination is strong. During her second session, she insisted on repeating the same curse. I returned an hour later to watch her persist for another fifteen minutes before passing out. Now she speaks less. Her silence is a form of victory in itself."

"Will she obey us?" the sovereign demanded, causing Seth to jump back a step. Aurion wondered if Sovereign Polfius realized what he was doing, but he quickly corrected himself. Polfius was undoubtedly using it to find some amusement, despite his discomfort.

Aurion had to soothe Seth to get him to stop stammering.

"Not reliably," was the ultimate answer, although it took several minutes to get it. The devotee attempted to justify himself. "I have tried many times to confuse her, yet she always knows what time it is. We have led her past false windows with darkness and stars beyond, and yet she will look me in the eye and tell me it is midday, and she is always right."

"She still eating?" Aurion asked.

Seth nodded vehemently. "We poisoned her a few days ago, too, but that has not deterred her. She still eats when we give her food."

"Poisoned?" The sovereign choked on the word. "We need her alive."

Aurion's thoughts flew back to the carriage, and he made a mental note to check the arrangement between Polfius and Councilman Galfium. He hoped the sovereign was not still planning to trade the Warrior.

"Jjjj... ju... ju... just... just..."

Aurion stepped in. Otherwise, the reply might take hours.

"A drug which confuses the mind but has no ill effects on the body," he explained. He'd kept tabs on the efforts to date. "Ideally, the prisoner becomes too confused to lie." He turned his eyes to Seth.

Devotee Seth frowned deeply. "She went into some half-sleep. She hung there for hours, repeating the same words over and over as if we did not exist. Nothing could pull her out of it until the drug had worn off."

Aurion cocked his head. "What did she say?"

"'I obey, Priestess. I will stay with you.'" Seth curled his lip. "While she was like that, nothing got through to her. I have never seen its like." Seth paused as if expecting the councilman to produce an explanation. Aurion had none, but his research into Nurmi had only recently become intensive.

"Where is she now?" Aurion asked.

"In a cell," the devotee replied. With a cautious glance at the man with the black and gold trim on his robe, he added, "A necessary pause. You wished her alive."

Aurion thought Sovereign Polfius would have had enough of the filthy little priest and the hot, sticky room, but the sovereign instead demanded, "Bring her out."

While the guards rushed to obey, Aurion shrugged. If the sovereign was curious, there was no harm in letting him see the savage again.

Seth pulled a small purple sphere from a tray as the soldiers fetched the Warrior. He fiddled with it as they waited.

Lania was dragged in, not because she resisted, but because her legs could not hold her. She had been stripped of everything except the shackles and chain. Her short hair cut irregularly and her face dark with filth and blood, she looked as dark-skinned as a Santanese. Thin cuts decorated her body from her neck to her feet, some nearly healed, some still crusted with blood. Aurion was immediately disappointed, although he knew enough to hide it. Suspended between two soldiers, he saw the sick wild cat again. Seth had done his work well, for Lania offered no fight.

She barely lifted her head but must have known the meaning of the white and black robe, for her glorious eyes narrowed. As her head raised in apparent defiance, her eyes seemed to spark. Unsteadily, she brought herself to standing and, with a mocking smile, spoke in Nurmi. One of Seth's helpers stepped up, blade in hand. Lania's jaw clenched in anticipation. She took the cut across her shoulder, a little too close to the throat for Aurion's liking, without so much as a whimper. Her stare was unrelenting.

The sphere in Devotee Seth's hand spoke in the Warrior's voice, but in Lionian, "You flatter me. Now I have gotten you all up so late at night."

Aurion paused, staring at the little tool Seth was holding. Magical items were rare; he'd never expected to find one in the depths of the prison among the dark corridors. But here it was, translating the Nurmi into Lionian for them.

"You give me a proper opportunity to curse you all in person," the sphere said, rendering another string of Nurmi words into Lionian. "I am pleased." To prove it, the woman smiled viciously, her teeth bared.

Seth's face flushed.

Ten days, and Lania had come to know Seth well enough to torture him back, Aurion recognized.

Seth snapped instructions, and the assisting disciple moved forward again. This time, his strike fell across Lania's face, and the cut reached below her right eye like a sliver moon reaching toward her ear. Although her head moved to the blow, she did not cry out. She took one long breath, then fixed her vicious smile on Seth and snarled words at him.

"Surely you can do better than that," came her translated reply.

The priest's face burned crimson. If Seth had remembered who else was present, he might have hesitated, but his rage was blinding. "To the salt water!" he shouted, gesturing with one squat hand to the barrels by the fire.

Aurion glanced at the sovereign. But before he could speak to the pale man, he was interrupted by the purple sphere still held in the open palm of the torturer.

"*Kri tehk bekil ku!*" Seth's voice said.

The spark in the Warrior's eyes flared into a bonfire.

"Both ways!" she shouted. The sphere obediently emitted her voice in Lionian. "You tell me all other tongues are evil, yet you speak Nurmi! I have made you speak to me on my terms!" She jumped in place as the guards dragged her forward. Her triumph was cut short as they plunged her head into a barrel of water.

Seth closed his fist around the sphere, and Aurion understood. The sphere did not translate Nurmi to Lionian; it converted any language for the listeners' sake. By closing his fist around it when Lionians spoke, Seth deactivated it. He had failed, just this once, to close his hand in time.

Lania was still sputtering laughter as the guards lifted her from the barrel to let her breathe, but by the time the priest finally called them off, she had no breath left with which to laugh. Beside Aurion, Polfius was dreadfully wane.

Nearly faint, gasping for air, and again being supported by the guards, Lania's face was hidden under a mat of wet hair. Her feet were under her, but she stood nearly bent in two. Seth's eyes glimmered as he enjoyed the victorious silence.

A sore victory, Aurion thought.

Aurion could barely hear the Warrior's soft mutter from his position, but Seth tilted his head like a hound hearing his master call at the sound. The devotee again opened his fist and held out the sphere, but the words were too quiet. He stepped forward and placed the sphere closer to Lania's face, searching for a reason to punish her further.

She had only time for a single strike. Lania yanked her arm loose with more strength than Aurion would have guessed she still possessed. Before anyone could blink, she slammed her hand into Seth's throat.

The Priest of Ramath collapsed, the purple stone falling from his grip and tumbling into the barrel.

The guards tackled Lania, pinning her to the stone. From under the soldiers, Lania laughed insanely, oblivious to the blows landing against her, mockingly, madly. A chill ran down Aurion's spine. When he could stand it no longer, Aurion ordered her back to a cell. As her laughter faded down the hall, Aurion knew the sound would haunt him over the next several nights. He suspected the same to be true with the sovereign who stood at his side, mouth gaping.

The disciples were the first to the devotee's side, each trained in healing arts. Aurion was only mildly surprised when they reported, their faces grim, that her single blow, perfectly executed, had crushed Seth's windpipe.

Seth died within the hour.

The part of Lania's mind closest to the Priestess knew she'd gone mad. Despite this, Lania could not stop laughing. Lost in her irrational hilarity, she distantly felt fists pounding her. She remembered nothing of the trip back to her cell. Once left in her prison room, she found her way to the hole in the floor to cough up blood; she had bitten her tongue.

The pain from her exhausted, aching muscles finally calmed her. Aware of herself once more, Lania stared down the hole, checking herself over.

In addition to her many bruises, they may have cracked one of her ribs, and her face was still bleeding from a new cut. Shackles still bound her hands, but they had dumped her on the floor without attaching the chains to the wall this time. Her jaw was sore. She stretched it, proving nothing was broken. Overall, she was better than she had expected.

Nothing had changed. She was still in a Lionian prison awaiting torture and death, chained and locked behind barred doors. She had no way out.

But her gut told her she was done. She needed to do something. Eventually, she decided to sleep.

She woke to the distant sound of water again. As the haze of sleep lifted, she became increasingly confident in her mental state, the presence of water catching her attention. How could water be running anywhere near her?

More than once, she had fallen asleep near the hole, dreaming of the Solon River, but she had dismissed the sound as fantasy. Now, in the cold silence of night, it was clear the noise came from down the hole.

As unexpected as the discovery was, it made her grin. If water flowed in, it had to flow out. Where water went, Lania could follow.

Ignoring the smell, she stuck her arm down the hole but found only stone. Curious, she reached down with her leg. While the stone tunnel led down a stride's depth, her foot reached a place without walls. It opened up below.

To her delight, the edges crumbled as she investigated it. She clawed out chunks of stone to widen the hole by hand. Once her fingers could no longer make headway, she turned to the shackles. Ready to leave, she pulled two pieces of thin wire from their place woven in her matted hair. Folding them, Lania worked the pick and shear. She popped open both locks, then strung the two shackles together to create a flail.

She swung at the hole with her makeshift weapon and sent chips flying from both the shackles and the stone. Laughing aloud, this time with delight and not delirium, she recognized how her early dances had aided her.

No matter the ruckus, no guard investigated the sounds.

Polfius' voice was taut.

"Well?"

Bleary-eyed, Aurion looked up at his sovereign. "She is most definitely gone." The reports lay scattered over his oak desk, each bearing worse news than the one under it. Four days since she had crushed a priest's windpipe with a single blow, Lania had vanished.

Sovereign Polfius snorted. When he turned to pace across the office, the white and black robes flared out like fire around him. "Out of the prison? Out of Lione? Out of the province?"

Aurion rubbed his temples to fight his fatigue. As predicted, he had been haunted by her laughter fading down the prison halls. For the last three nights, he had seen Lania in his nightmares.

The notion was unsettling. He had hunted deserters, sentenced murderers, and faced barbarians that fed upon their enemies. Nothing had ever had such a profound effect on him as that insane laughter and the flaring blue eyes of the caged mountain cat.

Not caged, he corrected. *The loose mountain cat.*

"Out of her cell," Aurion replied. "They are searching, Sovereign. If she is still in Lione, they will find her."

When it became clear Aurion could provide nothing further, Sovereign Polfius tossed his hands grandly and stormed out. As soon as he crossed the threshold out of the office, his poise returned. The public would never see the sovereign in an uproar.

With a sigh, Aurion swept his hand over the reports, stacking them roughly to the side. He'd memorized them. There was nothing for him to do but wait. Still, a feeling in the pit of his stomach warned him that they would never catch her, not now.

He turned to matters of Council business. A servant had delivered a message from Julluam earlier, an informant's update from the far-off province.

With a letter opener slotted under the seal, Aurion paused. He was grinning. He sat forward, thinking about the news from the prison, and he could not help but chuckle.

"Disappeared," he muttered. The chuckle intensified into a full laugh. He'd heard the various rumors. "Vanished like a ghost. Walks through walls, they say. Never mind the damn hole in the floor!"

He was interrupted by a voice to his left.

"You are impressed by her," Grizzle said from the shadows where his black garb concealed him. Unsurprised by his spymaster's presence, Aurion's laughter continued uninterrupted.

"Of course, I am impressed! Those cells have housed desperate criminals: traitors, murderers, deserters, and worse! Those sentenced to death, to torture. Some of them would never see freedom again! And in two hundred years, none ever succeeded in going down the piss hole. I wish I could have been there when they discovered she was gone!" He popped open the seal on the letter. "They must have turned the most incredible shade of purple!"

Grizzle left him to read, although Aurion heard him muttering about the insanity of his employer as he went.

Crouched in the sewer, Lania watched the lamplight pass. She waited for the sound of footsteps to fade, then waited a moment longer to make sure none of the Conquerors were close enough to hear when she propped herself up again and resumed her work on the hole above her. She needed only a little more space to be able to squeeze up.

The sewer was strange and damp. Most of it was continuous flowing water, but some areas were covered by walkways leading to openings. She had found them barred or guarded, neither of which suited her. She found another place where the water flowed out, presumably to the ocean. There, it was blocked by a grate Lania was confident she could easily overcome.

But she had promised Akara. Now that she had escaped their cells, she wanted back in.

It was time for the Warrior to answer the calls of her people. Lione would feel her fury.

CHAPTER 6

The unoccupied cell Lania found her way into was similar to the one she had escaped with one notable difference: the door was not locked.

When the patrols were in the sewers, she hid in the cell. When they were walking the upper levels, she hid in the sewer. Her strength slowly returned, her wound healing protracted on her diet of stolen crumbs and captured rats. Her leg bothered her the most. The crossbow bolt wound was to the bone and constantly ached even after a halfcycle of healing.

Within days, the searches below stopped. Content that she must have escaped, the prison fell back into its normal rhythm.

The Warrior of the Nurmi was waiting for it.

Avoiding the all-too-quiet night, she decided on dusk at the shift change to begin her run. Now wielding her chain as a weapon, Lania stepped into the path of two patrolling soldiers.

Their shock made them hesitate. Her first swing knocked one soldier off his feet. Before the second could react, she'd looped the chain around his neck, yanked him back, and hung him from a door's handle. As he choked, she stole his dagger and quickly slew the downed Conqueror. A second slice ended the dangling soldier's life.

She dragged the bodies into the empty cell after stealing both diuses. By necessity, she took one blue cape and put a hole through the center, then draped it over herself. As the sun set along white walls, the Warrior moved out again, finally armed, clothed, and on her way.

Tracking the movements of the patrols, she searched the new prison block. Most of the cells were empty, but Lania found what she was searching for in the fifth one.

The man was Nurmi and held by chains, his arms high. His legs were whip-marked and the right one was twisted and broken. His left eye was swollen shut. He hung naked and filthy, as Lania had done, covered in cuts she recognized as Tac's handiwork.

The lock was keyed, as the shackles had been, and it took only moments to pick. The man squinted at the light when she opened the door. He did not speak, but as soon as the first shackle fell from his wrist, he grunted and hoarsely said, "Hail, Warrior."

Lania felt Akara distantly nudge her.

"We heard you call," she whispered, catching him as he fell loose. "I have come for you." She was unsure if he heard her, for he did not respond.

It would be difficult enough to escape the prison, but carrying a wounded man threatened to make it impossible. Still, Lania knew their freedom was the will of the One God, and He would see her succeed. As Lania had promised Akara, she would answer those who called for help.

Leaving the man momentarily in his cell, she searched the hallway again. In the next cell, she was again successful. The second prisoner was the largest Nurmi she had ever seen. He was not even shackled.

He did not react when she opened the door but stared at her, his face shadowed. Once she determined his relative health, she told him to wait and ducked back into the other cell to bring the first Nurmi over.

She nearly collided with the large Nurmi upon her return; he had moved to the doorway. He pulled away, watching with childish curiosity until sudden recognition struck him. Instantly, his confusion vanished. He lifted the wounded man with a single muscled arm, taking all the weight from Lania. "Hail, Warrior," he rightly said.

Lania sighed in relief and passed a thankful word to the One God. If this Nurmi could support the wounded man, they may yet see the outside skies.

She hushed them when she heard the Lionians approach. Together, the three Nurmi ducked beside the door, out of sight. The patrol of two marched on by, not looking in.

Lania began counting again the moment the soldiers were gone. Eventually, someone would look into a cell. How long would the two missing soldiers remain unnoticed? When would they spot the blood in the hall or spattered down the door where she had hung a Conqueror?

She could not wait around to find out.

The large warrior came to her as she scanned the hall. Smiling weakly when she looked at him, he said, "You do not recognize me? I am Haro."

"Haro?" Lania replied in surprise. Most warriors taken in battle were enslaved, but those bearing the silver armbands, as Haro and Lania both had, were always tortured for information. Under those conditions, Nurmi died.

She did not understand how Haro had survived for so long. Perhaps her capture had pulled attention from him, buying time. Or had the Lionians not known the value of the prisoner? "You are... We thought you dead."

"I should have been," he answered with such sincerity she examined him again in the torchlight. He did not meet her eye but shook his head. "We will have to discuss it later. If you seek others, know three more are in a cell at the end of the hall. But first..."

Haro briefly left the wounded Nurmi and fetched a silver armband from under a stack of debris in a corner. Seeing it,

Lania smiled. *Lucky, he managed to hide the armband before the Conquerors took it from him.*

By donning it, Haro brought the One God's eye onto them.

He was right; questions were for later. They had to escape before they were discovered.

"Move with me quickly." She stole into the hall once more.

True to Haro's word, three other Nurmi warriors were imprisoned in a single cell at the end of the hall. Unchained, they exited quickly once she opened the door. All bore new brands on their arms in readiness for slavery, but none let it slow them.

Together, they made their way along the maze of corridors. The single guard manning each intersection never seemed to recognize the threat until after her blade took his throat. She led her warriors out like waves, Lania leading each advance.

After a dozen hallways, a gong rang out. Guards flooded from their side rooms into the hallways. Chased now, she passed other cells containing Nurmi. She expected her people to hate her for passing them by, but instead, the Nurmi helped where they could, calling away the guards or making a clatter to confuse the pursuit.

She swore she would return for those she had missed.

They forced their way out, collecting the helmets and cloaks of fallen Lionians as they went. The prisoners cut holes in the center of the folded cloaks and wore them draped front to back, held with belts. Even the man with the broken leg was at last able to cover himself. They were poor substitutes for a Nurmi's traditional garb, but the attire helped disguise them as well, being in Lione's blue.

When they finally burst through an outer door onto the prison grounds, there were three Lionians on guard.

Lania threw one unbalanced Lionian knife into the wall behind them, making the men turn their heads from her approach. By the time they turned back, she had her dagger in one of their throats, the most accessible gap in their armor.

She threw the dead man into the next Lionian, used her dius to parry the third Conqueror's lunge, and stabbed her opposite hand into the man's neck. When he stumbled back, she followed him down, ducking between him and his dius. She buried her knife to the hilt in his throat.

She spun in readiness, only to find Haro between her and the final Lionian. The larger Nurmi stood like a bear, hammerlike fists raised in readiness. When the Lionian stabbed, the fighter knocked the blow wide and punched, bouncing the Conqueror off the wall. The blue and black uniform crumpled to the ground, helm dented deep enough to draw blood from the flesh within.

Lania gave Haro a nod of thanks. Stealing the two unbroken helmets, then snatching a nearby torch, she led them across the grounds. With the light high above them, she hoped the enemy would only see the reflection off their helmets and the distinctive blue of their cloaks and assume they were soldiers joining the search.

It seemed to work. No more soldiers challenged their departure.

Dumping the light, they moved by moonlight once they reached the exterior wall. Haro boosted her over.

Lania landed in an area of Lionian homes and quickly climbed the wall of a house to reach the roof. Although she had planned to use the vantage point to decide on her next move, she found herself staring at the answer; she had stumbled across a laundry business where the clothes were drying on the roof in the warming spring air. Lania reached to touch her armband in thanks to the One God, but her finger hit only skin.

Moments later, she was helping five warriors over the prison wall with a rope of Lionian clothing.

Traveling straight and using the view from the top of the roofs to guide them, they reached the wall of Lione without being seen. The smooth outer walls loomed ahead of them, insurmountable and unbreakable. Lania already had a plan.

She spoke to Haro.

"What about you?" he protested.

"The One God brought me here," Lania replied. "Take the others; get them to the river. The Priestess sends warriors south to meet you by the Nartle Inn in Pohlia. Move fast. The One God will watch over you."

He wanted to object more, she could tell, but he visibly held himself back.

Nodding, Haro cut a piece of his hair, which he handed to her like a precious stone.

"You have saved my life, Warrior. With honor, I give you my debt."

Her stomach knotted, the reminder of the debts missing from her hair stinging. She smothered the memory, dismissing how she could taste the blood in her mouth from one of Nasib's blows, and fixed Haro with a false but calm expression. As she forced gravity and respect into her voice, she prayed the darkness could hide her unease.

"I am honored by your gift, Haro." She braided the lock of hair into her own to show him she was genuinely grateful. He beamed at the recognition.

"Now prepare yourself," she said, desperate to keep going for fear of stopping and finding herself still in a dark cell.

She left the shadows and walked to the gate in the open, sword in hand. As the gong sounded, Lania dodged and ran. Overeager to capture her, half of the Lionians gave chase. Behind her, five smaller shadows slipped up to the remaining guards, took the gate, opened it, and disappeared into the night.

Lania let her instincts drive her feet. The once-intimidating buildings became thickets and groves filled with hiding places. Alleys were deer paths guiding her through the underbrush. The carts and debris of the street were bushes and stones that would conceal her. Once her mind saw the forest, not a city, around her, she was uncatchable.

By the end of the night, she found herself by the gate once more. She led her pursuers there, then hid until they decided she had gone through. While they sorted out a pursuit, she turned away.

It was not hard, knowing to look on the roofs, to find clothes. In the dawn, merchants set up their stalls, whispering the latest news of the escaped prisoner to their neighbors as they went.

Lania's seeking brought her to a market. The smells overwhelmed her: flatbreads, fruit, honey, the blood of freshly slaughtered meat, and the musk of beasts. Her skin tingled with the fresh air of the open square, so different from the stagnation of the prison. The noise that had deafened her before began to rise once more as the city woke. The market threatened to drown her.

But a lone Nurmi wandering the streets was too obvious. As much as she hated it, she needed the crowds to hide her.

She lingered near the market, keeping to the shortening shadows as dawn encroached. Around a common drinking fountain, Lania found a slave trader preparing for the day. Just as a tailor would display finished shirts, the trader had picketed places along the road and, one by one, tied slaves there. Her hand clenched over the spot where her silver armband would have sat. Her stomach twisted, hollow, and aching.

She had the solution she was looking for, but she could not bring her legs to move.

Fear of the shackles enveloped her. Her wrists still felt light, the memory of the metal weighing against her skin like a withdrawing nightmare. She could not stomach the idea of being tied once more.

But a lone Nurmi walking in Lione would bring the soldiers. She needed to hide. In the city, the people were her camouflage.

Swallowing her fear, Lania assessed herself. Her clothing was smeared by the dirt of her flight through the back-streets of Lione and she'd not swum or bathed in a month now, at least. The diet of rats and scraps had shrunken her in many ways.

She looked the part.

With a final shuttering breath, Lania snuck out from her shadows and joined the back of the crowd of awaiting slaves. It struck her odd that so many were unbound, but then these people did not look ready to run. Consciously, Lania matched their downcast stares and hunched posture.

The slave trader, yawning widely, attached her to a post next to a Yeahsin slave, obliviously. Even the Yeahsin who ended up sharing her post did not look up. His head of black curls was patchy and dull as he stared at the ground.

She remained there as the day woke and the guards, who loudly came through the market in search, passed by without a second thought. The sun rose over the city, although the tall, white buildings blocked much of the light. The city warmed, smoke and masses of people suffocating the streets. Although she had no coat, she sweated.

At midday, a richly-clad buyer approached the shop.

"Need a Nurmi," the portly man told the slaver's son, who came forward to field the sale. "My daughter is grown. I seek a quiet, capable slave for her. It must speak Lionian flawlessly. I'll not have a bumbling savage."

Lania glanced up at the man but quickly lowered her stare again as the others did. He wore fine black trousers and a cotton shirt with matching red stitching. It would have taken days to embroider so much cloth; it had to be worth a lot.

The young man rolled his eyes. "All slaves talk properly around here, Master Gitarius," he said.

The buyer heaved his belly up as if straightening himself when he could not physically grow taller. "It needs to be healthy. No diseases. No cavities. No lice."

"Of course, Master Gitarius." the slaver's son said. Slumped and clearly wishing he could be elsewhere, the slaver's son led the prospective client to the posts and went through the motions of showcasing the slaves. The buyer stopped at a few women, but he moved on when closer examination proved them unhealthy.

When he reached Lania, he paused.

She immediately lowered her eyes, modeling her behavior on stories from the fire-pit in the Corelands, posing meekly as the man looked her over. Without a word, he checked her vision, mouth, and limbs, including her wounded leg. He felt the strength in her arms.

"Seems strong as an ox. Are you sure it is not as dumb as one, too? The strong ones are the most daft. Hard to train."

"No, no, she is just hard-working! Clever enough to know her trade and her place," the boy immediately offered.

Master Gitarius eyed him skeptically, but seemed pleased enough by what he saw that he did not bother to roll up the sleeves concealing her many cuts. The leg was a different matter; she flinched when he touched it. Without speaking to her, the stranger rolled up the leg of her leggings.

"Hell of a cut," the buyer said, scowling at the boy. He frowned disappointedly at the injury. "She's the best of the lot though, despite it."

"Cut her leg on a flagstone," the boy flatly lied. "Was cleaning up the kitchen just yesterday despite it. Father likes her to do the cleaning 'cause she's so quick."

Lania struggled not to react, outraged at the audacity of the seller spinning such confident falsehoods. The ease with which he lied made it hard to recognize, yet it was so clearly wrong.

The buyer shrugged. "I don't like that scratch," he said, pointing at the scabbed cut that hooked under her right eye. She'd forgotten about the strike that had cut her deep enough to scar over her cheekbone "Implies she's caused trouble. No slave of mine can look like a troublemaker." His eyes narrowed. Lania noted his hand unconsciously fondling his purse. "Lowers its resale value."

"Hard to find an unmarked slave, Master Gitarius," the boy pointed out. "But she's not a mine slave. Cleaner face than them."

Master Gitarius leaned back, running his gaze up and down her again. He wrinkled his nose, but his purse jingled under his hand. "What is your name?" he demanded.

The Warrior nearly snapped at him. Her name was sacred, and demanding to know it was a grave insult. How dare they presume to demand her name, she the Warrior of the Nurmi!

But he was Lionian and an idiot. His ignorance was a testimony to the distance between Lione and the One God in her eyes.

While she could not lie about her name, she certainly could not tell him her true name either. Like all enslaved Nurmi, she chose a descriptor instead of a name.

"*Tatkil*," she replied. She was, after all, a "sister."

"You understand me?" the man pressed.

"Yes, Master," she answered, trying to sound meek.

The answer seemed to suffice.

"How much for it?"

Aurion marched through the palace halls as if he were in the ranks once more. With his eyes forward and his steps short, he arrived at the walled garden.

Sovereign Polfius, ruler of the vast Sovereignty of Lione and supposed demi-god, reclined in a padded chair by the fountain. Cropped gray hair and a well-groomed beard showed off his senior years. The man's expression was always pensive, and age had carved that thoughtfulness into permanent, deep wrinkles around his thin lips. The beard, Aurion's adopted father had once explained, was a way of hiding those wrinkles. If that was its purpose, it was unsuccessful.

The sovereign could not, by law, choose his wardrobe. His pleated white robe was trimmed in black and accented by a black sash similar to a high councilman's but with golden embroidery. Unlike councilmen, who wore their chains and seals only during Council, the gold chains of office hung around the sovereign's neck regardless of the time of day.

The older man sat up, clapping his hands like a child at play. "What news? Has the Warrior been found?"

Aurion's step did not waver until he stood directly before his sovereign. He bowed, but it was short. "No, Sovereign. I do not believe she will be found. I did, however, hear news about the East Army today."

The older man arched one eyebrow at him. "Oh?"

"You have been making arrangements while I was otherwise occupied. Galeni Lonthius is apparently on his way to Lione." Aurion paused, but the sovereign did not volunteer any information. He no doubt hoped his secret was not fully revealed.

But the news Aurion had heard concerned personal affairs that had to be addressed. He turned away to pace, with a wave dismissing the servants. They scurried away obligingly. The guards were permitted only because Aurion knew them well.

Polfius' eyebrows rose, recognizing the move for privacy.

"Please, Sovereign, you must abandon these negotiations."

The sovereign pursed his lips in a disappointed scowl. "How did you...? Never mind. I know; if you were to reveal your sources, they would vanish. But I thought only Galeni Lonthius and I knew about our deal. You hear about things quickly."

"Particularly if they concern me," Aurion answered. "Please call it off."

The sovereign favored Aurion with a sidelong glance of curiosity. "Why? What is the matter with Olena Lonthius? Not too old for you?"

As much as it was necessary to keep the truth secret, Aurion did not dare lie to the sovereign. He put little stock in the man's status as a demi-god, but enough doubt remained to make him cautious.

"She would be unhappy," Aurion replied obliquely.

The sovereign leaned back and folded his hands on his recently expanding belly, ready for a lengthy discussion. "Unhappy? What could she possibly be unhappy about? Marriage to the sovereign's son! It's every girl's dream."

Hardly a girl, Aurion thought. They shared a birth year. Olena would be soon reaching her twenty-fifth birthday.

"Olena Nalla Lonthius," Aurion said cautiously, "has spent her entire life in the army. She knows nothing of life in the city."

"If you are worried she will not know how to keep the home clean, she will learn. She is intelligent, I am told. If anything, I thought you would be interested in that. Or is that the problem? You think she will be too much of a challenge to maintain?"

"No, Sovereign," Aurion said with a sigh.

"Sovereign?"

"No, Father," he amended.

"Good. For a moment, I worried you had lost your senses."

"She belongs with her father," Aurion tried.

"Who has reluctantly agreed to let her go. You know how hard it is to refuse a sovereign's request," Sovereign Polfius replied, and Aurion stopped pacing. *Oh yes. I know exactly how hard it is to refuse a sovereign's request.*

The sovereign cocked an eyebrow suspiciously. "Is this about the soldier's sister? What was her name?"

Aurion swallowed hard with a grimace. "Ailsa."

"Not high enough standard for a councilman or the sovereign's son, Aurion," Sovereign Polfius scolded.

"That ended. She has nothing to do with this," Aurion assured him, and the sovereign frowned. Aurion dreaded what he knew was coming but could find nothing to prevent it.

"You are not telling me something."

He searched again for an escape but only lies presented themselves.

"Do I have to command it from you?"

Aurion gave up. With all his heart, he obeyed his sovereign. If Sovereign Polfius gave the order, Aurion would have to answer. It was better to save him the formality.

He spun out the confession in a single thread; "Galeni Tactus Lonthius is losing his memory. Sometimes he forgets the names of his braxi or even where he is, yet you would never know that if you observed his strategy and command. As his mind worsens, his daughter never leaves him, and I assure you, she is as clever as you suggest. Galeni Lonthius no longer runs those armies, Sovereign; his daughter does, with the blessings of the braxi. If you give her to me, the armies will become aware of Tactus' weakness. Either he will retire or the ranks will fall into disarray as succession is debated. Either way, we lose a valuable galeni. We cannot afford that."

Sovereign Polfius stared at Aurion with his mouth agape. It was the best-kept secret of the army, and, with the sovereign knowing it, Aurion doubted it would remain as such. Whether intentionally or not, the news would be out soon.

"Please understand the need for this to stay quiet, Sovereign. If the wrong people find out, we are guaranteed to see it in the news sheet within hours. Then we lose our galeni and the East Army will be destabilized."

"Fine," the sovereign said in a choked whisper, a sure sign Aurion had upset him. "You have your wish: there will be no wedding. But I expect, *Councilman*, that you will inform me better in the future."

Aurion bowed deeply, more to hide his remorse than because custom required it of him. "Of course, Sovereign."

"Dismissed."

CHAPTER 7

Lania, now called Tatkil, sat cross-legged in the moonlight filtering between the bars of the window. With a thin blanket under her, she kept her thoughts off her squalid conditions. A single woven blanket for the daughter of the Black Arrow. The cold stone floor as a bed. A costume worthy of a dancing fool on a holy day. This was not what the Warrior deserved. She belonged in the Corelands.

The summer cycle had crept in, but there was no warmth in the Lionian house. Lania's mistress, Julti Lola Gitarius, slept under four quilts—Lania had counted as she made the bed—and had not bothered to have the fire stoked.

Convincing herself she did not have time for such nonsense, Lania did not shiver. Her focus was Julti, her ears trained on the gentle breathing. Sleep settled in.

With bars on the window, locks on the doors, and soldiers in the halls, the bedroom hardly differed from the prison. The main difference was that Julti's door locked from the inside, provided an easy exit. Now that Lania had learned the house, she plotted a route out.

That, she comforted herself, was not how slaves behaved. Despite her uniform and the control over her life she hid within, she was no slave.

They believed she was, and she could smile at that thought. Tatkil was expected, as the property of a young woman, to be on her mistress' heel at all times. She carried baggage, made beds, dressed the fourteen-year-old, and fetched anything the child desired. The work was strange but not unpleasant or difficult. Julti had revealed herself to be somewhat absent-minded, allowing Lania a degree of freedom even in daylight, so long as she dodged the attention of the Master of the Household. Falmio Caltian Gitarius, her owner, was a wealthy Lionian who ranked just under the upper class of the councilmen. It only took the slightest invitation to drive Master Gitarius into recounting the proud history of the Household of Gitarius. Unlike many lesser Lionians, the Household of Gitarius had two house colors, not three, which marked them as one of the more ancient and respected households.

It only took a little more prodding to gain a full account of his family's fall from favor. That story always ended with the assurance that, with Falmio Caltian Gitarius at the head, the family was heading back to the Councilhall where they belonged. His fur trading business was thriving in Lione, and he spent his fortune on gifts for important people or displays of affluence. He passed most of his day amidst councilmen and their associates, trying to sneak in connections and better his position.

What confused Lania most about these odd behaviors was that he seemed to be succeeding. The rich men liked to be catered to and complimented. Many eagerly let Gitarius into their circle. This pleased Gitarius to no end, although, as a result, his sense of importance, at least in the Warrior's eyes, was out of proportion.

Her master had it in his mind that Nurmi bred much like the rabbits of his fur business, and, as he already owned one male slave, he could expect to be surrounded by little Nurmi in a matter of mooncycles after the purchase of a female. When Lania heard his plans, she had barely managed to keep her silence and look at her feet as a slave was meant to. She avoided the other Nurmi slave pointedly, which was not difficult. The small man, who called himself Kaco, or "tiny," was the keeper of the dogs. Shy and generally absent, Kaco did not seem to notice her.

To Lania's delight, her master had also decided female slaves, the weakest of the sexes, would not survive the use of brands. Thus, upon her purchase, he had not applied the branding iron to her as he had to Kaco. She did not correct his misconception and accepted wearing the Gitarius black and red household colors as her only form of identification.

The moon slipped by the window, the breathing of the child now slow and deep.

Lania crept to the door on her toes. There, she placed a hand on the wood and listened with the ears of the hunter until she could again hear the regular breathing of the child in the bed. She heard nothing from beyond the door, so she slowly released the lock, lifted the latch, and cracked the door open.

In the silence of the night, the movement of the door sounded painfully loud. Hinges, she reflected, were the ultimate defense against thieves. When kept improperly, they creaked an alarm.

Any Nurmi sentry would have investigated or called the alarm by the time she slipped into the hall. Fortunately, she was dealing with Conquerors, not Nurmi. The guards had never reacted to any of her experimental openings, leaving her to assume that, in a household so poorly maintained, the noise was too familiar to attract attention.

The corridors were not lit as they had been in prison, but the post at the end of the hall had a decorative oil lamp on the table between the two guards. With their eyes adjusted to the lamplight, they would have a hard time seeing into the dark where Lania crept.

She flattened herself against the ground and slid along the outer reaches of the light and under a table. Hidden from view, Lania slithered up the corridor and once more out of sight.

At the next intersection, she eased through a door into an enclosed garden. The courtyard's ornamentation was sparse: a hole filled with water and a handful of plants in stone pots. She had heard Gitarius claim rare fish lived in the pond, and they required the murky water which, conveniently, prevented anyone from actually seeing them. A slave fed the invisible fish at least twice daily.

Lania slunk into the courtyard, closed the door behind her, and scanned the area for occupants. Small as it was, the only hiding places were the small pots and a bench by the murky pond, and none of those could hide a person.

Taking off her shoes, she retrieved a rope, stolen from Gitarius' hunting equipment, from under a pot. In one corner, Lania dug an anchor for her rope with a shard of firewood and the weight of a pot. That secured, she found the largest pot she could move and set it at the corner where the house walls met the walls around the garden. With the rest of the rope tossed over the wall, she balanced atop the pot.

After a moment of preparation, she leaped, pushing off the wall with her bare foot. The tips of her fingers came a head short of the top of the wall, and she fell back onto the cold ground.

After two more attempts, Lania came no closer to escape and decided she needed more height. As the bench was too heavy, she settled for a second pot on top of the first. Perched atop the stacked pots, she aimed her jump and leaped.

Lania was mid-air when she heard the crash behind her, and she nearly missed her grab because of it. She had toppled the second pot and sent it smashing onto the stone of the garden, where it shattered into a hundred pieces and dumped the unfortunate shrub onto the rock.

Lania cursed loudly, and in Nurmi, but she caught the top of the wall.

Pulling herself up quickly, she stretched along the flat top of the stone wall and turned to the doors. She drew a stolen dagger from under the red and black uniform and waited for the dozen Conquerors pressing to investigate.

She lay and listened for an alarm. When that did not come, she listened for footsteps. She heard nothing.

When she could no longer wait, she stood. The Conquerors in the Corelands had been dangerous warriors. But here, in the safety of their opulent city, they were lazy. She feared them less every day.

Keeping the rope tight against the corner, she climbed down the other side and dug another anchor. Now secure on both sides, she stepped back and admired her work.

The result was as effective as a ladder. On the inside, her rope was snug between two walls, hidden in the shadows.

She was out. The city awaited.

She had not forgotten the people she had been forced to leave behind in the prison. But before she sought a road back to them, she needed a way out of the Falling City.

The Warrior glided along the wall of her owner's home and out onto the streets to map the city's hidden paths and find its weaknesses. Then she would bleed the wretched city until it released her people from its white streets and towers and begged her for mercy.

Aurion found the blue tent easily among the bland whites and grays of the encamped army. He paused outside, enjoying the nostalgia it brought. The mark of a galeni stared back at him from the standard beside the entrance, bringing back memories of the far reaches of Namera and the distant south jungles of Santan. Once he felt the eyes of his bodyguards on him in query, Aurion gave a final sigh of surrender and ducked his head under the lifted flap, leaving the guards outside.

The tent enclosed two areas: one general space containing a map table and short, padded chairs, and one curtained sleeping area with a field cot. Six people occupied the main room, all in the blue and black uniform of the Lionian army. At the head of the table, Galeni Tactus Grantar Lonthius reclined over two chairs.

The galeni looked worse than ever, and his lounging position caused Aurion concern for the old man's back. He had folded his hands together, but Aurion still spotted a tremor in them. The old man's hair was perfectly white, including the wisps of the beard hardly visible against his tanned skin. His face was, despite wrinkles, still alert, and his eyes filled Aurion with confidence that the man was not yet ready to be pushed aside.

Beside the galeni, Olena stood stoically. Although she strongly resembled her father, having inherited none of her mother's more elegant features, her long hair and lashes ensured she was still beautiful. Her dark hair was braided intricately, likely by a professional, but she wore a modest dress more common to the lower class. The hem reached only the middle of her calves, as if the tailor had made a mistake, but this same error allowed her to match the hurried pace of marching soldiers. She wore soldier's boots below the too-short hem and stood as straight as any man of the ranks.

As a proper upper-class woman, Olena had folded her hands daintily in front of her. When she met Aurion's stare, however, there was no hint of delicacy. The hands, likely as callused as a peasant's feet, flexed anxiously, eager to be out of the humiliating pose.

All save the galeni, rose to Aurion's entry and bowed to the White and Black he wore. Aurion greeted each of the gathered officers by name, which put them in a slightly better mood when Galeni Lonthius dismissed them. Only one of the offi-cers, a loraxi of little note by the name of Krinus Otavious, was requested to remain. Olena, as Aurion expected, also stayed.

Aurion waited a dozen heartbeats to allow the other sol-diers to distance themselves before approaching the table. "Thank you for agreeing to meet me, sir," he said, bowing in acknowledgment.

The galeni laughed. "Sir? Accepting that white and black robe made you surpass my rank, Aurion. But why the for-mality? You have been calling me Tactus since you were fif-teen. Unless that wretched city has changed you?"

Aurion clutched the outstretched hand of the galeni in friendship and let himself laugh. "In some ways, perhaps, but never in that, Tactus, I assure you."

Smiling with the correction, the galeni gestured to a chair. As he took his seat, Aurion glanced at the loraxi. To Aurion's mild surprise, the man was at ease.

"Congratulations on your promotion, Loraxi Otavious," Aurion said, "but I expected you to be even farther by now." He glared at Tactus. "You are holding him back."

Tactus chuckled as he reached up to take his cup from the table. "If it were up to me, he would be commanding by now, but these things take time, as you know, Aurion." When he put the cup down, Aurion filled it from a pitcher on the table. At a gesture from the galeni, Aurion filled three other cups as well.

"The galeni has been more than generous," Krinus argued lightly once he had taken a sip from the cup. Aurion wondered when the loraxi had learned to pace himself when drinking in the company of his superiors. That was a hard lesson many never got a chance to learn.

"As always, Tactus? You get rid of me, and now you need a new protégé?" Out of the corner of his eye, Aurion saw the loraxi's expression of confusion. Most people only knew of Aurion's command in Santan, where his galeni had been slain, leaving Aurion to command the forces through two seasons alone. Few were aware he had spent the first year as an officer under Lonthius.

"You weren't my first attempt at smoothing out some rough clay," Tactus pointed out. With a short sigh, he added, "I wanted to thank you tonight for your involvement on Olena's behalf, Aurion."

The good mood flew instantly out the door.

With the topic at hand, Aurion glanced at Olena. "I could hardly take away your daughter, Tactus," Aurion said. "I mean, of course, no disrespect to you, Olena."

"Of course not," the woman answered. Her words were spoken in a matter-of-fact tone copied perfectly from her father. "Your reputation would be wrongly earned if you did not know the game we play. You have saved the army a great deal of embarrassment."

Aurion nodded, taking a drink from his cup. *Good wine from Salbero*, he noted, something he'd likely have had at home as a young man.

The galeni narrowed his eyes. "But you did not come here for my thanks, did you, Aurion? A councilman does not ride out of the city to visit an army camp without good reason." With a strained smile that bordered on a grin, Tactus added, "Especially not this councilman."

When confronted, Aurion hesitated. He let his eyes fall to the cup in his hand and stared at the red wine. Not for the first time, his position of power unsettled him. So often, he had looked to Tactus for help or advice. He had not considered how far they had come since those days.

But he'd asked for the meeting for reasons that needed to be addressed.

He drank the rest of the cup in a single swallow. "I need to ask you some questions." He deliberately avoided phrasing it as an order.

Galeni Lonthius barked laughter. "Of course you do! Always asking questions; that is my Aurion!" The galeni looked meaningfully at Otavious. "A good thing to take note of," he said. A moment later, his attention was back on Aurion. "Ask away."

"It was not your idea to see Olena wed, was it?" Aurion began.

Olena snorted in disgust but held her tongue.

"You know what I heard?" Tactus said with a dismissive wave of his hand. "I heard you never ask a question you do not already know the answer to. That is the perfect example. Spare me the performance."

Gratefully, Aurion continued, "Do you know whose idea it was?"

The galeni frowned, his expression dark. "You suspect something."

"Does it not strike you as odd?" Aurion asked, rolling the empty cup in his hands. "A wedding like this would normally be drawn out. The sovereign's adopted son and Olena Lonthius, the most sought-after bride in the Sovereignty, to be married. I would have expected mooncycles of activity and planning. Half the Sovereignty would be expected to attend. Perhaps I am being arrogant, but I would have expected much more excitement."

Olena put words to the question Aurion needed answered; "So why did they set the date barely more than a mooncycle away?"

"In forty-three days," Aurion agreed. "I would hardly have time to contact my mother and have her come to Lione. Why the hurry?"

It was forbidden for anyone not of the army to sit at the galeni's table, an old tradition that few knew the reason behind. But now Olena broke from standing beside her father and took the chair at his side. Aurion suspected it was her customary place. With her hands folded on the table, she leaned toward Aurion. "Is it possible Sovereign Polfius is sick?"

Aurion shook his head. "I considered that, but I have not seen or heard anything. I believe he intends to rule for many more years. He already has grandchildren, so I do not believe it is a desire for more family, either."

"So, he was put up to it," Olena concluded.

"My fear exactly. I need to know where to begin searching. I thought you might be able to help."

Tactus leaned back and bit his lip in thought, and Olena assumed a similar position in mirror, showing their strong similarity. The silence continued until the galeni slammed his cup down and barked laughter again. Aurion jumped like a criminal when the galeni pointed at him.

"Someone wants you out of the way." Aurion stared at the galeni in bewilderment. The man laughed again. "You have obviously never been married!"

"It does make sense," Olena said in a more controlled voice. "What better way to keep you busy?"

"It is simple enough," the galeni elaborated. "If you had a wedding to plan in a mooncycle, you would not have time for anything else. Add to that the wooing of a spirited new wife, and you would hardly be able to attend Council meetings, let alone pay attention to them. A lot of people could take advantage of that."

Aurion let his eyes fall to the cup he was fiddling with. "So, I need to look for someone who knew Olena would be a difficult woman but was unaware of her true role in her father's army."

"In other words, smart enough to spot the obvious but dumber than you," Tactus offered.

Despite himself, Aurion chuckled. "That has narrowed it down by two. It's a start."

Olena's head snapped up from its thoughtful bow. "Start with High Councilman Meltatio."

"Oh?" Aurion answered. He thought back to the wrestling match by the Councilhall. High Councilman Meltatio's slave had been talking to a slave of Maurio's a lot that day.

"I noticed him at the dinner on the twenty-first," said Olena. She lowered her eyes, suddenly looking like the proper rich woman of Lione she was meant to be. He took it to mean she was outside of her comfort zone. She no doubt had surpassed him in strategy and affairs of the armies, but politics were foreign and uncomfortable. "I am accustomed to being stared at, whether as a curiosity or as a prospective wife, but Meltatio kept smiling at me as if he knew something I did not. I heard of the marriage the next day. At first, I thought I was to be married to Meltatio. I was slightly relieved when I learned you were to be my husband."

Aurion did not miss the word "slightly." The idea of marriage would not sit well with the feisty woman. Had the wedding gone ahead, he suspected he would have spent at least a halfcycle trying to locate his wife-to-be.

Meltatio had served the Council for six years, first as the Councilman of the Market District, then as a high councilman. He could manipulate a mob well and had sufficient connections from his days in the financial district to control other councilmen, which made him dangerous. Fortunately, Sovereign Polfius had proven entirely immune to Meltatio's charm.

Meltatio would be a dangerous opponent, but there were worse.

Aurion rose from the chair and placed the cup next to the pitcher, noting in passing that Krinus had still not finished his. Olena was refilling her father's cup.

"Then I will start with him. Thank you, Tactus, for your hospitality."

The older man waved a dismissing hand once more. "You are always welcome here, Aurion. You should visit more often, preferably without more conspiracies; I have enough of those! When was the last time you had a good laugh?"

Aurion shook his head and looked at Olena, wondering just how many cups of wine Tactus had already drunk. The woman was eyeing her father with a skeptical glare. She understood the pressures, even if Tactus no longer did.

"Perhaps when I have a moment," Aurion said before bidding them farewell and wishing them a good trip back to Santan.

CHAPTER 8

Lania watched as the slaves helped each other onto the roofs of the shacks. From there, they crawled higher, onto more unstable rooftops leaning against the wall of the Newhope District. Three ropes dangled down the wall on the other side. The twenty-four slaves from the Market District, stolen from under the watchful eyes of the hired guards of some unfortunate slave master, made their way to freedom.

The once watchful eyes, Lania corrected. They saw nothing any longer.

After a halfcycle of waiting, the Warrior had come to Lione in full.

Among the slaves, Lania had found a handful of recently captured warriors from the Corelands to lead the more placid slaves home. These were the first, blazing a new trail for others to follow. A group of warriors, including Haro, was heading down the Solon River to meet the freed slaves. These would establish a road from the White City to the Corelands for the many to follow. Lania's work would be within and theirs without.

Every night, Akara reminded Lania of the voices calling her in their nightmares. She could not let them, or the One God, down.

As the last people disappeared over the wall, Lania felt Akara send a quiet prayer to the One God for their safe passage. If all went well, they would meet up with Haro's band, who would take them the rest of the way home.

Lania collected the ropes and hid them. As she wandered into the Docks District, she glanced at the water clock above and made note of how the hands pointed. She still could not make sense of it, but at least she knew how the two black pointers moved. It was getting toward morning; she knew that by the sky. Julti would not rise until the sun was up.

As she cut the lines to a few small boats and shoved them off, she remembered her mistress would be staying home the next day to learn from her mother. That was fortunate, she thought as she carved a hole in one of the boats before pushing it away from the docks. She had gotten very little sleep this night. It would be best if she were able to rest.

As she left the docks, a shout went up. One of the drifting boats had been spotted.

Lania headed home, musing whether the Conquerors would see the boat with the hole as it sank or if, as she had intended, they would assume the escaped slaves had stolen it. She did not care as long as it kept the soldiers from listening to Newhope District homeowners complaining about strange sounds on their roofs.

The white paint on the rope leading back into the House of Gitarius had soaked in and dried thoroughly in the warm summer air, making the rope hard to spot in the corner. She used the pond to clean herself and stripped off the extra clothes, which she stashed under one of the plants. Bloodstains were a little too obvious, even for Gitarius.

Her new room, suggested by Gitarius as a pleasant place to raise many children, was only two doors from the garden. The room had been converted from a storage closet when the slaves in the kitchen had complained they had no interest in seeing two Nurmi mating. Now, the room contained a small wooden bed and a straw mattress with a thin blanket. For some reason, Gitarius insisted upon repeating how very bright and pretty the blanket was, as if she were a five-year-old with a colorful stone.

Although the mattress was usually uncomfortable, Lania fell asleep at once. A moment later, the water clock was chiming, and she had to get up.

She helped in the kitchen for the better part of the day under the watchful eye of Master Gitarius, who felt things went better when he was supervising. A councilman's brother was coming for dinner, and the meal prepared could have fed the Nurmi army for a quartercycle. Half the food would be thrown out that night, a waste when others were hungry.

The rumors of the Warrior's attack reached Gitarius' household mid-afternoon. They were sure of the attacker's identity as she'd left a guard alive. She snorted when she heard Gitarius' version, which had her wielding four weapons at once and resembling a she-bear, but the exaggeration served the legend.

The Lionians filled the afternoon with speculation about the Warrior and where she had gone, supposedly on boats taken from the docks. They'd failed to find the sunken one.

As she stoked the fire, Lania smiled to herself.

She had been so busy listening that she had not noticed that Kaco, the little keeper of dogs, had come in with firewood from the market. As the Nurmi man placed it beside the hearth, he did not meet her eyes but whispered in Lionian, "I came to see you last night."

Lania's heart jumped, and, in her surprise, her hand knocked a log from the fire. The sudden flare of sparks attracted attention, and she endured Gitarius' glare as she tried to get the log back into the fireplace before it burned the carpet. Knowing Gitarius was watching, she answered in an unsteady voice befitting a slave.

"I will be sure to leave the door open for you tonight." Kaco's expression was confused, but he said nothing. Without looking back, he headed outside.

When Lania shyly glanced at her master, Gitarius was grinning.

The entire household was late getting to bed due to the feast, so it was nearly midnight when her door creaked open. Lania sat on her bed with a stolen sword under her knee.

Kaco still wore his uniform but had removed his shoes. Like many slaves, he bore scars across his face as evidence of the mines. His eyes were as blue as the sky on a warm day, but they had an emptiness Lania knew had been spawned in the mine's darkness.

He stood in the doorway like a child afraid of a monster hiding under the bed. She nearly laughed at the thought. *Maybe tonight the monster is on the bed.*

Lania drew out a lit candle from where she had concealed it and placed it on the corner of the bed. Kaco came to life; he scuttled into the room and quickly closed the door. His back against the thin wood, he stared at the candle as if never having seen one before.

Lania had been given no light but had taken it. He knew as much. His blank expression, eyes fixated on the candle, made it clear he did not know how to respond.

But he had closed the door. Lania considered that a good sign.

Slaves were not meant to speak unless first spoken to, so Lania waited in silence to see if he could break that rule.

After a long pause, Kaco stuttered, "I came to see you yesterday. You were not here."

"No, I was not," she replied. In place of Lionian, Lania answered in Nurmi.

He jumped, and she bristled to see the fear in his eyes. A breach of the Language Law clearly terrified him.

But if he could not speak a few words of Nurmi to one of his people alone in the middle of the night, how could she expect him to move against Gitarius? After all, that was precisely what she wanted of him.

Seeing his worry, Lania said, "If the master wants little Nurmi, he will tolerate a few words exchanged in a bedroom in Nurmi. Besides, he cannot hear us."

She was certain the cowed slave would not have argued if she declared the sky was green. He did not object to her logic now.

For a long time, Kaco looked down as he planned his following sentence. She waited again.

"Where were you?" he asked, to her immense pleasure, in ill-practiced Nurmi. She did not try to conceal her grin but did stifle her shout of victory.

"I was out in Lione," she replied, pausing to let him ponder the answer.

"Are you..." Kaco said, initially unable to finish. After a deep breath to steady his nerves, he asked, "Are you the Warrior?" He finally looked up.

Feeling the need for her full authority, Lania stood up. "Yes, Kaco, my name is Lania. I am the Warrior."

His eyes dropped. "My... my name is Binoran," he said, and she permitted herself another smile. He had a true name and had connected her to the escaped slaves. Binoran was not as simple as the master believed.

"A warrior's name," Lania answered. "It suits you."

When Binoran nodded absently and reached back to the door, Lania's heart skipped. She had not seen enough strength in him to convince her he would not tell Gitarius about her. Would a Nurmi betray their Warrior?

Unwilling to order him to stay, Lania said, "I see scars of a whip on your face. Did Gitarius give them to you?"

He paused at the exit, thinking. It occurred to her then that he might have trouble understanding Nurmi. How long had it been since he had heard a Nurmi voice?

After significant consideration, he shook his head. "The mines, many years ago."

"Did you do something wrong?" she persisted, knowing the longer he waited, the less likely he would report his discovery to Gitarius.

Although reluctant to speak, he turned slowly toward her, his head still bowed. "When I first was captured, I served the iron mines. We spent every fourth quartercycle in a cell. Some called it rest, but it was meant to break our spirits. Like the whips." He pulled his right arm forward to expose his upper shoulder. A thick white scar shaped like an X looked back at her from his biceps. Beneath that mark, a lion head brand identified him as the property of the Household of Gitarius. Both would have caused a great deal of pain, she was sure.

"Did it work?" she asked.

He had not hailed her. Even when she confirmed her identity, he had not looked hopeful or excited. She felt as if she was trying to reach someone who had fallen down a deep well. What could she do with someone who had lost all hope? When a Nurmi lost faith, what did they have left?

Lania saw the battle he fought against himself for the answer but, after long breaths of contemplation, he lifted his head and met her eyes for the first time.

"At first, it seemed it would," he said, "but we never stopped believing in the One God or the prophecies. We never forgot about the Black Arrow or the Twins, Warrior. It was hard, but we would never surrender."

"Then you are Nurmi and can be trusted. I warn you, Binoran, I have no intention of freeing you. I need to keep my hiding place. But if you are willing, I could use your help."

The small man's eyes lit up with a spark she imagined had probably been common before slavery. He was curious and eager. "How can I help?"

"I am here to free as many slaves as I can before the Lionians drive me out. I need contacts within the city. I need places to hide. I need more people helping me."

The spark in his eyes glittered with previously forbidden excitement. "Can I be of service?"

"Tonight," Lania decided, "we are going to fight. Tomorrow, I will refuse to have anything to do with you. If Gitarius still wants little Nurmi, he will be forced to get rid of one of us. I expect it will be you, if only to avoid Julti's tantruming." He nodded, knowing the young lady had taken possession of Lania and would object strongly to having any toy taken from her. "If he sells you outside of Lione, I will come and get you, but if you are sold within the city, I want you to light a flint in a window every night until I come. From there, you should be able to assist others in escaping."

She knew a cruel master might buy him, but Binoran accepted the risk without hesitation. The Warrior, the legend he had once doubted even existed, was asking for his help. It terrified her to realize he was now hers in all things.

Once he had left, that realization kept Lania awake.

Aurion watched the councilmen depart from the Councilhall, assessing each glance or hesitation, gleaning all he could. His gaze paused on High Councilman Meltatio for a moment longer than the others, but he found nothing. That much had been expected; the man was too practiced to break any facade this close to potential enemies. But yesterday one of Grizzle's contacts had spotted Meltatio conversing with another councilman, Transitory Councilman Maurio. And as he watched, Aurion spotted the mistake he had been looking for; Maurio moved to intercept Meltatio and, with a subtle gesture, Meltatio waved him off.

Meltatio had introduced a weak link to his inner circle. It would only be desperation that would bring Maurio into the other high councilman's orbit, which did nothing to assuage Aurion's concern that something more was afoot. He needed to know.

As Aurion watched Meltatio, the councilman paused under one of the many arches leading out and looked back as if admiring the Councilhall. His eyes drifted over the fourteen lower boxes on the main floor, up over the High Priest's central podium, and into the five high councilman boxes below the public benches. They passed over Aurion, who was still at his seat, appearing to be engrossed in a scroll.

Eventually, Meltatio's eyes reached the twentieth box that stuck out of the far wall above all the others. Sovereign Polfius had already stepped off his golden throne and retired behind the curtains.

The councilman then let his stare wander over the rows and rows of carven faces circling the dome above the Council seats likely, as visitors tended to when they entered the Councilhall, imagining his face among the ancient sovereigns. Sovereign Polfius' face was there already. According to the sovereign, nothing was as unnerving as seeing yourself overseeing your decisions.

Perhaps that was why Meltatio had gone to the arch. From that position, he was hidden from the old sovereigns.

As Meltatio finished his scan of the Councilhall, Aurion stood to follow. He was interrupted by his name when he reached the main floor.

"Councilman Volustio," he greeted with a polite nod.

Councilman Craxus Trano Volustio was fifty-eight years old and had a long, bearded face that reminded Aurion of an eagle, if eagles could grow beards. His nose was hooked, and his eyes were close-set and small, giving him a pene-trating glare that set many on their heels. The white and black robes he had worn for a decade accented his pale face poorly, making him look sickly. Aurion spent afternoons in the gardens to avoid the effect himself.

When the older man spoke, he wore a pleasant smile that turned Aurion's stomach. "I wanted to congratulate you on your wedding, but I am too late."

Aurion buried his displeasure, keeping his expression polite. "Things change quickly. It is good you can keep up."

He would not be able to catch Meltatio now. Had that been Volustio's intent? Was he involved?

"Some things change for good reasons, too. You are as well informed as ever, I see."

When it came to secrets, he and Volustio were equals. Early in his career as a councilman, Aurion had been impressed by how Volustio kept all of Lione in his head. Eventually, respect had been replaced with an active dislike for the man and his heavy-handed methods.

Aurion had quickly dismissed Volustio as the person behind the marriage; Volustio had known Olena's secret and would never have expected Aurion to be unaware.

"Everything happens for good reasons," Aurion said.

Volustio smiled pleasantly once more. "But you must be careful, Councilman. You have reached your mid-twenties, have you not? And you are yet unmarried."

Aurion did not bother to answer. The real threat was still to come.

"And in all your years in Lione, there have only been a handful, at best, of women. If news of your quickly canceled wedding gets out, I suspect the people may begin to wonder if your favors lie with the women at all or if they are pointed toward *others*."

There it was. He had the power to spread the rumor and the motivation to start the speculations, too. It was, however, a threat with no weight behind it.

"If you are looking for such a simple weakness, Councilman, you will have to look farther to the right than my seat," Aurion replied with a laugh.

They both looked to where Aurion was referring. For a rare moment, they agreed. It was no secret that most of the Council disliked Councilman Atoron Ganon Galfium. Very little concerning Galfium was a secret. Most of the city knew of his odd pleasures, including the people taken to privately owned houses across the city. It would not have been so bad if the councilman had been capable of keeping it to Lionians. Even respectable councilmen sometimes hired from the streets. This was forgivable, as many had lost wives and needed company.

The trouble with Galfium was his preference for slaves. It did not seem to matter what race they were, nor did it matter if it was a man, woman, or child. The idea of a Lionian lowering himself to the level of the beasts was sickening, and the added indiscrimination of gender made it worse. While everyone knew, no one spoke of it, and Galfium was somehow always re-elected when the vote came.

"You heard of the activities in the Market District a few nights ago?" Volustio asked, continuing the "pleasant" conversation once their attention returned from the seat where Galfium sat during Council.

"I did not think the Warrior had so many arms," Aurion replied with an empty smile.

"Ah yes, I had forgotten you have become the expert regarding the Nurmi. The description of her attack does not fit?"

"The original description fits well enough. The resulting exaggerations are products of fear and superstition."

"Always the case," the older man philosophized. "People need a monster for the heroes to slay. Easier to have her look the part." Without missing a beat, which prevented Aurion from excusing himself, Volustio went on, "And how is the new spy doing?"

Aurion held his expression perfectly neutral and dropped three fake names without hesitation. "Mani, Trevio, or Chal?"

Aurion wondered whether Volustio would check into the names Aurion had "given" him. *Probably*, he thought. The names might be real, to add to the humiliation when the truth came out.

Before Volustio could reply, Aurion asked, "And how is Safarik enjoying his new position?"

He scored a mental point in his favor when he saw a brief expression of annoyance take the eagle's face. The councilman recovered quickly, but the wound was still fresh.

"Well enough," the older man replied with forced calm. "He has a great deal of potential."

"Indeed. He learned from the mistakes of his predecessors well. I noticed he does not go anywhere near my house."

"He wishes to avoid making the same errors of judgment as he should. As we all should," Volustio concluded, sufficiently irritated to finish with a strained "Good day," and storm off.

Free of the conversation, Aurion left, joined by his two bodyguards once he was outside.

The wounded pride was still there, which was good. Volustio's previous spymaster had threatened one of Aurion's spies a cycle ago. Grizzle had found out, and the offending party had been dead by morning. Grizzle did not allow anyone to threaten his subordinates.

It had fallen to Aurion to manage the aftermath. Throwing salt onto Volustio's wound was his way of trying to prevent another indiscretion.

But the incident was one of many going back years. It was unfortunate, in Aurion's opinion, but he had come to accept the rivalry. If he had not risen to the challenge, he would have been forced to yield to Volustio, and he was not going to do that.

He walked home, preferring his feet to a carriage. Despite the crowd of the Market District, he had little trouble navigating the streets thanks to the white and black robes and the silver chain he still wore around his neck. The crowds gave him plenty of space.

He bought a cantaloupe as he walked and gave half of it away when he spotted a beggar under a cart. He was still licking juice from his fingers when he entered his gate.

It was more land and space than Aurion would ever have bought, but the house had been a gift from the sovereign as part of his incentive for coming to Lione. It was built on a small hill within the city and enclosed by walls. Through the gate, the yard flowered all year, making it a satisfying splotch of color in a white world. The road to the house branched to the back, where apple trees shaded a pond and bench.

He greeted the gardeners as he passed and let the two bodyguards wander off once he was inside. After selecting two reports off his desk, Aurion planned to return to the garden but was interrupted by Antori Trailus knocking on the office door.

The house guard wore his casual clothes, as he was not on duty, but he still sported the green, brown, white, and red of the Household of Illica to advertise his loyalty.

"A moment?" he asked.

Aurion put his scrolls down on the desk without hesitation. "Always," he said, leaning against the desk to show he would listen for as long as Antori needed. He avoided the chair behind the desk, not wanting to become the official master of the household.

"I am worried about Ailsa."

"Is she unwell?"

Antori nodded, hesitated, then shrugged. "She goes out at strange hours, sneaking out when she thinks I am sleeping," he said. "She will not tell me where she is going and tells me I do not trust her when I ask. She is bothered by something but snaps at me when I try to find out what it is. I worry she might be in trouble."

Aurion kept the knot in his stomach from showing. Even if they were not together, he cared. He wanted to believe he would feel the same for any member of his household, but he could not deceive himself.

His words were tight with concern. "What kind of trouble?"

Antori licked his lips and avoided Aurion's stare. They had served in Santan together through more than one rainy campaign, but Aurion had never seen Antori so unsure.

Fighting enemies was easy. Managing younger sisters was uncharted territory. Aurion sympathized wholly.

"I followed her one night," Antori finally admitted. "She went to a house in the University District. Other people entered, cloaked or hidden, sneaking along like Priests of Havi. I had to leave before I was discovered, but something about it does not sit with me well."

Aurion pushed off the desk. He had heard little from Ailsa recently. The last time he had passed her in the hall, she had seemed happy. Suddenly, that seemed wrong.

"Could you find the way back to this house?" Aurion asked as he headed to the wall and knocked twice against the stone.

"I could," Antori confirmed.

Before Aurion could return to his desk, the secret panel of the wall opened, and Grizzle stepped into the room.

Unlike Antori's modest armaments, Grizzle wore no less than eight visible weapons. A dozen more, Aurion knew, was concealed somewhere in the loose shirt and breeches combination of black, and one was certainly in each of the soft leather boots. The whiskered face sported a dozen thin scars, hidden well under a tan so deep it would never fade.

Aurion repeated Antori's concerns to Grizzle, and the older man accepted the mission with the distant, uncaring demeanor Aurion expected of him. Antori was starting to smile with relief at recognizing the spymaster.

"Care to go for a walk, Grizzle?" Antori asked.

The spymaster harrumphed like a porcupine bristling its quills. "I'll go. You'll need someone with intelligence handling this."

"That, and you'll have an excuse to leave the house," Aurion pointed out.

"I'll get changed," Grizzle said. "Meet you downstairs." He gave Aurion a sidelong glance. "I need to pick up some new flowers for the office, anyway."

Aurion laughed aloud at the thought of Grizzle purchasing a bouquet of daffodils from a street vendor.

As Grizzle disappeared down the hall behind the hidden door, Antori bowed to Aurion. "Thank you, Aurion."

"If it is something worth worrying about, Grizzle will find out. I am sure Ailsa will be fine."

Antori's sad expression made Aurion's gut churn.

"I hope so," he said.

CHAPTER 9

Ailsa slipped out of the shop, her cloak drawn tight over her shoulders. It was not cold in the early summer night, but a drizzle made the streets shine in the lamplight. The road home was too long this time of night: she knew of a nearby inn that would be open despite the late hour. Her brother would be grateful she had sought shelter rather than risk the streets alone. It had worked before.

With her head bowed and her mind elsewhere, she thumped into a large man's chest before seeing him. Her foot slipped on the wet road, but the stranger's hands flashed out from under his dark clothing and found her wrists. The rough hands steadied her expertly.

Her heart jumped into her throat. She had thought the street empty. Alone, she had little hope against an attack.

Relief flooded over her when the stranger released her and stepped away politely. "I'm sorry," he muttered like a drunk, although his quick movements had demonstrated more grace than any drunk she'd met. "You should watch where you walk."

Her anger rose, but she wanted nothing more than to get to the inn. She did not have time to deal with suspicious drunks in the early morning.

Without replying, she pushed past him.

He stepped back into her path. Ailsa's heart sped.

"I am very, very sorry," the man continued saying with no hint of a slur, "but I am glad you stopped."

It was an ambush. With one step, she was in front of the alley between houses. She cursed herself for the mistake.

She could run, summon a guard. There had to be dozens on duty in the district. One had to be close.

But the stranger did not try to grab her; he stood relaxed. "You see, he wanted to speak to you."

To her disappointment, Ailsa's voice trembled when she asked, "Who? Who wanted to speak to me?"

"Who do you think, Ailsa?"

Involuntarily, she spun to the alley and stared with wide eyes as Aurion, her once-beloved Aurion, stepped into the light of the street.

There was no point in running.

But does he know? Her mind raced. How much did he know? Was he here only because Antori had told him she had been leaving at night or because he knew the conversations taking place in the shop a few streets back? Eerily, his expression offered no clues. He did not seem angry, or sad, or even relieved. If she looked closely, he had a touch of worry on his face.

She had to hope he did not know. He was here to look out for her.

"Aurion! Thank the gods it's you! With this brute," Ailsa pointed at the man in her path. "I was worried."

"I can see that. You are shaking," Aurion answered, and she cringed under his gentle touch when he put a hand on her shoulder. Softly, as if he still loved her, he pulled off her hood and pressed a hand against her cheek. "You are cold."

His touch made her wish she could turn back time. Once, they had spent days together in the garden or around the city, laughing and talking. She could not accept that she had lost that relationship, that magic.

There was hope.

He took her arm, and they walked together like old times. She followed without protest as the strange man disappeared into the alley. To her surprise, he led her deeper into the district instead of back to the Freeman District and home. His questions distracted her away from asking why.

"You are out late," he said gently.

Deciding on the same story she had prepared for her brother, she replied, "I needed some air, so I thought I would go for a walk."

Aurion did not meet her eyes as they walked the streets of the University District, then passed through the gates to the Market District. "Without your slave?" he asked. "Until one o'clock in the morning? To the house where three councilmen plot to kill the sovereign?"

Her steps faltered with his final statement, and she would have fallen if he had not been holding her arm. Once stable, she ripped herself from his grip and glared at him. "Why do you bother asking?" She tossed her arms wide in frustration. "How could I have forgotten? You never ask a question you do not already know the answer to!"

"Mind how loud you speak," Aurion replied softly. He retook her arm steadily. For all its firmness, the touch was tender. "You will attract attention."

Alarmed, she searched the nearby streets. Discovery would be dangerous. If guards overheard the word "assassinations," or if any hint that Aurion knew about their plots got back to the councilmen, Ailsa could end up paying the price.

"I asked," Aurion continued, "because I wanted to know if you would lie to me." He was avoiding the center of the market, heading north toward his district along the wall.

Ailsa snarled but kept her voice low. "I do this for you! I do this so you will be free of your obligation to this cursed city! It is killing you, Aurion. Please! I beg you, leave it!"

When he pulled her to a stop, he finally met her eyes, and the pain she saw shocked her into temporary silence.

"You know little then, Ailsa. I would be just as loyal to the next sovereign as I am to Sovereign Polfius. His death would change nothing." He quickly added, "But that does not mean I will stand aside. He is a good man."

With nothing to say, Ailsa gritted her teeth. Aurion's hand held her arm gently.

"What did they want with you?" Aurion asked to her silence.

Ailsa avoided his stare. He seemed so sincere, as if he loved her still. But if he loved her, he would have left behind the wretched Council! No other sovereign would put so much on his shoulders, she was certain. Once Sovereign Polfius was gone, he would understand. He might even thank her for saving him.

"What part were you to play?" Aurion pressed, his voice tender.

She wanted to answer him, to please him, but she knew he would catch her in a lie. The truth would upset him. "I will not say anything." Briefly, she tested herself against the sadness of his expression but could not hold his stare. She had hurt him, and she hated herself for it.

She expected anger at her refusal. As the master of her household, he could order the information from her, but she would not yield, not when his safety was at risk. She readied herself for the defiance, knowing it could see her jailed or executed, but the blow never came.

Instead, sounding disappointed, he sighed.

With a pained voice, Aurion pointed back down the street they had walked. "Do you know who lives there?"

She looked back and recognized the house at once. Her voice dropped to a whisper. "Councilman Meltatio."

Aurion confirmed her observation with a single nod.

"He returned from the meeting ahead of us. His room looks over this street. He has a strange habit; he never goes to bed before two o'clock, preferring to watch the streets in the early hours. I am told he has seen many strange things in those late hours."

Ailsa's stomach dropped, leaving her sick.

They knew. High Councilman Meltatio would recognize Aurion, and, with her hood down, he would recognize her too. They would think she had betrayed them. They would kill her!

She turned to Aurion and found him waiting. Silently, he took her arm and led her toward the Freeman District. There was no pressure on her arm; she could have left, and he would have let her go. That, she reflected sadly, was because he knew she would not do it.

They left the Market District through the arch and gate, and Aurion nodded to the guards on duty there. None of them saluted, but they all acknowledged him with a smile so sincere it wounded her.

She waited until they were well past the soldiers, then found her voice. "I was to distract you. Since you canceled the wedding, I was to keep you busy."

Aurion nodded as if he had already known as much. She wondered if he had. "How long?"

She eyed him skeptically. "You already know."

"Tell me anyway."

"The sixth of the fourth," she replied.

He frowned. "They intended to kill the father of the groom on the day of the wedding. One of them has a pitiful sense of humor."

Ailsa peered at her lover in surprise. "You never called Sovereign Polfius 'father' willingly before. Why would you begin now?"

Aurion shrugged his shoulders as if lifting a cart above him. Rather than answer, he asked, "What else did they tell you?"

"Nothing," she said. "I didn't know who was to kill him or how or really when, besides the date, and I only knew that because I was told to distract you. 'Too impassioned to remember his own name' was the phrase High Councilman Meltatio used, I believe." With his hand still on her arm, she felt Aurion's shutter. Ailsa's eyes burned with tears. Was she so revolting to him now?

He led her through the gates of his house, where a dozen household guards waited. "Then you will, as far as they know, do as they have asked."

"Meltatio…" she began, but he raised a hand, and she stopped.

"At the time of our stroll, Councilman Meltatio was meeting with an associate of mine, well away from his windows. They do not know of our conversation. As far as they know, you have begun your work." His tone lacked the kindness she was accustomed to and sent a shiver down her spine.

He turned from her, and his voice became strict. "She is not to leave the estate without an escort from Grizzle," he commanded the soldiers. "No messages are to be sent or received. Until the seventh of next mooncycle, she is a prisoner here."

The men accepted the orders stoically. One of them—she did not even know his name—stepped forward and invited her, almost as if she had a choice, into the house to see her room. The tears that had been burning began to fall.

Her heart aching, Ailsa watched Aurion wander along the side path into the garden's shadows. She wanted to shout, to tell him she had made a horrible mistake siding with the councilmen and beg his forgiveness. But it was too late. His indifference cut deeper than his anger could have.

She turned to the guard.

"Take me in."

As the silhouette of Aurion Illica Polfius disappeared around the side of the building, Ailsa marched into the white house with her head high.

Binoran stepped away from the window after lighting three sparks in succession. The other slaves in the room above the warehouse looked at him suspiciously, but none had objected or told their master of the new slave's behavior. They had not even asked him what he was doing or why he had been doing it for the last four days with no result.

She was out there, and Binoran would continue to light the signal as she had asked until the world ceased to be. After so long without hope, he was unwilling to let his faith slip from his grasp again.

The shared room, one of several in the warehouse, had a single barred window. All windows in Lione were barred, even if, like this one, they looked out from the second floor with no balcony.

The room housed thirteen men and women, with only four blankets and a single pot for nightly business. The prize of the room was a single candle, although no one seemed to know who had stolen it. It remained unlit in the dusk, set at the center of the room, awaiting attention. Binoran had not discovered whether the candle stayed in its place because the slaves liked to remind themselves of their potential for rebellion or because no one dared touch the stolen item.

The bars on the second floor were not as tight as they should be, Binoran realized. The gap between them was wide enough for a relatively small person to slip through.

A shadow slid into the room through the window as if on the strong breeze. While the others backed away with frightened whispers, Binoran stepped forward, ran his hand from forehead to chin, and greeted her as loud as he dared. *"Reah, Belaul."*

The mood in the room changed. A few people whispered their greetings, and every last one of the slaves inched forward to see the Warrior among them.

When she hushed them, they obediently fell silent.

"Well done, Binoran," she said, her voice low.

"My thanks, Warrior," he whispered. Elevated before the others with three words from her, he filled with pride. He was now a source of faith, their connection to the Warrior.

She sent her gaze across the room, pausing on the rag around his right arm above his elbow. The fresh brand stung in answer to his thoughts, and he resisted the urge to put a hand to it.

"How many others are there?" she asked without commenting on the rag or the brand beneath it. It seemed to hurt her to know she had forced him to endure another branding.

"Thirteen in this room, twelve in the next," he said. For slaves, they were reasonably well off. Most were fit and healthy. She would see little evidence of mistreatment.

"I told you..." Binoran heard one slave whisper to another. "I told you it was the Warrior who had freed the slaves. I told you."

"Yes," the Warrior answered, although the comment had not been to her, "I am the one freeing slaves, but I have not come to free you. To continue my work, I need a place to hide slaves. This means I cannot free you, any of you, until I am finished. Will you help?"

He could tell they were disappointed, but they could easily conceal another face among their ranks. Surely, they could see how useful it would be.

A single man stepped forward and ran his finger from his forehead to his chin. Binoran grinned widely, for it was Nalo, the man who had confessed to the nightly meetings others denied.

"I will do as you ask," Nalo said.

Others followed quickly.

The Warrior did not smile, but a nod was all any of them required. "Binoran," she called, "come with me. I must show you the route you wil..."

Her sentence fell off, and she tilted her head to the window. They all hushed, wary of discovery, but the night was silent. After a few moments, Binoran dared venture, "Warrior?"

"Someone is calling me," she said, her voice heavy. "I must go now. I will return in a moment."

"You hear us?" one of the other slaves suddenly exclaimed far too loudly. Others shhhed the fellow before the Warrior could. In a more controlled whisper, the same man added, "You truly hear us when we call?"

"The Priestess listens, and I answer," she replied as if no other answer was even possible.

She disappeared through the window, sliding between the bars as easily as passing between parting willow branches.

With a great grin, Binoran lit the candle with the flint and steel the Warrior had given him for the signal. They all stared at the flame, beaming.

Lania dropped down from the window, landing on the hard streets with only the slightest sound.

The push Lania recognized as a call from a dreaming slave was firm from Akara. Somewhere nearby, someone was calling her. It could not be far if Akara was so insistent. The Warrior had to answer.

Lania pushed aside Binoran and his room of helpers, intent on her new goal. For a moment, she turned her attention inward, seeking the connection to Akara. Testing a few steps down the road, Lania felt Akara's approval and so moved on at a jog. A block away, she came to a lit building. As she approached, feeling Akara's appreciation in each step, Lania heard the sound of people within.

With the rats in the nearby alley, Lania located a shutter-less window and peered through the bars.

Between the dusty shelves and the sagging counter, there were three visible men. The first two were diasists in a color combination unknown to her, but their uninterested, negligent expressions allowed her to dismiss them; they were no threat to her. The other one, who was old and gray, sat haughtily on a stool against the right wall, where a back door led into the alley. *Rich enough to be wearing White and Black*, she mused.

As they spoke again, the fourth Conqueror stepped into Lania's line of sight. The man was lean and dressed in black. Although she could not see his face, she spotted a knife on his belt and a menace to his step that could put both soldiers within to shame.

The Lionians were unimportant to the Warrior. Akara would only call her for a Nurmi's sake. This made no sense.

Lania searched again, this time finding a Nurmi woman lying prone by the back door. Akara mentally nudged Lania. The Nurmi was calling her in her dreams. Akara seemed to believe the need urgent, having driven her with purpose.

Lania headed around to the back. She found the door ajar. As she approached, she heard voices within.

"Do you consider the task reasonable?" the old man asked.

"I can hit a needle off a post at fifty paces," said a deep, gruff voice that must have been the man in black. The voice was deeper than she would have expected of one so thin. "Provided I have the proper equipment," he added, prompting them.

Lania heard the shuffling of uneasy feet. *Diasist?* she wondered.

"The hand crossbow will be ready tomorrow. The finest, as ordered," the older man answered.

"Then tell me when," the man in black replied.

"In good time. Not long, I assure you."

Akara's persistent push paused, changing to confusion. Lania heard a light moan from within, near the door. The slave in the shop had woken up. She had stepped out of the Dreamworld and lost contact with the Priestess. It was up to Lania now.

"Damn Nurmi's alive," the old man said. "She heard us. Kill her."

The rage of the Warrior exploded. She would not permit such a thing to happen in front of her, not when she was so close.

Bursting through the doorway, Lania threw her knife, catching a diasist in the throat before he could draw his sword to attack Lania or the Nurmi woman. With a rough hand, Lania plucked the older man from his stool and placed him in front of her. Her sword was in hand, held to his throat as she eyed the remaining occupants from over the old man's shoulder.

The second soldier had drawn a dius but was too far away to be of immediate use. The problem was, then, the man in black. He had a small crossbow out, cocked and aimed at her. He hesitated only because of the old man she was using as a shield.

"Get up!" Lania called. The Lionians would not know what she said, she trusted.

The slave, who had been cowering in anticipation of a blow, darted behind Lania with a muttered, *"Reah, Belaul."*

The way she clung to Lania's clothes would be a problem. They needed to get out before any of the Lionians figured out a course of action.

"I want you to run out the door behind you and turn right. From there, take the first right and keep running. Run until your legs burn, then walk, calmly, in that direction until I find you. Understood?" The woman swallowed loudly and hesitated but then choked out, "Yes."

"I will not be far behind," Lania comforted. Despite his vocal objections, which were copious and varied, the older man was not, seeing the proximity of the blade, squirming. More to her benefit, Lania knew, since his noise was stopping the others from hearing what she had told the slave. Not that they would understand Nurmi.

"Go!" the Warrior commanded, and the slave ran out the door. Lania shifted the old man to cover the escape, preventing the man with the crossbow from shooting the slave down. He squawked and cursed,

"Do you have any idea who I am? How dare you! You'll be on the chopping block by morning..."

She dismissed his irrelevant threats.

It would not be hard for them to find the escaping slave if they gave chase, and evading pursuit while accompanying another would be tricky. She could not let them follow, nor could she leave the slave to fend for herself for too long. A conundrum.

The answer came from the man in black.

Deliberately, Lania kept her head in the open a moment longer and, by her conscious carelessness, invited him to fire his crossbow. If he was half as good as he boasted, he should have been able to shoot the center of her eye from across the room. She gave him an opportunity he could not resist.

She knew the speed of their crossbows. Had she waited for his finger to move, she would have been shot. But she waited for his intention to pull the trigger, ready to move once he was committed to the action. Seeing it in his eyes, Lania pulled the older man over, ducking her head behind his body.

The sound of the crossbow firing and the thud of the quarrel's penetration into flesh were almost simultaneous, and they matched well the screech of agony the old man released at having a quarrel dig into his shoulder. To further immobilize him, Lania kneed him in the lower back, sending him to the floor. Before the man in black could load another bolt,

Lania was out the door and running. She heard the cries of the older man, yells of fury more than pain now, as he rebuked the man in black and everyone else in the room and, as Lania had hoped, prevented anyone from passing him to give chase.

Lania caught up with the slave and escorted her back to the warehouse in the University District. She called down Binoran, who snuck through the bars and awkwardly landed in the street.

The three Nurmi climbed the walls of the city and escaped to the woods along the river. The woman, Malni by name, shyly followed, attentive when Lania called her over but otherwise happier to remain a silent shadow. Binoran comforted her gently. Lania did not interrupt. He was better suited to that role than she was.

Once out of sight of the city and under the forest canopy, Binoran took his place beside Lania. He was holding Malni's hand to guide her but held something silver in his other hand.

He offered her the item. "Warrior, a friend found this mooncycles ago in a trash pile. We thought it best you take it."

Lania barely glanced at the small strip of metal he passed to her as she tucked it into a pocket. It was an armband, one of the silver ones that Akara used to recognize the greatest Nurmi warriors. Binoran was right; she would return it to the Corelands, where it would honor another.

When they reached the twisted maple tree in the darkness, Lania paused, Binoran and Malni with her.

"I am the Warrior," she said to the forest. "I lead one of our people home."

To the untrained eye, it looked like the tree's trunk broke along its length, but the stretch of wood did not fall. Malni squeaked in alarm, covering her mouth in the next breath. Even Binoran flinched back as if ready to run.

But the shadow by the tree was no magic. The Nurmi sentry hidden there lifted her hand and replied, "Hail, Warrior. I will tell the others you come."

The young woman dashed off over the rise at their back.

At a calm walk, Lania led the two slaves on, pleased that Binoran checked behind them several times. He was memorizing the trail. That was good.

Haro's hidden camp by the river was quiet in the night. The boats lay propped up as a shelter, covered with branches to conceal them. A small fire smoldered in a pit, tended by a warrior making paddles. Several other trees had been felled and were being stripped during daylight hours to transform into vessels.

Haro emerged from the shelter, the small sentry in his wake.

"Hail, Warrior," he called softly, running his hand from his forehead under his eye. "Already more? Come." He beckoned for Malni. "You are safe now. We will get you home."

Malni readily released Binoran's hand for Haro's outstretched hand. He guided her to the company of the others who were advancing to check on the commotion. They gave Malni a coat and set her by the fire, starting their day early as the dawn threatened over the water. With excitement, they told her of their preparations and of the slaves they had already met up with. Already the first waves of free slaves were touching the banks of the Corelands.

Haro stood at Lania's side, eavesdropping on the accounts of their adventures.

"You're responsible," Haro said. "You're working the One God's purpose in the Falling City."

Binoran nodded on her left. "You are the beginning of the end for the Lionian Sovereignty."

It felt good to hear their confidence, especially in Nurmi, when Lania heard precious few words of her language within the Falling City.

Malni glanced up from her place ensconced among the other Nurmi, her bright blue eyes catching the light of the new dawn.

Dawn. She had to go.

"Take care of her," Lania said. She reached into her pocket and retrieved the silver band to give to Haro, thinking he could send it to Akara in the north.

Lania extended the armband to Haro, and she felt Akara snap at her.

Pulling it back, Lania took the armband to the firelight. She recognized every scratch and dent along the metal. She could not help but grin; it was *her* armband.

"They took this from me in the prison," Lania whispered, awed, "and now a slave in Lione has given it back to me. How can this be?"

Haro laughed lightly and placed a hand on her shoulder.

"The One God works strangely. He comes to us when we think he has passed us by. I have always known He favored you."

Armband in hand, Lania shared his confidence. Nothing would stop her, not now that she was blessed once more.

CHAPTER 10

"Ah, councilmen, how fortunate I am to have caught you both!"

Transitory Councilman Navius Julian Maurio froze when the sentence was only half finished. For a moment, his heart stopped. He knew that voice. He dreaded that voice.

He was not alone, and there was some comfort in that. High Councilman Parum Meltatio looked surprised to hear Councilman Polfius address them, but instead of fear, the high councilman's expression was profound annoyance. They'd been talking in one of the more obscure corridors of the Councilhall, well away from prying eyes, but Councilman Polfius had a reputation for having eyes everywhere. How had he found them?

Navius' skin prickled with sweat as he waited for Aurion, who seemed to be taking as long as possible to walk down the corridor to reach them. He must know. Why else would the councilman come after them? He had come to tell them the guards were waiting outside. They were doomed.

Instead of the string of accusations Navius expected, Councilman Polfius offered a small, insincere smile and a quick bow as he stopped before them.

"Oh, wonderful," he said. "I was beginning to think I was going to have to hunt you down individually." Navius tensed at the word "hunt." He was surprised when Aurion leaned in and lowered his voice. "I have heard of your recent..." The councilman paused and wondered aloud, "How should I say it?" With a sigh, he finished, "...goals."

Navius again swallowed hard, thankful when it seemed to go unnoticed. Parum stared at Aurion and he stared back. Neither of them seemed to be paying Navius any attention.

"I am not certain what you are speaking of, Councilman Polfius," the high councilman said in an even tone that matched his volume. *Perfectly smooth*, Navius thought Aurion would have to believe the assertion.

Aurion shrugged. "Perhaps that is a good thing. Still, midnight meetings? Sovereign Polfius has been a good leader."

Amazingly, Parum smiled broadly and made it seem sincere. "Why worry over the safety of the sovereign? We all know there is no way into the sovereign's room that does not lead past dozens of loyal soldiers. He is, by far, the safest man in the city."

Despite the persuasiveness of the high councilman's tone, Councilman Polfius did not look convinced. Instead, he frowned. "I know what I have heard. I will ask you only once to set aside your plots. If you stop now, I might be able to spare your lives, make sure the right details reach the right ears. Still, I need to know you are willing to let the good of the city rule your judgment. Please consider carefully."

He examined them both, and Navius felt the blood drain from his face under the scrutiny. It was as if the man, with a glance, could read his mind. He passed off a quick prayer to his household god that whatever magic the councilman was attempting failed.

With a formal nod of satisfaction and a bow, Aurion finished with, "Good day, Councilmen." The councilman turned in a military fashion and marched down the hall, leaving them.

Navius was finally able to exhale. He wanted to ask a hundred questions: How much might Aurion know? Was his threat real? Would he dare bring accusations upon councilmen? Could he be trusted to keep his word? He had not been among the councilmen long enough to know how much his rank, albeit a transitory one, would protect him.

Only one question at a time would be tolerated. "Does he know?" he asked. He garnered a sharp glare from High Councilman Meltatio.

"Of course not. He was guessing, trying to get us to slip up. He has no proof."

"We could tell the sovereign what he said about withholding information," Navius suggested timidly. "Sovereign Polfius hates knowing Aurion is cleverer than him."

Parum shook his head. "Who do you think the old man will believe? Us or Aurion?" The question needed no reply. The high councilman dropped his voice further. "We move ahead." He paused, staring at Navius and gauging him.

Navius straightened himself and cleared his throat to recover the large piece of his pride taken by the confrontation.

"Be ready," the high councilman finalized. Without hesitation, he turned away and headed down the south hall.

Navius stayed for a moment longer, pondering. If Aurion had genuinely known about the plot, why had he bothered to tell them? Was he looking for more votes in the Councilhall, or was he, as Parum said, bluffing?

He headed through the white halls absently after Meltatio, only to discover his path blocked by two palace diasists. Before he could protest, the voice called to him, *that* voice again. A shiver ran down his spine like cold water.

Aurion waved off the guards and stood in Navius' path, looking grave and horribly serious.

"Please forgive the intrusion, Transitory Councilman," the younger man said as Navius began to sweat once more. "Rest assured, High Councilman Meltatio will not hear anything said here, so you can speak in safety. Only you have the sense to pay attention to my warning. Meltatio will fail, and he will pay for his mistake with his life. I give you one chance to escape that fate."

"I do not know what you are speaking of, Councilman," Navius stuttered in echo of the high councilman's earlier lie. Even he knew it was not nearly as convincing.

The sovereign's adopted son looked genuinely saddened by Navius' response. "Pity," Aurion said. "You do not believe that I know, do you?"

"I know that you are trying to make me say something I should not," Navius answered. "It will not work."

"Eight days," Aurion said. "In eight days, you are planning an election because our sovereign will be dead."

"How...?" Navius heard his voice whisper.

Councilman Polfius shrugged. "I know a lot of things. Meltatio ignored my warnings and is going to fail miserably. I want him caught in the act. I want you to help me."

"If I do not?" Navius inquired.

Aurion gazed at him with curiosity and replied matter-of-a-fact. His concern and sorrow vanished. The emotions had been fake, Navius saw.

"If you refuse now, or if I do not believe you at any point, you will be arrested for treason, tortured until you betray your co-conspirators, and then executed. If you agree, I can convince the sovereign you went along with it to sabotage the plans. It is your choice."

"That is no choice," Navius choked out.

Aurion shrugged with indifference. "I know."

6TH DAY OF THE 4TH MOONCYCLE, 994

Aurion stood on the balcony of his Freeman house with his dius on the railing. In the last of the fading light, the palace's colored lanterns reflected off the white walls into a cloudy night. The lamps along the roads looked back at Aurion through distant music. Lingering songs drifted up from the streets of the Stadium and Market Districts, reminding him that the city was still very awake.

"Unlucky day for a wedding," Grizzle muttered with a shrug that pulled his dark cloak over his shoulders. The rain had stopped for the moment, but the clouds were still thick. "A rainy wedding means a hurricane marriage. Good thing you canceled it."

Aurion could only sigh. He began pacing, but his eyes remained on the colorful palace.

Transitory Councilman Maurio had been very helpful. The Councilman of the Stadium District, whom Maurio served, was ill and dying. Having been elected by his peers to stand in for the true councilman until the man's recovery, or death, Maurio had found the position to his liking. His plots with Meltatio had been aimed at stabilizing the arrangement. If they got rid of Polfius, they seemed confident that they would be seen as heroes among the Council and would be able to pass any edict they wanted. It was wrong, but it was what they believed.

There was more to that one, Aurion was certain. Meltatio wanted the High Seat, of that he had no doubt. He apparently had not mentioned it to Maurio, probably fearing the transitory councilman would set his goals higher if he knew.

Now threatened with losing everything, Maurio had turned against his co-conspirators by filling in the details Aurion had been missing.

He had dealt with it. The assassin had been arrested that morning on a petty thievery charge that would keep him in prison, under the watch of specifically chosen guards, until well after the assassination date. The man would be released, as Aurion had little actual proof and would rather not bother Sovereign Polfius with the details, but he would leave with a stern warning. Next time, if Aurion or any of his spies so much as suspected involvement, the assassin would die.

"What bothers you?" Antori had come up behind him, on duty. Grizzle snorted and crossed his arms but waited for the answer. Aurion had the feeling the old spymaster had been about to ask the question anyway.

"We have the man," Aurion said without pausing his pacing.

"We do," Grizzle confirmed.

"Sovereign Polfius was told the wedding was a ruse and knows this was the night they had intended to use."

"He does," Grizzle answered.

"But we arrested a man whose weapons of choice are darts and a dagger. Why would Meltatio commission such a specific crossbow when it was not to be used?"

Grizzle shrugged. "A fake trail?"

Aurion paused, frowning at him. "What if darts and dagger mark the fake trail?" He glanced again at the palace. "And what about that slave? The man has nothing to do with the palace itself, only the gardens. What use was that?"

It was still bothering him. All the pieces were not lining up.

Antori broke the silence; "You checked the guard?" he asked, and Aurion nodded. He had verified each of the names on the guard that night and did not believe any of them would allow an assassin to pass. "Then you have done all you can. There is no way into the sovereign's bedroom that does not go past those guards. They will…"

The concern that had been nagging him flared, and Aurion understood instantly how the last piece fit.

"Demons!"

With the final curse, he snatched the dius from the railing and ran from the balcony, taking the steps down four at a time. He paused long enough at the stable to throw a bridle on a horse, and both Antori and his second bodyguard, Balvor, followed. Grizzle watched in mild amusement as Aurion explained.

"There is no way *into* the sovereign's room without going past the guards. That was why I was so surprised when Meltatio seemed to have no intention of altering the rotation. It would take an awful lot to kill them all, especially without setting off an alarm and bringing the entire palace down on them. I did not think it was possible." He threw himself onto the horse bareback. Antori and Balvor were quick to follow, and he paused for them. Grizzle looked up at him with disinterest, expecting the rest.

"There is no way *into* the sovereign's room, Grizzle," he answered, "but there is a way out through the gardens that I have no doubt a slave knows."

He rode from the estate at a gallop, glancing at the water clock as he went. If Meltatio kept his love of ironies, he may have ordered it for midnight, but an assassin concealed in the sovereign's room would have no way of knowing the exact time.

None of the guards at the gates tried to stop him, nor did any of the men at the palace door, where Aurion had to leave Antori and Balvor by law. The palace guards raised an eyebrow, but he was too well known for them to worry over his appearance. More than one glanced at the sword and exchanged confused looks, but none spoke. Councilman Polfius often walked the palace after hours. They feared no treachery from him, even if he marched with a dius in his hand.

The two men standing on guard at the entrance to the east wing intended no more action than the others, but their plans changed when he called to them.

"Diasist Salvius, Diasist Fotian," he ordered, "with me."

With hardly a glance at one another, the two soldiers left their post and fell in behind the councilman. He forced himself to walk, determined not to raise the alarm. If the assassin heard them coming, he might panic. When it was the sovereign's life under threat, Aurion could not afford for anyone, least of all the enemy, to make mistakes.

There were three other sets of two guards along the way, and he called to each in turn. He saw the final two, standing outside the doors into the sovereign's room, tense when they spotted the half-dozen men marching along the hallways, but when they recognized him, their anxiousness faded. Here only, Aurion paused.

"Delanto, go to the left and get to the sovereign's side."

"Yes, sir," the diasist replied. Aurion did not have time to correct the error.

"Tomori, Fotian take the right side. The rest with me to the tunnel entrance. I want him alive." None dared ask who he wanted alive. With a final deep breath, he burst through the doors.

The moon was on the far side of the window and hidden under too much cloud to be visible. In the dim light, Aurion headed immediately past the bed to a small, mostly concealed doorway that led down to a one-way exit out of the palace.

The top entrance, hidden in an armoire, could be opened from either side, allowing an assassin hiding within to enter. The only trouble would be getting into the one-way exit at the bottom, but with no guards—secrecy defended the entrance more than anything—all he needed was someone to open the way.

And having a slave who knew the gardens at your service would make that easy.

When the doors suddenly burst open, Sovereign Polfius considered calling for the guards. Once he saw the guard was already present, he reached for the glass orb on the bedside table as an additional precaution. He glimpsed a blur of white as Aurion raced past the bed and yanked open the armoire. By the time Aurion pulled the man hidden within the corridor from his cover, the guards had surrounded their sovereign, and Polfius could see no more.

The shocked intruder within the tunnel had hardly enough time to yelp in surprise before the councilman had thrown him from the secret passage and into the arms of the guards. The pounding of fists, in substitution for swords, saw the intruder pummeled from consciousness.

Polfius put back the sphere with a trembling hand, seeing the powers drain from the faces around him as his fingers left the enchanted object. Aurion seemed to be the first to recover from the mind-altering magic of the sphere, but the sovereign knew that was likely because the magic had not had to change Aurion's thoughts at all; his adopted son had not come to harm him, anyway. When Polfius failed to give the order, Aurion commanded the assassin to be taken to the prison and interrogated.

The guards slowly filed out with the would-be assassin in tow, but at least two checked the passage for a second time.

Knowing he was incapable of standing, Polfius sat straight instead as he asked, in a voice lacking most of its typical confidence, "What was that about?"

Usually, Polfius was angry when Aurion withheld information from him, but as Aurion explained the plot, Polfius was more worried about the other councilmen.

How many more were there? Meltatio, Maurio … others? How could he not have suspected? They stood before him daily, lying to his face, and he had not seen it. He could not say he had ever truly trusted the men, but he certainly had never expected they would be plotting an attempt on his life.

But Aurion had known.

"Are there others?"

Aurion looked away, a sure sign he was about to say something he did not want to, but he spoke honestly when his sovereign questioned him. "Those two were the only ones acting against you, but many more are unhappy, Sovereign. You did, after all, cut their salaries by a hefty amount. Despite all the good it has done, the councilmen would rather see the funds in their pockets. We should not see many more attacks for some time, but they were not alone in their dissent."

His calming voice did not do any good. Polfius did not want to be reassured. He wanted the truth.

He ordered Meltatio's arrest without waiting for the assassin's information. He kept Maurio free, as it was easy to recognize that they now had a powerful hold on the transitory councilman. By keeping Maurio in his place, even possibly allowing him to become the new Councilman of the Stadium District, Polfius extended his sphere of influence by one.

Aurion spent the rest of the night answering questions and discussing the corruption of the Council. By morning, neither man had slept, and Polfius felt no desire to do so. He knew he would not be capable.

The order went out first thing in the morning for an emergency assembly. In the presence of the incomplete Council, Polfius revealed the arrests and the evidence against Meltatio, but not Maurio. Later that day, the assassin was paid quietly to say what they wanted him to say and imprisoned indefinitely. No one bothered to ask where he went after that.

CHAPTER 11

Although Gitarius occasionally showed signs of having found the proper substitute for Binoran, it was a full two mooncycles before he finally brought a new slave home.

Like so many others, Recmtupi had been scarred by the whips of the prison at the mines, but when they told the master he was an attractive slave who would win over any Nurmi woman with his charm, Lania had laughed. The slave master, a whelp of a man, beat her for the insult. For the next several hours, she had been forced to bite her tongue.

She did not understand what they saw in the slave. Although the direct translation of the name he used meant "handsome," the man was too tall, too thin, and too arrogant. He was as obedient as Binoran but lacked the feelings of inferiority that had kept Binoran in his place. Recmtupi seemed to think the Lionians were better and, as a result, sought to spend his time with them, as if to forget he was Nurmi. Although he charmed the master with compliments, Lania found his speech pretentious enough to make her want to grab his throat every time he opened his mouth. The distance she put between them was deliberate; she feared she would succumb to her desire, to the doom of Recmtupi.

Julti decided the new slave was not as interesting as her latest purchase from the market, a small dog, and thus Lania saw little of him. The little she did see him was too much.

But what shocked her most was the way he was sitting on her bed when she went to her room to sleep on a late summer's night.

Lania closed the door behind her quickly. Recmtupi began to knowingly smile, but her angry stare made the smile falter. After only a fleeting moment, the hesitation was corrected, and he leaned back against the wall with a less sincere smirk.

"Perhaps you have made a mistake," Lania said in Lionian. "Your room is a few farther down the hall."

He stretched out as she spoke and smiled in a way that made Lania grimace. Some would have called that smile attractive, but it only served to upset her stomach.

"I have made no mistake," he replied.

While contemplating the easiest route to the stolen sword she had stashed under the mattress, Lania switched languages. "I suspected as much," she said in Nurmi, making him jump. "Get out."

His smile wavered. "One as beautiful as you should not dirty yourself with such foul language," he said, still in Lionian.

"Dirty?" Lania demanded in Nurmi simply to spite him. "Our language is not dirty. Any who say so are Conquerors."

He did not, she judged by his expression, understand what she had said and that made her heart sink.

"Come now," Recmtupi replied. "Why must you carry on like that? Come sit by me and I will show you why such talk is fouled."

She wished for her sword. When she spoke, it was in Lionian, but she made her voice as harsh as she could. "I share no bond with you. Leave me be."

His smile thinned, but he refused to let it surrender. "How foolish of me!" he exclaimed. "Looking at the beauty of your face, dearest star, I forgot all else in the world. My name is

Recmtupi," he said, but he did not bother to stand or bow as he would have to a Lionian. Although he was seated, she still felt he was somehow towering over her with his eyes turned to the gutters below.

She was going to enjoy proving him wrong, Lania decided. Akara warned her to be gentle, but the Warrior in her was already snarling.

"That," she said slowly, "is the name you give Lionians. If you do not trust me with your true name, then how can you expect me to trust you?"

For a moment, he seemed genuinely puzzled. "That is my only name."

"How unfortunate you have so wasted your time. Leave," Lania replied flatly. Her voice was firm, leaving no room for discussion.

The performance was over in a blink. The smile gone, the slave flipped his legs over the side of the bed and sat up. He did not shout, although his voice strained.

"You must be a new slave," he said, "so I will explain to you how things work here. The master wants baby Nurmi, and what the master wants—"

"Does not concern me," she finished for him. He scowled, and Lania smiled. "Do not take me for some pathetic, beaten slave, Recmtupi. I am no cow to be set upon by the bull."

He stood, fists at his side, and took menacing steps toward her. He was only slightly taller than her. Lania met him eye to eye without flinching.

"You do not understand then. What the master wants, the master gets. Lionians rule this world, and those who do not obey, die. They are like gods when compared to you."

"Gods?" she repeated. "There are no 'gods,' Recmtupi. There is only One God, and He does not tolerate the insolence of his people."

The Warrior saw exactly when Recmtupi made the decision to strike her and, ever ready, she acted first. She slammed the butt of her hand sharply into his ribs just as his hand raised for the blow, forcing him to double over. Although he recovered fast enough to grab at her, she twisted out of reach.

"How is it you have lost faith so completely?" she spat at him as she put the bed between them.

When he spun to face her, his expression held deep menace.

"What faith was there to lose? Look around you, Tatkil! Lionians rule everything in this world. It is their money we use, their language we speak, their laws we obey. They rule all the world! Clearly, they have got it right."

"Do you know nothing of your people? The Black Arrow has been freed! The Priestess and the Warrior have been born. How can you tell me we are wrong when the prophecies are coming true before your eyes?" she shot back, her voice tense but not raised, not when there was the risk of being overheard.

"Lies! There is no Warrior! There is no Priestess! The prophecies are as false as that One God!"

Lania stumbled back as if she had been struck. Never in her life had a Nurmi denied the One God so flatly. How could the One God let someone become so lost?

He leaped across the bed to grab her as she staggered under the weight of his words. He caught her, but hard-forged instincts were quick in answering even when her conscious mind remained stunned. Lania yanked her shoulder free from his grip, caught his wrist, twisted it, then released just as he squeaked out a cry. He seemed surprised enough by the practiced ease of the motion to pause as she moved to the other side of the bed.

She had to whisper to keep her voice under control, but she still heard it tremble. "What of the slaves escaped from Lione? What has become of them if there is not a warrior leading them to freedom?"

Snorting in disgust, Recmtupi crossed his arms across his chest. With his shoulders square and his chin raised, he tried to look the part of a charmer once more.

"They are not escaped. They are dead. The Lionians merely made up that story so they would not have to count the bodies thrown into the trenches. There is no Warrior! There is no freedom!"

He ran at her again, but she did not move away. As fast as a firedrake, she struck him across the chest with her open left hand, forcing him to turn. With her other hand, she pulled her stolen dius from its hiding place under the mattress and placed the blade against his back.

"Enough!" she snapped, shaking with anger. "Do not deny my father's work, do not deny the existence of my sister, and DO NOT DENY MY NAME!"

With the tip of the blade on his back, Recmtupi froze.

He needed only darkened hair, and she would never have known the race he had been born into. She could kill him as surely as she killed any Conqueror who crossed her path, without her conscious troubling her. It would be a release for him, although he did not know it.

Gently, the Priestess' calm trickled into her mind, and Lania felt her hand steady. She could not kill him. He was a Nurmi, even if his heart was blackened. The Warrior could not kill a Nurmi.

Annoyed by the Priestess' insistence, Lania shoved Recmtupi away, lowered the blade, and pulled her armband from its hiding place.

"Do you know what this means?" Recmtupi faced her on his knees and dared not answer. "It means I am a member of the Black Arrow's army. It means I have fought many battles against your so-called gods and killed many. It means I have battled for my people and am blessed by the One God for my work. I am here not as a slave, Recmtupi. I am here because I am still fighting them and..." She spoke each word slowly. "I am winning."

"Im... impossible. It cannot be..." he managed to stutter.

She stared at him coldly. "I am Lania. I am the Warrior. Do you deny my name?"

Raising his hands open-palmed to her, he shook his head and lowered his eyes to stare at his knees. It was a Lionian gesture, but even Lania knew it meant he was unwilling to fight. "No, Warrior. No, I would not deny your name," he said.

Realizing she had lifted the sword in defense of her name, Lania forced herself to lower the blade once more. He had gone so pale, he nearly matched the sheets of her bed. Moments ago, the universe had made sense to him. Now she had stepped in and corrected him. She had not done it gently, either, she reflected.

She put her armband on and sat on the bed, trying to look calm. It took many breaths before her heart rate slowed, and many more before she trusted herself to speak. When she was ready, Recmtupi had not moved.

She waited longer, listening to Akara's calm. She waited until Recmtupi's trembling stopped, and he finally, hesitantly, looked at her.

"How long have you been a slave?" she asked gently.

"I... I was born a slave," he replied, slowly lowering his hands and speaking as if answering his master.

"You do not speak Nurmi?"

"I was never taught it. I hardly saw other Nurmi, let alone spoke with them."

"So you were given no name?"

"Toval," he admitted. "I was called Toval."

Her relief covered her. He had a name. Even if he did not speak Nurmi, even if he had lost hope, he had a true name. If he had a name, then the One God was watching over him. All was not yet lost.

"That is a priest's name," Lania replied.

"A priest?" she heard him mutter to the floor. "More proof of a false god."

She resisted her frown and instead lightly laughed, which made him look up with curiosity. "I met a warrior with no strength, who now stands by my side in this battle. Now I meet a priest with no faith. Not all of the One God's plans are clear to us. Come, sit by me. Although I am not the Priestess, she will speak through me, and you will learn the faith you have lost."

When he sat beside her, nothing remained of his coy advances. Humility, Lania thought, suited him.

Sympathetic looks from the guards chased Aurion as he made his way back into the palace shortly after the water clock had chimed the start of the eleventh day of the Fifth Mooncycle. To Aurion, it was the forty-fifth day of Polfius' paranoia.

Aurion recognized the palace guards dimly but did not pause to speak to them. The call had come to his home less than an hour before, interrupting the few hours of sleep he had been enjoying since leaving the palace only three hours earlier. He was in the palace at the command of the sovereign, just as he had been every night since he had burst into the sovereign's bedroom and pulled an assassin out of hiding.

The angry talk against Polfius' cut of the councilman's salary had disappeared since the executions of the two conspirers, but the sovereign did not so easily forget the surprise intrusion of his "son" that had saved his life.

Polfius trusted none of the councilmen save Aurion. No decision could be made without first consulting him. Aurion was required to spend more time in the palace and Councilhall, to the detriment of his home and other duties. Somewhere during the last mooncycle, Aurion had acquired Meltatio's high councilman sash. Although his ascension to the black sash had been planned for over a year, Aurion felt as if he had cheated. Polfius had insisted Aurion be named high councilman and, in the wake of the executions, no one had dared argue.

Polfius continued to decline. In the mooncycle following the failed assassination, the sovereign had four other officials, one of them a councilman, arrested on petty charges that led to their public executions. It was whispered among the palace servants that the sovereign no longer put out the lamps before going to bed and that his sleep was disturbed by visions of angry men carrying daggers. His lack of sleep had seen him grow ill, and visits to the doctor were a part of the quartercycle routine. Aurion suggested a trip out of the city to help relax the sovereign's tense nerves several times, but Polfius felt safe only in his palace with Aurion at his side and refused to travel.

It was growing harder to collect information. With Polfius demanding so much of his time, Aurion feared he would miss something soon.

"Another late night, eh Aurion?"

Startled by the voice he did not immediately recognize, Aurion rotated mid-step to face it. He forced his tight muscles to relax when he noted the familiar, friendly smile of the man wearing the black sash.

"As always," he replied. His mind spun a thousand reasons for High Councilman Dobrius to be in the palace so late at night. Half were reasonable and perfectly valid excuses, but the other half ranged from fantastical to paranoid. *Who would have thought paranoia was contagious?* he mused.

"You do not look well," High Councilman Dobrius commented in a kindly tone. "Even then, you look better than he does." Neither man felt any need to clarify of whom they spoke.

"He will improve," Aurion insisted, a little taken aback by the high councilman's apparent concern. His tired mind was sluggish, and he was only now beginning to realize why Dobrius might care.

High Councilman Dobrius had been appointed by Sovereign Polfius. They were not close friends, but the high councilman had more to lose than gain if something happened to the sovereign. Dobrius was also a very logical man at heart. Unlike some of the selfish men manning seats in the Councilhall, Dobrius might even see the good Polfius could do.

With another concerned look, High Councilman Dobrius lifted a hand in a pleading gesture.

"They are not plotting anymore," he said. "I swear I would tell you if they were."

"I know," Aurion said, groaning, "but what difference does it make, what is real, as long as the people that matter believe it?"

He got a sad smile from the high councilman in reply. "At least you know," the councilman said. "That must count for something." The man turned away and wandered off down half-lit halls. By way of farewell, Aurion wished him well.

"And say hello to your wife for me," he finished.

High Councilman Dobrius waved one hand over his shoulder in acknowledgment.

It was not until he had his hand on the handle to the sovereign's door that Aurion finally realized what had brought the high councilman to the palace. He permitted himself a small smile as he remembered the rather imposing form of the high councilman's wife and the lengths to which Dobrius would go to avoid her. He re-centered himself with the little humor the thought provided and prepared to deal with the anxious man on the other side of the door.

"Are they out there?" the sovereign whispered as Aurion entered the brightly lit room and closed the door. It was no wonder the sovereign could not sleep: the lamplight reflected off the tiles and gold trim of the room with enough glare to blind.

"There is no one out there but soldiers," Aurion replied wearily as he set the scrolls he had brought on the table by the door, his dius beside them. He had brought it at Polfius' insistence, and the soldiers no longer even commented on it.

"Which soldiers?" Polfius asked quickly.

"Good soldiers," he answered. "Good men who honor their word and are loyal to their sovereign. Braxi Fraltium is getting rather annoyed because of the number of times I have changed your guard, Sovereign."

"Some people cannot be trusted."

"Most of those I switch are merely not well known to me, not disloyal, Sovereign. You need not fear them." But he could tell his words did nothing. "I am here now, regardless. I will watch over you."

It was not the first time he had been asked to sit by the sovereign during the dark hours of the night, so he merely sighed and turned to the scroll he had brought to give the sovereign time to settle.

By the time the water clock chimed two, he was able to dim the lights.

CHAPTER 12

When the sun finally dragged itself into the sky, it shone without warmth. Clouds hovered on every horizon, some of them dark and threatening rain. Although thunder was not yet audible, the priests of Toa, Myn, and Min all agreed a storm was on its way. Divine intervention was not required; the air smelled of rain and carried the feel of a storm.

From a white room in the Market District, the Warrior watched the rising sun. Something was on the wind, she was certain, and she met it with a wide grin.

Aurion analyzed the city skyline from the palace window with even less energy than the unenthusiastic rising sun. Polfius' sleep had been broken by nightmares, as always, but they had been short and calmed more easily than before. Perhaps, he dared hope, the sovereign was beginning to recover.

He would try to convince Polfius to head to his country cottage. The weather was warm in the late summer. Surely, the world would look better from the shores of a private lake somewhere, with fresh fruit and a cool drink in hand. As it was now, the sovereign had a meeting with at least three councilmen the coming day.

If only they would leave him alone, just for a while.

Aurion himself had not slept. For the moment, he was the only thing holding the sovereign to any kind of trust, and he could not let himself betray that confidence by being caught asleep. Instead, he had read, spoken to the guards, and written letters to his mother and sister. The letters, he reflected, he dared not send until he had a chance to read them again.

Although it was early dawn, the city was already awake. He could hear the bustle getting louder through the window to the bedroom.

When he had first arrived in Lione, Aurion had spent hours watching the elaborate city. Looking out through the crack in the shutters, he realized he had forgotten how much he loved the White City. With all the distractions of his duties and the added trouble of the corrupted Council, he had not stopped to look at his city in years.

But Lione was still a wonder to behold, especially when part of her still slept and Aurion could watch the red dawn slip along her ivory buildings. In the distance, he saw the masts of the countless ships finding their way into the docks. The gates were already packed with visitors waiting to gain access to the greatest city in the Sovereignty.

He returned to the table where he had left his scrolls and sword, picking up the blade. The standard issue dius, nothing special, had been the only thing he could afford when he had joined the ranks of the greatest army in the world. Councilmen were not meant to carry blades. Aurion was expected to let others defend him. "When a councilman needs a sword" was a synonym for something never happening.

Yet he had taken the sword with him when he had come to the aid of his "father" a mooncycle ago and, even now, he brought it to the palace. He felt better knowing the sword was nearby.

There was a light knock on the door, and Aurion put down the sword, afraid of being caught with it, before answering.

The guard outside carried a message not for Polfius, but for Aurion. A soldier had just come off duty in the prison, where there was talk of a Nurmi fighter offering information in exchange for freedom. The news was passed along the soldiers to be whispered in Aurion's ear at the earliest opportunity, as he had requested.

When he searched his mind for the names of the guards on duty, Aurion came up empty. What only a short while ago would have been common knowledge for Aurion was now impossible to retrieve from his memory, further proof that he had indeed been neglecting his other duties. Giving up, he asked the guard. Hearing the answers, he decided the rumor deserved investigation.

But he could not leave, not while the sovereign slept.

He gathered his things, knowing it was useless.

"What time is it?" Polfius asked, rolling over and groaning like a dying man. The sound worried Aurion again, but the sovereign's face was brighter, the bags under his eyes a little less dark.

"Probably about seven," Aurion replied, unable to remember the time he had just seen displayed on the water clock tower. "The sun is just rising. I'm glad you slept."

The sovereign nodded weakly. "You clearly did not," he answered.

Aurion shrugged and rubbed his eyes to try to clear them, if only to look more awake. He knew it would not help the way he felt.

"How many nights has it been, then?"

"Several," Aurion answered. He wanted to say four, with only a half night in between that and the three before, but he did not want to put that burden on the sovereign.

Polfius sat up like a man twice his age and rubbed his face in mimic. He noticed the scrolls gathered on the table. "Leaving?" he asked like a boy who had just had his only yorin taken by a bully.

"As soon as you were awake, Sovereign," Aurion corrected. "There is talk of a Nurmi in the prison who wishes to bargain. With Lania's recent attacks, I am interested in what he has to say."

Polfius nodded again. His pouting expression looked less offended. "Then I shall go with you," he said as he rose from the bed and headed for the dressing room.

"The prison is hardly the place for the sovereign," Aurion objected. "And I am not certain if these claims are true. The new Councilman of the Market District has a meeting with you at eight and I may take too long. Go, eat, rest longer."

Polfius stood in his nightgown, with his arms crossed and faced Aurion sternly. "I am coming with you, or I will order you to take me."

Their arguments were growing increasingly short, Aurion noted. If the sovereign was not impressed, he gave the order and Aurion followed. He missed their discussions.

"Some clothes..." he tried, but the sovereign dismissed his concerns with a wave. He muttered something incomprehensible about a lack of time, then gave orders to fetch the escort and carriage. Aurion conceded, as he always did. Soon, they were heading across the city.

While Aurion spoke to guards, the sovereign stood behind him like an obedient old hound. He said nothing and drew so little attention to himself, they walked by without anyone bowing at all. For Aurion, it was common practice—all the soldiers knew High Councilman Polfius did not care about formalities—but no man would have dared be caught not performing the gesture to the sovereign. The soldiers were simply not paying enough attention to the old man behind

Aurion to see past the plain white robe without sash or chains of office.

Familiar with the prison, Aurion found his way through the dark hallways, sympathizing with the tired soldiers as he went. He had once had to stand for endless hours staring at empty halls like them, wishing for some excitement with one breath and begging the gods to forget the request on the second.

Minor arrests from the day before, which were a constant in the great White City, managed to provide occupants for most of the smaller cells lining the walls without filling any of them. He did not pay much attention to them until he heard a cry.

Somewhere behind him, a man shouted in pain, and Aurion spun in search of his sword, only to realize he had left it in the carriage. At first, he thought a guard had been struck, but when he saw the plain old white robe collapse, his heart jumped.

A prisoner had reached through the bars and stabbed Sovereign Polfius.

Aurion rushed back to the sovereign as a nearby soldier stepped up to the bars of the cell and ran the man inside through in a single action. By the time Aurion reached the sovereign, blood had soaked through the nightgown.

Ocracion had been born a thief. No matter how far back he went, his memories were of the white streets and the many pompous nobles' purses he would eye daily. He had no history and no papers, for he did not know either of his parents, and his non-existence had given him a ghost's life in the White City.

He had been caught. After nearly twenty years of success, he failed. A simple picked pocket had seen him arrested and held for over a quartercycle while the guards searched for some way to identify him. In the end, they fined him and created an identity for him based on a distinctive scar they gave him on his shoulder.

Within a year, he had been caught again during an unusually bold raid of a home. He had spent another few days in the prison at the mercy of the city guard until they found his papers. When he was finally identified, they brought a priest of Mintova, Goddess of Justice, to see him. His lies to the priest had allowed him to leave with just a fine and a promise of having been reformed.

Bitter at his treatment, he had taken to stealing from soldiers. He discovered quickly that the arrogance of many soldiers made them good targets. He had been enjoying his success until the morning of the ninth day of the fifth mooncycle.

The personal guard that had already once arrested him had recognized him and foiled every lie Ocracion tried. This time, they had beaten him. As a criminal, Ocracion had no rights. Knowing they might kill him outright, he had tried to escape and, in that attempt, almost killed a man.

He had never before slain anything, not so much as a chicken, but he did not regret the hit to the man's forehead that had knocked the soldier back and seen him crack his skull against the wall. Ocracion had spent his life fearing and resenting soldiers. Striking back felt good.

He could have done worse, he knew, but had not drawn the knife he kept under his shirt. Early lessons had taught him the hazards of bringing a knife into a fight.

Now locked in a holding cell along a hallway in the prison, he wondered how long it would take them to identify his scar. First, they would take him from the temporary cells where he could see the people passing to one of the small stone cells in darkness. Then, they would ask him all sorts of questions, and he would lie to them. Despite this, soon enough, they would figure out who he was once more, and then he would die.

It was his third arrest. His body would be tossed into the trenches as soon as they figured that out. He was a dead man already, and that knowledge made him hate the soldiers even more. Unwilling to let them have the satisfaction of executing him themselves, he was determined to deal the death blow himself.

His knife was still under his shirt. Apparently thinking any weapon would have come to light before he arrived at the prison, they had not searched him.

But the more he considered it, the less certain he was he could kill himself. There was no question that he wanted to be dead before they came for him, but the knife in his hand felt cold and awkward. Throat? Would that even work? He did not want to bleed out through a gut wound; he had seen how long that took. The heart seemed the best choice, but he was not confident in his aim. What if he missed?

Commotion woke him from his reverie. Ocracion, confused by the visitation to the prison, straightened and moved to the edge of his cell to get a better view. A high councilman? He would have expected more pomp following such a man. Where were his red-plumed personal guards? Where were the pages and servants? There was a single servant—an old man dressed in a simple shift of white—looking lost behind the councilman. The councilman himself was talking to the soldiers and ignoring the servant and everything else in the room, including Ocracion himself.

A plan formed in his mind as he watched the White and Black approach. Councilmen ran the city, and the city ran the soldiers. This one man was responsible for everything Ocracion had endured over his thirty years. He had his one chance at vengeance.

But the god of thieves was still being mean, and the councilman walked by with a soldier between him and Ocracion's cage, still oblivious to the occupant of the cell and his blade. Ocracion considered taking the soldier in exchange but doubted he could sneak his knife through the armor. He thought his opportunity had passed when the servant walked by.

It was not a councilman, but at least it was a blow to the councilman personally. In addition, the lack of defenses made the man an easy target, even for an inexperienced attack from a doomed thief.

Ocracion reached through the bars and caught the man's thin shift. A yank brought the old man against the bars. He raked the knife across the lower part of the throat roughly, the knife catching and tearing in places where it should have cut. Upon his cry, Ocracion released, and the man collapsed.

The resulting chaos left him reeling. Men came and went from all directions. The councilman rushed forward to see to the fallen servant, but Ocracion only understood why when a nearby soldier, making a holy sign across his face, whispered, "Oh gods, Sovereign Polfius."

Another soldier stepped up to the bars, and Ocracion's belly hurt sharply. He looked down; a sword reached through the bars and cut into his gut. He tried to laugh, filled with victory, but no sound emerged.

Aurion shouted for a soldier to fetch a doctor and vaguely noted that some of them left. He tore at the robes over the wound with practiced hands, but he could already hear the wheeze of a dying man from the ragged cut in the neck just above the collarbone.

He packed the wound with cloth, trying to staunch the flow, but the face of his sovereign was paling, and there was a sickening cough coming from the severed trachea. He was terrified; Aurion could see it clearly in the older man's eyes. His throat cut, he could say nothing to tell Aurion of his fear. He stared ahead, choking, shivering, and sweating, for minutes that lasted forever. Finally, the brain starved of blood and the body emptied of air, everything relaxed, and the eyes lost focus. On the floor, staring into the black stones of a damp, sickening prison, the sovereign lay dead.

Aurion could not find words to curse with. The sovereign was dead, and the blood was on his hands. He should never have come. He should have convinced the sovereign to stay away.

He tossed aside the guilt when the gravity of the situation struck him. He had to take control or there would be a riot.

"Yoraci," Aurion snapped to the nearest guard, "get me the men who went for the doctor quickly and tell no one else of this. No one here is to leave." Had any of those who had left known who was struck? Did they think he was a servant, or did they know he was the sovereign? If he could keep things quiet, he could call the Council together and have a new sovereign elected before the people even knew Polfius was dead. He could stop the riot. He had to.

But as he waited for the return of the yoraci, a sound rose in the distance. It started as a shout, then grew to a roar.

The sovereign was dead, and the people needed to make known their support for a new candidate.

From the kitchen of the Gitarius home, Lania heard a shout. A man burst into the house and delivered a message in panicked, incomprehensible Lionian. The terrified master of the

Household ran through the house, called the slaves and servants out, and ordered them to pack at once. The panic that followed was ideal for the Warrior. Ignoring Gitarius' orders, she collected Toval and headed for the roof.

The shouts of the people were clearer above them, and she heard enough to understand the encroaching panic. The sovereign was dead. The people headed to the streets, to the councilmen's homes, and to the common areas, in support of their candidates for the High Seat.

But not everyone was chanting the same name, and fights broke out between the Lionians as if a victory over another man's supporter proved theirs to be the better choice. Diasists previously off duty were forced into the streets as quickly as messengers could get to them.

Besides the upper-class Conquerors, who hid away in their homes with their doors barred and their personal guards vigilant for troublemakers, the city was in the streets. Those with connections to the sovereign, like Gitarius, feared for their lives. Without looking back, he packed up his family and left. In his haste, he forgot his two Nurmi slaves.

Lania watched the havoc, grinning. From her place on the roof, she saw guards being reassigned off the walls to deal with the riots in the streets.

Now was the time.

She stole a sheet from her master's room. Mixing ashes with the best wine she could find, she drew a circle with four lines extending from it. She stopped in to see Binoran and called out to the slaves and, with Toval on her heel, they ran for the water clock.

The central area of Lione was the pride of Lionian scientists. She did not know exactly how the water clock worked, but she knew that the waterfall that pushed the lever below counted the minutes and hours of the day. She wondered with a smile what would happen if it ever broke.

The clock was unimportant to her; her eyes were on the tower. Although the water fell from only a man's height above the pool, the tower rose above every other building in the city.

She sent her escaped slaves along a path to the wall, led by Binoran. Lania herself clambered up the tower and tied the sheet from the highest point she could reach. She had just started her descent, making a point of breaking at least a few components that looked important, when fires began in the Dock District.

Hundreds of Nurmi flocked to the sign of the One God flying above Lione, and the Warrior of the One God was there to meet them.

Aurion found his way from the prison dazed but resolute. He sent orders to the councilmen—he did not care what they said of taking orders from him—and called the emergency assembly. Only in passing did he notice the blue cloth flying above the water clock with the false god symbol plain to see. It was not until much later that he gave it another thought.

Carriages had no hope of navigating the choked streets, forcing Aurion to walk to the Councilhall. Although he had only one district to traverse, he barely made it through the screaming masses. The University District was already flooding with people as they headed for the enormous white building where the leaders would gather.

It will not be terrible, he told himself. They would get to the Councilhall, elect a new sovereign, and the people would be happy. Most did not really care; they would accept whoever was elected. They had no choice.

Escorted loosely by prison guards concerned for his safety, he traveled to the Councilhall so wrapped up in his thoughts that he failed to listen to the crowds. When he finally arrived at the mound where the Councilhall was ensconced, there were only seven other councilmen present. The rest eventually sent word through unfortunate messengers that they were trapped because of the crowds and would have to be excused.

"If the messengers can get through, so can they, damn them!" Aurion cursed. Surely, they knew the vote could not pass with less than half of the Council, and any fewer than fifteen of the twenty would upset the crowd. He needed them to come. Without them, the riots would just continue.

It was there, sitting in his box within the Councilhall, trying to come up with a new alternative, that Aurion finally heard the crowd in earnest. There was marching outside and it wasn't the soldiers.

The name they shouted was Aurion Polfius.

Leaving others to continue leading people from the city, Lania slipped into the Prison District and freed the prisoners, pausing long enough to turn the Windraso, Santanese, and even Lionians loose. The streets were becoming harder to navigate, and she relished adding another level of chaos to the riot. The criminals and prisoners ran amok, attacking any who attempted to stop them.

Lania returned to the water clock, a trail of freed Nurmi prisoners in her wake.

Around her, the name she heard was Aurion Polfius, but it did not interest her.

It could not be done. The councilmen had to come. The crowds had to be calmed.

Aurion hit the seat in his box, just below the public benches, hard, feeling as if the world had been spinning too fast for too long. He could not be sovereign. He would have to do things the people would not understand. He would lose support, and his network of information would collapse. He barely survived the corruption when he was a part of the Council. He could not do it as sovereign. He simply could not.

The smell of smoke made his head ache.

Aurion was still in a daze as he washed his hands of the blood and changed his clothes. His mind kept spinning, trying to think of something, anything. The other councilmen present were looking to him for guidance now—the crowd outside was shouting his name—but he could do nothing as he watched the city burn and break from the upper window of the Councilhall.

When Lania returned to Binoran, the flow of people had slowed.

"How long has it been since it began?" she asked.

Binoran pointed to the water clock. "Four hours, by the water clock," he replied, laughing at his pun, "and I have lost count of the slaves sent out. How much longer do you think it will go on for?"

"Not much longer," she answered. "People grow impatient. They have not chosen a new sovereign, but they will have to soon. This is the last group we send. Go with them." She made to scale the tower and retrieve the flag.

"What about you?" Binoran interrupted.

"You need not ask me that!" she replied sharply, but her tone did not even serve to discourage the little warrior.

"You will stay? Will Gitarius not have noticed?"

"Doubtful. If he returns, I should be able to sneak back in without him suspecting. I am not finished here yet."

"Then I will stay," he decided.

Lania softened her tone. "What of your master? Will he not punish you for your escape?"

"I will hide in the warehouse and tell him I got frightened and hid rather than risk the streets. And if he wants to punish someone for the escape of the other slaves, I will get a few more bruises. What does it matter? As you said, we are not finished here yet."

He would do it too, she knew. He would risk his life again for her, and she did not even need to ask.

"You need not restart again, Warrior," he insisted. "There are so many more that need to escape. It is better when there are more of us."

She could not argue. The chain of people leading the way out of the city was a result of Binoran's assistance. She led them out of their prisons, Binoran hid them and got them out of the city. Warriors outside led them to the river, and Haro took them home. Many were still caught during their flight, and many more were being recaptured from the Nurmi lands every quartercycle. The added influx from the mines only made it worse.

Her work would never end, but it was only with Binoran's help that she even stood a chance.

"Go then, and may the One God watch over you. I will go to the river first, then return. I will see you soon," she accepted.

The little warrior vanished into the crowds.

Collecting the remaining slaves, Lania left the city and followed familiar markers between cottages and through dense forests until she found the river outpost concealed among the trees. Haro greeted her. One boat, weighed heavily down by slaves, pushed off the bank.

"There are still many more to follow," she warned, but the larger man did not seem fazed. He ordered more boats into the water.

"What happened?" he asked once done.

"The sovereign is dead, and the city is in a panic. Half the slaves in Lione have escaped today," she told him.

He laughed. "A panic? Because there is no old man to lead them? Conquerors will fight even each other over nothing."

"A fortunate thing for those ready to use it," she replied with a more reserved smile. "But we must be careful. Once the city calms, they will want their slaves back, and we cannot let them know where we have gone. How well do your men know the river?"

The look he gave her was a mixture of curiosity and admiration. "Enough to follow it from the bank or the water," he answered.

"Send the next group by land. Have them follow the river up until at least the second post. After that, they can use boats. We cannot have too many on the river during the day."

He selected a group of four men to lead the next group of slaves and had them gather supplies.

"After the coming slaves slow, send a group of your men back to the villages and leave a trail by land. You know the path?"

He nodded. "As do most of the warriors. It is, after all, the way they escaped Lione."

"Good. If the Lionians follow you by land, it will be easier to hide the river boats. You will see to it?" she asked, and he agreed before smoothly moving on to collect men and horses for the trail.

That was it, she realized. She would return now, find Gitarius, and go back to the cold, unfriendly streets. Her place awaited her in Lione.

Letting Haro wander ahead, Lania turned to face the forest for a moment and tuned her ears to the excited laughter of the newly escaped slaves.

It was summer again; she had been in Lione for over half a year. How many had escaped since she had come? A hundred? Two? Had she been so successful? More slaves were trained, more were captured, and more were born. There would always be more. The work that waited for her would never end.

The woods were buzzing with insects and birds, the call of which she would never hear inside the White City. She had missed the smell of the forest. The sweet music of the forest felt peculiar. But, even as every little detail about the dense forest felt foreign, her heart leaped to know she was home again.

"You do not have to go back," Haro interrupted quietly, having returned silently to her side.

"There are so many still left," she said with a sigh.

"Others would take your place if you ask it," he replied.

"How could I ask them to risk their lives as I do?"

"You are worth it. You know you have my life, Warrior."

Her stomach knotted, and she became acutely aware of one particular braid in her hair. How could she be worth dying for? It was true that she fought the Lionians but, if she was dead, it would go on. Someone else would fight. They were Nurmi. They would always fight.

"It will not be too much longer," she said instead. "The Lionians draw closer every time slaves escape. Soon, they will know."

"And then? They capture you once more? Execute you?" Haro asked, his voice heavy with worry. "You cannot let that happen, Warrior. Too many people need of you." She felt him moving as if to lift a hand and touch her arm, but the raised hand did not contact her before being drawn away consciously.

She was the Warrior. She was beyond such things.

"The Black Arrow leads the army," Lania said, straightening herself to perfection. "What use am I except here? They will not take me. Once they know, I will escape myself. Until then, I will continue. I cannot give up, not yet."

She turned her back to him and began her steady run back to Lione, pushing her longing for the forest aside.

Once she reached the walls, she wondered why Haro had not argued more.

Aurion could not let it continue.

The people outside were calling his name. Beyond them, innocent people were being trampled or killed in fights over the High Seat. The councilmen cowered in their homes, ignoring it. The fires had spread. The riot did not seem to be slowing.

Aurion moved up into the public seats, where he could see down over the entire room. Only the High Seat was at his level; the boxes where the councilmen sat extended in rings below.

Looking over the seats in the oval room where Lione's fate had so often been decided, he mentally placed the people in their seats.

First on the right from the throne where the sovereign sat was High Councilman Valtorio, originally from the Highreach District. The high councilman was a stubborn old man, bitter against anyone younger than he, uncaring of the people not of his district, and only marginally caring of those within it.

No good.

High Councilman Telvius? *Too deep into the corruption of the Council,* Aurion replied to himself. Besides that, the councilman was greedy and would stop at nothing once in place, which was why Polfius had watched him so carefully.

Councilman Norisius? *Young, selfish, rash, and power-hungry. Easily corrupted and too new to the Council.*

High Councilman Dobrius? *A slow-witted man with too many well-known weaknesses that could be exploited.*

Councilman Volustio? Thinking it nearly made Aurion laugh. Volustio hated Aurion and everything to do with him. *If I want a burned city,* Aurion told himself, *doing nothing will suffice.* Why waste energy on electing Volustio?

Councilman Galfium's seat he skipped entirely.

And what about High Councilman Dracus? *A little rash at times, with a temper that put a few slaves into the trenches, but always kept in check in the Councilhall.* He was old enough to die before becoming too corrupt, but strong enough to keep a firm hand on the Council. He had supported a few of Aurion's endeavors and, although Aurion did not feel ready to trust him with his life, he felt he could certainly trust the man to do the right thing for Lione.

He went over the rest of the room, trying to find someone better, but none of the others seemed even a possibility. *So that's it,* he told himself firmly. He had made his choice.

With a heavy heart, he ordered the guards to open the huge public doors of the Councilhall.

The sun had hidden itself behind a layer of gray clouds that covered the sky from horizon to horizon. Rain could be felt in the air, but it did not fall, not yet, as the great White City burned.

The crowd hushed as he came out into the street, anticipating his answer to their call, but he did not have the heart to speak to them. He walked instead, navigating the streets by foot, at every step followed by the chanting masses. Guards and soldiers marched alongside him. The crowd threw gifts and tree boughs in his honor. It became a march for a festival day.

Aurion was relieved when he arrived at the home of High Councilman Palviro Wavius Dracus.

When he knocked, surprise finally stilled the crowd. The door took a long time to open. It allowed only Aurion to enter and quickly shut behind him.

With weary eyes, Aurion regarded the front entrance of the high councilman's home. It was more elegant than most, including his own. The polished floor ran without seam into the walls, which were in turn covered with patterns of glass and metals that made them sparkle. The slave who had opened the door had been helped by a group of no less than five personal guards, who returned to their places by the door once Aurion stepped inside.

Was he missing something?

But there was no one better.

He was led from the decorated main entrance, through halls that rivaled the elegance of the palace, to a small central courtyard where he found Dracus waiting for him.

"Quite an entrance you make," the older man said, looking up from where he sat at a fountain. Tired as he was, Aurion could not tell if it was said with a sneer or a laugh.

He shrugged weakly. "Not my plan," Aurion said, accepting the cup a slave offered him. He distantly felt it burn as he swallowed the strong wine. Everything seemed to burn, and he was becoming numb. The offer had been no more than formality, anyway. It was not as if Dracus was being friendly.

"Not much seems to be today," his host replied with a light tone and a toss of food for the fish in the central pond. Aurion could see Dracus keeping his attention on him, even as the older man watched the fish. When Aurion did not speak, he continued, "Why have you come here, High Councilman?"

When the host sat on a padded chair nearby, Aurion chose the fountain edge as a seat. He swallowed the rest of his drink quickly, finding his tongue more agreeable.

"I am looking for a sovereign," he replied.

The older man laughed. "It seems the crowd has made their decision."

"I do not want it."

The host leaned back in his chair and took a drink from his own cup. Beside Aurion, a slave refilled the guest's cup.

"The power behind the power, is it? You want to rule but without the danger of being the figure on the coin? Is that it?"

"Nonsense," Aurion answered. "You cannot possibly think I had any control over Sovereign Polfius. The opposite was true, I fear."

Dracus smiled wistfully under his thin beard, like a grandfather reminiscing. "Yes, Polfius did have a way of keeping us in our places." He sighed in a way that made Aurion painfully aware of the sovereign's death once more. His sovereign, his father, had died because of his mistake and there was nothing he could ever do to atone for it.

Aurion shook his head to clear the thought. Other plans were in the making. Polfius was dead. The city was burning. Lione needed a sovereign.

"Can you do it?" Aurion asked.

The old man snapped to attention. "Do what?" he asked. "Do not be vague, High Councilman," he chastised when Aurion glared at him.

But the choice had been made. There was no other way.

"Can you rule Lione and rule her well? Can you lead the Lionian people to victory? Can you control the Council? Can you stop the corruption poisoning her?"

Dracus suddenly looked twenty years younger.

"You will support me?" he asked, eyes wide in wonder.

Aurion could barely find the energy to nod. "All I want is your promise to act only in the interest of Lione and her people."

"You have it, High Councilman Polfius. Consider the deal sealed."

All Aurion could do was sigh.

PART 2

THE ENEMY OF MY ENEMY

CHAPTER 13

The enormous white house was decorated from the top of the flat roof down to the paint covering the doorways. Flowers had been brought from afar at an enormous cost, each quickly replaced when it wilted in the unexpectedly hot sun. Slaves and servants busied themselves at a wild pace to fill the cups of distinguished visitors. Musicians played dance music from the central courtyard while lazy men and women dressed in finery stood around and watched, unwilling to dance in the unseasonal heat.

Conversations were hushed, as if fearing eavesdroppers, but Aurion still heard the words he expected.

"Another new Councilman for Market…"

"…if the ships are finished…"

"…just half of what the Nurmi Warrior is capable of. I heard…"

"He'll catch her, have no doubt. No one hates the Warrior like our sovereign. He's spent every day of the last two years hunting…"

Antori arrived at his side and handed him the cup he had requested. The soldier then repositioned himself by the wall as if acting as a bodyguard.

When Aurion glanced at his guard, Antori offered, "Same talk all over. Lania's activity recently has the city mumbling, and Dracus is taking it poorly. A few people wonder about the Windraso War, mostly upset it's taking so long."

Aurion sipped his cup as he scanned the room.

Four councilmen had attended the wedding, but the sovereign had not, which did not surprise anyone. The ceremony had been overly long, and the house smelled like a winery. They had moved on to the cheaper drink that most, given their state, would not notice. Falmio Caltrian Gitarius—Councilman Gitarius, Aurion corrected himself—had taken one of the other councilmen aside to show off his garden, and was just now leaving the room, probably hoping to talk to the man about Dracus and win another vote. It was unlikely to work. Gitarius was not known for his persuasiveness, no matter how much pressure the sovereign put on him.

Where once a flattering merchant had dwelled, now a councilman bent like a weed in a riverbed to the swell of the sovereign's word. *What an irritation Gitarius has turned out to be*, Aurion reflected. *Just one of many*, he answered himself. Dracus had recognized the ease with which Gitarius could be manipulated. Gitarius' strength in the Council was minimal, but he had been eagerly taken in by the ten other supporters for Dracus, giving the sovereign the eleven votes he needed to get almost anything he wanted through the Council.

The moment Gitarius' supervision left the room, Aurion saw Councilman Vanius, the newly appointed Councilman of the Highreach District, leave the crowd watching the musicians and stumble toward Aurion, bumping into passersby and disguising his approach by starting more than one useless conversation.

Knowing the man wanted to speak in private, Aurion turned from the room and, with a shake of his head, told his two guards to stay behind.

"You sure?" Antori grumbled. "That brat's a supporter."

Aurion smiled at his friend's assessment. "And Dracus is mistaken in trusting him. I need to tell him to stop being an idiot, something always best done in private."

He got a nod of understanding as he left the room, shadowed distantly by a man he knew was plotting to kill the sovereign who had given him power.

Someone was always plotting. Vanius had only just come to power, thanks to Dracus, and the sovereign still believed Vanius was one of his reliable eleven, but Vanius had tasted power. What had Dracus expected? Treachery followed when the power-hungry got a taste of authority.

The best Aurion could find was an empty courtyard, perfect for shy couples wanting to star gaze. To prevent such indecencies, the host had posted a guard by the entrance. The open-faced helm, while of a modern design Aurion found strange, allowed him to recognize the soldier.

"Good day, Paccinon," Aurion greeted.

The gray-streaked bearded man smiled and half-bowed, but no one else was around, and the formality was unnecessary. "A good day, Aurion, unless you are the bride," the guard answered, and Aurion smiled wearily. Indeed, Julti had looked miserable during the ceremony. It was understandable—she probably had as much interest in marrying Councilman Galfium's son as Aurion did—but Julti's father had been well-paid to see her wed.

"I cannot blame her," Aurion answered, making the guard nod in sympathy for the child.

"A bad match, they say," Paccinon confirmed. "She broke her marriage statue too. Bad omen."

Not surprised that Gitarius had kept the unfortunate sign secret, Aurion put the fact to memory for later use. "At least your boy is a little distance from marriage. How is Saber doing?" Aurion asked, and the guard beamed with pride.

"Developing a liking for books. History mostly, along with anything on mechanics he can lay his hands on. He's attending school at the Farilan temple in the Stadium District."

"Have you given any thought to Krivior temple?" Aurion asked. "Farilan is for men of the crafts, not for boys who want to learn history."

Paccinon shrugged. "Cannot be afforded on a personal guard's salary, even a councilman's guard."

"Well, there are three scholarships at the library that have not yet been claimed," Aurion offered, and Paccinon smiled again. "If Saber wants to learn, have him visit the library and ask. I'm certain something can be arranged."

"Thanks, Aurion," the guard replied, grinning wider still. "I will."

After taking a moment to savor the knowledge that he was still making a difference, Aurion said, "If you will excuse me, Paccinon, I believe I am being followed."

As Aurion turned to face the fountain and await his pursuer, Paccinon's face darkened. "Anything you need a help with?" he asked, a hand on his sword hilt.

Aurion waved him off. "Doubtful, but thank you for the offer. Please keep an eye on it."

The guard nodded and returned to attention by the door, just as Councilman Vanius took his first step into the courtyard.

"High Councilman Polfius," the newest Councilman of the Highreach District greeted him. "I had wanted to speak to you."

"If this is about that guard you sent to me, Councilman, I think this conversation will bore me quickly," Aurion replied.

The man's hand, about to reach around Aurion's shoulders in amity, paused. Knowing he had rendered the man's first several planned sentences useless, Aurion waited patiently for the councilman to revise his approach.

"Your reputation is well earned," Vanius said instead, letting his arm fall.

"You knew that," Aurion said, "and yet you sent someone to tell me what was going on, presuming I did not know."

"I wanted to make sure you were—"

"You wanted to control what I knew, and when, Councilman," Aurion corrected. "Your games annoy me and annoying me is not wise."

Vannius smiled thinly, his beady eyes flat. "Councilman Volustio will attest to that, I'd wager," he said. "I gave you credit; I knew you'd figure it out, eventually. So, you know, but you've not told Dracus. That is why—"

"And why do you assume I've not told him?" Aurion interrupted.

As the man flipped a rock into the fountain, Councilman Vanius eyed Aurion. "Because you're just as worried about him as I am. You didn't like that farce about the Fanlant farm, and you are one of the few people keeping an eye on Julluam right now. You know the province is in trouble, and Dracus is spending all his time, and all Lione's money, on boats destined for Northreach. The entire Windraso War is a joke! The savages are running from us, not fighting! How can we win when no battles are being fought?"

"Enemies don't have to die to win a war," Aurion replied.

"Well, the enemies in Julluam were supposed to die, and yet the Esparan King has been seen."

"I know that, Councilman," Aurion pointed out.

"And the dragonkeeper is not the myth they claim he is," Councilman Vanius added.

"The dragonkeeper is a boy living in a mountain range, who promised not to get involved and is even now bargaining with one of our paki," Aurion said, but Vanius did not seem to hear him.

"If the dragonkeeper allies himself with the King of Espar—"

"Unlikely. The line of Kings in Espar betrayed Dragon Pass."

"—we will be reliving the War of the Pass!"

"The War of the Pass," Aurion argued, "was fought against a well-prepared and very healthy Espar, utilizing both the strength of men and the strength of dragons at a time when we did not anticipate dragon involvement. We know that the alliance fell, and Espar has been kept weak. There will never be another defeat like the War of the Pass." Before the man could argue, Aurion continued.

"No, if the King of Espar allies with the dragonkeeper, it will not be epic. We will have subterfuge and bickering, then we will see a burst of attacks in Julluam, and we might lose our holdings there, but they will not move beyond the borders of Julluam. The alliance between dragons and man will not last. We will simply repeat the conquest of Espar, and Dracus will burn the Dragontail Mountains to ensure it never happens again."

The councilman cleared his throat noisily, pulling at his collar. "So, you see—"

"I swore an oath to the sovereign, Councilman," Aurion said. "By that oath, I cannot assist you."

When he turned, Councilman Vanius grabbed his arm.

Aurion could have knocked the councilman off his feet for the insult, but he was too bored with the conversation to feel threatened. Paccinon tensed ever so slightly but, as Aurion had requested, did not move.

"But if you join..."

"I want nothing to do with you," Aurion replied.

"...we could have the support of the army as well," Councilman Vanius continued as if Aurion had said nothing.

"I will not give you the army. If you want it, convince them yourself," he answered shortly. "I am not a token."

"Dracus grows too influential, and you know it! He has eleven votes in the Council, Councilman!"

"Ten," Aurion answered, "if you were to leave his service."

"Eleven votes allowed him to seize the Fanlant farms for himself! It is what allows these ridiculous boats to be built for the promise of funding he does not have! And how fares your previous libraries under the strain? You cannot say you do not feel threatened."

Aurion pulled his arm free gently. "I have little love for the man," he said, "and he knows that full well. I disapprove of his tactics in the Council, and I dislike him assigning benefits to himself when they should be going to the people. However, I swore an oath, Councilman, as did you."

"But will you act?"

"Do you think I would tell you if the answer was 'yes?'"

Councilman Vanius laughed sharply. "Probably not!"

"Then..."

"One last thing." The councilman stepped into Aurion's path. "Something you might not know but should." Finding it unlikely the man would tell him anything he had not heard from other sources, Aurion was surprised when Councilman Vanius said, "Dracus is recruiting your spymaster. Rumor has it he will not tolerate rejection."

Aurion kept his expression even and his voice smooth. "Are you finished?"

With a disappointed sigh, the councilman stepped aside. His short stature made the gesture sharp. "Talk to me if you want to get involved," he finalized, turning toward the fountain.

Aurion shook his head to Paccinon as he left. He had no idea if the guard had heard much of the conversation from across the courtyard, but he did not want him telling others about the meeting. He got a nod of understanding, then amused himself with imagining what Councilman Vanius' face would look like when the man turned around and noticed Paccinon.

As soon as he returned to the main courtyard, Aurion nearly ran into Councilman Gitarius. He was not certain if he jumped to see Dracus' lackey so close to the hallway, but Gitarius greeted him with enthusiasm that made him doubt he had betrayed anything. Gitarius was notoriously bad at concealing his intentions.

"Enjoying yourself, High Councilman?" Gitarius asked.

Aurion barely remembered to smile, but he managed it. "It has been a wonderful celebration, Councilman," he replied with false enthusiasm.

Gitarius loved to hear his title, and he puffed himself up in a way that reminded Aurion of a content pigeon. "I am glad so many have taken pleasure in my little gathering," he said. Without pause, he indicated Julti next to her new husband. "A splendor, is she not?"

Indeed, the dress, jewelry, and flowers were extravagant and beautiful, all done up in the red and black of the Household of Gitarius to boast their dual-color status. Gitarius had spared no expense on the wedding. Having re-secured the respect the household had held long before, Gitarius was more than happy to flaunt his success.

Despite this, Aurion could not help but notice the places where the expensive makeup had been washed with tears. Clearly, the customary trips to the temples had had little effect: Julti looked miserable. Now, Gitarius' daughter walked around smiling weakly with her eyes lowered like a slave. The groom did not seem to notice her as he, like so many others, got steadily drunk.

"Indeed," Aurion answered. "She is quite a sight to see." It was not even a lie.

As Aurion watched the bride, Julti's slave arrived at her mistress' side. Aurion allowed Gitarius a moment to smirk in pride before asking, "Councilman, what plans have you for Julti's old slave?"

Gitarius shrugged and gave him a sidelong glance. "No need for her now. Why? Are you interested in a personal slave?"

"My sister is visiting Lione, so I need one. What's her name?"

"Tatkil," his host answered. "She's a good slave: quiet, obedient, maybe simple. She doesn't speak much but is very capable. I could sell her to you."

Already Aurion was nodding, his eyes following the movements of the slave girl as she had the cup refilled for her mistress. Serena would not like having a slave, but no Lionian girl went into the city without one. A Nurmi would never be loyal to him, but he could at least expect it to not ally with any other Lionian either. If what Gitarius said of her obedience was true, he may even be able to get some information from her about her old master's household.

Grizzle would complain—it was the spymaster's policy to avoid slaves—but Aurion felt this was an opportunity that should not be missed.

And he had to talk to Grizzle, anyway.

"How much would you like for her?"

It took all of Lania's effort not to show recognition. Without any doubt, she knew her new master from a jail cart, from a prison cell, and from a room with a furnace and a palm-sized purple sphere. She remembered him taking her silver armband, the same band she had reclaimed and wore on her arm when her sleeves could cover it.

He did not seem to know her. Although she watched him carefully from under lowered eyelashes, he did not seem to think she was dangerous. Gitarius informed her that his household was done with her, and she was to serve the new man instead.

Tatkil accepted with a shy nod, then followed her new master out. Lania absently wondered how much she was worth.

Her new master watched her as they traveled in a covered coach, surprising his servants with his acquisition and then further by insisting she travel with him. Lania initially thought he might ask her questions but soon discovered his only interest was in watching her. Knowing she was being judged, Lania buried the Warrior deep under Tatkil. With her uniform covering most of her faded scars and her cap hiding her hair debts, he had no grounds to suspect her.

Up a rise in the Freeman District, the carriage came to a halt, and she was taken inside, where she met a black-clad man with a freckled beard and far too many weapons.

"What have we here?" the man asked as Tatkil stood for inspection. "One of Gitarius' by the colors, but a Nurmi?"

Seeing they expected no answer from her, Lania kept her eyes ostensibly on the tiled floor, trying to take in as much as she could through the corners of her eyes without appearing to.

"For Serena," the high councilman informed his man.

The man in black circled her. "No brand," he pointed out.

"And no papers," her new master added.

The man in black took a step back, sneering. "Some people should be tattooed with a bulls-eye on their forehead. No papers? On his slave? As a councilman?"

"Probably an illegal breeding colony," her new master said with a shrug. "I'll have new papers drawn up so we don't get caught out, but in the meantime..."

"I'll figure out where she came from," the bearded man confirmed.

Lania felt the stare shift to her, and she tried to bury herself into Tatkil farther. "And you'll be a good cooperative slave, right, little one? You'll tell me what I want to know about the household of Gitarius, won't you?"

Despite feeling like she was being addressed like a five-year-old, she did not look up. "Yes, Master," she said in slurred Lionian.

"And that's the other reason I bought her," the high councilman said. "Gitarius blindly appears to have offered me an opening into his household."

"She's still a slave and not to be trusted. I'm sure you're well aware of that, High Councilman Polfius." The title was covered in sarcastic pomp, as the man in black said it.

Lania felt her heart skip a beat. She remembered his name from the Day of Defiance two years before. Rumors said he had refused the High Seat. She had never known the name of the councilman who had confronted her during her imprisonment. Strange that it would be the same man.

"Of course I know, Grizzle. But speaking of not to be trusted... when were you planning on telling me about the offer you got?"

With their attention on each other, Lania felt it was safe enough to glance up. She could sense tension. The master was angry. The man in black knew why, she judged. His bearded face scrunched in disappointment.

"Demon-shit," he said. "I'd ask who told you, but you'd never tell."

"Why didn't *you* tell me, Grizzle?"

"You know damn well why, Aurion!" the black man replied. "It wasn't your problem, and gods know you have enough problems already!"

The Master of the Household frowned deeply. "Not my problem? And how would you feel if it had been one of your employees? I'd ask Volustio's spymaster for the answer, but, of course, he's dead."

"I should probably drop by Volutio's district again in reminder," the man brightly offered.

"Don't change the topic, Grizzle. Tell me what happened." The high councilman's voice was a growl.

The broad man in black crossed his arms and leaned back. His glower seemed pensive, if annoyed. "He asked, that's all. He just asked. I told him I wasn't interested as politely as I could."

"As politely as you could?" High Councilman Polfius echoed, incredulous. "I hope you had someone read the letter before sending it. You're not known for tact!"

Grizzle smiled briefly. "I put lots of flowery words in it."

"And?"

The smile went out. "And I got a note back this morning saying he didn't like my answer."

The master and the spymaster stared at each other for a long moment. The councilman's jaw was clenched for several breaths before he asked, "Do we have a plan to deal with this?"

The grin from the bearded man looked feral. "Two options, neither of which you will like. Fortunately, I only don't like one of them."

Despite the abstract commentary, both men seemed to be following the other's thoughts.

If she could find out who had sent the letters and why the two men considered it such a threat, she could use the information. A weakness in the high councilman's house could be advantageous.

The pause lingered, and Lania turned her eyes back to the stones at her feet. She felt each man glanced at her as they considered their un-specified options, but she did not meet their gaze.

"I," the councilman said at length, "am going to tell Serena about her new slave. We'll talk after I've had a chance to think." Turning to her directly, the master commanded, "Tatkil, you will obey Grizzle in all things. Answer his questions as best you can, and I will provide you your own room and bed."

"Yes, Master," Tatkil's timid voice replied.

"Good."

The master was gone before the man in black spoke again. "So, little one, shall we talk about Councilman Gitarius?"

Two options. One: Give Grizzle up. Two: Have Dracus stop asking.

Aurion knew which one Grizzle didn't mind.

Grizzle would never leave. The man had come out of retirement for Aurion alone. His loyalty was not to anything material that Dracus could provide, and the spymaster was only as good as he was because it was his passion. No passion meant a poor job. Then what would Dracus do?

There were temporary ways to have Dracus stop asking, but only one permanent one.

Aurion was going to have to intervene. Dracus had forced his hand. The man Aurion had supported had now damned himself.

Aurion knocked on his sister's door before registering the giggling on the other side. One of the girls squeaked in alarm, causing all the others to burst into further giggles. Aurion winced. Had he known Serena was with friends, he would have delayed his visit.

"Come!" Serena's voice, so like their mother's, shouted over the ruckus of the girls.

By the half-finished patchwork on the chair, they had been putting together a quilt at one stage, but the job had deteriorated into games. Threads hung from her canopy bed almost at regular intervals, and a piece of material made from tied scraps wound its way up the posts. All five girls had colored threads draped over their heads and caught around their arms, making him think there had been a spool-throwing contest.

"A word, Serena," Aurion requested, "in private?"

The girls tried to pull the threads clear discretely as they lined up for him, several fixing their hair or straightening their sleeves as they went. Every last one of the five blushed heavily.

"Of course, brother dear," Serena answered. She did not attempt to adjust her appearance before shooing the girls out the door, promising to meet them in the garden shortly.

The instant they were clear of his sights, Aurion heard the giggling resume. The sound of their running feet faded down the hall. He closed the door.

Serena stood in the room, a hand on her hip and thread trailing off her on all sides. Seeing her, Aurion laughed in earnest.

"All right, come here so I can fix your hair!" he said, pointing to the chair. "You look like you've been on a ship for a mooncycle!"

"I," she declared as she flopped into the chair and let him pull the pins from her hair, "am fourteen. I can fix it myself."

"I have no doubt of that, sister," Aurion answered, untangling green thread from her temple and ear, "but you've got a spool stuck in your collar. Should you try to pull the thread from your head, you will be here a while."

He handed her the offending green spool, which she took to re-winding.

"I'm glad you were having fun," he added.

"It would not kill you to relax a little with the girls, brother," she said. "The people should not be shocked if a councilman is more casual within his home. Any more of those strict stares might give Laynni a heart attack. They are trying very hard, you know. They do not want to offend you, but you—"

"I'd rather they go around telling everyone you are being suffocated."

"So all the young men offer to rescue me?"

"So they see in you an ally and an opportunity." The threads removed, he handed her back her pins and gave her a brush off the nearby vanity.

Tacked around the mirror, Serena had pinned her sketches of her newest friends. The drawings were uncanny likenesses to the models, including mischievous sparkles to eyes where appropriate. A sketch of Serena dominated the room from the top of the mirror's arch. Aurion felt he was looking at an image of his mother.

"There, you are unthreaded," he said, turning away from the pictures and bringing his mind to other things. "I fear I am no expert at lady's hair fashion, however, so you are on your own."

As she brushed her hair, he went to the window over the garden and watched the many colorful dresses burst from the lower door. The girls walked, arms locked, in step to the orchard and found the benches.

"How was the wedding you refused to let me attend despite my having an invitation?" she asked.

"Boring and hot. You would not have liked it."

"Says you!" Serena replied, tossing her long black hair.

"I bought you a slave, though."

She had her hands in the air, deftly pinning her locks in a twirling pattern atop her head when he looked back at her, but the statement made her pause, then perk up.

"A slave! Does that mean I can go out alone?"

"Yes, so long as Grizzle checks her out and says it's..."

She leaped to her feet, her trailing hair forgotten, and grabbed him in a hug that squashed the rest of his sentence into a grunt. "I've had another invitation, you know," she said, pulling away. "Julti Lola Gitarius has..."

"Julti Lola Gitarius Galfium," he corrected as she untangled herself from him.

"Whatever-her-name-is asked me to call on her in a few days at her new home."

"A piece of normality, I suppose."

Serena rushed to her vanity, checking her reflection and giving up on the elaborate hair pattern. Instead, she quickly wrapped two bands of dyed beads around her head.

"You've also had a request from Otavopon Navius Maurio," Aurion offered. "He is—"

"Son of Navius Julian Maurio of the Household of Maurio. Eighteen, tall, dark, handsome, and as bright as a rock." Seeing him dumbfounded by her recitation, she flashed him a smirk.

"Well, I'd say we are related," he said.

"Grizzle felt I should be educated," she told him. "His idea of 'educated' involves memorizing the entire population of Lione."

"So you know…"

"Otavopon is siding with Vanius officially, but we're suspicious he's passing the information to his father? Yes."

"And Maurio works for Dracus, naturally," Aurion added.

"Maurio follows any who leads," she said, "which makes me wonder why you are not leading more, brother."

He took to undoing the tangles from around the bedposts as he answered. "I selectively lead. It's less dangerous and means I can usually get results. If I did it all the time, someone might argue with me."

"So, when is Otavopon wanting to rescue me from my oppressive brother?"

"He's offered to give you a tour of the Stadium."

"And I can go with the girls and the new slave?"

"You can go," Aurion replied hesitantly.

"And if it turns into another proposal?"

He paused his work on the knots and frowned at her. "Then elope."

She burst into laughter. "It would be the fourth offer of marriage, you know. So many…"

"Seven, sister. Three came to me directly."

Seeing her proudly puff out her chest made him realize how much older than fourteen she looked.

"After only five days, too! I must be nearing your total!" she declared.

Shaking his head, he pulled the last of the knots from the bedpost and threw the material onto the bed.

"You have a ways to go yet. Go downstairs when you are ready and meet Tatkil, the new slave. I will see you at dinner."

He had his hand on the doorknob when she, a smile in her voice, goaded, "You must dread marriage to have refused them all. You're getting too old to be saying 'no' anymore. Who will take you in now? You are old and gray!"

"Twenty-eight is not old and gray," he said, "and I've never had an offer I liked. I've never met anyone I wanted to curse with this life."

"Mother wants—"

"Mother has to wait for grandchildren, Serena. You go first."

"She would have a fit to hear you suggest anything of the kind!"

"Then don't tell her. I won't."

He left her chuckling.

CHAPTER 14

After Grizzle's many questions, which she provided detailed replies to in broken Lionian, Lania was deemed safe and passed along to be branded.

She contemplated the branding as they prepared. She did not fear the pain but objected fundamentally to being marked as someone's property. Her only alternative, she recognized quickly, was to escape immediately. Could she get to the others fast enough and get them out? Could she clear the city with the high councilman searching for her?

She decided the importance of getting the rest of her people clear of the city outweighed the discomfort of a brand. Lionians might believe it marked her as property, but she knew it meant nothing.

She let Tatkil cry and squirm. Lania pushed the pain to the back of her mind and forgot about it.

Once done, she was introduced to her new mistress.

At first, she thought Serena would be much like Julti, for the girl presented herself, dressed fashionably, amidst a group of twittering friends. She even seemed to have Julti's high-pitched squeal of delight, but there remained something distinctly un-childlike about Serena. Although she rambled about her favorite stores or how pretty dresses could improve a temple service, the way Serena never stopped paying attention warned Lania that the councilman's sister was much more intelligent than even her friends knew.

For eight days, Lania stayed within the grounds of the Illican household, assisting her mistress. She was given a room, which she promptly arranged an exit from. Knowing both her new master and the master's spymaster were keeping a close watch, she gathered information subtly for her imminent escape. She was profoundly pleased to catch one of the spymaster's men coming in from the garden through a secret door.

Between duties, Lania studied the garden. The secret entrance was well built, hidden by plants but set apart so that anyone coming in would have to cross the open yard to approach the house. But if she was leaving, she didn't need to worry about the soldiers at the house, which made it a fine escape route.

After the eight days, Lania was finally given a task outside the walls of her master's manor, chaperoning the girls on a trip into the Stadium District. Tatkil took over quickly, Lania aware of the many eyes on the high councilman's new slave. Compliant and helpful, Tatkil accompanied her mistress to the outskirts of the Stadium District and behaved impeccably.

The boy who met them was dressed formally in his colors, complete with two daggers on his belt that were eyed by Lania but ignored by Tatkil. While the rest of the girls flocked ahead and then behind, Serena playfully pulled Otavopon into their conversations by dropping occasional prompts for a story or two about himself until he happily discussed his household, father, politics, and business.

Lania nearly laughed aloud at seeing, through mock ignorance, Serena was now learning intimate details about Councilman Maurio.

The markets were bustling, the spring opening the gates to produce from the far reaches of the Sovereignty. With two years of experience, Lania recognized many of the foreign fruits, vegetables, and sometimes animals now. It never ceased to amaze her how much food sat out on the carts being picked up and rejected by wealthy citizens, while regions of the Sovereignty struggled in near-starvation. The amount that was thrown out continuously boggled her mind. The Nurmi still did little farming, preferring to forage and steal grains, but if they grew enough in numbers, that would have to change. She couldn't fathom being so careless with food.

Proudly, Otavopon ushered the school girls through the gates, waving the guards away with an exaggerated gesture. No tickets or payment were required when in the presence of the current Councilman of the Stadium District's family.

The stadium was one of the largest structures in Lione, feeling like a mountain surrounded by foothills to Lania. Entering under its arches put them in a corridor that circled the walls. The event was a hunting demonstration and filled more than one of the flat, sand-filled arenas with contests and crowds.

The area was packed until Otavopon brought them through a guarded side door and into smaller, less crowded corridors.

The stone walls blocked the noise sufficiently to allow conversation again, although the immense crowd continued to have a presence like the roar of sea caves in the distance. Here, the people had to raise their voices to be heard, but there was space between viewers to move and plenty of seats available around the ring.

"Welcome to the private games," Otavopon said, pausing by a sunlit arena that was only a dozen paces wide. Lania couldn't tell if they were beside or above the main arenas, but it felt underground still. Lione had been built up over centuries, leaving layers of tunnels below. She suspected this was one.

A dog fight had just finished, the victorious bloody dog being dragged back by a loop and pole while the defeated animal lay far too still on the sand in the thin sunlight. The smaller crowd was now loudly collecting or paying bets, the surviving animal already dismissed from their minds.

Lania had heard they used sand because it was easier to rake clean of the blood, but it turned her stomach to see it in play. It would be worse, she assumed, in the games in the larger arena, where mountain cats and boars were hunted in manufactured terrain to entertain the crowd.

"This way, ladies," Otavopon called. "Archery is on right now, and we have the absolute best seats!"

Lania followed her mistress, remembering to stand at the base of the stairs so Serena could use her to balance on the uneven, worn step in her ridiculous shoes should she wish. Serena paused, her calculating stare on the downed hound in the ring. Lania suspected she was memorizing the faces of the onlookers as her friends went on ahead.

A shout of alarm sounded from the far side of the ring, and movement caught Lania's attention. Without thought, she darted into the path of the hound that had broken from the catcher's pole, putting herself between her mistress and the attacking dog.

The dog lunged for Lania's throat, fast as any sword thrust, but Lania dodged, caught the dog's scruff, and spun the hound around on its momentum. She sent it flying back the way it had come, where it crashed into the stones around the arena and rolled once before coming to its feet.

Lania met its angry stare, teeth bared, as everyone else in the room retreated. She was aware that a master was somewhere, shouting for a new catcher pole, but she did not take her eyes off the dog.

She understood its fury at being trapped and being used for nothing but death. She did not hate the dog, nor did she fear it, despite knowing it was a threat. No, she pitied the dog as Serena withdrew up the stairs behind Lania. Still, pity was not enough to let the Warrior break the stare. If she turned or ran, the dog would have her. She was not prey. She would never be prey. So, she stood ready, her hands out, her eyes locked, and growled back at the dog.

So intense was their stare down, the hound was taken by surprise when the loop came over its head, the rope tightening quickly to hold it to the hollow pole and allow the handler to keep it at a distance. Lania didn't stay to watch after that, not wanting to know the fate of the poor beast. Neither death nor ongoing life would be pleasant for the dog.

It didn't take long to find her mistress again, for the stairs lead up to private boxes, which Otavopon had reserved entirely for the occasion. The colors of her uniform gave her access as she was recognized as a slave of the guest.

She stepped out into shaded sunlight. The canopied box was set high on the wall between two arenas, the walls made of smooth wizard stone. To the right, in a large arena filled with rows of targets, Lionian athletes performed trick shots while riding horses or swinging from ropes. To the left, a smaller arena with five targets contained a line of wide-eyed slaves being organized. The crowds differed between the sides; to the right were families of Lionians with parasols and lenses viewing the performances, but the left had soldiers and workers and a lower, latticed viewing area for slaves.

The rich on the right, and the poor on the left, Lania remarked. Would Serena and her friends find the sides equally entertaining?

While Otavopon talked the girls through the demonstrations on the right, Serena took it all in then quickly assessed the left. As Lania joined her mistress, she realized her shoulder was wet. The dog's tooth had caught her skin as she'd thrown it back, leaving a shallow scratch. It revealed just how close the enraged hound had come to tearing her throat out instead of that of its next opponent.

She should not have leaped in to defend Serena. But then, Serena was not able to protect herself. *Wouldn't that have been interesting?* What would Councilman Polfius have done if his sister had come to harm or, worse, died while under another councilman's care? And what would he have done to Tatkil, the slave meant to protect her?

The very fact that she had stepped into the hound's path now struck Lania as insane, but she'd not given the action any thought. She had been playing the role of slave for too long; Tatkil had taken over. The slave knew only to protect her mistress; she would not have fought or thrown the dog. But the Warrior could not be taken down by a mere beast.

If not for Lania hiding in the depths of her mind, Tatkil's devotion would have claimed her life.

With a cold shock, Lania finally understood. Too often, the slaves she pulled from their shackles feared her and the freedom she offered. It had never made sense to her. But Tatkil was not a person; she was a slave. Like the other slaves, she had nothing but her service to her master and mistress. Lania, by freeing a slave, took that duty—the thing that defined them—away. It was no wonder the change she brought terrified them. The soul of the Corelands gave them a new identity over time, but it was a long journey back to peace for them all.

Serena acknowledged Tatkil's return with a grin and an overenthusiastic hug that suggested the slave had been gone for a mooncycle, instead of a mere moment. Doing so, Serena attracted the attention of the other girls and Otavopon, who quickly inserted himself to explain the slave games. The girls had put the dog attack out of their minds but Otavopon was still pale. Lania suspected had similar questions as she did: what would have been his fate if the dog had gotten Serena instead?

Otavopon was formal in his speech, his words strangled by fading adrenaline. "Since some slaves are still used for working and hunting, their contests are often close matches, but they are nothing compared to the skills you will see demonstrated with the very finest of Lione's—"

"If it's a slave match," one of Serena's friends quickly interrupted, "Serena should enter her slave!"

Serena shook her head. "We have no bow."

Otavopon assessed the disappointed frowns around him and offered, "I am certain something can be arranged. The prize is a hundred hiYorin. Not much to a councilman, but good fun regardless!"

How quickly he changes sides depending on what he thinks will garner the desired reaction, Lania mused.

The friend, who had colored her head pink for the day, clapped her hands enthusiastically. "It would be such fun, and I would bet on her! She is Nurmi after all!"

It was evident Serena was hesitant, but with four girls against her, it became increasingly difficult to object. At length, she conceded and asked Lania, "Can you shoot a bow?"

Lania shrugged in the most pathetic manner possible. "Most Nurmi women can," she replied.

"Perfect!" the pink-haired friend called. "Please, Serena, please? It would make the betting so much more fun!"

The influence of the girls, Lania had to remark, was more substantial than she had at first believed. She had not expected Serena to surrender to the pleas of her companions, but soon Lania found herself being escorted down to the arena to compete. Serena paid a stipend to enter then took a seat behind the shooters, Otavopon sourly standing at her side instead of back in the box above.

The game, they explained for the newcomers, was simple. The one whose arrow was the farthest from the center of the target was removed from the competition until only one contender remained at each target. Those would then move to a single target and carry on until only one remained, who would be named victor.

The bow they handed her was weathered, worn wood bent to the left, but it was still a bow. She had not held a bow in two years.

The wind was weak in the walled space. Because of the cramped quarters, the targets were hardly more than thirty paces away, making the Warrior scoff. Thirty paces with a dead wind was hardly a challenge at all. Perhaps, considering the condition of her bow, she could expect a little difficulty. Perhaps the long pause since she had last held a bow would slow her.

Most of the slaves enrolled in the games were Yeahsin with curly black hair and bright blue eyes, although a few of each race were present. Only two other Nurmi were in the game, and they both looked at their bows with a mix of confusion and fear. There were also Nurmi in the crowd behind the latticed wall, many of whom she recognized as belonging to the rich patrons enjoying the more advanced games on the opposite side. A few risked the sign, hiding the gesture under a cough or the swat of an insect, but most could do no more than smile without giving her away. The majority would not know her, not yet, but those who did had a glimmer to their eyes that was painfully uncommon among slaves.

They expected her to win.

She could, she felt certain, despite the aching of her recently branded right arm and the cut on her neck that had faded into a faint itch of dried blood. Most of those who stood around her now had never held weapons. She could defeat them, but did she want to?

The Nurmi audience smiled at her from all sides. They knew she would win. They knew she was the Warrior.

It would not be strange for a Nurmi woman to shoot a bow at least reasonably well, she decided.

When she pulled the bow, the sensation was so familiar it pained her. Compensating for the twist of the bow, she aimed her shots to always fall within that of another but not the closest to the center. When only she and one another remained at the target, she surprised the onlookers by hitting the bull's eye and took victory of her target.

Of the four others to win, two were hunters of moderate skill. One even had his own bow and arrows and thus did not have to waste time, as the Warrior did, looking over the arrow before firing, trying to guess which way it would drift. In the end, it came down to her and this Yeahsin hunter.

Having consistently landed her arrow outside his on each turn, she could not fault him for smiling confidently when he made his shot. He was rewarded with a clean shot that landed within the smallest of the circles, a finger's breadth right of the center dot.

She was attracting attention she could hardly afford in the White City, and his shot was too accurate for her to best without suspicion. If her master discovered who she was, it would end her time in Lione. Was a game worth losing Tatkil?

It was no longer Julti and Gitarius she had to fool, it was Serena and High Councilman Polfius. High Councilman Polfius was already going to find her out, probably soon. She did not know if this would make it easier, but she knew it would give her people one more thing to talk about.

It was worth it.

The arrow embedded itself into the perfect middle of the target, drawing gasps from the crowd. Her opponent dropped his jaw while his master came over thebarriers, shouting groundless objections and demanding a second shot.

From her seat, Serena jumped up and down, screeching, babbling, and giggling about her victory as if she had just made the miraculous shot herself. She hugged Otavopon, which made the man flush. The commotion she caused was enough to draw attention away from the angry slave owner who had lost, especially after the winning girl was identified. They handed over the one hundred hiYorin, and Serena pranced all the way home in the company of her chittering friends. She included Otavopon in her excitement expertly, a calculated decision.

As they left, Lania passed a prayer to Akara mentally, asking her to thank the One God for guiding her crooked arrows.

She had provided a new legend.

"You are pacing again," Serena told Aurion after he had taken only a few steps along his distracted path. "Have I upset you?"

Aurion stopped himself and made an effort to smile at his sister. Outside, night had fallen, and they had finally had a chance to talk about the day's events. They had chosen Serena's room, where the cool air through the window from the garden lifted some of the musk of the late spring. Serena sat at her vanity, shamelessly dressed in her night-gown in front of Grizzle. The old spymaster ignored the indecency as they had all expected he would.

"Not you," he told his sister. "No, you did very well to flush out what you could from Otavopon, but his lack of caution offends me."

"Offends?" Serena smiled knowingly as she checked her reflection in the mirror. "You are getting defensive of me, brother dear. You need not worry about my safety. After all, it is Otavopon's reputation that was at risk." Her eyes went to the man in black who stood in the corner.

Grizzle nodded to show he was listening, but said nothing. Aurion and he had already discussed the events. They could use the dog attack to discredit Otavopon, showing him as weak and cowardly if ever they wanted to undermine Maurio or his household now. There was no need to acknowledge how he had not been in the room for the situation; Serena's safety had been guaranteed by Otavopon's family, and they had failed. A handful of people knew so far. Aurion could change that when it suited him.

"Tatkil was very lucky today," he muttered, his thoughts on the quiet Nurmi woman who had already been sent to bed. "First handling the dog, then the contest."

"Gitarius had hunting dogs, but it was another slave who managed them," Grizzle offered.

"It was pure reflex, not training," Serena replied, her eyes on the drawing she was working on. "She is stronger than she looks."

Aurion frowned. "Many Nurmi know how to shoot a bow, even the women, but I never expected it from her," he added. "With her obedience, I thought she was born a slave."

"She had no brand," Grizzle reminded him. "I've traced her back to the shop where Gitarius bought her, but there it ends. I'm still going through the rest of the inventory to see if we pull up any other mysterious arrivals."

"Dangerous oversight on Councilman Gitarius' behalf," S erena pointed out. She was using charcoal to elaborate on a sketch of Tatkil when Aurion checked her work. Aurion wondered if she would hang it with the others over her mirror, but he would not have been surprised if she decided to.

"She was likely illegal to begin with," Aurion agreed, "but then, where has she learned to shoot a bow, especially that..."

His eyes fell onto the drawing and the crescent-shaped scar along the slave's cheek.

His heart paused as, for the first time, he truly looked at the face of the slave.

"Oh demons," he said, his voice choked.

Serena and Grizzle looked at him, but the thoughts running through his mind were too disjointed to put into words and explain. Instead, he stammered, "Grizzle, did she say how she got the scar on her face?" Serena, self-conscious, lowered her charcoal.

The spymaster looked at the drawing, then shrugged. "Said the cook gave it to her. Gitarius' cook has a temper."

"It was not a cook," Aurion said, memories streaming through his mind, ending with the laughter that echoed for a lifetime through the dark hallways of the prison. "I saw her get that wound. I was there."

"How is that possible?" Serena asked, peering up at him.

"No wonder I could never find her route into the city!" he exclaimed. "She never left! She could sit and wait for the perfect opportunity in front of us, leaving us to chase obscure rumors in the north!"

"Brother…" Serena started.

Grizzle leaned back as if prepared for a long wait. "Don't worry. When he finishes thinking, he'll become coherent."

"No wonder she was such a good shot with the bow!" Aurion carried on, a smile now finding its way onto his face. "And no wonder she didn't look me in the eye! How could I have missed it?" He stopped, his chest tightening and making his smile fall off. "Demons, what am I going to do about it?"

He analyzed the options.

Trap her now? Kill her? Reveal it? Shame Gitarius?

The moment he settled on the answer, he faced Grizzle to find the spymaster waiting.

"Get me every available soldier and bring me a lamp. We have a very big problem."

The spymaster conceded the point without argument and left. After Aurion had gathered all the soldiers and explained what he wanted of them, and why, Grizzle finally spoke up.

"Too many damned conspiracies," the spymaster grumbled, but he headed outside to wait with his assigned guards as Aurion took the lamp and went to Tatkil's room.

He would not have her escaping. Grizzle now guarded the garden.

He did not try to sneak in, fearing a delay would give Tatkil an advantage. Bursting into the room, Aurion rushed the sleeping form in the bed and yanked back the blankets.

To his shock, Tatkil sprung up from behind the bed as he exposed several arranged sacks in the bed. He caught sight of a knife and brought his sword up defensively, but by the time his sword pushed aside the lunge for his throat, she had kicked his arm sharply, making him drop his weapon. All at once, she was behind him, holding the back of his robe at the collar and a knife to his throat.

He had never met a better fighter. He had barely blinked and was at her mercy.

The diasists crowding the hallway froze. Aurion knew one or more had gone to fetch Grizzle, but he doubted the spymaster would get the summons fast enough. She'd blocked the window, he saw. She had been expecting this.

They stood there, no one moving, for long minutes as, for some reason, she did not rake the knife across his throat.

"You don't want to kill me, Lania," Aurion said, slowly realizing why she had paused. "You'll never get out of the house."

"You want to test that theory?" her rough voice said from behind him. Tatkil had spoken in an accented, shy whisper, but this woman was self-assured and sounded like the legend she was. Even the accent he expected from his conversation with Lania in the jail cart had completely vanished. "How many do you think I can kill?"

As she spoke, her knife-wielding hand drifted slightly wide, likely in backswing for a thrust, but it gave Aurion an opportunity.

He grabbed her hand, shifted his weight, and tried to catch one of her feet on his own. She moved her weight back too quickly, and he was left spinning out of her grip.

She dropped into a wide crouch, her knife at the ready. Aurion stepped back to the cover of his soldiers and reconsidered the slave he had bought.

As she met his stare with the barest hint of a smirk on her face, she looked nothing like Tatkil. She had removed her cap to let her hair fall loose. The little braids he had thought so practical were obvious now as hair-debts. The eyes that had amazed him from the back of a jail cart were on him, and he felt a chill climb down his spine. She was poised with the strength of a confident fighter. The Warrior, a murderer, and a thief, stood before him proudly. She even wore her silver arm-band below the sleeve of her uniform in blatant disobedience.

Yet the only answer he could give was a cross stare. The command for her capture stuck in his mouth. For once, he did not know what to say.

"Now you must decide what to do with me," Lania said, as if prompting him to action. The Warrior rose slowly from her crouch, her eyes narrowing on him as if to test his resolve. "The way I see it, you have two choices. You could try to capture me or you can let me go."

The comment broke his silence. "Let you go? Why, by the gods, would I let you go?" he snapped. He could not believe he was even having the conversation, and yet…

She raised an eyebrow and stood straight, extending her hands in a submissive gesture he knew could kill a man. The knife was still in her grip.

"Hear me out, *High* Councilman," she said and, as if bewitched, he did not respond. "If you try to capture me," she said, "one of two things may happen. First, although I doubt it, you may catch me. I imagine I will make a fine prize to show the Council, although there would then be the trouble of explaining how you caught me, which would then force you to admit that I had been sitting here, in your very home, without your knowledge. What a tarnish to your reputation, Councilman!

"Of course," she continued, "there is no promise you will capture me at all. I may escape your grasp, leaving you to explain the disappearance of Tatkil and, possibly, the death of many of your guards. Nothing more than an inconvenience, I realize, but still." She glared at him with seriousness. "Then there is the matter of letting me go."

With absolute confidence, she challenged, "Tell me, High Councilman, why has the sovereign not figured out the game the other councilmen have been playing against him for more than two mooncycles?"

Aurion was unable to believe his ears. Had he been so careless with his words near the Nurmi slave? Perhaps she had heard it from other slaves. Perhaps she had overheard the soldiers or...

She was waiting for him to reply. The answer was obvious to any who knew Dracus' mind.

"They plan their meetings quickly after you attack," Aurion said.

"Because?" she prompted.

"Because they know the sovereign will have been up the night before plotting against you. Because they know that for the next three days, Dracus will do nothing but think of the Warrior. Because they know you have distracted him."

She nodded, wearing a grin that seemed to say she had defeated a great enemy. She looked proud and, for a reason he did not understand, that impressed him.

"The same thing that stopped you from figuring me out right away is stopping the sovereign from figuring out the plot against him," Lania said. "You were distracted, High Councilman. Now, if you let me go, I can stay on as Tatkil. I can continue to be the sovereign's headache, and you can continue to dream about the sovereign's death and the salvation of your household. I offer this to you, High Councilman, at the cost of freedom for a few Nurmi."

She faced him with her hands on her hips, waiting for the reply.

It was true, all of it. He stared at her, marveling at the reasoning the savage had just put forward. He was convinced, he realized sadly. Dracus had to be removed, and Lania could mean the difference between the success and the failure of the plans already in place. It would not be long.

He would give the sovereign a distraction and save the other councilmen from discovery. To save Grizzle...

"Very well," he said, hardly recognizing his own voice. He could see he had taken them all, even the diasists in the hall, by surprise.

Lania cocked her head in amusement. She was probably wondering if he was serious.

"Never use this household in any of your plans. If I find evidence leading me to you, I will come for your head." He sighed and lowered his sword. "You are right. I want you to remain. Carry on, Warrior. Distract my sovereign for a while longer."

He took the sword with him when he left her muttering to herself. Probably, he thought with an ironic smile, saying something very Grizzle-like under her breath about the insanity of her master.

CHAPTER 15

31ST DAY OF THE 2ND MOONCYCLE, 997

Knowing that High Councilman Polfius was angry with Sovereign Dracus had not prepared Lania for his willingness to release her. Since he was disinterested enough to avoid direct involvement in the assassination attempts, she had expected him to call the guards and make an attempt at capturing or killing her.

For five days, she watched every move the councilman and his soldiers made. She refused to seek out her other contacts, fearing they would use her to flush them out. She watched High Councilman Polfius most of all, seeking deception, and found none. She ensured she was confident of her ability to open the secret escape from either side, ready to climb the walls by the trees if she had to.

But nothing came of it. Nothing changed. She was treated like a slave.

On the fifth day, Tatkil followed Serena into the Market District for shopping. Determined to see the trap before it sprang, Lania scanned her surroundings. She was certain the high councilman had delayed only to catch her unprepared, perhaps under the eye of the Council or perhaps to embarrass her before her people to discredit their confidence in her. She could not let him succeed.

"How were you not spotted before?" Serena grumbled in chastisement when the crowds were too thin to overhear. They were out for the day, buying foolish things in the market and gathering rumors, but Tatkil was awkward in Lania's distraction. "You walk like expecting battle."

Lania tried to put Tatkil back in charge and become the slave, but the presence of too many people sabotaged the attempt. In the market, strangers were everywhere. It would be easy to hide a knife among the shoppers.

Since she had been addressed, Lania was free to answer, "I hate shopping."

"Well, we're heading home then. Try to calm down. Outsiders will know something's wrong with you prancing like that." To make her point, Serena turned to retrace the steps home, stopping occasionally to browse or chat as if the world awaited her every whim and no conspiracy was chasing her, carrying purchases.

As the white home appeared ahead of them, Lania eyed it, wondering if the high councilman had arranged for Serena to take Lania out solely to ready their return with soldiers. Five days had passed in silence. She could not expect it to continue.

Lania paused in the street. She was not usually fearful of confrontation; she loved the thrill of conflict, especially when the odds were stacked against her. The challenge of outwitting High Councilman Polfius should have excited her. She feared no Lionian!

Her fear was not her own, she recognized. Akara was worried about something. Her twin, distantly safe in the Corelands, was calling to her, passing on fear, and pain.

As Lania considered the sensation, it was as if a wall broke within her mind and the emotions flooded in.

Somewhere far north, Akara was screaming in frustration, and Lania felt her sister's voice as a throb that made her drop the shopping. The feelings were so potent, Lania could practically hear the voice of the Priestess amid the sudden desperation. Someone was in pain, calling for her, begging for salvation with their final breaths.

Lania spun without thought and instinctively caught the body that collapsed out of the shadows. Before she could identify it, she heard a voice croak, "Forgive me, Lania."

It was Binoran, although she had trouble recognizing him. Mostly unconscious, she could feel his mind waver through the sporadic prodding from Akara. The Priestess was insistent: in his broken dreams, Binoran called for her by name. The man who had given his life for her was dying.

A glance told her everything she feared was true.

His side had been sliced open by a whip, and his face was scarred to match his old mine wounds. One hand had been smashed bad enough that she made out tiny bones sticking out through the mangled mess. His face as pale as the bones, his skin gleamed with sweat as he trembled in her arms. He tried to speak for a second time, but only succeeded in gasping and groaning with pain in his struggle to stay awake. Her voice caught when she recognized the familiar signs of a man who had lost too much blood.

Not Binoran, she begged the One God and her sister. *Not Binoran...*

"Forgive..." he said again, and, for the first time, she heard the voices shouting through the market about an escaped slave and a reward for capture. The Lionian onlookers whispered and pointed.

"If I forgive you, you will go and die on me," Lania snapped at Binoran in Nurmi. "You will not die, Binoran. You will stay alive so I can tell you how cross I am."

She had to move before the guards arrived, and before the spectators figured out that the corpse she held was worth yorin to them. There was nowhere safe nearby, with only one possible exception, and she had to risk it.

Serena had walked on without acknowledging her; she would be at her house shortly. Lania did not dare use the front gate. Propping Binoran against her, she navigated back alleys to the rear of the high councilman's house at a run. "You will stay conscious, Binoran," she ordered. "I will not drag a dead body to the river. If you want more than the trenches, stay conscious."

Fumbling through the vines once she was certain the alley was vacant, Lania located the secret back door to the high councilman's garden and opened it. She did not have time to clean away the blood left behind as she dragged Binoran into the garden and shoved the entrance shut with one foot.

The biggest problem with the secret door was that it led directly into the garden, with only a handful of shrubs as cover. No matter which way one went from there, reaching the house required crossing in the open.

To her disappointment, it was not just soldiers who saw her emerge from the bushes with Binoran at her side. High Councilman Polfius was sitting under the trees with a book in hand. She stumbled to a halt as he slowly looked up.

For the second longest moment in her life, nothing moved. Lania froze with the half-dead man on her shoulder. Her hands were wet and sticky. She could feel blood seeping through her uniform where Binoran was pressed against her.

Hearing Binoran groan convinced her to speak. Her pride would not allow her to be seen, even just before Binoran, begging a Lionian for help. Instead, Lania lifted her head high and told him, "This man will stay here."

At last, the expression changed: the high councilman frowned. He took his time putting down the book and standing. "Our agreement is not even a quartercycle old," he said slowly, as if he did not hear the voices shouting beyond the walls, ordering the search of the houses in the area.

"And I am going against it," she snapped. Her shoulder ached with the weight it carried. "Either you help me, or I will take this entire household hostage," she threatened. Vaguely, she noticed the guards tense, but she did not care. While their employer considered what she had said, the guards slowly drew their swords. Lania reached for her knife.

Out of the corner of her eye, Lania saw the spymaster step into the garden from another door. A servant stood in the man's shadow as he said, "A diasists at the door, Aurion. They're looking for someone."

For a dozen more moments, the high councilman did not move. Lania held his stare in determination.

Finally, he lowered his book.

"Balvor," High Councilman Polfius called to one diasist, "take our visitor to one of the guest rooms. Tatkil herself will be needed at the door."

The guard took Binoran reluctantly from his Warrior. As quickly as she could, she told Binoran, "I will be back soon. Do not fear." In Lionian, wanting to ensure they understood her words, she added, "They will not harm you. Their lives depend on it." She could not tell if Binoran had understood, but she thought she saw him nod. The comment had, at the least, irritated the guards further. Or, she thought viciously, is it fear?

"Have Noria look him over. Tell her I want him treated like a Lionian patient," the high councilman said without acknowledging her threat. "Get changed quickly, Tatkil, and come to the front hall to be with your mistress. The rest of you," he ordered, "get back to work."

As he turned from her, she knew his eyes met those of the spymaster. She heard no words, but the man moved through the garden to the secret door.

She ran to her room and changed her uniform as quickly as she could. Once she had clean clothes, she returned to the garden to wash her neck and hands. Between rinses in the pond, she held her silver armband and prayed the One God kept Binoran alive long enough for her to get back to him.

Unable to believe the councilman, Lania took a detour to ensure Binoran was where the councilman had instructed. She was almost surprised to see a Lionian woman leaning over the small Nurmi man, whispering complaints but working on the bloody cuts with skilled hands.

She could not bring herself to be thankful, not to a Lionian. What now? What was he planning? Her master stood to lose everything. Even the charge of treason could ruin his entire household, regardless of the trial's success. Why would he take the chance?

She had no answer as she reached the front of the house where her mistress was at her loom in the library.

Hearing her arrive, High Councilman Polfius went to the door.

Although Serena initially shot Tatkil a glare, it vanished at once. Even Lania was impressed by the girl's self-control.

As the Warrior sat at her mistress' feet, Lania could hear the high councilman apologizing for the delay and asking the soldiers what they wanted. From the library, Lania overheard their report about a missing slave who had killed his master and escaped into this district. The slave had last been seen just outside his door, with a slave of his.

The high councilman told them in a calm voice she imagined he used mostly in the Councilhall, that he had only one slave, and she was with his sister in the other room. It was not even a lie.

For a moment, it seemed they would believe him and leave, but one voice insisted they see his slave to be sure. After all, the voice said, this was not merely an escaped slave, this was a murderer. In the silence, Lania imagined she saw the high councilman shrug in his casual way before leading the city guards to the library.

The moment a diasist arrived at the entry to the room, Lania spotted a smear of blood on her right hand. Before she could get the hand out of sight, Serena surprised her by knocking her cup off the loom and onto the floor. Scoffing at her slave as if it were her fault, Serena sharply told Lania to clean up the spill.

Tatkil's reaction was slowed by Lania's concern for Binoran and her shock at Serena's perceptiveness. But she recovered swiftly under Serena's stare and fetched a rag and cleaned up the spill, the cloth in her right hand concealing the evidence. Absentmindedly, Lania wiped the floor with her thoughts on Binoran.

Would he even be alive by the time she got back to him? She felt inside for Akara's feelings but detected only the Priestess' calm confidence. Either resting, Lania considered, or dead. How could she have left Binoran in the hands of a Lionian? How could she have trusted a Lionian? She had to get to him!

High Councilman Polfius, clearly practiced at diversion, started a conversation about the recent news of the White City. His friendly disposition succeeded in turning the attention from the slave. The diasists hardly looked at her again.

The floor had been dried and polished by the time Lania brought her attention back to her task. Serena ordered her to fetch more water, presumably because having her slave wipe a perfectly dry floor was becoming suspicious. Lania returned with the water and sat by the girl's feet as she worked at the loom, but the Warrior's eyes stayed on the hall. She had to get to Binoran. She had to help him.

With the high councilman nonchalantly discussing the gossip of the city, Lania feared their conversation would go on for hours. She could not tolerate the delay. It had been long enough already. What excuse could she give? Or would she even bother? Why not just run?

Before she could decide, the high councilman politely told the guards he had work to do in his reading room. Seeing Lania dressed in her slave uniform and now content with the high councilman's story, the soldiers bowed, thanked their superior, and left.

The instant they were out of view, Lania ran.

He was alive. The Lionian healer protested Lania's intrusion, but the Warrior ignored her flatly and took over. Frustrated that the Lionian would neglect it, she immediately drew a careful line of blood from Binoran's forehead to his chin to bind the mind to the body and prevent the mind from drifting loose in the Dreamworld and to the Gate. Feeling the line on his face, Binoran breathed easier.

The hand, Lania knew, would never work perfectly, but the part of her mind closest to the Priestess knew how to place the bones and splint the broken limb. She used the Lionian's supplies.

Let the One God watch him, she prayed with her sister as she cleaned, applied poultices, and stitched the rest of the injuries the Lionian had not gotten to. *One of your children is in pain*, Akara prayed with her. *Guide him, lend him strength, and stay with him...*

Without a thought to her duties as Tatkil, Lania stayed with Binoran long after darkness took the city. Closer than ever, Lania healed the injured body, and Akara tended the turbulent mind. With her soft confidence, she assured Lania that he was still alive.

When her mind felt it would slip into sleep, Lania sang.

The sung prayer had once been her lullaby. Long beyond the days when her father's voice had lulled her to sleep with the song, Lania used the prayer to clear her mind and brighten her soul. This time, Lania was surprised to feel Akara sing along.

The Corelands are quiet.
The people are sleeping.
The sun is slipping away,
slipping away
And the moon has risen high.
The dream time is nigh.

Sleep now, my child,
for He has come to watch you.
Sleep now, my child,
all is well around you.
Sleep now my child,
I am here to defend you.
Sleep now, my child,
and let the Dreamworld take you.

I dream of a home.
I dream of a land of peace.
I dream of freedom,
and I come home.

Long after the words had been sung, Lania soothed her spirit with humming. She sat, waiting, praying, refusing to let herself sleep, and watching the candle nearby shrink. It was not until later that she realized she was not alone in the room.

High Councilman Polfius stood at the door watching her. He had gone to a Council meeting earlier, she knew, and she had no doubt he had been asked about the confusion over the missing slave. Had he come to capture her? He might be able to. She would not leave without Binoran.

To comfort herself, she gripped the knife concealed under her uniform.

He was leaning against the doorway with his arms crossed and his eyes half closed so peacefully, Lania could not help but wonder if it had been the song that had caused him to stop and watch her. She had heard Lionian musicians play. Lionians had to be able to find joy in music at the least, even if their strings and horns were so different from Nurmi flute and drums.

She wished for a flute or drum to play with, to let him hear the song as she heard it in her memory.

He snapped out of the trance when she looked at him and met her stare with a look meant to get her attention. Binoran would rest better with the pollution of the Conquerors farther away. As Lania rose to follow him out of the room, she pulled her sleeve over the armband.

"The slave was found dead an hour ago," the high councilman told her in a whisper once they were clear of the room and heading down the stairs. "Apparently, he succumbed to the injuries his master inflicted. The body was dumped in the trenches."

Lania stopped walking without thinking. He had planted a body and distracted the guard.

"I want him out of the house, Lania," he told her as he continued down the hall. "I cannot be hiding escaped slaves."

She nodded and, restarting her feet, followed him into a sitting room at the bottom of the stairs. "He will be gone tomorrow," she said.

"Good." While he found a seat and collapsed, she paused on the step and worried for a moment if Binoran was all right. Akara answered her concerns with reassurance but, like a whisper blown on the night air, she added, *Sleeping deeper than most of my priests can meditate.*

Lania smiled in thanks for the thought, but also to acknowledge the Priestess' accomplishment. The Twins had always shared feelings, but the speech was new.

He must have seen her smile for, when Lania looked again at the high councilman, he wore a baffled expression.

Lania erased her smile. "Why did you do this?" she asked.

It was his turn to smile, which struck her as odd. He would have laughed, she suspected, if it would not have woken those nearby.

"Because the thorn has to stick in Dracus' side for a few days more. You have five days. I want slaves freed. I want Dracus distracted. I am now dictating the time."

He had said if any evidence led him to her, he would turn her in, yet he had not. He had said she must never use the household for anything, and she had done just that. She had walked into his grasp as the Warrior, and he had turned a blind eye. His hatred for Dracus could not be the only reason.

"Besides," he said, proving her right, "you defended my sister, and I have not forgotten that."

A Lionian who believed in honor? Impossible!

Despite Lania's dislike for the circumstances, the fact was that he had saved her life. He could have turned her in as he had promised and let Binoran die, but he had not. He had put himself at great risk to protect her.

By her name, she had to honor his selflessness. The idea confused her, yet she knew it was right.

"Do you know what a hair-debt is?" Lania asked. The question, put so bluntly, made him startle back. *He knows, of course he knows,* she scolded. He had books all over his office about Nurmi.

"When a Nurmi saves the life of another, they are given a lock of hair as a token of the debt between them. It can be claimed later for any task," he replied factually. His expression remained suspicious.

"Any task that does not go against one's family or tribe," she corrected. "That is the restriction of the debt."

He nodded to accept the new information.

Seeing the black hair and the sharp features of a Lionian turned her stomach, but she clung to the facts: he had saved her life. He acted with honor. Somehow, he was not the same as the others.

Avoiding his stare pointedly, Lania cut a lock of her hair.

"You have saved my life tonight. I honor that and offer you my debt."

She expected him to laugh or otherwise scoff, but Aurion merely stood and took the hair from her hand without a word.

She saw gravity in his expression and was content he understood. It was right. The One God was pleased.

"I must go back to Kaco," Lania said, returning down the corridor to escape his stare. He let her go.

She did not go back to Binoran's side immediately but stood around the corner, at the top of the stairs, her back pressed to the wall, trying to organize her thoughts.

She had never thought it possible. A hair-debt was sacred, and she had just given one to a Lionian. Had she done wrong? Her gut felt like she had swallowed stones.

As she stood around the corner, she heard voices in the room she had left.

"You are insane," Serena's voice said. "Grizzle is having a fit. The rumors of the escaped slave—"

"I pulled a body from the prison," he answered, indifference in his voice. "It was branded and everything."

Lania heard shuffling footsteps, but the voices remained in the room. Pacing again?

"This is such a risk!" the sister chastised her older brother. "Think about it! Lania! The Warrior herself. You have allied yourself with an enemy of Lione! And a Nurmi! How could you—"

The high councilman's voice sounded tired when he answered. "Councilman Balfidius went missing yesterday. Dracus is targeting those who oppose him."

Lania presumed the long pause was out of shock. What could Serena possibly say?

The councilman's weary voice continued a moment later, "My name is on the list, Serena. Demons, it's probably next. He knows I have votes in the Councilhall, and he wants them. Either he goes, or I do."

"But... but this is not..."

"I made an oath to not harm the sovereign, Serena, but I never said I would actively stop others. He has forced my hand."

The finality of the comment left even Lania feeling cold.

"I feel like I understand *her* right now better than I understand my fellow councilmen," the high councilman added. "She risked her life for one of her friends. Demons, she just gave me a hair-debt, a sacred tradition that predates all Lionian contact. She stuck to a code of honor despite my being her enemy! How can I ignore that?"

Lania heard the disbelief in Serena's voice as she replied, "You are impressed by her."

"And you are the second person to tell me that," the high councilman admitted. "I didn't think Grizzle was wrong then, either."

A Lionian who defends his family, believes in honor, and is flattered by the hair-debt...

Feeling her gut relax, Lania nodded to herself as she returned to Kaco's side, content that the Lionian understood perfectly the sanctity of the gift she had gifted him.

The slave was gone by the next evening, and Aurion did not even want to know how she had done it.

Serena, and Tatkil for that matter, spent the day with Tatkil's old mistress Julti, and Aurion's sister returned with plenty of news. Julti was unhappy with her husband and did not hesitate to complain about her unlucky life to anyone who would listen. Serena, the innocent country girl fresh to the White City, was happy to.

Hearing how much Julti had so told Serena about the plans to have the assassin report to Galfium in the palace library made Aurion wonder how much was reaching the wrong ears. Dracus must have known something was amiss, but it was hard to see if he knew what.

Aurion was relieved, as was much of the Council, when the Warrior attacked. Aurion nearly laughed in the Councilhall when he heard that the Warrior stole, like a taunt, thirty-three slaves from the home of Councilman Volustio in the Newhope District. Other escapes had been poor men, markets, and other scantily protected areas, but this time, the slaves had been from a councilman, essentially the sovereign's front door.

Volustio was furious at the savage who had robbed him of half his slave population. He called a meeting with the sovereign and would have called an emergency Council meeting if he had not been stopped. The effect on Dracus was perfect. The sovereign spent over four hours venting frustrations and plotting retaliation during a meeting with Volustio. In the background, final preparations were made.

After all the information was in his hands, Aurion called Grizzle and, with Serena, met in the office. Lania sat at her mistress' feet, acting the part of the slave perfectly.

"They have only the support of half the guard," Aurion said, thinking the day through. "The loyal half will want blood for the death of their sovereign, and they will not be alone. The people of Lione are prideful. No assassin should escape with their life, and Vanius knows it, yet he has done nothing to arrange for a scapegoat. I do not think Vanius knows the guards plan to kill the assassin to save face. If he does know, he certainly does not seem to care."

"What of the blade hidden in the sovereign's room?" his sister asked.

Aurion could only shrug. "They have ignored it. Ideally, Dracus will not have the chance to even get to it, but..."

He paced again in silence. Serena looked to Grizzle for an explanation, but the spymaster knowingly waited to see where Aurion's train of thought would end.

"Polfius never reached for the sword," Aurion said. "When I pulled the assassin from..." Mindful of the Nurmi in the room, he stopped the sentence and revised it. "When I stopped the assassination, Polfius never reached for his sword. He reached for an item."

One of Grizzle's eyebrows rose. "Magic?" he asked.

"A green glass orb with gold," Aurion remembered. "It… it did strange things to my head as soon as he touched it, only I didn't realize it until after he'd let it go and the powers were gone."

"Strange things?"

"I wanted to defend Polfius anyway, but I don't think I could have done him harm with him holding that orb."

They considered the information until Serena offered, "Well, I don't think we want him getting his hands on that item while the assassin is in the room. You are a councilman, brother. Could you possibly get into the bedroom?"

Aurion and Grizzle both shook their heads.

"I would have to change the guard," Aurion explained for Serena. "Those that are on guard tomorrow are with Vanius—he made sure of that—and I do not trust them. If it meant saving their heads, which it could, they would turn against me as quickly as they did Dracus. If I do anything out of place now, Dracus will have me arrested outright. If it was not for Lania's attack last night, I suspect we would have seen arrests today. He knows far too much."

Tatkil did not react to her name, and Aurion was pleased. Since she had given him her debt, she had calmed dramatically. If he had not already known her real name, he would not have guessed it from her vacant stare.

As he looked at her, Tatkil seemed, as Gitarius had once described her, simple. The blankness in her eyes suggested she would only understand if spoken to directly, slowly, and using short words. He suspected she wanted to know why he was staring at her, but no slave spoke without being bidden to.

"Lania," he said to her, and the ignorance drained from her face. The blank stare was instantly replaced by sapphires that showed only determination.

"What?" she asked, and the last illusion of Tatkil was gone. Her voice was sharp, telling him without needing any further words that he had better have something worth saying.

"I want to claim the hair-debt," he replied.

Her expression softened. Her answer, though, he did not understand.

"Brek cem ug pi ouy refi?" she said as she stood, placed a finger to her forehead, and ran it under her eye. For him, she translated into Lionian, "What need have you of me?"

He could tell by the way his sister shifted that she was uneasy with the dealings. Lania was already a criminal living in their house, and she flaunted it by speaking blatantly in Nurmi in his presence, as if taunting him, but Aurion doubted Lania had spoken maliciously. To him, it seemed she was responding to the debt as she would have if he had been a Nurmi. He could hardly be offended by the respect she was trying to show him.

Besides, breaking the Language Law was the least of his concerns.

"I want you to move the sphere from atop the sovereign's bedside table to beneath it tomorrow night before he retires for the evening."

With a thoughtful frown, Lania nodded. "I hope you have a better plan than simply asking me to break into the sovereign's bedroom. The palace is difficult to get into, even for me," she warned.

"I do," he replied with a look to Grizzle, which won him an understanding nod. They had once planned for such an eventuality. With the spymaster's help, it could be done.

"And the blade your sister mentioned? It would not do for him to pull a weapon on your assassin."

"Not my assassin," Aurion corrected.

"Whatever," she answered, smirking slightly.

"There are several weapons in that room. If you have time to move them, then move them, but your priority must be the orb," Aurion answered, unsure if her smile should comfort or worry him.

"Then destroy the lock of hair I gave you and consider me bound to your task," she replied.

For his sake alone, he was certain, she bowed in the Lionian manner.

CHAPTER 16

As she smuggled Binoran out, Lania opened the path for her companions outside the walls to come in and led them to a hiding place in Binoran's warehouse room, Haro among them. The thirty-three Nurmi slaves stolen from Councilman Volustio now also resided in the warehouses, as the building had not yet changed hands and the Lionian master, being dead, no longer needed it.

Although the Lionians were aware of Volustio's losses, few had heard of the scattering of other escapes across the city. Any remaining Nurmi helping her were waiting for the moment to depart. Lania knew her time in Lione was done. It was time for all of them to go home.

The death of the sovereign tonight would mask their departure perfectly.

As she walked, Lania adjusted her new uniform and again cursed the way it slipped around her shoulders and bagged around her waist. It had not been made for her, probably not even for a Nurmi. The high councilman had not said where he had gotten it, but Lania suspected it was something he had stolen as a precaution. It was an outfit of tights and a coat in purple and black, with sparkling clean white lace and silver buttons. *Likely difficult to keep clean*, she thought, especially for the slaves who worked cleaning up after Conquerors.

The sleeves were short and only reached part of the way down her upper arm, where they ended in a puff of lace that tickled her arm constantly. At least, the high councilman had pointed out, it would help conceal the incorrect brand she wore.

She thought he had come to regret branding her, although she could not be certain if his frown at the mark was because it would tie her to him if she was caught or if he regretted having harmed her. It was equally possible he feared he had offended her. Many Lionians had died for having offended the Nurmi Warrior. He seemed to know the details of those cases intimately.

The leggings were similar to those of her old uniforms and did not quite reach her knees. She had already decided to get rid of the shoes early as they were too big and made running difficult, but the councilman had insisted that they be black leather shoes, with a silver buckle to match. At least it had a cap to go with it, and she took a moment to tuck her braids under the lop-sided bunch of purple material.

The silver armband, with the shorter sleeves, could be seen if the sleeve slipped up at all, but it had been Lania's turn to insist on something, and she had refused to leave it behind. She would need the luck of the One God.

He had managed to convince her out of her knife, which annoyed her. She hated, with a passion, being unarmed. All her life, with precious few exceptions, she had carried a blade. Even as a slave, she had always had a knife ready, which was illegal, and had both offended and surprised her master. He had insisted that she be rid of it. It would hardly do, should she be arrested for something so simple at the wrong time.

Despite being rather tempted to make another run for slaves, his warning stuck with her and sent her, in the hours before honoring the debt to the high councilman, to the warehouses.

As she walked among the freed slaves, she was careful to comfort and reassure them but, once beyond their eyes, she became restless. The high councilman expected her to be in the palace before sundown, but he was busy with other things in the meantime. Tatkil was not needed. Even Grizzle had decided she need not be followed; she had checked but found no one spying on her. Lania had nothing to do but wait.

She could not paint her face or let her hair debts down, making her feel sorely ill-prepared for her chore. Haro showed her to a small room on the second floor where they could plan, but they quickly found there was nothing to discuss. Everyone knew the role they would play come nightfall. Lania took to pacing, a new habit for her until Haro brought out covered swords.

Feeling the sword again in her hand, Lania calmed. For the first time in years, she was back where she belonged. She threw aside the high councilman's hat and let her debts, now dozens in number, dance around her face. She breathed deeply, taking in the scents of the room with a focus priests would envy. Although the room was musky, she closed her eyes and smelled the perfume of evergreens in the air around her. In the darkness, she saw each needle on the dark green pines of her home and felt the breeze cool her blood.

Haro was similarly armed and offered her a spar.

When they clashed, Haro proved he had returned to his previous greatness since escaping the prison years ago. Lania, so long without a sword, felt herself marked by the coal-coated covers of the swords as often as her sword caught Haro's skin. As her heart raced, the swords moving methodically, something unforgivable stirred in the Warrior.

Beyond many horizons, the Priestess met with a priest in the Grove as the sun set above the living ceiling of giant cedars. In her role as Priestess, Akara had shared her bed with many others, but these had been chosen by the One God's traditions. Now, visited by one of her priests, Akara's heart fluttered innocently, and warmth, buried under priestess robes, arose powerfully.

When her prayers were done, the observing priest entered the cedar circle and offered the Priestess an Altio's bloom, whose petals were used in the creation of love potions by Lionian alchemists because of their beautiful scent. A confession followed, and the priest kneeled before her, swearing on his soul that, for his love of her, he would die. The thought terrified the Priestess but, at the same time, wooed by emotions that were as unfamiliar to her as a Lionian sword, she found herself drawn to it.

But her duty was to the Corelands, not to herself. She could not allow herself to be unduly tainted by others.

Despite the distance between them, Lania felt Akara's desire keenly but, not bound by traditions, Lania did not reject the emotion.

As she pivoted around Haro's lunge, passing close enough for skin to touch skin, she felt her body answer. She could smell only Haro, sweating from the dance, and felt her heart pound to see the passion in his eyes. She would never have expected his desire, but, even as she noticed it, she was aware it had always been present. Even more unexpectedly, Lania found she wanted him in return.

For nearly three years, she had been abandoned to the enemy's city and forbidden the company of her people. She was a grown woman. Her body surged with the thought of the fighter's body near.

In the forest grove, Akara collapsed into the wildflowers at her feet and pushed away the priest when he rushed to her side. Shaking and clutching her head, the Priestess demanded Toval depart at once.

As she spun to avoid Haro's attack, Lania slipped up inside his guard and against him. Pressing her back to his chest, she felt his empty left hand wrap around her waist like a serpent. Her stomach knotted.

She could have escaped. She could have pulled away or used the sword to mark him and carry on, but the Warrior had no wish to break their contact.

The sword fell to the ground. Lania slid her hand into his, palm to palm.

His restraint dissolved. He spun her around violently, forced her back against the nearest wall, and covered her mouth with his in a single motion. Ages of suppressed emotions flooded in, smothering her. The grip of his right hand in hers pinched. Moments later, as his left hand tore at the buttons, they both toppled backward onto a Lionian mattress.

And when the pain was too much, she cried out and Haro, his face buried in her hair-debts, answered with two words; "My thanks."

The minutes passed furiously. He was fierce with her and she ached when at last he stopped, but she did not resist. He collapsed at her side with a hand on her exposed stomach and, with his head against her shoulder, fell asleep.

After a prolonged hesitation, the room came back into focus. Blankets and pillows lay strewn about the room where Lania lay naked on the Lionian mattress, bruised, sore, and bleeding. The whole world pressed against her skull, threatening to crush her. The words "My thanks" repeated in her head, making her cringe.

Thanks? For this? Was he so grateful that only the Priestess had been strong?

Exhausted and trembling, Lania forced her eyes closed to shut out the world. Somehow, she drifted into dreams and arrived in a small white room made of Lionian stone. Although there was no source of light, not even a window, the room was softly lit as if by moonlight. On a mattress at the center of the room, with her knees drawn to her chin, sat Akara.

The dreamed room seemed to shrink to include only the Twins.

When Lania rose slowly, the ground was wet beneath her, and she realized that she had been lying in a pool of blood. The inside of her legs felt raw and her mouth was dry as she moved silently to Akara's side and waited. Feeling her sister with her, the Priestess lifted her head from her hands and the tears falling down her face in the false moonlight became evident.

The Warrior was not surprised to see them, but she found it easy to pull herself from the Priestess' pain, just as she distanced her own emotions. She did not acknowledge how her stomach twisted when she realized where the blood was from.

Sitting beside Akara, Lania put an arm around her sister as if to comfort a child.

"I sent him away," Akara said with a shiver. "I could not let it happen. I could not... Not now, not him. My body is for the One God. I could not allow it." The Priestess' head rested against the Warrior's shoulder, as if they were children once more, hiding from the outside world and knowing no other would hear them and understand. The Warrior could not be weak. The Priestess could make no mistakes.

"You felt..." Lania began, but she knew it was unnecessary to finish.

Her sister nodded against her. "To be touched, to be held, to be loved by another," the Priestess mumbled. "It felt so wonderful. He loved you for a moment. He truly cared."

"And now?"

Akara lifted her head and looked at the Warrior's face as she searched deep inside for the emotions of her twin. Because of the distance that separated their bodies, the weak emotions remained faint. "Nothing," Akara finally answered. "You are ... empty."

With one arm around her sister, Lania smiled feebly. It was gone. All the passion, all the desire, all the love, was gone. Thinking about Haro now, she felt void of anything.

"Regret," Akara told her. "You regret it."

Dropping her stare to avoid meeting that of her sister, Lania accepted Akara was right. She regretted the weakness she had shown. "He does not understand," Lania said at length. "He will never understand."

Akara nodded, knowing all the words Lania had not spoken aloud, all the feelings that wandered in her heart, and the painfully absent ones.

Haro was one of the people closest to her, and she knew he would be there when she needed him, but beyond that, their relationship was weak. She could not ask for his help or advice without destroying part of the legend he followed. His obedience was blind.

And now? Nothing would remain the same if she allowed that to fail. A change in her relationship with him would cause a change in everything. She would become mortal in their eyes. She would be Lania, and the Warrior would lose strength.

He needed the Warrior, not Lania. It was the Warrior he had lusted after, and it was the Warrior that had accepted him. Once the moment passed, Lania was again alone. Worse, for it left no room for doubt, she realized she would forever be alone. She needed her solitude, needed to disappear at an instant's notice and be accountable to none. Haro would never give her that freedom if he loved her.

"Not alone," Akara whispered, resting her head once more against the Warrior's muscled shoulder. "I am here."

The comfort felt as distant as the Priestess herself.

As Akara cried for them both, Lania closed her eyes and tried to force out the knots in her stomach. She shuddered as her mind slipped away from the Dreamworld, knowing what she had to do.

The sun had touched the horizon when Lania woke to the disarrayed Lionian room with the large warrior beside her, a satisfied smile brightening his face in the shadows. Slowly, but with all the haste she could manage, she wriggled out of his arms. Fetching his knife, she tucked the blade into her hair and turned her attention to her body. Revolted by it, she set immediately to clean herself.

Before she finished, Haro slipped up behind her on feet meant to pass in silence on the fallen leaves of the Corelands. Softly, he kissed her cheek, a hand reaching around her waist to hold her against him.

She ripped herself from his grip and spun. Her hand snatched the knife from its place, and she found herself holding it before her as she would have faced a Lionian. For the first time in her life, she felt timid by her nakedness and wished she had thought to cover herself.

Haro took a step back as he saw the blade, but once past the initial shock, he smiled and let his eyes look her over.

She was still partially red from her blood, and she felt dirty even in places where she had no mark from the sword. Her skin tingled where he had touched her.

"What troubles you?"

There was no answer to give. She tore her eyes from Haro and looked for her clothing, letting the knife lower. Was she mad? Would she use the knife against him? How could she have done that to one of her people?

But the reason was clear. She could not have him near her. The Warrior could not be human, be weak.

He seized the opportunity and reached for her. The moment his finger touched her arm, she dodged away, and the knife twitched in her hand. She refused to let it strike, but it took effort.

"Stay away from me," she heard her voice say frigidly. She felt she should have shouted, but only the hoarse command escaped her.

He paused and did not follow as she found the uniform and rapidly donned it. As she finished, he said, "I did not mean to hurt you, Warrior. I know it can be painful."

She lifted the knife. Although she was unsure if she was capable of using it against him, she was desperate to put some distance between them. Seeing the blade, Haro stopped his advance.

"What have I done to wrong you?" he pleaded.

She felt her body tremble, ready to defend herself, and the thought frightened her. She was the Warrior. She could not harm a Nurmi.

With more determination than she thought she possessed, she drew her mind in and breathed deeply. Her eyes closed for only a moment, but when they opened again, she had buried her regret. In the shadows of her mind, she regretted being cruel, but it was a necessary precaution.

"It shall not happen again," her voice said.

Had she used the knife to pierce his heart, she doubted he would have looked more pained, but the moment of agony was brief. In the next instant, Haro's face twisted into a grimace that could have frightened children on Spirit's Eve. Lania ignored his rage and set her stare coolly, betraying nothing. During the moments it took him to find his voice, she spoke again.

"You know what is expected. I will meet you at the Palace District entrance. May the One God guide you surely." With memories of a stubborn high councilman in her head, she tossed the knife aside and picked up her cap. Before Haro could reply, she was out the door and down the stairs.

As she exited, something crashed against the wall. Lania did not even pause to consider what furniture Haro had broken.

Sitting by the window that let him see the water clock, Aurion waited, counting the minutes. There was nothing left for him to do. Either it worked or it did not. It was out of his hands.

He was still sitting there when he heard the news of the arrests. Dracus had recovered from his distraction too fast. Vanius and his supporters had been caught. The assassin was among those imprisoned.

Aurion did not know if she was in the palace yet, but there was no way for him to find out. He could not warn Lania that the situation had changed.

He moved to the garden to wait for Lania to return, not knowing why he was confident she would.

CHAPTER 17

Once in the streets, Lania's defenses shattered, and she fled into the White City blindly. She ran until her lungs ached and her legs burned, numbing her to their tenderness, stumbling often in the ill-fitting shoes. It was not until she arrived at High Councilman Polfius' house that she realized what she had done and was able to stop. She felt her eyes flush with tears as she leaned against a wall in the fading light, her chest heaving.

She forced the tears back, swallowed to clear her throat of the lump, and set her gaze to the stars.

With only a few words, she had broken Haro's heart. Somehow, she felt the pain as well.

Akara's mind was untangling, and Lania knew her twin was meditating within the Dreamworld. The peace of her sister slowly filtered into the Warrior. Lania's heart slowed its pace. Although she wished for the river and its cleansing waters, she contented herself with the mental calm of her sister and the tears that the Priestess shed for her, knowing she would cry none of her own.

As Lania set her feet onto the path that would take her to the Palace District, she pushed Haro's voice from her head. The slaves were leaving tonight. It had been too dangerous to send them out with Volustio and others, striving to find them.

If all went as the councilmen had planned, they should have plenty of distractions to make their escape. The sky was clear tonight, and the stars would guide them easily. Haro would lead them.

She turned her head back to the path she was walking as that thought cascaded down an unwanted path. *My thanks…* It was nothing. It had meant nothing. Akara had done as much on Spirit's Eve every year, and even on New Year's Night. It meant nothing to the Priestess. Lania saw no reason it should bother the Warrior either.

To be held, to be loved. For a moment, he actually cared…

The entire Palace District consisted of the sovereign's enormous palace. Very few people passed under the arch leading into the district, and the guard stopped every person. It was the cleanest of the districts, with the streets swept of the daily dust and kept empty of merchants or vagabonds. There were, some said, more gardeners and slaves in the district than spires in the city, and it showed in the elegant displays of flowers along the roadways.

But it was still a tall, white, boring building with bars over the windows and shutters that locked tightly. Even with guards more numerous than the rodents, the Lionians seemed to fear every shadow that passed them by.

It was still light, but the sun was casting long shadows from behind the immense palace. Three times as large as any other councilman's home, the palace could have sheltered the entire Nurmi population with enough room for their animals as well. It was home, the high councilman had told her, to an assortment of Lionian servants and other slaves, as well as the sovereign, a good part of the guard, and any family the sovereign had. Regardless, more than half of the rooms of the building were empty.

It was a symbol, she thought with a sad smile, of the way the Sovereignty was run in general.

She slipped her hand up the sleeve and touched the cold metal of her armband to her fingers. *One God, lead me,* she prayed silently. *What have I done?*

No one gave her answers.

Getting into the Palace District proved to be simple. The high councilman had ambushed a Nurmi slave and smuggled her out of the district the day before. Thanks to Naino, who would escape with the others later, Lania knew the layout of the palace, the expectations of the guards, and the procedures the slaves in the palace were meant to know. If all went well, Lania would be cleaning the sovereign's room before bedtime, able to move the orb to a place the sovereign would not find. Then Lania could leave, and the debt given to a Lionian would be paid. Then—she felt her heart dance lightly—she could go home.

The freedom to go home was worth the pain. It was just one more battle. She would bear it, then she would go home.

She was stopped at every gate and asked about her business, but it was clear the guards did not remember Naino enough to even notice the age difference between the woman they normally saw and the intruder. Lania's quiet stature and shy glances meant she was allowed past the reinforced metal doors into the inner palace.

She did not pause to gawk at the palace, although it was tempting. Every surface had been carved or plastered with a mosaic of colors bright enough to shame a new spring rainbow. Where there was no color, gold predominated, from the candelabras to the tips of the spears of the statues that lined halls. Purple was prominent in many rooms, with silver curtains that sparkled in the sunset and cast shining specks.

Lania's mind remained fixed as she made her way through the halls, recalling Naino's instructions as she went to keep herself from getting lost, either in the palace or in her thoughts. Fortunately, the older Nurmi had known every turn well enough to walk it blind. Soon Lania found herself holding cleaning rags and a bucket of water in front of the sovereign's chambers.

Her experience as Tatkil kept Lania's posture submissive. These guards knew Naino and questioned Lania on the regular slave's whereabouts. With a little hinting, they eventually decided that Naino was ill, and the master had sent another in her place. Lania was allowed in.

The suite was elaborately decorated, but the novelty had already worn off, and Lania cast only a cursory glance at the golden trim and glowing brass hangers. Magic radiated through here, adjusting the illumination as if reading her mind. Through the lounging room, she found the bedroom. Passing a wall-sized mosaic that depicted a silver dragon with the sovereign's seal around its neck, she went straight to the bed and found the orb tucked behind the lamp on the bedside table. Cautious of magic, she poked the item first gingerly. When she felt no response, she tentatively picked it up.

It felt cold, heavy, and useless in her hand. With a shrug, she tucked it into a corner under the table where a less suspicious person might assume it had fallen.

Beside the bed was a sword as well, a surprisingly plain dius at odds with the rest of the ornate room. It lay pinned by the bedside table, the grip within easy reach.

Lania pulled it down and slid it under the bed.

Done, she started for the door, thinking up an excuse for the guards should they ask. Perhaps she had forgotten something...

The door to the chamber opened, and Lania quickly slid back into the bedroom. Seeking a hiding place seemed foolish; she was Nurmi. She would hide in the open.

When the intruder burst into the bedroom, Lania was cleaning the floor. As a disinterested slave, she lifted her head long enough to see the intruders before looking back at the floor in mock inattention.

It was the sovereign, of that Lania had no doubt. She had not seen this sovereign before, but he had the same expression of supremacy all sovereigns shared. His beard was freshly cut around his thin, pale face that seemed pink only when compared to his spotless white costume. He was dressed in his proper robes, sparkling from walking only freshly scrubbed halls. The edges were trimmed in black with gold on top and gold chains decorated him like a Santan dancer.

He barged into the room, taking no visible notice of Lania. Following him quickly came a councilman in a sash-less white robe with billowing black sleeves. It took her a blink to recognize Gitarius, but she put her head down and prayed he would not recognize her.

"So, it was for tonight!" Sovereign Dracus shouted as he threw open the doors, and Lania's heart stopped for a moment.

"Yes, Sovereign," Gitarius behind him confirmed with a bow that dipped much lower than Lania was accustomed to seeing. Gitarius had always excelled at groveling.

"They have been arrested?" Dracus demanded.

The councilman recovered poorly from the bow and, for a moment, bore the expression of a man on whom a bee had just landed. The man faced an unhappy choice: he could simply leave it alone and hope it went away, or he could swat it, risking being stung. Either way, he was in danger of getting hurt.

Seeing this, the sovereign demanded in a deep, foreboding voice, "What is it?"

"All the councilmen were arrested moments ago, as you ordered, Sovereign..." Gitarius squeaked like a dog that had just had his tail stepped on. He would have stopped, but the glare of his sovereign insisted he continue with, "...except High Councilman Dobrius."

"Except?" the sovereign shouted, and the guards at the door flinched as if anticipating a blow.

Gitarius bowed and backed away, which ran him into the wall by the door.

"He knew of our coming and had already fled the city, Exalted One, claiming holidays. It is thought he is heading east to—"

"Go get him!" ordered the sovereign.

Gitarius nodded hard. "Of course, Sovereign!" This time, when he bowed, he could have kissed his knees. "We are already pursuing him." This seemed to calm Sovereign Dracus, and Gitarius relaxed enough to begin slowly straightening.

"You have the assassin?" Dracus said in a dangerous half-whisper.

"Yes, Sovereign," Gitarius joyously reported once he got himself standing straight.

That was the end. The assassin had been captured, and the councilmen involved were already chained somewhere in the prison. Lania thought of High Councilman Polfius and wondered if he was among them. She had not seen him during the last day because of time spent—an uncomfortable feeling creeping into her chest and stomach—with Haro. Surely her master was clever enough to keep his involvement secret.

"There is new information," Gitarius added reluctantly before the sovereign dismissed him. By the man's dithering, Lania suspected it was bad news.

The sovereign was not yet concerned. He filled a cup from a ready pitcher, then watered it down with unexpected calm. Lania felt more than saw his eyes on her for a moment, and she scrubbed hard on the stain she had discovered by the foot of the bed to assume the role of the slave. Her mind was still on the high councilman and the failure of the assassination. Would Sovereign Dracus be ready in the morning to follow the trail of the thirty-odd men and women running north? How did this change things for her people?

"What new information?" the sovereign said once it became evident that Gitarius needed encouragement.

Gitarius went to the doors and closed them, and the sovereign's eyebrows rose in answer. The next sentence fully explained why he had shut out the soldiers. "It seems High Councilman Polfius may have been involved," Gitarius whispered.

Lania risked looking up just in time to catch a view of the sovereign's face as he heard the news. There was no attempt at restraint. The sovereign snarled like an animal, caught the nearest object, which happened to be the cup he had just filled, and threw it across the room.

"Aurion!" he yelled, dissipating the attempted secrecy instantly.

Gitarius cringed, but he dared not speak.

Tatkil answered as the slave: she picked up her rags and bucket and went to the spill. The Warrior risked another glance in the sovereign's direction as she crossed the room.

"You clever demon! I knew it!" the sovereign accused as he knocked the rest of the things from the tabletop and stamped on them furiously like a child throwing a tantrum. Then he stormed to the bedside table.

Lania's stomach dropped, knowing what he was looking for. When he failed to find the magical orb, his stare roved through the room accusingly. "Who else has been in here?" he demanded. He was more coherent. Having regained his composure swiftly, he recognized the absence of the orb.

Gitarius' eyes darted about as if seeking someone to redirect the blame to. Overlooking the slave and finding no one else, he fumbled out, "The guards outside might know."

With a victorious grin, the sovereign leaned over and pulled the orb from where Lania had hidden it. The moment his hand touched the magic trinket, something powerful swept over Lania, but it slid off her like a mountain stream breaking over a river stone. Gitarius stood straighter, his eyes flashing black before returning to dark brown. His breath was tense.

"Now," Dracus said, "I ask again; who could have moved this?"

"The guards, a servant, a slave..." Gitarius said, his words running together.

Lania realized she was staring at the sovereign and his magic trinket, but when the sovereign noticed, he didn't seem offended. Instead, he spoke to her directly, "Slave, do you know who moved this? Was it you?"

Lania stood, keeping her posture defeated and low. "No, master." She stuttered deliberately. The lies came easily. "I do not know how it moved."

"Part of the plot," Sovereign Dracus decided. Keeping the orb in hand, he stormed to the doors. Gitarius scrambled to open them for him. "We will have to ask the man who knows everything in Lione. Come, it is time we bring this trinket to visit High Councilman Polfius."

The doors clattered closed behind the two men, leaving Lania again alone in the dim chambers.

Relaxing Tatkil, Lania stood straight.

The orb was magical, as Aurion had suspected, but if it forced obedience or truthfulness, it had failed on her. That did not surprise her. Nurmi knew that magic was broken by truth and, sharing a soul with the Priestess, who was truth incarnate, protected her.

Now left in the room alone, knowing there was no assassin to rid the world of the sovereign as Councilman Polfius wished, Lania's plans were foiled. She had freed a large number of slaves: they were staged in the warehouse, ready for escape over the walls. But she had been counting on another Day of Defiance with a dead sovereign to keep the Lionians occupied. Now, they had no cover through which to escape.

Keeping a wary eye on the doors, Lania tidied the mess on the floor and replaced it on the table. Spotting an array of ornate weapons and jewelry, Lania turned her cleaning into a search. A plan forming, she rushed after the sovereign with a bejeweled dagger hidden in the folds of her tunic.

Aurion sat with Grizzle in the office, a tense silence between them. The spymaster had delivered the news; Dracus had arrested the would-be assassin and was now rounding up councilmen involved with the plot against him. Vanius was already residing in a prison cell, awaiting trial and expected execution. Aurion had not heard from Lania yet and wondered if he would. It would make sense for her to leave now, although with the guard out in force and looking for conspirators, her job would be more difficult. But she had no reason to return to Aurion's household now, at the least.

The knock on the door was harried. When admitted, the servant, Guilion, was paler than Aurion had ever seen, and he'd known Guilion through more than one rough pregnancy with his wife. Guilion was always a man of few words, preferring to do his duty than talk about it. He wordlessly handed Aurion the letter.

The sovereign's seal was fresh enough to be warm. The instructions were short: a summons.

"No guessing then," Aurion said. "Wish me luck."

"Make your own luck," Grizzle grumbled, a familiar mantra that made Aurion smile and shake his head in helplessness.

"I've either done so or I haven't. Now I find out which."

Aurion decided on haste, hoping it would leave Dracus less time to prepare and show obedience if this was not merely an execution order. He liked to think there would be more ceremony if Dracus had decided to see him killed, something to appease the soldiers and the masses, but he wasn't sure anymore. There was an assassin loose. If Dracus thought he was involved, the sovereign might not stand on ceremony.

None of his soldiers could accompany Aurion beyond the palace gate. He was on his own.

The palace was busy and bright, and so perfectly normal it confused Aurion as he was admitted and led through the familiar hallways to what he ultimately realized was the observatory. It seemed every sovereign eventually chose their favorite room; Dracus claimed the view of the stars helped him feel closer to the gods. It was in the circular, tall room that Aurion met Sovereign Dracus to hear his fate.

Aurion mentally assigned suspected names to the palace soldiers he passed on his way into the darkened room, but their helms were an older style and closed over the faces. It did not help that many of the men likely to be closest to the sovereign this night would hold loyalty to Vanius more than Dracus. Surely, Dracus knew as much, seeing as he had arrested the assassin and many of the conspirators. Perhaps in response to that, Dracus appeared to have a dozen slaves attending him instead of Lionian servants and only two bodyguards at the door. A bustle of Yeahsin, Santan, and Nurmi slaves moved around the room, adjusting lamps and shades over the high windows hiding the stars, while others fed him fresh, candied nuts and poured him and Councilman Gitarius wine.

As soon as Aurion's foot touched the tiled floor of the dim observatory, a wave of energy flowed over him. He felt as though he had walked into a sauna, the pressure of the air making his skin prickle, even though it carried no heat. His heart jumped into his throat, and he stumbled in shock. Only as he righted himself did he spot the glass and gold orb Dracus held in his hand on the armrest of the plush chair.

Despite delicate inquiries—a substitute for the more intensive research he planned to undertake once he was no longer under scrutiny by the sovereign—Aurion had been unable to learn much about the magic of the orb. Polfius had never explained it to Aurion, not even to admit to its presence. But while he did not fully understand its powers, the effects were undeniably potent.

As he righted himself, Aurion realized the slave now presenting a tray of wine to Councilman Gitarius, standing at Dracus' side, was neither the sovereign's nor a slave. At first, he feared Lania would be recognized, but the fear quickly left; Gitarius did not acknowledge her and certainly did not look at her face to identify her. She fit in eerily well among the slaves, but she let her slave persona slip as she passed Gitarius, meeting Aurion's eye. It amazed him the difference between Tatkil and Lania. Even the way she stood for that instant was confident, not cowed.

She was showing him something as he stepped forward to present himself to the sovereign. She had a dagger in hand, but as she slipped behind Gitarius, the blade vanished. When she served the wine, she drew Gitarius to one side, revealing that she'd placed the ornate, sheathed dagger under Gitarius' belt.

The man couldn't reach it to fight, and neither of them could harm Dracus, Aurion was certain, thanks to the magic orb. But then why arm Gitarius at all?

It struck him in the next breath, and he was further impressed. He couldn't nod to show her he understood, but she had already dropped her stare and moved on, leaving the room as a subtle slave.

Aurion bowed to the sovereign, but when he tried to speak, his tongue stuck. He revised what he planned to say and managed to get out, "To what do I owe this summons?" He would have rather said "pleasure" instead of "summons," but the word would not come. If the orb was controlling his words, this was going to be complicated.

Dracus smiled, his beard splitting wide to show his teeth as if ready to snap his jaw shut on passing prey.

"I have heard terrible things, High Councilman."

It took all his skill to keep a calm facade. "What things, Sovereign?"

"I heard you knew of this threat."

Aurion debated trying to deny it, but the strange powers over him would limit his lies. He had to find a way around. "I never had a hand in a threat against you. How could I? I am not in your confidence, unlike others who stand here." The magic did not have a problem with his words; they were true, each in isolation.

"But you knew," Dracus spat, his voice echoing in the empty space.

Aurion's mind felt sluggish as he sorted through answers. Nothing he *could* say, he wanted to say. Finally, he decided on a limited truth. "I swore to follow my sovereign's every order. But I am not responsible for his safety if others endanger him."

Dracus broke out laughing, making Aurion nervous. It seemed a semi-crazed sound, the stress of the late night full of hidden threats leaking through in his voice.

If he was searching for another person to blame, Aurion had to provide one. He had made his luck. He had sent Lania to the palace.

Aurion turned his gaze to Gitarius pointedly, and Gitarius jumped. Somehow, the man always looked guilty. That was fortunate today.

"I am also not the one coming armed before the Sovereign of Lione," Aurion said slowly, keeping his eyes on Gitarius. "Some people like power too much, Sovereign. Giving them a taste leads to a desperate desire for more. I have proven I am satisfied with my status. Others here have not."

Dracus' laugh dropped as if sliced off by a blade. Gitarius flinched when Dracus fixed his stare on him, making Aurion wonder if the man *was* guilty of something. He had always seemed oblivious to his blunders. Perhaps he'd recognized a mistake somewhere. But then, everyone had secrets.

"What are you implying, High Councilman?" Dracus insisted, his gaze now boring into Aurion.

Aurion revised his sentence once in his head, but the pause only gave his words more weight. "If the assassin was to fail, would there not be a backup? Who could they count on being at your side?"

The slaves had left, Aurion noticed, except for one on call by the door. The low lamps made the room feel cavern-like, although the windows above, unbarred, showed the moon high above them in three-quarters. It made expressions hard to read, leaving Aurion unsure if Dracus was following the bait Aurion was threading before him.

"You can't mean me!" Gitarius squeaked. He threw his arms out. "Madness!"

But Gitarius' movement highlighted the flash of gold from his belt, the dagger Lania had planted.

Dracus' expression fell into deep shadows, although his eyes widened in shock. "You!" Dracus accused, his pointing finger damning Gitarius. "I foiled your allies and so you, you dare try? The assassin... was it you as well? If they failed, you were there, waiting, armed! And you had the gall to point fingers at another, to imply it was Aurion! You pushed your advantage too far! I see what you did!"

A more powerful man would have seen his fate and lashed out, but Dracus did not even need the magic orb in Gitarius' presence; the man lacked a spine in every way. All he did was stammer excuses that went unheeded.

"I find you guilty, Councilman Gitarius. Guards! Kill him!" Dracus rattled off in a single run.

Aurion had expected accusations and trials, not instant retribution, but the soldiers were swift in their response. The man on duty at the door drew his dius and, despite the councilman's skittering, pleading cries, and desperate avoidance, cut Gitarius down. There was a reason palace guards were considered elite; the cut was expert and so swift that Gitarius' screech of pain happened almost after it was already done.

Aurion was careful not to move, not even to flinch, as the guards moved in and executed the councilman. It was not a good time to draw attention.

But once Gitarius gave his last sighing gasp, the slaves knew the protocol. They collected the councilman's district seal from around his neck and took back the dagger, presenting both to Dracus like a dog with a retrieved dead bird.

As the body was removed and maids came in to clean the stains before they set on the tile and grout, Aurion stood by in false patience. He did not know if this would appease the sovereign sufficiently. He might be next, and now he had seen that Dracus did not feel the need for trials tonight. The only comfort was knowing he had weakened the sovereign by stealing one of his supporters. That, at the least, would make things easier for the councilmen who survived this night.

At length, Dracus retook his place, a slave cleaning the seal as he held it then washing his bloody hand with perfumed towels. Dracus had the orb in hand again, his knuckles white as he clutched it. The pressure of magic had not lifted from Aurion in the slightest, its presence like a weighted blanket over his shoulders.

"I believe I have you figured out, High Councilman Polfius," Dracus said, his tone conversational, as if no one was washing the stones behind him of blood with scented water.

Aurion stopped himself from laughing, knowing he could only afford so many offenses before the sovereign tired of him. "How so?" he asked instead.

"You are a soldier," Dracus told him, folding his hands over his belly as he leaned back. The orb was now on display, and Aurion's eyes involuntarily snapped to it. He dragged his eyes away, not wanting the sovereign to know how well he understood what was happening to him.

"You and I both know that on the battlefield, all you have is your sense of honor that keeps you bound to the men who command you. A soldier does not need love for his commanders; he does not even need respect. All he needs is the oath he has given. Nothing could change that, could it?" Dracus grinned again.

If he believed that, he wouldn't need magic, Aurion thought, but he did not dare even try to say those words.

"You never had to break your oath, not like the conspirators did. If I had asked you what the plans were, you would have told me, no?" he continued.

Aurion shrugged rather than answer.

Dracus' levity died in a blink. "I could have you killed, you know," he warned, puffing himself up.

"Yes, you could," Aurion replied.

"But then... I have slain the guilty already. But maybe this example needs more blood, guilty or not," Dracus mused, dangling Aurion's life with his words. "Maybe I should imprison you. Time in the prison could make you see things my way."

Something shifted in Aurion, the fear for his life wearing too thin. He could not be bothered with the games. He either lived or died here.

So be it.

His words, bare truths, came easily through the magic in the room.

"You know damn well I will not simply roll over because you made my life inconvenient. Make up your mind. I disagree with you, Sovereign. That does not matter ultimately. I disagree with people all the time. It's part of my job, really. But I will not tolerate you trying to steal my people from me."

Dracus' face scrunched in a scowl. "Is that what this was about? Your spymaster?"

"My inaction during a threat to you? Yes, that is what that was about. He won't work for you and you threaten my household with your insistence. I do not see sufficient gain from you sitting on the High Seat for me to accept that transgression. Thus, I saw no reason to assist when there was potential for a change in sovereign. I did not agree with those who acted against you, but I also did not stop them. That is truth. Leave my people alone. Your fight is with me."

"The sovereign is owed the loyalty of all Lionians," Dracus corrected pompously.

"Grizzle doesn't care," Aurion replied. "He swore no oath and will never. Forcing his hand is as good as signing your own death certificate." A wry smile found Aurion's face. "Maybe I have helped you after all. By shielding you from Grizzle, I verily saved your life, Sovereign."

The pause lingered between them, the moon above slipping behind clouds and casting the room into a gloom only broken by the dim lanterns. Aurion had to hope the shadows over Dracus' face were pensive, not angry. The sovereign's hand rotated on the orb, never letting it go.

"I think we have a possible arrangement," Dracus said at length. "I will leave you your minion, Aurion." With one uplifted finger, the sovereign added, "I want you… no, I order you, Aurion, as your sovereign, to report any information you have reason to believe I would want to know. This includes assassinations, the activities of the councilmen, trouble in the city… anything. Anything you think I would want to know, I order you to tell me. You do this, you be my spymaster, and I will let both you and your minion live."

Aurion finally felt the pressure ease around him, the threat of execution lifted. The guards had been on edge, hovering next to the wall with drawn blades as if expecting to be called into action once more. But they would not be needed tonight. It was not perfect, but it would do.

Aurion was not sufficiently defeated to lower his head, but he was careful how long he held the sovereign's stare. Confidence and competence were desirable, but a threat was not. Finally agreeing, Aurion bowed. The gesture also served to hide his grimace.

He had said it before; what he did now was not possible from a higher position. If he could not filter the information, he would lose the precarious hold he had on the web of the city. The army might remember him as a hero, but if he was turned into Dracus' lackey, he would lose that. And without his contacts, information collection was further hampered.

It marked the beginning of the end, he was certain, but he saw no option. It was better, for now, than immediate execution.

"Excellent!" Dracus declared, as if they were now best of friends. He stood up, the chains of his office clattering loudly, but kept the orb in hand. Aurion took that to mean his trust of Aurion had limits. "We will make a wonderful team!"

The words stayed with Aurion as he returned through the busy palace. He passed a slave pouring the blood-tinged water into flowering bushes as he left and gathered his relieved soldiers for the ride home.

"Get me Tatkil," Aurion requested as soon as he passed through his gate, wondering what the answer would be. She had had plenty of opportunity to get back, but was she coming?

As he waited in his office, he threw open the shutters of his window to try to remove the smell of blood from his nostrils.

To his surprise, the little slave appeared in her Illica uniform, her head bowed, her hair debts hidden. The servant who brought her in frowned at the inconvenience being caused by the Nurmi, but left when Aurion requested.

The office doors were lined with layers of cloth to act as soundproofing, and the walls here were solid stone to muffle voices. Lania appeared to know it; as soon as the doors shut, she asked, "Did you at least keep the dagger? It was a pretty one."

Aurion felt a smile tug on his mouth.

"I assume from the sovereign's bedchamber?"

Lania shrugged, her coy smile showing teeth. "The sovereign found out about you," she explained. "He was angry that one of the councilmen he had wanted to arrest had escaped, and Gitarius said you were involved in helping Vanius. He came for your head."

Aurion took a place behind the desk, feeling like it gave him more authority. But as he looked at her now, he realized it meant nothing to her. "You gave him a different target," he said, avoiding the seat but leaning onto the desk.

Her mirth faded with the gravity of his words. The scope of the evening's events had settled upon Aurion, and he knew there would be long-reaching consequences. For the moment, he was simply grateful he had come out alive.

He followed the logic through. "Dracus intended to kill me. You did far more than I ever expected of you. I owe you my life." As he spoke, he picked up a pair of scissors kept on his desk. Keeping his actions slow and obvious, he cut a piece of hair from his head. He offered it to Lania. "I am in your debt," he finished.

For a moment, she stared at the hair blankly, and he felt foolish. Why would a Nurmi accept a debt from another race? But when she moved, it was with reverence. Gently, cautious to not allow their skin to touch, she closed her fingers around the lock of black hair. She was, for a moment, hesitant.

"I... I fear I cannot wear it," she admitted.

He laughed and shrugged, grateful she had accepted the gift in the spirit it had been intended. "I did not expect you would."

"I am leaving," she said abruptly, as if not having planned the words. "Tatkil is coming with me, of course. We will blend into the many slaves who escaped this night."

"Through the chaos of the Market District?" he asked, goading her slightly. He had not expected her to reply so was not surprised when she only tilted her head. It almost got a smile, but the joviality didn't last long enough for the smile to emerge. She seemed to struggle with her words now, leaving him suspecting she had not intended to tell him of her departure.

"I hope that will not be trouble for you. Your city is free of the Warrior for a time, High Councilman. I will return, and I will see you again; the debt between us ensures it. Goodbye."

Aurion stood watching as she snapped open the doors and strode through. She was heading for her room, but that was for appearance's sake only, he was certain. He watched her until she was out of sight, wondering what had possessed him. Why, in the name of the gods, had he let her stay to begin with? Why had he even considered getting her involved in the sovereign's attempted assassination?

After a few minutes that brought him no answers, Aurion called, "Serena!" His sister arrived at his side quickly. "Tatkil has escaped. Surely this upsets you?"

Serena grinned, and Aurion wondered if she enjoyed the game they played with the rumors of the city. It was just one more lie, one more show. Like an actress with months of rehearsing, Serena stepped into her part.

"Tatkil! Come back here you swine!" she screamed until the whole household could hear her. "Intruders! In the garden! Guards!" The commotion caused was enough to wake the neighbors. By morning, the news was all over the city: the Warrior had stolen High Councilman Polfius' only slave and escaped the city.

CHAPTER 18

By the time the meeting ended, Aurion had a bad headache. Sovereign Dracus had leaned into his contacts hard after the attempted assassination. Vanius' replacement was behaving very well, catering to the sovereign. There had been even more turnover of councilmen in the wake, his paranoia similar yet disparate to what Aurion had seen consume Sovereign Polfius. Instead of fear, Dracus met conflict with anger and attacked any who dared step out of line.

Aurion himself had his mind elsewhere most of the time. Word from the province Julluam had been scarce and peaceful so far, but he felt like he was watching clouds move over them. It would not be long before the storm swept in. There was rebellion in the wind.

The north was no better. Dracus had wasted no time in declaring war against the Nurmi and, in the same breath, declared the war with the Windraso victorious. The people, as predicted, wanted revenge for the slaves Lania had taken. It was hard for Aurion to tell just how much Dracus was personally invested in the war in the North. It was a useful smokescreen for his dealings with the Council, but Aurion suspected Dracus also wanted to lead a victory parade.

At the moment, they were discussing the sovereign's brilliant plan to attack the Nurmi. Two pakanons, just over three thousand men, had snuck across the Solon River. In a matter of days, they would be in a perfect position to attack what the Nurmi had named Slufi—which translated as "Grove"—where, according to the reports, both the Priestess and the Black Arrow were in residence.

Since Lania's departure from Lione, the Black Arrow had pulled away from the front and left the command in the hands of his daughter. Aurion assumed the Black Arrow had at last retired, since, according to the records regarding Maltor before his escape, Maltor was over sixty now. How he had survived this long was a miracle, although Aurion preferred not to think of it in such a way. He had little faith in his own gods, and he did not want to worry about the Nurmi ones.

If all went well, the Lionian forces should be able to attack Slufi and take both the Priestess and the Black Arrow in one swoop. With the capture of the two legends, the Black Arrow could finally be killed, and the Priestess silenced. He intended to use Akara to lure Lania, confident the Warrior would come to rescue her religious half, into a trap. By the end of the next quartercycle, all three menaces would be gone. Dracus' confidence as he outlined the plans almost made Aurion believe it.

As Aurion listened to the comments of the councilmen, numbers mixed in his head, and he realized his unease was not because he could feel the stares of the dead sovereigns on him.

The city of Tran, facing the Nurmi city Lafilrupi, had been drained of men when the sovereign assembled the company to attack Slufi. Lania, in Lafilrupi, would know exactly the number of men in Tran, but she had probably decided a siege was not worth the lives should she choose to attack the city now. It could be conquered, he figured, but it would be costly to take and even more costly to hold. Although Aurion did not consider her reckless, he did think her unforgiving when it came to revenge.

The army would attack the Slufi on the eve of the twenty-first. At that time, the soldiers destined for Tran to replace those who had marched north would still be at least a day's march away from their goal, even if they were rushed.

Aurion told the page beside him to show blue, and the boy flipped the painted wooden flaps until the appropriate side was facing the center of the room where High Priest Guital was controlling the speakers. After a short wait while others had their turn, Aurion was asked to make his statement.

"The attack against Slufi should be delayed one day to allow the reinforcements to reach Tran," he said. A gesture to the boy had the flap flipped back to white.

Councilmen muttered to one another briefly, then Councilman Volustio showed red, and the hall acknowledged him for his answer to Aurion.

"Even if a messenger from the grove was sent the very moment of the attack, they would not reach the river until, at the very least, four days later. If fresh mounts were waiting for him at every city and he did not sleep, perhaps he could arrive in three days." The councilman laughed to demonstrate how unfeasible this feat was. "The reinforcements will have enough time to reach the river before Lania knows what has happened."

The page looked at Aurion, but he did not signal the red of rebuttal. Dracus was watching him; Aurion knew he had attracted the attention he required. There was only one person that mattered in the Councilhall these days and, thankfully, it was not Volustio.

The rest of the Council had no other objections to the sovereign's plans. Many were so excited by the prospect of crushing the Nurmi that they failed to question it thoroughly. *Surely*, Aurion thought to himself, *if it was so simple, we would have done it already.*

"Council is dismissed," Dracus interrupted the latest speaker prematurely, but no one complained. The same points were being argued, and everyone was thankful to end what had turned out to be an unusually long meeting. "Return to your districts with the gods' favor."

The replying, "As always, we honor the sovereign," was muffled by the lack of enthusiasm.

"High Councilman Polfius, remain."

Aurion bowed to the sovereign's high, central seat in acknowledgment. "As you request, Sovereign."

Dracus waited until the entire hall was empty before rising from the High Seat. Since the attack, Dracus had chosen to shave his face clean, as if he wanted to be younger, more vibrant, but he moved like an old man down the steps; an injury made his knee stiff.

"You are still holding to your oath, aren't you, Aurion? Braxi?" Dracus asked as he made his way down the steps of the Councilhall.

"I've not been called 'Braxi' in years, Sovereign," Aurion answered mildly. "Just as you left your military rank when you joined the Council."

Dracus let out a tart chuckle. "You didn't say 'pakani' rank. Afraid to remind me you were once my superior?"

There were hundreds, if not thousands, of men like Dracus—soldiers, trained and disciplined—and Aurion considered himself one of them. Despite their similarities, Aurion saw distinct differences between himself and the sovereign.

Dracus saw Lione as the greatest city in the world, but Aurion knew the depths of lies that marred it. Dracus considered the army undefeatable, but Aurion knew every battle they had fought, win or lose. True, they had never lost a war, not a real one, unless the defeat at Dragon Pass counted, but he knew they did not win every battle. He knew, for instance, that the recently declared victory against the Windraso was jaded; there were still Windraso out there who would kill a Lionian if they could, and they were still living free in the inhospitable northern reaches.

Dracus also believed in the supreme power of the sovereign and aspired to a sort of immortality that worried Aurion.

"It wouldn't be useful," Aurion replied. At least Dracus wasn't carrying the damn orb, allowing Aurion the freedom to choose his words. He still was careful to avoid lying.

Dracus made a face. "Be useful then, Aurion. Any update on affairs regarding my safety?"

Aurion's comments in the council had provided an excuse for a conversation, Aurion acknowledged.

Aurion did not hesitate. "You have been curating your councilmen, but the experience and knowledge of those who served longer have been lost in the turnover. People are noticing. Your safety is assured; none are attempting a coup. You have people working outside the Council, though, people who might have otherwise been considering councilman rank. They are not happy. In particular, watch Councilman Galfium's staff carefully; they are using him. He is likely to become a liability in his senior years. And Vanius' supporters will grow uneasy if you do not do something about the arrests. Given enough time, they will forget, but you must be cautious that Vanius does not turn into a martyr."

Dracus nodded as he listened. He carried on up a few steps, a petty move to position himself above Aurion when he was naturally shorter. "Good," the sovereign said, and Aurion bowed. "You do have a flare for gathering information."

Aurion detected a hint of resentment in the comment but saw no reason to answer it.

"Now," the sovereign said, taking a seat on one of the benches where he would still be above Aurion, "tell me why you suggested the delay. You would know better than most that the timing would be fine. The longer we wait in Nurmi territory, the greater the chance of our discovery. A delay could prove fatal."

"A lack of one may still," Aurion answered. "The Priestess and Warrior, according to Nurmi prophesy, are one spirit divided between two bodies. It is said that parts of their minds are still connected, although the bodies are separate. There are stories of times the Warrior knew her sister was nearby before messengers arrived, or the Priestess knowing exactly when the Warrior escaped her prison in Lione. The two, it is said, can be on opposite sides of a city and still know what the other is doing, perhaps even thinking."

"You believe that nonsense?" Dracus interrupted.

"I did not say I believed it, Sovereign," Aurion corrected, "but I feel you should at least know the possibilities. If the Warrior knows the Priestess has been captured at the assault on Slufi, I am certain she will attack Tran as retribution. If that is before the reinforcements arrive at the river, it could be disastrous."

"She does not have enough men to take Tran even now," Dracus argued, and his tone dared Aurion to contest it.

Knowing better than to directly oppose his sovereign, Aurion answered, "She will not be cautious if it is revenge she seeks. As soon as she finds out the Priestess has been captured or killed, she will seek vengeance. I do not doubt that. I only worry that it may be sooner than we expect. Without reinforcements, Tran could suffer high casualties."

"By the time she knows what has happened, they will have been there for three days, Aurion!" The sovereign stood and tossed his hands into the air. "You are suggesting changing these carefully laid plans because of some superstitious nonsense. I will not be frightened by such rubbish!"

Aurion could only bow in consent.

"Dismissed," Dracus hissed as he turned to the exit, his sneer evident.

Aurion caught himself smiling as he watched the man limp into the hallway's light beyond the arch. He could not be blamed now when things went wrong, and he suspected they were about to. Magic or not, he knew Lania had coordinated attack after attack from Lione, with clear communication to her sister throughout. Aurion would have bet his entire fortune that they had not relied on riders or runners.

Now, he would have a chance to see for certain.

21ST DAY OF THE 4TH MOONCYCLE, 997

Although the rain had stopped, the damp air threatened to drench the Nurmi army at a moment's notice should they venture outside. Lying in his bed, one arm around Malni, Haro heard the thunder roll over the wind, promising the storm's return. The thunder sounded like the growl of a great wolf.

The growl turned into a voice.

"Haro!"

The Warrior's voice, coming from the entrance to his shelter, startled Haro into rolling over so quickly he tumbled straight from the bed. She was no more than a silhouette against the glowing background of the central firepit's embers, but he could have levitated back onto the bed sooner than fail to recognize her.

"I go to wake the men."

The Warrior did not acknowledge the woman in the bed, and Haro barely managed to speak before she departed without any explanation at all. "Yes, Warrior," he first said as he sat up stiffly and felt his back ache from his fall. As he tried to clear his eyes, he asked, "May I ask why?"

The question came as Lania disappeared out of the doorway, and he was forced to wait, sensing her standing just beyond his view. When she returned, her stance was tall and purposeful. The tremor in her voice was of rage.

"They attacked the Grove," she said.

The fatigue blurring Haro's mind instantly cleared. He leaped to his feet, reaching for his armor and sword. "The Priestess?" he asked.

This time when her voice shook, Haro wondered if she was afraid, but he corrected himself rapidly. It was surely no more than a shared emotion from Akara. If that was true, then Haro's fear had come to pass.

"Taken," she said.

Haro knew Lania's time in Lione had left her scarred, and she would not, for as long as there were alternatives, go back. If Akara was to be dragged to that cursed place, then Lania's rage was understandable.

If the Twins were separated once more, the Black Arrow would be furious. He may even come back to Lafilrupi to lead the army and let the Warrior go after her sister. Then Maltor would lead them to yet another victory and show the Conquerors...

Haro cut off the thought mentally and paused as he tightened the straps of his armor.

Maltor had been in Slufi, with Akara.

The Warrior was waiting for his question at the entrance.

"The Black Arrow?" Haro asked.

It took a moment for the Warrior to respond. Haro could not say how he knew she was watching him in the shadows, but when she spoke, he was certain her eyes were locked on his own. He shivered when he felt her rage in the air.

"Dead."

The word struck him like a sword's thrust. His shield clattered against his foot as the cry of outrage, pain, and grief caught in his throat.

He had been born free and taught the legend of the Black Arrow before he had learned to speak himself. Growing up deep in the Corelands and far from where Maltor fought, it had taken a Lionian attack to bring Haro's childhood hero to his rescue. He did not hesitate to say it changed his life.

The rescue had come by night. Once the arrows were flying, Haro, as a boy of seven, had been snatched from his cage and carried down to the river to escape. The man carrying him had been struck down, that much Hero remembered. He had lain in the mud by the river curled in a ball, terrified Lionians would find him first and slaughter him as they had so many others, but too frightened to move toward safety.

Maltor had found him and carried him to the safety of the river. That very moment, Haro had decided to become the warrior his name denoted. He wanted to lead raids so no other child would ever be left to die in the mud.

With Haro's parents dead in the raids, Maltor had helped him find a family to take him. The two of them had often laughed at the way Haro had insisted on staying with the man who had saved him and training to be a warrior like him. He had eventually agreed to be adopted by one of Maltor's closest friends.

And now the Black Arrow was gone.

They would die for this, Haro promised. He would see the body of the man who had killed his mentor nailed to a tree and left to bake in the sun before his end. Aloud, he could only curse the black-haired Conquerors to the darkness beyond the Gate.

"I do not believe it was them," Lania said, her voice even. "His spirit has moved beyond the Gate."

The Priestess would know if her father's soul was trapped outside the Gate to the afterlife, and the Warrior would surely know from her sister. The implications were clear; the Black Arrow's death did not require avenging.

"We attack," the Warrior said in a voice that instantly reminded Haro of Maltor, a fact that both stung his heart sharply and caused it to beat doubly with desire for her. "Tonight," she continued, as her voice darkened. "By morning, there will be only smoking ruins. We take no prisoners and show no mercy. Then I shall ride to Lione and take back my sister."

Haro lost the echo of the Black Arrow's voice in the vehemence of her declaration. As she stood with her back to the embers of the firepit, she stood with absolute certainty.

There would be a massacre.

Maltor would never have commanded such a strike, but Lania seemed ready to enjoy it. Haro had not seen such fierceness in veterans, and he did not expect it from a woman who was hardly into her twentieth year.

He felt he was to blame and, yet, could not justify his guilt. If she had not wanted him, why had she taken his hand? Why had she not resisted? He had thought that, given enough time, she would come to see reason, but she had only distanced herself from him and then from everyone. Now, he only saw her smile during battle, and that smile never failed to chill him.

"Yes, Warrior," he said, picking up his helm and brushing off the dirt. "We will avenge them."

As the Warrior slipped away, Haro glanced back to Malni, huddled naked in the bed and watching with her eyes wide.

"That was..." she whispered as he donned his helm.

"Get the children out of camp," Haro interrupted. "When we are finished, there will be no reason to remain. Tonight, they all die."

As he left, he prayed it would be enough to bring a dead man's spirit some satisfaction.

CHAPTER 19

29TH DAY OF THE 4TH MOONCYCLE, 997

Sovereign Dracus had been furious enough at the Council meeting that, for the most part, the sovereign had been incapable of forming complete sentences. It would have been comical to watch the ruler of the Lionian Sovereignty stammering like a shy teenager after his first kiss if it were not for the cause of his frustration.

He had started by reporting the success at Slufi: they had captured the Priestess and killed dozens of defiant Nurmi. Most of note, although the body had mysteriously disappeared, was the confirmed death of the Black Arrow. Without the support of their founder, many seemed to think the Nurmi army would collapse. Akara was nearly back at Lione, escorted by hundreds of men and ready to be turned into the bait the sovereign thought he would need to trick the Warrior. Things seemed to be going well.

The moment the word "Warrior" was mentioned, the Council grew restless.

Aurion was forced by official inquiry to tell the Council what he had told the sovereign more than a quartercycle before. Most of the Council, to Aurion's amusement, still concluded that it was mere coincidence, not revenge for the attack on Slufi.

They were wrong. Despite extensive gathering of information, Aurion still did not have a clear picture of what had happened that night. All he knew was that there were no survivors and whatever she had done, it must have been spectacular. The city of Tran was dead, every last soul. Nothing remained of the city but a smoking pile of rubble, bodies, and death.

They would rebuild it, he was certain. It was not the first time the Nurmi had attacked the river city. He doubted it would be the last.

By the time the meeting ended, Aurion was ready to throw Councilman Volustio out the upper-level windows. More obnoxious than usual, he lobbied relentlessly to kill the Priestess immediately. He claimed to fear that, by the time she arrived in Lione, the savages would plan a rescue.

Aurion did not need to object; other councilmen countered Volustio's suggestion by pointing out how valuable the Priestess was as a demonstration, one the people would not believe unless they witnessed it, and as bait. Dracus already had plans for the religious icon, including a trap for her twin, which was the final decision on the matter.

Sitting at the desk of his second story reading room after the Council meeting was adjourned, Aurion wondered what grounds he would have used to object to Volustio if he had been forced to. He did not, by any means, support the Nurmi, yet he did not want to see the Priestess dead, which he thought odd. The Priestess was a clear threat to Lione, almost as much as the Warrior. He could not justify doing anything to spare her life.

And yet he had spent the last day trying to figure out how to do it. The evidence of his efforts was still on the desk under the lamplight. He had resorted to reading a book of legends, although the author admitted many of the stories had contradictory versions. No one knew if it was because the slaves lied about the tales.

Akara had arrived in Lione that evening, escorted by enough men to conquer the province of Julluam for a second time, with no sign of Lania. Many figured she was leaving Akara as Lania had been left, but Aurion did not believe it for a moment.

As much as Aurion wanted to see how similar the twins were, it would have to wait. Dracus was letting no one near the Priestess, or at least that was what Aurion had been told officially. Other sources gave a slightly different story.

Councilman Galfium had not let his fascination with the Nurmi sisters wane over the last three years and, despite Aurion's cautions, Dracus had agreed to something, although the details were vague. Thinking about it turned Aurion's stomach, but he could find no real means of objecting.

Hearing a soft step across the room behind him as he neared the end of a Nurmi legend book, Aurion pulled his sword from where it had lain beside him, jumped to his feet, and spun to face the sound.

Lania stood beside the window with both hands open and spread side to side, indicating she was unwilling to fight. The gesture usually also implied one was unarmed, but a dius lay on her left hip and a dagger on the right, probably the only visible one of many others. A bow hung over her quiver as well, which made him wonder why it had been her footstep he had heard instead of the clink of weapons. When he looked closer, he spotted the dark cloth wrapped around her sword and dagger hilts to muffle the noise.

Since he had last seen her, Lania had developed a dark tan. The spark he had glimpsed in her eyes when she had taken the role of the Warrior and spoken of her people had flared into a permanent blaze in the frozen blue of her irises.

She raised one eyebrow and said, "A councilman bearing a sword?"

He dropped the dius out of the defensive position and onto the table, embarrassed and muttering, "Old habits."

She cocked her head, probably wondering just how old a habit it was if he could still look the part of a soldier so easily. Instead of asking the question, she lowered her voice and said, "I come to claim the debt."

"I had expected as much," he replied as she advanced into the light of his lamp. "The sovereign has asked me to report anything I think he would like to know, and I know he would be most eager to hear about this visit, Lania. He will know anything I tell you and probably take my life for it. You should be careful."

He spoke without emotion as best he could, but he heard his voice tense. But no matter what the consequences, the sovereign's order was law, and the oath he had given left him no choice but to obey. The gods would have to be in a very good mood to see him live past the morrow.

To his surprise, the Warrior's expression did not change as he confessed. He could have said nothing and trapped her later when he told the sovereign. It could have even saved his life if he could convince the sovereign that he had intended to capture the Warrior all along. She must have known.

"You will honor the debt?" she asked as she arrived at the desk to flip a careless hand over the pages he had been studying. Although Tatkil had acted ignorant, he was certain Lania could read when the corners of her mouth twitched slightly to see the book's contents.

"I owe you my life," he told her. "I gave you the debt as my word that I would repay you, but I cannot go against the sovereign, Lania. I will not."

Councilmen spent years perfecting an emotionless gaze; the Warrior proved she could do it flawlessly when she regarded him.

"Have you so easily forgotten the limits of a Nurmi hair-debt, High Councilman? I cannot ask you to go against your family or tribe. Whether or not you realize it, Lionians are your tribe and the sovereign is your chief, the way Maltor was for us."

Had circumstances been different, he would have offered condolences for the death of her father, but he was as happy to see the Black Arrow dead as the sovereign was. Maltor's death was one step toward ending the war and giving Lione victory.

Admitting defeat, he sighed and said, "What need have you of me?"

He was certain that, when he saw the slight smile grace the Warrior's face, it had been permitted only to inform him that she was pleased that he had remembered the words she had spoken to him cycles ago. Although she seemed to want to show she approved, her smile had no more feeling than her disinterested expression earlier.

"I want information, and then I want you to forget I ever came."

He finally understood her strange assurance. In the book he was reading, there was a legend about a hero called Canir, who had used a hair-debt to tell his wife he had not been gone for two years, which meant she could not accuse him of the adulteries he had committed. As the story went, because of the sacredness of the debt she owed, his request became truth for her, and she lived happily with him for many years to come. Further, if anyone asked, even a priest to whom it was a great sin to lie, she could tell them truthfully her husband had never done any of the things he had done during his time away.

If Lania asked him to forget she had been here, then that was truth, and he could not report her.

"What information?" he asked. He was smiling, Aurion realized foolishly. He could not remember the last time he had let himself show emotion unintentionally.

"Where is my sister, and what are their plans for her?"

He hesitated. Lania would go after her twin, even if it meant death. Aurion wanted her to be safe, but the debt had been claimed.

"They have put her in the palace prison, with the guard doubled and at least two yoracs moving around." She was thinking as he spoke; he could see her mentally counting the men and comparing them to their known positions. He knew she would not like the conclusion. "Even you cannot get in there, Warrior. They expect you to try. If you go now, you will be killed."

She nodded in silent agreement but avoided his stare while he answered her second question.

"She will not leave there until Sovereign Dracus takes her to the speech podium tomorrow morning in the Market District. He intends to see her executed," he said with a final frown.

Lania nodded once, a gesture almost military-like.

"It's a trap," Aurion warned. Her head snapped around to look at him as if she would see lies on his face. "Dracus expects you to strike," he explained. "He will have half the Lionian guard waiting for you. If you go, he will kill you."

For a long moment, she did not answer or move. Then, to his disappointment, she nodded again.

"The debt has been repaid," she said as she pulled a pouch from around her neck, opened it, and took out his lock of black hair. As he watched, she ceremonially tossed the loose hairs through the bars of the window. Turning to face him briefly, she bowed stiffly as Lionian custom required and moved to leave.

"Lania, wait."

He had not meant to speak at all, and now that he had, he found himself without anything further to say. She had not heeded his warnings if she still thought to save her sister. Dracus knew she was coming. Not even the Warrior was that powerful.

She paused near the door with her hand hovering near her sword and, when she scanned the room, it was with her head tilted like a hunter stalking prey. Eventually, she met his gaze, but her stare demanded that he state his purpose swiftly.

"Why risk your life so needlessly?" he asked as gently as he could.

"I will not allow the Priestess to die," she answered sharply.

"Your own legends say she may not die until you do," he protested with a gesture to the pages he had been reading. "If you are safely away from here, then she cannot die. Or do you have no faith in your prophecies?"

He thought perhaps she would draw her blade in answer, but what had been anger faded when she looked at the pages lying on his table.

"You do not know of what you speak, Lionian," she told him, and he noticed keenly that she had called him "Lionian," not "Conqueror." "Conqueror" was always spoken like an insult, and he was surprised she had not used it. He was uncertain if "Lionian" was any better, but she did not sound as vicious when she said it.

"The prophecy does not say she may not die until I, nor the other way around," Lania said. "That is a Lionian translation. It is flawed." As she wandered back into the room, Aurion retook his chair like an attentive student.

"I always thought it odd," he admitted. "If she could not die before you, but you could not die before her, then you would both be essentially immortal."

When she shook her head, the tips of the hair-debts braided into her hair caught his eye in the light. "Not immortal," she grumbled in a most un-womanly manner. He suspected there was far more to that statement than she would tell.

Since that was the limit of her reply, he pressed, "What is the correct translation, then?"

"If I wanted to," Lania said, "I could drive a knife through my heart right now. The One God would not stop me. When He gave the prophesies to the priests, he knew I would not do this. It is not that my sister cannot die, or even, as you say, 'may' not, die before me; it is that she will not. I am the One God's servant, and I act in His name because He does not walk this earth. I do not believe He wishes to see the Priestess die at the hands of the Conquerors, so I will intervene. He will guide me, but I will be the one to keep the prophesies from failing."

Taking a deep breath, she finished, "What the prophesy says is that the Warrior will not perish until the Priestess can show her the way to the Gate. The Priestess will not enter the realm of death until the Warrior opens the Gate for her."

The Gate that she was referring to was the gate to the afterlife, which was supposedly located somewhere in the Dreamworld. Aurion was fairly certain that only the dead could see the way to the Gate, and he was absolutely certain that only a content, dead spirit could open the Gate; that was the purpose of the barrier. Spirits requiring vengeance could not move beyond and would continue to wander the Dreamworld until avenged by their living relatives or securing their vengeance by haunting the dreams of the ones responsible for their deaths.

But if only the dead could see the Gate and only the dead could open the Gate, then the prophecy said that Lania had to be dead for the Priestess to be dead and vice versa.

It was something he would have to think about further, he decided.

"Some would believe that she and I are bound together in death," the Warrior continued. "I am less certain of that. It is only prophesy. The future is ever-changing. The One God knows this."

Many gods were worshiped in Lione, although Aurion had never found comfort in any of them beyond the Illica family god, Travorson. In Lione, all major officials played a role in a temple somewhere by serving at least one of the most powerful nine or, in the case of the sovereign, the Lord of the Gods, Lioni. Aurion officially was a follower of Anthi, the god of war, and had worshipped for many years as a soldier before too many friends had died, including his father, and his faith had wavered. Anthi was supposed to be stronger than Damith, god of death, yet even Aurion's father, more loyal to the god of war than many of Anthi's priests, had fallen to Damith.

Coming to Lione had crushed the remnants of his faith. The men of Lione were worse servants to the gods than even the soldiers. Aurion had heard of worshipers disguising inexpensive, useless trinkets as expensive offerings, or "sacrificing" already dead animals to avoid having to kill a healthy part of their herd. He knew the tricks of the temples, the truths behind their prophesies and miracles, and it had caused him to reconsider the role of gods in his life.

Temple services happened constantly around the city. Two positions in the Council were reserved for the High Priest of Lione and the High Priest of the God Lioni. For a good crop, farmers made offerings at Blarvinor's temples. Mariners visited Seritan's temples daily with prayers for good weather. The Goddess of Justice, Mintova, oversaw the courts while her brother Havi was paid tribute by a successful thief in the shadows of his sewer temples. The list went on.

Yet it was all for naught. The assortment of gods was constantly at war with one another, causing never-ending feuds between their followers. The gods were meant to bring order to the world, but Aurion could see only chaos where they passed. Even Anthi did not seem to notice that Aurion no longer went to the temples.

The Nurmi faith was very different, but he knew little of it. The priests were best known in Lione for their prophesies. The most famous of these had been the words of the last Nurmi to be captured, who had told of Maltor's coming, even calling him by the name a priest was to give him at his birth. Some scholars believed he had taken the name after escaping, fulfilling the prophecy. But those who believed the child had been named Maltor at birth argued that he had escaped because the prophecies had given him the courage to do so, and those who had followed him had done so because of their confidence in the foretold future. The prophesies were seen as self-fulfilling, diminishing their power in Lionian eyes.

"Are you satisfied now?" Lania asked, peering at him with her head cocked to one side and, if he looked closely, a mildly amused look on her face. He could tell without a mirror that he looked pleased, probably more than she had ever seen. Gathering knowledge, especially information so genuine, was one of the greatest joys he knew.

"So, you will save Akara because that is what the One God would expect you to do?"

She nodded and grinned in a way that made him shiver.

He had seen her smile like that before and it was always followed by blood. He struggled to finish his thought. "And, guided or not, how do you intend to do this when she is being guarded by the best soldiers Lione has, in the heart of the best-protected district in all the White City?"

Her answer was the same vicious smile.

"Or do you intend to save her when the sovereign expects you to while he makes his demonstration in front of half a city with guards stuffed into hiding as tight as stacked melons?"

"You will be in the market tomorrow," she answered with a toss of her head. "I will show you."

He could not help smiling. He wished he knew what she did, or had even a fraction of her faith in her One God. She was doomed, he was certain, but she was ready to face it. He should have never expected her to turn away when Akara was in danger.

Once her smile had faded, she took a moment to bow to him in farewell. He stood and bowed in return with respect, the first time he had done so in many years.

She took a single step toward the exit, then gasped. She doubled over and fell as if she had been struck, her breath struggling and making her sound as if she was choking.

Without a thought, Aurion hastened to her side and helped her up by her arm, but she twisted free of his grasp with a dagger materializing in her hand. He startled back but not because of the weapon.

Shocking him, he saw tears running down her cheeks.

"Demons," she whispered with such vehemence, she seemed to be baring her teeth like a wolf. "Monsters, ashes burn you." He was forced back farther, fearing she would strike at the black hair without recognizing him.

Instead of striking, she moved to wipe her cheeks. When her hand came away wet, she looked at it in puzzlement.

"They will die for what they have done," she told him in a voice that made him shiver. "I cannot let them escape vengeance." While he struggled to form the inquiry he wanted, her expression softened for a blink. "I am sorry for the grief it may cause you." As if catching herself, her sternness returned in the next instant. "But I will destroy them for this." Before he could ask what had happened, she had turned and vanished down the hallway without another glance back.

He moved to pursue but stopped himself when he realized the futility and the stupidity of the action in the same instant. He wanted to pray they had not done something foolish like kill the Priestess, but he could not see the god Travorson listening to him if he asked for the life of a Nurmi.

He collapsed back into his chair and looked to the book.

"Might have to write one myself," he grumbled, flipping over the pages about the legend of the Warrior and the

Priestess. He started reading the Nurmi legends about the Falling City, waiting for more bad news to reach him.

30TH DAY OF THE 4TH MOONCYCLE, 997

The crowd had gathered as early as the dawn, anticipating the execution with loud music and vendors despite dark clouds above. It would have been a festival, if it had not been for the grim faces of the brightly clad slaves who had been brought to witness the end of their faith.

There were soldiers about, many of them concealed, but they did not concern Lania. Lionians and their powerful crossbows could shoot far but lost accuracy due to the cumbersome sights and the size required. Short of mounting a crossbow, they could not make good at significant distance. And their archers were not born to shoot. Lania had lived with a bow in her hand, with the exception of her time in Lione.

Their perimeter had been checked out to over a hundred strides. She didn't need to be that close.

As she made her way to a perch, Lania wondered if Aurion was already in position on the speech tower. She was thankful for the high councilman's warnings, although she wondered why he had given them. It was not possible that a Lionian was helping her willingly, yet she did not believe he had betrayed her either. High Councilman Polfius continued to confuse her.

The building she chose had a new slanted roof of mud shakes that was distinctly unlike the common flat roofs of the other houses nearby. It was a little harder to keep balance on, but it provided extra height, a boon for her purpose.

While lying on the slanted roof, Lania notched the last of the light, hawk-feathered arrows in her bow. Like every one of the blackened-shaft arrows from the collection her father had left in Lafilrupi, the tip had been treated with poison. She knew he would be pleased that his namesake would be used in defense of his youngest daughter.

Long before the procession was visible, Lania heard it coming. Instead of rising to watch, she sought the emotions of her sister. Through that now-potent connection, Lania knew the Priestess was weak, that the soldiers were many and close at hand, and that councilmen were there with their personal guards and slaves. Altogether, the Conquerors were more numerous than the entire company of Tran.

Still, the Warrior did not look.

Vendors and entertainers were forgotten as the gong sounded, and the people filed together to crowd the speech tower that stood three stories high at one end of the square. When the man dressed in the white robe with black sleeves trimmed in gold stepped up onto the podium, the silence became Lionian cheers. The roar was cut short with a wave of the sovereign's regal hand.

Lania did not hear what he said for the first part of his speech. Although she had felt Akara's pain during the night, the feelings had been slightly muted by the distance separating them. At their current proximity, Lania's body ached with each movement she imagined her sister made. In addition to the physical pain they shared, something within Akara felt horribly hollow. Even now, Lania felt her sister crying, although she doubted any tears were falling.

That was not just Dracus' doing. That had been Councilman Galfium.

Grinding her teeth against her fury, Lania clenched the bow until her fingers went white. She wanted to stand, drive the black arrow through the man's black heart and out the other side for what they had done to her twin, then laugh as the blood stained the wretched white robes of the councilman. Dracus' turn would come as well. It was time to avenge Slufi and the lives lost.

Through Akara's sorrow, Lania felt her sister deliberately cultivating calm for the sake of her twin. The rage subsided, soothed like a wave passing over disturbed sands.

They were of one mind, their connection strong enough for Lania to hear through her sister's ears and see shadows through her sister's eyes.

Councilman Galfium lounged under a sunshade, goblet in hand. His slave, a large Santanese man with tribal tattoos marred by scars, stood by with a pitcher. Situated behind Akara, Galfium was protected from Lania's arrow. His stare still made Akara's skin crawl and her stomach toss. Rage swelled in the Warrior at her sister's pain, and the slumped form of the Priestess shivered with the emotion.

High Councilman Polfius was also present, Lania noted, trying to distract her sister. Sure enough, Akara was aware of him standing over the sovereign's right shoulder in a position of authority.

When the sovereign finished his speech, a gesture brought the Priestess forward. She was not bound, although Akara did not seem to have the strength remaining in her body to stand and hung suspended by two soldiers. Persistently, Lania felt patience from her sister. She knew the plan they had devised across the dreamscape. They had to hold to it, no matter the screams and jeers from the people.

With stately force, a single word cut above the howl of the crowd: "Bow!" the sovereign commanded the Priestess.

On the cue, the guards holding Akara simultaneously released, expecting her to fall without support.

As Akara gave Lania her calm, Lania lent her sister strength. Akara hovered for a moment before, as if lifting a man's weight above her, straightening her back and standing as Maltor had taught her.

The stunned crowd fell silent.

Although she teetered, the Priestess raised her chin and, drawing power from Lania, declared, "Never."

Lania smiled. They'd not discussed pissing the sovereign off quite so directly, but she did not begrudge her sister the chance to one-up the man who was responsible for the attack on Slufi.

While many did not understand the Nurmi word, the meaning was clear enough. The Priestess of the One God would not bow to a Lionian, no matter what rank.

The sovereign's voice rose above the crowd loud enough for Lania to hear it at her great distance. She heard his fury.

"BOW!"

Lania felt the hands of the guards and flinched. It was Akara they pushed down, not her, but her skin tensed where they had touched.

Akara's wounded legs crumpled. Inside, Akara fumed at her body's inability to withstand the trial. Her voice was soft now. Perhaps some Nurmi nearest the speech podium would hear her, but for Lania, the words were clear as mountain water.

"I may fall, but I do not bow."

The sovereign laughed, not understanding the defiance. With his own hands, he lifted Akara to her feet and held her before the crowd. "Speak to them, Priestess," he commanded. "Tell them the future you see for yourself now!" He had drawn a soldier's dagger and was lifting it toward her throat as he spoke. While others knew the Priestess' fear by her trembling, Lania felt the fear as if it was her own and closed her eyes to resist it. *They will pay,* she reminded herself to steady her and her sister's mind. She would make them pay soon enough, but not everyone was in place yet.

Lania clasped her armband tightly enough to embed the symbol of the One God in her palm. That blade was too close. *Patience...*

The Priestess was still wavering, and her voice shook violently as she spoke. The three words she whispered were broken Lionian.

"She ... is ... here."

Speaking dissolved her remaining energy, and Akara fell against the sovereign, who held her up with one arm. He raised the knife to her throat until it was only a finger width away, but the Priestess' eyes had fallen shut. Akara's fear faded as her consciousness slipped along the edges of the comforting Dreamworld.

"Call her," the sovereign said, a whisper in Akara's ear that Lania heard clearly.

When Akara only whimpered, the sovereign tightened his grip and moved the dagger closer still. "Call her out!" he shouted, shaking Akara from semi-consciousness.

The Priestess swallowed hard and slowly opened her eyes.

Lania peered over the edge of the roof, her bow and arrow ready. Her father had claimed she had borrowed the eyes of the hawks, but even for her, her sister and the sovereign were small targets. Still, she did not need perfect accuracy, not with a black arrow. And the sovereign's display had moved Akara to the right, leaving Lania a clear line of sight on her target.

"Sister," Akara obediently began in accented Lionian, her voice echoing through Lania as the Warrior aimed. "The monster you seek..."

The sovereign's grip, once holding the knife, switched to the Priestess' throat, irritated by her continual, if mild, defiance. He tightened his hold. Akara's breath failed her.

Sovereign Dracus' shout boomed over the crowd and through the emptied streets. All of Lione seemed to be in that square, watching with rapt attention.

All of Lione except one man, a Santanese slave, who stepped forward to fill his master's goblet and slipped between Akara and the councilman.

"Lania! Come out, Lania, or she dies!" Dracus screeched.

Akara's mind panicked, desperate for air, but the body was too weak to escape the hold of the sovereign. The Warrior struggled for control against the fright, but everything in her, even the part of her mind usually calmed by her sister, screamed that now was the time.

She grinned as she considered the irony. For the first time, the Warrior obeyed the Lionian sovereign.

Lania stood up and loosed the arrow.

Akara's thoughts came through, an urgent whisper in her ear. *He sees you.*

He was not the sovereign. *He* was Aurion. Her old master had spotted her before the shot.

The arrow struck its mark.

The Santanese, a slave called Benninja, snatched Akara from the sovereign's grip.

Lania did not wait to see the results, knowing Akara's ties to her would provide all the information she needed. She slid from the roof, dropping down and breaking into a run.

Aurion had known what to look for and was still taken by surprise.

The guards patrolling the Market District square were constant and numerous. They had established a perimeter and were checking every corner, every slave. They had a good chance of spotting Lania, knowing she had a scar over her right cheek and, considering the importance of this venture to her, would be wearing her silver armband. They cleared and blocked the roofs and alleys, leaving no sale cart or wagon unscrutinized. There was no chance she was within reach of the sovereign.

It was the change in the horizon that caught his attention. Although it was a tiny difference at this distance, he spotted when the roofline silhouette moved.

Aurion snatched the sovereign aside, a reflex he almost regretted when he saw the arrow whiz by. But rather than striking Dracus, the arrow slipped behind them and cut into Councilman Galfium's arm.

"Get her!" screamed the sovereign, although the command was surely superfluous. The soldiers were scrambling, commands relayed as fast as word could travel. The soldiers rushed to catch her trail, but they had to travel at least a hundred and fifty strides. She had quite the head start.

Her shot had missed Dracus, but that it had hit the Market District's speech podium was impressive, Aurion thought. She'd picked a lighter arrow and shot from a distance that would have left her target not much more than a splash of white. But the light arrow wasn't likely to kill without superb accuracy, something she'd never achieve at that distance. It seemed wasted.

The crowd had surged, and people were trying to move swiftly in cramped spaces; the sea of people was dangerous now. The soldiers were torn; many were in pursuit of Lania already. The remaining ones would not suffice to control this number of people.

Time to go, Aurion thought. He could deal with the fallout once...

In turning, Aurion spotted Councilman Galfium stumble. The thump he made as he went down was enough to bring the eyes of the entire present contingent to him. In the noise of the people, Aurion hadn't heard the councilman's gasping, but his heaving chest was obvious now.

The light arrow Aurion had dismissed as a wasted shot, he saw, was black.

Lione had killed Maltor, but his legacy lived on. Although the arrow had not pierced deep, it had cut the skin, and that was all that was required. Lania hadn't needed precision after all.

Seeing Councilman Galfium, the man who had kept Akara overnight, spasm and convulse on the smooth top of the sheltered speech tower, Sovereign Dracus' face paled. Aurion was sharply reminded of the shades Polfius had taken when the prisoner had drained his blood with a well-placed knife. Although unwounded, Dracus gaped for a moment in shock before, shaking his head, he commanded to be returned at once to his palace. Sovereign Dracus didn't even thank Aurion for pulling him aside as he stormed off, leaving Aurion in a torrent of memories and indecision.

Had Lania missed in truth? Galfium had been the cause of her tears last night. Was it any wonder the Warrior exacted justice?

Akara…

Akara was gone. Aurion had missed when she'd escaped as had, he assumed, the guards caught up in defending the sovereign and councilmen.

Although he felt exposed standing where the sovereign had been a moment before, Aurion stepped up to the edge and cast his gaze over the crowd that was being forcibly broken up. It was questionable still whether the guards or the chaos would rise victorious in the square, but Aurion remained for a moment more, searching.

Akara had never been to Lione. How would she find a hiding place? Had the slaves helped her? Which ones? Was Galfium's retinue looking a little thin, perhaps? It wouldn't surprise him. Galfium had taken Nurmi slaves before, and even other races would share their fear and hatred of him. No, Aurion recalled. Galfium had brought a Santanese slave, not a Nurmi one.

Had they worked together?

The more he thought about it, the more confident he became that Lania had struck where she had intended. Dracus had been using Akara as a shield. To get her sister out, she had needed a distraction, and what better way to issue a threat than to kill the man next to the sovereign? The sovereign had retreated now into safety, but the main goal— freeing Akara—had been accomplished.

Near the back of the square, a cart collapsed under the weight of frustrated, fearful people. The soldiers were slowing the departures from the square, and at least some of the observers were now panicking. The crashing cart dumped cooking oil and uncooked meat across the ground, causing more chaos as people alternated between trying to move away and stealing the free food.

Definitely time to go.

Like the sovereign, he would return to his home and...

If Lania had indeed struck exactly where she had intended, then the results of her shot were highly predictable. He did not believe she had forgiven Dracus for his involvement in the raid of Slufi. And what better way to ensure she knew where he would be? Lania had broken into the palace before.

If he was right and Lania was heading for Dracus, he was bound by his oath to tell the sovereign.

Maybe I don't need to run to do it though, he decided.

As Aurion descended from the tower, his personal guards moved in, but the sight of the black and white robes seemed to work as a deterrent to the people. He passed a doctor rushing up, and he felt for the unfortunate man who was already too late for Galfium. With some manipulations, Dracus could put the blame on the doctor if he wanted to prevent Lania's legend from getting credit for the amazing kill. Aurion wondered if the doctor knew.

"Home?" Antori asked as Aurion finally got beyond the Market District walls and to where the streets were of a manageable volume.

Aurion shook his head. "Palace District." He kept walking, Antori at his side. "But we'd better go wide around the square." He gave his yoraci a stern look. "It's exceedingly dangerous in there right now."

Antori nodded, and Aurion heard humor in his voice when he added, "A very wide berth it is. Hold on. I need to fix my belt first. Sword loop's a bit loose."

The march Aurion and his personal guards made through the Market District, taking a long, circuitous route, was anything but elegant. One by one, the guards came up with an excuse to pause. One had to retie a boot, another to get a stone out. The youngest one, Calre, claimed to see a lurking shadow and insisted the party go back by three blocks to go around a possible threat.

Once at the Palace District gate, the good mood lifted, and Aurion was relegated to going in alone.

He dragged his feet, hoping all the while he would be too late.

CHAPTER 20

Councilman Galfium's slave had done as promised. Akara had predicted as much. During the chaos of his master's death, Beninja swiftly hid Akara under a Galfium uniform and fled the area. He met up with Lania beside the Market District gate, and together they used a smuggling tunnel to pass into the Docks District. The soldiers were moving in, chasing Lania's known location in the far north of the district.

The dark-skinned Santanese slave said nothing as he passed Akara over to Lania, but his eyes held deep sorrow still. Usually, the brown eyes so similar to a Lionian's worried Lania, but these eyes were depths of a cavern dark, not the Lionian's midnight. His broken soul was what had brought Akara to him for help.

It marked the first time Lania had put her faith in another race, but she trusted that their common purpose would rise above their differences, just as Akara had. Beninja bore the scars—physical and emotional—of Galfium's bedroom habits. The Santanese man would not live long, and he knew it. In killing Galfium, Lania had fulfilled her part of their bargain. In giving Akara back to her, Beninja had fulfilled his. What happened to him now was left to fate as far as Lania was concerned. Beninja simply handed Akara over and left without looking back.

Taking to alleys she had memorized while in Lione, Lania led Akara. They would take refuge for a short while before attempting to escape. Akara needed to rest, and Lania had one more unfinished task.

"Lania…" Akara muttered as her sister took her arm.

"I am here now, sister," Lania whispered back. "Stay with me. I will get you out of here."

When the Priestess nodded, Lania felt her slip into the Dreamworld, but she quickly dragged herself back to reality.

"Lania…" she moaned again. "Lania… they… I tried to stop them… they…" Lania jostled her gently to keep her conscious. The alleys were not busy, but crossing paths with an unwanted visitor could ruin everything. The warehouse wasn't far. She still had a road out of Lione even High Councilman Polfius did not know about.

"I know, sister," Lania said. She wiped her sister's tears away before clearing her face and cursing how her sister's emotions flooded her mind. She needed to think clearly, not be distracted by memories that were not even her own.

"You know?" Akara choked with fresh tears falling and sobs shaking her weak form.

"You were not the only one who cried last night," Lania told her, checking a road before choosing another. "Do not fear. They will pay for this, sister. I will kill them for what they have done." She wasn't sure how that would lift some of the corruption they had inflicted upon Akara, but it was all Lania could offer.

When she tried to move forward, Akara pulled her back with her full strength.

"No," she whimpered desperately. "No, sister. Do not go after them. It is not worth it. It is all right; I am all right now. Do not go! It's dangerous!"

Murder was pollution of the soul; it was morally reprehensible and a sin that even the One God would not forgive. But killing monsters was easy. War could be justified, and was this not just another battlefield? Was it that Akara was close on hand and some of the corruption would be spread to her? Surely, the One God knew the duty had to be done. Did Akara not see it? The monster had to die.

"Akara…" Lania began, but Akara shook her head, which caused even Lania's mind to waver again uncontrollably. Lania swayed under the effect.

"Do not go," Akara begged. The rest of her arguments were cut off as her consciousness fell completely into the Dreamworld. A hint of dream—or was it prophecy?—passed between them. The glitter of shattered colored glass flashed through her mind, then scattered.

Lania shook her sister as gently as she could and called to her in her mind. When she felt her sister's mind return, she spoke again. "Do not disappear, sister. I need you here. Stay with me a while. It is not far."

"Lend me strength once more, sister," came the whispered reply from the slumped Priestess. "My body grows weak."

Lania did not fully understand, but all she had was her sister's, and she did not hesitate to give it to her. "Do as you will," she answered.

A tingle in the back of her mind crept in, and she felt her sister closer than ever before; part of her mind melded with the Priestess. Lania endured the intrusion as her sister anchored herself within the Warrior's strength and determination.

They moved forward.

There was no Warrior and no Priestess, just two in one as they passed through the streets. Although Lania could see her sister walk beside her, she could also see herself through her sister's eyes. She could do nothing without Akara following perfectly. Their strength and their pain were equally shared, the distinction between them blurred into non-existence.

Soon, they were welcomed into the warehouse by Haro and his warriors.

Haro ushered the Warrior and Priestess into the warehouse, then latched the door behind them. In the light of a few stolen candles, with friends guarding the doors and windows, the Warrior gently put down the Priestess, who had collapsed asleep in her arms as soon as they had passed into the warehouse.

"Care for her," the Warrior commanded Haro. Haro's heart jumped, and he warmed when she brushed against him, despite how she was moving away from them both. "I will return shortly." And then she was gone.

She frightened him now. Haro had lived his life in war, but the memories of the massacre of Tran sent shivers down his spine. He continued to love her, trying to ignore how he shuddered to see her grin before battle and wishing daily he could somehow bring some serenity to her world.

How could he be the one to do such a thing when he had ravished her so viciously the moment she had allowed him near her?

He knew they were now divided. She had built walls around her soul so thick he could not reach her. The Warrior did not need him, leaving Haro with nothing. He had lost her. Perhaps he had never known her at all.

He brought his attention to his new duty, his heart turbulent.

Whenever Haro had seen the Priestess, she had stood tall and proud as the infallible voice of the One God. Beautiful and powerful, yet gentle and calm, she had been immortal in his eyes. Seeing her lie on the black cloak he had lain over a dirty straw mattress for her, soaked with blood, scarred by the whip, thin from the lack of food, and struggling to breathe with every gasp, Haro could not see the strength of the One

God. The Priestess was no immortal. She could be hurt, could even be killed, and it sent him into torrents of worry.

He sat nearby with his sword across his lap, watching over her until evening, ready to leave whenever the Warrior returned to them. The Priestess' training in the groves served her well; she drifted into the Dreamworld and slept so deeply that Haro expected only the Warrior would be able to wake her. It was exactly what her body needed.

Although he kept his back straight and directed the watches on the windows and doors as the night fell, Haro's mind wandered. Near midnight, the Priestess woke, giving him a new purpose; feeding her and providing what she needed to dress her wounds. There were no wounds where the blood had stained the Priestess' thighs. He tried not to think overtly about that.

Cleaned and changed back into the proper robes of a priestess, the Priestess again rested. But before she closed her eyes, she looked up at him with wide, sweet eyes. Her chestnut hair pillowed under her, long enough to reach her waist but soft and thick under her head now. Her eyes matched the Warrior's, but when she spoke, her quiet voice dispelled any doubts that she was a being of faith, not fury.

"Will you help me, Haro?" she asked. "I cannot make it home alone. I cannot make it through this life alone. Will you help me?"

His voice answered instantly. "Of course, Priestess." He could give no other answer, but if he spoke it to the Priestess, it had to be truth. By speaking it, he made it true.

She smiled softly, and her eyes shined as she lay back down and pulled a cloak over her shoulders. "Do not go far," she finished, her eyes already closed. "I may have need of you."

His sword on his knees, Haro watched her for a long time. How could she have known what he was thinking? Was she angry with him?

He had always followed the Warrior without question in admiration of her tactical mind and skills with the sword, but he had seen the Priestess only among the crowds as she performed ceremonies. Seeing her faith healing her in a manner Haro had not imagined possible, Haro admired the Priestess in a manner he had not previously. There was innocence there, lying by the candles. She was strong in many ways but, unlike her twin, weak in others. She could not defend herself as the Warrior did. She would need someone to protect her.

She needed him.

He would defend her, Haro decided. She needed someone to carry the sword for her.

He would be that person.

After getting into the palace, it was easy to track where Dracus was by his loud tirade. But Lania was patient. She knew he would come to her. Then he would die.

Getting into the sovereign's room was tricky until she remembered the window. Unlike much of Lione, only the lower windows were barred in the palace. She was fairly confident there was magic preventing entry while allowing for a high view of the city, but the enchantments seemed to part around her skin as she moved into the room from the roof. It was the sort of entry that had become easy for her, and the escape would be the same.

Whether there were spells on the windows or not, there were certainly spells in the decadent room. The lights adjusted themselves, allowing Lania to see by a strange light as she headed in, no lamp or torch required. The mosaic taking up the wall had a blue tinge, as if the silver dragon with the sovereign's seal was underwater.

Dracus was in the outer room now, carrying on about the risks being justified and how important it was to capture both Twins. He seemed to think Akara would be retrieved, speaking of it as if it were a foregone conclusion in light of all the many resources applied to the efforts.

Someone—a guard?—gently argued that the magic they had attached to Akara was not functioning as they had expected.

Of course not, Lania scoffed. Magic could not hold against the truth, against the power of the Priestess. But it was interesting that they had possessed the ability to use a trinket or similar to even try. She'd heard rumors of great rooms in the palace where magic items were hoarded jealously. Seeing evidence of it made her wonder what else they had hidden away.

Dracus had not carried his magic stone at the Market District, she realized. That was the sort of power she would not allow any Lionian to keep, remembering how it had affected people like High Councilman Polfius. And since she had time...

Lania found the orb on the table as before and turned it over in her hand. It felt dead, like a stone buried for centuries, yet she knew it held powers. Perhaps it only worked for the sovereign, or perhaps the bearer had to activate it in some fashion. Either way, she did not need it to work; she needed to destroy it.

Lania checked the room, wondering what it would take to break the trinket. It was glass, and it was old. She was surrounded by stone in this cold, white city. For once, that was a good thing.

Standing back, Lania aimed at the enormous mosaic over the west wall and threw the orb as hard as she could. It smashed into the head of the dragon depicted there, cracking as it splintered the colored glass. Shards burst into a shimmering explosion.

Akara's words, *"It's dangerous,"* echoed in Lania's ear in the moment before the magic struck her. She had only enough time to wonder what her sister had seen in her visions before the bursting powers slammed her like the runaway waters of a swollen river. Cold stone pressed against her skin and the world went dark.

Up, sister.

The words kicked Lania into consciousness. Her ears rang as she brought her eyes back into focus, blinking through watering eyes and peering into a foggy night. The walls around her had crumpled. The room was now tilted as if a giant had stomped onto the bed and broken the supports of the floor. Outside light—that of a long dusk—drifted around the otherwise darkened room, catching on the scattered glass of the smashed mosaic. Dust still settled slowly around her, choking the air and making it even more hazy now that the wizard light was gone.

Three figures loomed over her in the gloom. One unmistakably wore the white and black with the golden chains hung around his neck. The other two were dark patches of blue, although the silver sunburst symbol on their chests glittered through the dust.

Guards.

One had two swords.

My sword, she recognized.

Before she could fully gather her wits, the sovereign struck her, a candleholder slamming into her side. Pain hit her harder than the magic had. The sound of Akara's prayers filled Lania's ears over the ringing, a pleading cry for divine blessing. *One God, please, help her now.*

A second blow landed before Lani could breathe. The bones protecting her lungs broke.

Her body screamed, although she kept her cries to herself with a determination born in a Lionian torture room.

Without seeing where she was going, she rolled in time to see the sovereign miss, shout, and lunge at her like a wildcat. Unable to rise fast enough, Lania kicked the sovereign across the face, which stunned him long enough for a second kick, which shoved him off balance and onto the well-polished floor. Her side shifted. Sparks filled her vision. Her lungs spasmed, making breathing impossible.

The soldiers moved up.

Breathe, sister.

Lania held one hand against her side while the other lifted her onto her feet using the bed, filling her lungs despite the pain as she rose. Knowing she could not face them without a weapon, Lania skirted around the jumbled bed, heaved the side table clear, and looked for the sovereign's hidden sword.

The dius fell out of hiding onto the floor before her, the clatter muted by the ongoing ringing in her ears

Sensing an incoming sword, she snatched up the dius and blocked wildly. The roughly deflected guard's sword sliced into her arm below the armband, cutting deeply enough to leave a scar as she stumbled, cornered between the smashed mosaic and the disarrayed bed.

The injury to her arm brought to life all of her instincts set aside for battles. Ignoring all pain, her dance began.

She turned the next blow aside, opening a path under the metal plates of armor on the legs. Her sword, in her fury, cut right to the bone, and the soldier collapsed, grasping a leg that would never move again. A spin brought Lania face to face with the other soldier, who hesitated as he stepped over fallen rubble.

Drugged by the battle and moving too quickly to stop herself, Lania lunged at him, but his dius blocked. Without pause, she slid the blade off his and slashed toward his hip. Again, he blocked. Giving him no reprise, Lania struck again, then again, forcing him to remain defensive and retreat. The sovereign watched, for a moment seeming too shocked to move.

Even the guard did not seem surprised when she found his defense lacking. After driving his block high, Lania threw her elbow into his chest, shoved him back and, in the moment it took him to recover, sliced her sword across his throat just under the helm ties. His cries did not piece as much as usual, as if cotton had been stuffed in her ears by the explosion.

Although she'd been careful to use her strong right side, the final blow tore at her left, and the pain made her vision blank. Her head swam.

Into the lapse came new pain; she'd been struck again. The sovereign was screaming, although the sound was muffled by her deafened ears. When she regained her sight, she was facing him, having turned his next strike with her blade. He looked surprised. Had she done it with her eyes closed, perhaps?

Focus, sister.

The pain blinked out for a moment, replaced with warmth. Into that pause, Lania drove the blade into the sovereign's unprotected gut and dug deep. The sovereign crumpled like wet laundry onto the floor.

The world spun, and Lania stumbled back a step under the tilting vision as she wrenched the blade free of the flesh.

The One God was watching, the Priestess his voice, Lania decided. The monster who had raided their sacred land was dead.

Standing over the sovereign she had turned into a corpse, Lania slowed, and her head began to swim once more. She could vaguely feel blood on her arm and leg, although she did not remember when either wound had happened. It was not until she placed a hand against the tender area of her ribs that she realized that too was bleeding. Her movement had caused the broken bones to break the skin and, after the dance, the skin around was shredded. She could hardly draw any breath.

Her mind shifted wildly. She felt certain she would faint.

Move, a voice whispered in her ear, although she could not tell if was her own or Akara's. Regardless, she knew it was right. If she did not get out of the room, she would die. She had no choice. Although she staggered under the effort of standing, she found the energy to tear part of the sovereign's sheet and cover the wound on her chest.

The rest of the chambers were in shambles. She had started to wonder why the sovereign had brought only two guards, and now she saw the answer; the corridors had caved in. As her hearing improved, she could make out the sounds of those attempting to get through the rubble.

The door didn't seem prudent, so she returned to the window, not knowing how she would get through it without a functioning left side but seeing no other option. She stood in the rubble for long moments staring, her wandering mind unable to believe what she saw; the wall was missing. The blast had tossed chunks of stone into the garden.

And beyond those stones strewn about the garden was a man in a white robe with wide black sleeves.

Aurion met her stare in the dusk, his stare calculating and calm. She wondered what he thought of the hole she had made in the palace and what he'd think of the bodies behind her, but his expression gave nothing away. She knew he'd be glad to be rid of Dracus.

The wall had exploded outward, leaving a trail of debris from the opening down to the garden. Large chunks made scaling down the pile a bit like clambering around mountain trails, although she was careful to guard her wounded side as she climbed. Once she was in the shadows below the debris, the sound of marching soldiers caught her attention. Lionians could not travel quietly; their uniform was designed with dangling baltea strips that slapped their legs. Her father had once said it was to terrify their enemy and make noise to belie their numbers, but that seemed like a lot of work for some strips of leather studded with metal to do.

Lania sank into the shadows under the fallen stones. She did not need to meet more Lionians, whether it was one or sixty. She needed out of the garden and out of the palace. She was not yet sure how she would do it with her injured side.

The clatter stopped by the collapsed stones where Lania concealed herself.

"Get up there," Aurion's unmistakable voice snapped. "If the sovereign is in there, we must get him to a doctor!"

The soldiers skidded and scraped as they went up the stones, redirected by Aurion's words and given no time to search her hiding place.

Once the last of the soldiers had finished their climb, Lania slid along the shadows of the walls where she knew no one from the blasted room would see her. Her side ached horribly, the shifting bones grinding with each breath and making it harder to pant quietly. Her chosen path was the shortest one out of the area. It put her in Aurion's direct line of sight but, for once, that did not concern her.

He did not appear to notice her, but he could have been making a point of ignoring her, his eyes on the gap in the stone above that led into the sovereign's chambers.

As she exited the garden, she heard the soldier above make the grave discovery and announce Sovereign Dracus' demise. She hastened into the shadowed streets, knowing her movement was increasingly limited. After only a few steps, she had to pause to catch her breath, her head swimming.

She would never make it to Haro and Akara.

Aurion paced the palace garden, keeping his eyes away from where Lania had gone. He'd never imagined he'd regret not pursuing drama training. How did one act when worried about someone they were meant to care about but, in truth, did not? No one would be surprised by a bit of indifference from him. It had been a while since he'd loved his sovereign, although he was still duty-bound to the man. And what about when he knew so certainly the man was dead already but could not reveal that without showing that he knew this was an assassination? Lania would never have left Dracus alive.

But she had been moving gingerly, he was certain. Her movement was generally fluid when not masquerading as an awkward slave. She'd been injured.

She might need help.

When word of the sovereign's demise reached his ears, Aurion had his excuse to leave. Lania hadn't been gone long and, moving so cautiously, she would not have gone far. Still, running after the Nurmi Warrior was not wise and, if seen, would result in his execution regardless of who next sat in the High Seat. Part of him wanted to thank her still, but mostly, he wanted to ensure she was not found this close to the explosion and body. If someone recognized her as his slave Tatkil, it would spell disaster. She still bore his brand.

Collecting a carriage from the palace stable was straightforward enough; it was common for a councilman to require transportation home after meetings. The driver he held on retainer was already awake because of the explosion and jumped into action.

Having seen which way Lania had gone, Aurion directed the driver slowly down the streets outside the palace, his door open and lamp held high in search.

He saw the blood trail first, but Lania wasn't far. She'd c rouched low, her head ducked, under a doorway, and was not moving.

When lamplight reached her, the Warrior's head shot up, her bright blue eyes betraying her race despite how shrouded and dark her features were. She looked feral, a wildcat ready to flee into the mountains or fight to the death if cornered. Despite her injuries, Aurion still had the strong urge to run when her eyes fixed on him.

He dared not hesitate, not with the risk of nearby eyes. Moving more confidently than he felt, Aurion came up beside her and threw the blanket from the carriage over her. It seemed a signal, and she rose unsteadily to her feet once the blankets draped her head and shoulders enough to hide her. Then, as if she was a Lionian, he offered her his arm.

She didn't touch him. Although her hand reached out and hovered over where she could have accepted his arm, her skin did not touch the black sleeve of his councilman's robes. She walked better than he had expected to the carriage. She kept her head low enough that, with the blanket, even the driver would know nothing about her.

Once in the carriage, Aurion signaled for Jannus to drive on, letting him assume they were headed home. It would look better if the carriage took the expected route for now.

Her breathing was shallow and pained, but her head was up now. When she sat straight, the blanket parted enough to reveal that she wore only a pair of too-large breeches and a bandage over her chest. The bandage was made, if his eyes were not playing tricks on him, of the sovereign's bed sheets. Fresh blood stained the bandage through on her chest and arm, and it glistened to match the silver armband that, clean and gleaming, sparkled from her left arm in the lamplight.

He glanced out the window, parting the curtains as he usually did so the other occupants of his carriage would not be seen but leaving him able to watch the roads as they passed through. There was not much to see in the darkness of the streets, but once in the Market District, the lamps lit ongoing clean-up efforts and a strict curfew. Jannus would ensure they were not stopped. Councilmen did not have to adhere to curfews.

The people didn't know yet, Aurion reflected as the carriage passed a pair of anxious youngsters being corralled back to their homes. No one out here knew Dracus was dead. *For the best.* If he could find a place to get Lania out of his carriage without being seen, he could head to the Councilhall next. He was ready, his mind already on possible replacements.

"Why?" Lania's voice cut in.

He glanced at her, dropping the curtain. He didn't have to ask what she was referring to. "Because if you were found and connected to my slave, it would cause problems," Aurion replied factually. He was aware there was more, that he had not wanted to see her arrested or executed, but he was not acknowledging that to her.

"It was a risk," she added. She did not seem capable of longer sentences, her panting breaking her words into fragments.

"You are hurt," he replied. "You would be caught."

She smiled then, the smile that had haunted him after her prison time, the one that told him clearly what she thought of their odds of catching her and how much she would enjoy proving him wrong.

The carriage paused at the gate out of the Market District, but only long enough to identify him. The guards dared not make him pause and did not check the carriage.

"People could have seen you collect me," Lania reciprocated once they were moving again and not likely to be overheard. It seemed she was expecting him to meet that smile of hers with the same eagerness for conflict and potential blood.

"No one will think twice about a councilman picking up a woman from the street." He eyed the blanket, wondering if he'd have to wash blood stains from it before returning it. But concealing the identity of a prostitute was common enough. No polician would appreciate leverage against them. "You took my arm, or at least made it look like you did. As far as watching eyes are concerned, you accepted my offer. That is all."

She nodded and fell into a long silence, which allowed him to resume his watch through the curtains. They were in his home district, the main streets not bustling as much as the Market District would this time of night, but there were no soldiers at the intersections either. Were they still convinced

Lania had remained near Galfium's murder? When would someone sound the alarm that the sovereign had been murdered? Would anyone connect the events?

He was about to ask her what she would do now when Lania abruptly said, "Docks District."

Not wanting her back in his home, Aurion thumped on the roof of the carriage to warn Jannus, then slid open the port between them. Across from Aurion, Lania dropped her head and slumped over, hiding her features.

"Docks District, Jannus," Aurion directed. "The old Gantheran warehouse."

She glared up at him once the port was closed again but did not correct his assumption. He'd made the connection easily enough after tracking the slave she'd hidden in Aurion's home. The warehouse had been empty since. With Gantheran's death, the estate had gone into limbo between two heirs and then was sold. Knowing Lania was still active in Lione had prompted Aurion to set sentries on it; he'd not heard anything today, but he'd also not been home yet. He suspected there was a list of activity waiting on his desk now from the spies assigned to it.

Aurion had been tracking the turns of the carriage; he could tell when it turned toward the gate to the High Reach District. He'd not had to point out they wanted to avoid the Market District, but Jannus was taking the long way around. The High Reach District would be silent this time of night, although the Docks and Stadium Districts might have some activity.

Sure enough, the noise permeated the carriage as they crossed into the Stadium District. The bustle was contained in the bars and inns after a series of races in the stadium, the guards working to keep people off the streets where they might impede traffic or cause disturbances. Although the races had ended hours ago, the district was far from sleeping, the lights and sounds still carrying through the dark of midnight.

With all the ruckus, he almost missed it when Lania said, "I broke the magic orb."

Aurion pulled his eyes from the window and ensured the window's coverings were secured. She was looking at him from under the coat, her eyes as piercing as the first day he had seen her behind the bars of the jail cart traveling south. That wild cat had been caged; this one was feral and free.

"I'm impressed. I didn't think magic trinkets could be broken by normal means."

Her lips stretched in a smirk. "I am far from normal."

He could not help but smile. "Fair. Then I am grateful; you did me two favors. Dracus wasn't fit for ruling." This time, he met her stare directly.

"And now?" she asked. "I am no current use to you." Aurion shrugged and looked away to avoid staring at the seep of blood from her side. He didn't want to draw attention to the wound she seemed to be doggedly denying. Her breathing was short and shallow, but at least it didn't sound raspy. That was a sound he never wanted to hear again.

"I'm not of current use to you, either. You haven't tried to kill me yet."

Lania wrinkled her nose, although he suspected she would have shrugged if it hadn't hurt so very much to do so. "I have no reason to waste my energy on it."

"And I have no reason, for the moment, to waste my energy on attempting to capture you. I want you out of the city. This seems the most expedient means."

Jannus thumped the roof above, then pulled the carriage to a halt. Aurion checked the window; they had reached the docks. Jannus had brought the carriage to the back of the warehouse where it could be easily assumed Aurion was visiting any number of trade houses along the water.

Lania stared at him, and Aurion froze under the weight of her stare. Carefully, as if every gesture had to be negotiated against great hesitation, she lifted a knife and cut a lock of her hair from amidst the hair-debts woven here.

"You again saved my life. With thanks, I offer my debt."

He reached for the hair more quickly this time, confident. She was still being careful not to allow their skin to touch and released it smoothly. But it felt right to pocket the token from her. Perhaps it would provide some connection. Having the debt of someone as influential in the north as her would no doubt be of use.

When she said nothing further, Aurion got out and checked the streets, but it was quiet and dim in the minimal lamps.

"Don't stay past morning," he warned as he opened the door and let her step down from the carriage. Although he was checking the street, he still did not see any unwanted eyes, yet he knew the city could deceive him. "If anyone decides the Warrior killed Dracus, they'll look here. Besides, it's been bought and will have a new occupant next week."

She nodded, her movement otherwise minimalistic and pained. When she stumbled, Aurion reached to steady her.

Before he could reach the Warrior, he was blocked by the largest Nurmi he had ever seen. The man matched Aurion's height, but he was as broad as an ox across the shoulders, with arms like logs and a deep, warning glare. Light armor, a dius, and his long, Nurmi-style hair held back by a band of embroidered cloth made him the perfect Nurmi warrior. There was even a bone necklace around his throat, likely trophies taken from victims, and the stars reflected off a silver armband.

The man shouldered his way between Aurion and the Warrior, lifting his dius and snarling something incomprehensible like a snake spitting poison. Instinctively, Aurion retreated and reached for his sword, shocked that a warrior of this stature was present in Lione.

"*Aeti, Haro*. He will not harm me," Lania interrupted, and the mix of Lionian and Nurmi was sufficient to call off the larger man like the finest hunting hound called to heel. "Come, we have much to do."

Although Aurion thought he saw concern on his face, the Nurmi did not move to support his Warrior as she stumbled off. She would not be seen as weak, Aurion realized. Was it that the Nurmi man would not show her vulnerability to a Lionian, or did no one dare help Lania for fear of her?

The man glared back at Aurion, in a look warning the high councilman he could expect to join his sovereign on the pyres should any harm befall the Warrior. Aurion gave the man respectful space and climbed back into his carriage. He could still see the Nurmi watching him as Jannus drove him away.

Grizzle would curse Aurion for this, and it was only a matter of time before the spymaster found out. Aurion planned to tell him right away to avoid that embarrassment. Besides, they needed a good excuse for picking up women in the Palace District and visiting the docks on such an evening. They'd have to come up with something, but Aurion felt far too tired to devise something at that moment.

As the carriage took him back through the gates, Aurion stared at the blood on the seat across from him, wondering if she'd survive. It could be that the Warrior was not just one person, he mused, but anyone who dared take up the mantle. Perhaps when one died, another took her place. Yet those brilliant eyes and snarling gaze belied that theory. She was a legend; no one else could match her.

She'd live, he had no doubt.

He was surprised to realize he would miss her, but he was glad she was gone from Lione. Still, part of him hoped their paths would cross again.

Haro joined Lania by the door into the warehouse. She could pretend she was waiting for him, but, in truth, she had run out of breath and was resting. He tensed at seeing her but said nothing as he opened the door and led her through the room. Lania followed, keeping the guise of strength around her. Her side was screaming in pain still, but she dared not show that weakness.

They would collect the remaining slaves and make their way out through a sewer exit tied to the docks. From there, a pair of canoes waited to take them to the river. The water meant safety and freedom. For the last time, the White City was behind her.

"Did he deserve it?" Haro asked from beside her. Despite her frustration, mostly directed at her involuntary distraction, Lania could not glare at him for his question. He asked it out of concern for her health and that of her sister, not to pry or annoy her, but it was a question she did not want to answer, not now.

"You are always quiet like that after you kill someone," Haro said to justify his inquiry. "Not in battle, but that is different. When you fight a man face to face, when both of you are armed and you know one of you will die before the other will move on, there is no need to feel guilt. But when you hunt without a battle, it is different. You went in looking for one life in particular tonight. Did he deserve it?"

She could not stand to meet his stare. It was easier when he thought she was heartless. She had watched his desire for her fade since she had destroyed the Lionian fort on the river, leaving none alive. She knew how she frightened him. It was better that way.

"Yes, he deserved it," she told him in her coldest voice. "They both did."

The blood of Councilman Galfium had been remarkably easy to spill, even at such a distance. It had been a fitting use of the final black arrow, ridding the world of that evil. The only regret she had was not having done it sooner. She had not known the sovereign would hand her sister over to the man whose sex life was so discussed and disgusted. Now it would be the talk of the town, as soon as the Lionians stopped talking about their sovereign's demise.

Akara had begged her not to go, and the vision of sparkling, smashed glass returned to her. A vision of the explosion, Lania realized. She'd known the risk of breaking the magic orb. She'd tried to warn Lania.

But killing Dracus had been a certainty. There was nothing else she could have done. She was the Warrior. She was death.

She had disobeyed her sister.

"I wish to claim the hair-debt," Lania impulsively told Haro.

"What need have you of me?" he replied at once, although his eyes burned with questions.

"Protect the Priestess, Haro," she told him. "She will need a warrior who remains at her side, one who can be trusted to obey. I am not she." As she spoke, she undid the braid that ended with the lock of hair he had given her over three years ago.

He nodded and ran his finger from his forehead under his eye in answer.

"She will understand," Lania said as she let the hair loose into the waters, the debt fulfilled. "Let's go."

Freedom awaited.

The End

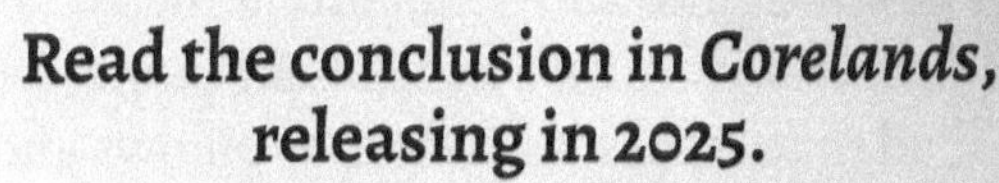

**Read the conclusion in *Corelands*,
releasing in 2025.**

Excerpt from *Corelands*

W hen Aurion woke, a light burned nearby. It was dim, barely illuminating his view of a ceiling that immediately struck him as wrong.

Not Lione, his mind whispered urgently. *Those walls are wooden, not stone. That roof is thatched. This is not Lione. This is not even a tent on a battlefield.*

His eyes hurt, as did his face, when he winced in pain. He closed his eyes again, content in the darkness, and concentrated on breathing.

Closer consideration proved his eyes and face were not alone: everything hurt. With each breath, his chest creaked and ached. His leg throbbed, as did the bottoms of his feet if he wiggled his toes. He tried to remember what had happened, or where he was, but his memory refused to answer.

His throat felt as dry as the Santanese desert, and that gave him purpose. He was thirsty. Opening his eyes, he rolled over in search of something to drink.

As soon as he moved, he discovered he had been mistaken; not everything had hurt. *Now* everything hurt. His neck, leg, and back all burned, and he tumbled back onto his back involuntarily, gasping for breath and blinking back tears. He wheezed like a man with blood in his lungs. His heart pounded, already exhausted by a little movement.

It's true. I'm dying.

As he lay back, struggling to catch his breath, he tried to focus. He didn't want to dwell on blood and death. He needed to think about something and get his mind working. Then he'd be awake enough to solve this problem.

The bed feels wrong, he told himself. In Lione, he had slept on down-filled mattresses with feather pillows and warming stones by his feet, but if he had been wounded, he expected the cheaper mattresses of the hospitals, filled with straw. Instead, he was lying on a piece of cloth drawn tight between four pegs and covered in ... fur? Perhaps bearskin? He had always assumed the northern animal's furs would be rough and, having never had much choice in wardrobe as a soldier or councilman, he had never been given the opportunity to learn otherwise.

The cloth was loose enough to let him sink into it, but still supported stiff and aching limbs without letting them dangle. He was not wearing any clothing at all, he realized abashedly, but he had been covered with a mix of wool and hide blankets that protected him from the cold air that chilled his face.

He had closed his eyes to fight back the nausea that swelled as the world spun. *Where am I?*

"Drink this," he was told and, despite his fear that the world would spin uncontrollably and leave him behind, Aurion opened his eyes little by little. The candle's glare felt bright enough to blind him, but, focussing past the remnants of the tears in his eyes, he made out the face of the most beautiful Nurmi woman he had ever seen.

By Lionian standards, she would have been a treasure worth a thousand lorax. Her pale skin was smooth and flawless, and she had a slight smile that creased her face minimally. Her skin sparkled faintly in the candlelight as golden. Black dyes drew the mark of the One God across her forehead.

Her brown hair, worn down her back save for a handful of braided hair-debts, caught the firelight and glittered as if it had spun gold for every second strand. The voice was softer than Lania's and lower in pitch, which gave every word the woman spoke the feeling of great wisdom and meaning.

The eyes amazed him; they were bright and intelligent, but so caring and so calm, his breath caught. He was ready to believe anything this god-sent woman said.

He obediently sipped the drink she lifted to his mouth, but tasted nothing of it as it passed over his parched tongue. Once he had done as she had asked, the woman sat back and vanished from his view.

In groggy waking, Aurion finally recognized her face.

"Lania?" he managed to say, but the word was no more than a whisper.

"My sister asked me to call her when you awoke. She is on her way."

He mentally chided himself. Of course it was Akara, not Lania. Lania, he knew, had a scar across her right cheek, her hair was considerably shorter, and her face would never have been so pale, but the woman he saw with his tired eyes was so different from the one he had seen escape Lione a cycle ago, he could hardly believe it. There were no stained robes, blood-soaked hair, or tears. She sat calmly, her shoulders square and her eyes looking at him curiously from under gold-touched lashes. Even looking down on him, a Lionian, the enemy who had done unspeakable things to her, Akara showed no hatred.

He tried to nod, but his throbbing head and throat stopped him. He lifted a hand to cover where the pain had flared, but soft hands caught his wrist.

"Do not touch," Akara told him in a loving voice, although he could not help noticing she released him quickly to let her sleeves fall back over the black tattoos that decorated her arms and hands. "It will heal."

His instinct was to nod, but he did not dare. After listening to the chirp of the night animals for a moment, his mind was awake enough to try to gather some information.

"I did not hear you call Lania." He had meant to speak it, but it escaped only as a murmur.

Akara smiled again, and her eyes sparkled just like Lania's. "No, you would not have," she said.

"I do not understand," Aurion replied.

"Forgive my sister, Aurion," Lania's strict voice said from the foot of the bed. Aurion could tell by her voice that the same mischievous spark was in the Warrior's eyes. "In her role as Priestess, Akara often must be mysterious. I believe she enjoys it."

Peering down over his feet, he could just see the Warrior as she stood with her hands on her hips next to a sword. She wore leather armor but put down her shield as she came to his side. For the first time, Aurion compared the Twins, as the Nurmi people had dubbed them.

Lania was deeply tanned and muscled, which made her sister Akara seem shorter and smaller. The Priestess' hair was longer, reaching down to the back of her thigh, and it lay flat with only a handful of debts tipped in gold. More than half of the Warrior's head was done up in hair-debts, braids topped by hair that did not quite match her brown. Lania was scarred and rough in her practical, although filthy, armor. Akara was pristine and sparkling in the un-dyed robe that had never seen a day of heavy use.

The eyes were the same. Both were brilliant blue, although Lania's glowed with energy and Akara's simmered with concern.

Seeing Lania, a testimony to the world outside, the beautiful place he had been drifting in with Akara broke into a thousand pieces. His mind dragged itself into action. Instantly, he lost the blind trust toward Akara and, when the

Priestess offered him the drink once more, he lifted his head away, wanting to know what he was about to swallow.

From the side of the bed, Lania snorted. "If you wish to disobey the Priestess, you should have told me sooner. I would have stopped her from binding your leg or sewing up your throat or treating your fever or…"

"I get it," he muttered before accepting the drink. It was sweet but foul and tasted entirely wrong on his tongue. It occurred to him he had probably never drank anything similar: he had never undergone Nurmi healing before.

The thought hit him. It was unlikely any Lionian had.

He choked and, in his coughing, felt his throat flare with heat and pain. Nausea struck again, and he closed his eyes to stop the world from spinning. He did not see the Priestess place anything over the wound on his neck, but the fire subsided quickly with a chilly compress.

"My men…" he whispered once he could breathe again.

"Dead." Aurion could not tell if Lania or Akara had spoken. "All three," the voice continued. "I am sorry."

Silence filled the room, and Aurion's mind drifted again.

"She says not to speak anymore." This time, the voice certainly came from Lania. "You need to rest. The drink will help you sleep."

He did not hear her move again and was not sure how long he remained awake. The drink helped keep the world still as he lay wondering about bearskins and strange herbs and fell asleep.

BOOK CLUB QUESTIONS:

1. What gender stereotypes were represented and which were distorted in this book?

2. Not all battles are fought with a sword. What other "battles" did Lania fight? How did her faith affect her success or failure?

3. What cultures did the author pull on when creating Lionians? What about Nurmi? Why do you think that?

4. There are several examples of arranged marriages, but none of them appear to be healthy or successful. Do you believe arranged marriages can work? Why might they work better than marriages for love?

5. In chapter 15, Aurion agrees to allow Lania to shelter in his home with a fugitive. What informed that decision? Was the logic believable? Do you agree with his decision?

6. How did Aurion's character change through the book? Was it for better or worse?

7. Is prophecy or fate real in this book? What makes you believe that?

8. Which of the two main characters (Aurion and Lania) do you consider more powerful? Why?

9. Which character did you most identify with?

10. A common theme throughout the book is loyalty: Lania's to her people, Aurion's to the sovereign. Is loyalty a fault or an asset? When should it be discarded?

GLOSSARY

DISTRICTS OF LIONE:

Docks: Docks and warehouses by the water

Freeman: Mostly rundown shops but has the largest Library

Highreach: Upper-class homes

Market: Sales and market squares

Newhope: Refugees and other poor. High crime rate.

Palace: Sovereign's palace

Prison: Barracks and large prison

Stadium: High-end shops and the stadiums

University: University, but also observatory, laboratories, research centers, and library.

PEOPLE:

Nurmi:

Akara: Priestess of the Nurmi people

Binoran (*Kaco*): Nurmi man who helps Lania

Haro: Fighter and friend of Lania

Lania (*Tatkil*): Warrior of the Nurmi people

Maltor: Black Arrow: first slave to escape the Lionians.

Naino (*Rahngun*): Nurmi slave in palace

Toval (*Recmtupi*): Nurmi Priest with no faith

Vela (*Pitiscil):* Nurmi prophecy, also known as Messenger

OTHER:

Tril: Prophet of the Esparan

LIONIANS:

Canion Hallius Guital: High Priest of Lioni in Councilhall

COUNCILMEN:

Aurion Arrius Illica Polfius: Councilman of Freeman District/ High Councilman

Balfidius: High Councilman

Craxus Trano Volustio: Councilman of Newhope District of Lione

Falcun: Councilman of West army

Falmio Caltrian Gitarius: Lionian noble, Lania's master, Councilman of Market District

Ganon Anton Galfium: Councilman of Prison District

Julian Caius Dobrius: High Councilman

Navius Julian Maurio: Councilman of Stadium district

Norion Polrion Vanius: Councilman of the Highreach District

Palviro Wavius Dracus: Councilman/Sovereign

Santio Valum Laliro: Councilman of South Army

Solorin: Councilman of East army

Stranstius: Councilman of Freeman

CITIZENS OR SOLDIERS:

Ailsa Femca Trailus: Lionian member of the household of Illica

Antori Yeon Trailus: Loraxi and friend for Aurion Illica

Balvor Vannio Conticus: Loraxi and friend of Aurion Illica.

Draina Kayla Illica: Aurion's mother

Drake: The little boy spy for Aurion

Dulci: Paki who interrogates Lania

Grizzle: Spymaster of the Illica Household

Horati Fulmar Falcium: Serving Yoraci

Jannus: Palace driver for the Illican Household. Santan War veteran.

Julti Lola Gitarius: Councilman Gitarius' daughter, Lania's owner.

Krinus Juin Otavious: Serving Loraxi under Galeni Lonthius

Noria: Healer of the Illica Household

Ocracion Pick Pocket: Lionian Thug/thief

Olena Nalla Lonthius: Daughter of the Lonthius

Otavopon Minton Maurio: Maurio's son

Safarik: Spymaster for Volustio Household.

Serena Concula Illica: Aurion's sister

Seth: Torturer in Lione, Priest of Ramath

Tactus Grantar Lonthius: Serving, famous Lionian Galeni (father of Olena)

PROVINCES OF THE LIONIAN SOVEREIGNTY:

Camsion

East Bank

Grift

Guildar

Isuiton

Jilluam

Lionion

Namera

Northreach

Penecia

Quebelo

Salbero

West Bank

PLACES:

Camian Sea: Sea near Lione

Cikrupi (*Newhome*): Nurmi village, center of Corelands, freshly established

Culbrupi (*Northhome*): Nurmi village cart to the North

Damiani: Lionian city, north-east of Lionian province.

Falti: Lionian city along Solon River to the east

Gatrupi (*Fishhome*): Nurmi village where Aurion is taken

Guhitkrupi (*Foresthome*): Nurmi village north of river, home to Lania and Akara

Lafilrupi (*Riverhome*): Nurmi river outpost

Lione: Capital of Lionian Empire, center of the world.

Manfari: Lionian village within Corelands.

Mount Dukhum: Mountain in Corelands, bordering Windraso territory.

Puyckeacrupi (*Mountainhome*): Nurmi city far north at base of Mount Duhkum

Salbero: Western province. Aurion's home province

Slufi (*Grove*): Northwest of Solon river, sacred land rediscovered, home to Priestess.

Solon River: River from Mount Dukhum, crossing through the south of the Corelands, forming the west border of the Lionian Province, and eventually emptying in the bay at Lione.

Tran: Lionian border city facing Lafilrupi over the Solon river.

Whum-bekil (*Blood-water*): River outpost that forms upon Tran's destruction.

LIONIAN RANK STRUCTURE:

Diasist: basic foot soldier

8 Diasists are one Yorac headed by a Yoraci

5 Yoracs are one Loraxan, headed by a Loraxi

10 Loraxans are one Pakan, headed by a Paki

4 Pakan are one Pakanon, headed by a Pakani

3 Pakanon are one Braxan headed by Braxi

A full Galen (an army) is headed by a Galeni

Find more about D. Lambert's writing at
www.dlambertauthor.com

Keep to date by following!
Facebook
Twitter
Newsletter

Remember that authors love reviews (and they keep us writing!). Please take a moment to post an honest review on your favorite book site!

AUTHOR BIO

At a young age, Deborah's rampant imagination kept her up, lending great detail to all the terrible things lurking in the night. In desperation, her mother suggested she invent her own stories to distract her brain. She has been doing that since, channeling her ideas into sword and sorcery-style fantasy novels and shorts.

In her other life, Deborah is a veterinarian. She lives in Sooke with her husband of 13+ years, their two sons, and three demanding felines.

Discover more at
4HorsemenPublications.com

10% off using HORSEMEN10

www.ingramcontent.com/pod-product-compliance
Lightning Source LLC
Chambersburg PA
CBHW020242010826
48973CB00006B/1624